Leaving Amarillo

A NEON DREAMS NOVEL

CAISEY QUINN

WILLIAM MORROW

An Imprint of HarperCollins*Publishers*

LEAVING AMARILLO. Copyright © 2015 by Caisey Quinn. Excerpt from *Loving Dallas* copyright © 2015 by Caisey Quinn. All rights reserved. Printed in the United States of America. No part of this book may be used or reproduced in any manner whatsoever without written permission except in the case of brief quotations embodied in critical articles and reviews. For information address HarperCollins Publishers, 195 Broadway, New York, NY 10007.

HarperCollins books may be purchased for educational, business, or sales promotional use. For information e-mail the Special Markets Department at SPsales@harpercollins.com.

FIRST EDITION

Designed by Diahann Sturge

Library of Congress Cataloging-in-Publication Data has been applied for.

ISBN 978-0-06-236681-8

15 16 17 18 19   OV/RRD   10 9 8 7 6 5 4

*For my brother, Michael—who filled our home
with music all hours of the day and night.*

"Music melts all the separate parts of our bodies together."
—*Anaïs Nin*

Prologue

Austin MusicFest—Day 5

IT'S TIMES LIKE THIS, TIMES WHEN I'M ON, GIVING IT MY ALL AS MY bow dances across the strings like it has a mind of its own, that I feel like I can fly. Leave this stage, this crowd—this world even—and ascend to a higher plane.

The deafening kick of Gavin's drums beats steadily along with my pounding heart while Dallas's guitar strums a rhythmic river flooding my veins and carrying me across the stage. The sound lifts and holds me while I play my heart out. The music flows around us and into me, lighting every single cell my body is composed of on fire from my toes to my head until I am blazing with the heat of it.

The section of the audience that my eyes can reach is cast in a neon blue glow with hues of red streaking on the periphery. The colors are as vibrant as I feel and would be distracting if I weren't playing, but I am focused. I am one with my instrument and its rich sound is so much a part of me it's as if it's coming from inside my soul instead of from the fiddle on my shoulder.

We take the audience on a fever-dream roller coaster of emotions with our sound. Dallas likes to begin and end on fast-paced songs and weave the slower ones through the middle. "Whiskey Redemption" comes just after a string of reworked R&B hits that had everyone singing along. We play "Ring of Fire" and then my favorite Adele hit. All three of us chime in on the vocals for our version of "Love Runs Out," playing it like a game of round-robin.

My favorite song is up next and I feel electric and on fire while we play it. It's a mash-up of a song called "Whataya Want from Me" and another called "Beneath Your Beautiful" that we've altered to fit our sound. It's our most downloaded cover online. Took me forever to get Dallas to agree to it and even longer for the three of us to get the timing right. But the hard work was worth it. I can see it on the faces in the crowd.

We play Dallas's favorite drinking song, one he wrote himself, and then our set ends with our updated version of "When You Leave Amarillo." The applause is so loud it vibrates through to my core and the sensation is electrifying. It's a serious struggle to catch my breath. We bow and thank the largest, most enthusiastic audience we've ever played for and escape backstage. I'm not even sure if my feet are touching the ground as we step off the stage.

My brother is immediately swept into a darkened corner by some suit chatting him up, a potential manager probably. But Gavin is right behind me. He's so close I can practically taste his adrenaline high as acutely as my own.

"That was amazing," I breathe, turning to face him. "I think it might've been better than sex."

He stops tapping his drumsticks on his knee and pins me with his stare. His hazel gaze darkens as he backs me into the hallway and out of my brother's line of sight. "That was amazing because *you* were amazing."

The dim lights backstage are reflected in his pupils, making him look almost possessed, otherworldly. Somewhere the next act is being introduced and my brother is shaking hands and making a deal that will change the course of the rest of our lives. But here, where I am right now, Gavin Garrison is making love to me with his eyes. And I don't want him to stop. Ever.

Lowering his head enough that his lips are almost touching mine, he says the words that send my already racing heart into overdrive and halt my ability to form coherent thoughts. "But if you think that was anywhere near better than sex, those pretty boys you've been screwing around with have been doing it all wrong."

Chapter 1

THERE IS A LOT TO BE SAID FOR BREAKUP SEX.

No pressure. No worries about being perfect. Just give me one last orgasm please and thank you and goodbye. Have a nice life, or don't. Peace out.

Not that I'm an expert or anything. I've only had sex with one person. But I'm pretty certain that the last time was the best time.

In Jaggerd McKinley's case the breakup sex was decent enough that I was now having some firm second thoughts about getting back together just so we could break up again and have one last round. Lord have mercy, the things that boy could do with his hands. Apparently they weren't just good for working on broken-down cars. He'd been holding out on me in the year that we'd dated.

"Dixie, that's twice you've missed your intro." My brother's voice startles me. "Can you join us here, please? This space ain't free, little sister."

"My bad." I feel my face heat from the attention of him and Gavin. Usually it's Gavin getting distracted and screwing up—typically because some chick has caught his eye or rung one of his drumsticks with the underwear she's flung onstage—and my brother would be glaring at him.

"You all right?" Gavin eyes me with concern. Last weekend we played at Midnight Rodeo, a nightclub downtown. My now ex-boyfriend had never been very supportive of our band, Leaving Amarillo, and had shown up drunk as Cooter Brown. Gavin and my brother both nearly pummeled him before security could escort him out and it wasn't pretty.

"Yeah, I'm good. Sorry. Let's go again." I shrug and bring Oz, my fiddle, up onto my shoulder.

Two bars into the song, the music surrounding us cuts off sharply once more.

"Damn it, Dix. It's three chords we're working with here." Dallas's ice-blue eyes are laser beams and I am the target.

I lower my bow and sigh loudly. "Sorry." Taking a deep breath, I shoot him and Gavin both an apologetic smile. "Promise I'll get it together. I'm good now."

"Did you ever get any sleep last night?" My brother's gaze softens, and I'm slightly surprised by his unexpected show of concern. When we're rehearsing or recording, the music comes first. Usually. I don't know if it's the dark rings around my eyes caused by long nights of caring for our grandfather or my recent breakup that has him worried, but he waits for my answer before continuing.

"I did. I'm really okay. Let's go again." I force a smile and raise my bow once more.

We play half of our set without stopping and I fight through the exhaustion and the non-Jaggerd-related painful memories plaguing me. Instinct honed by years of practice takes over as my bow flies across the strings.

"Hell yeah," Dallas calls out, fist-bumping Gavin when we finally stop to catch our breath. "That's what I'm talking about!" He grins at me and I smile back at his enthusiasm.

"Think we're ready for Nashville?" I feel ten pounds lighter from playing, and from making my brother proud.

"We're on our way, little sister. On our way," Dallas tells me before turning to Gavin. "Okay, let's pick it up at the top of 'Ring of Fire' and push through to the end of the set."

It's all I can do not to roll my eyes at the *little sister* part.

Despite the fact that I'm nineteen, Dallas acts like I'm twelve most of the time. And like he's my dad. Since our parents were killed in a car accident when we were kids, he actually filled that role every now and then.

Gavin's hazel gaze meets mine and he nods to make sure I'm ready before he counts us into the next song. My heart does the little stuttering flip-turn it likes to do on the rare occasions we make eye contact for more than a split second.

Just like that, one lingering look and I'm transported back in time to the first time I saw him.

Gavin Garrison, our drummer and my brother's best friend, was the first boy I'd ever had a crush on. From the moment he stepped onto my grandparents' porch the day of my parents' funeral, with his cautious silvery eyes and his torn clothes and messy hair that was in serious need of cutting, looking like a stray puppy, the three of us had been inseparable.

That day had been so surreal, with everyone—strangers mostly—tiptoeing around us, offering cookies and tea, and whatever else they thought would distract us from the fact that we were suddenly a nine- and twelve-year-old pair of orphans.

Dallas and I were sitting out front on the porch swing in silence, which was unusual for me as I typically had a hard time shutting up. But the heavy hands of shock and grief were still firmly clamped over my mouth.

Gavin had walked up, nodded at the throng of people flowing in and out of the house, and turned to us.

"Party?" he asked without introducing himself.

I watched my brother for cues on how to answer the stranger. Dallas swallowed hard and shook his head. "Funeral. Our parents."

Gavin ran a hand through his mussed hair, mussing it further. "Well . . . fuck."

It was the first time I'd heard the word out loud and on purpose and a thrill shot through me. My heart sped in my chest, which was surprising since all it had done since my aunt Sheila had told us that our parents were dead was thud heavily as if it were considering saying to hell with the whole thing.

"Wanna go break shit?" Gavin asked.

I turned to my brother, sheer panic and pure adrenaline pumping fiercely through my veins. *Say yes,* I pleaded silently.

"Guess so," Dallas said, hopping down off the swing as if we followed strange kids all the time.

I walked with the two of them off the porch. Dallas introduced us. And Gavin did the same. He turned and shook my hand like adults did, and I swear on all things holy, lightning flashed right up my arm. It flickered in his eyes at the same time and I froze.

"What were you doing? Why were you at our house?" Dallas asked, narrowing his eyes and watching our exchange suspiciously.

"Um." Gavin pulled his hand back and scratched his head. He glanced around as if looking for the nearest escape route. His eyes darkened, the wary edge they'd first held returning when he shifted his guarded gaze to my brother. "Looking for something to eat. Figured a party would have food."

The sound of drum cymbals shatters through my memory. My intro comes and I'm snapped back into the present and out of the past. I lift Oz and play my part until Dallas nods, satisfied that I haven't royally botched anything this time, but he can probably tell that I'm distracted. While he belts out the lyrics to the song we wrote about the past being more than just a memory, I glance back at Gavin.

He's changed a lot since that scrappy, overly thin boy he used to be. Thick muscles strain and flex against his charcoal-colored T-shirt, intricate tattoos painting a mural up and down his arms. I can't tear my eyes away from him as he rocks the drums with everything he has.

He's different. More . . . vibrant. And his hygiene has certainly improved since he was a ten-year-old kid pretty much fending for himself. But there is still hunger in him. Still a deep, dark need that consumes me body and soul when I look into his fiery eyes.

"Let's take five," Dallas announces when the song ends, throwing me a pointed get-your-crap-together look. "I've got a few phone calls to make."

I don't say a word to either of them as I leave the room. Grabbing a bottle of water, I make my way to the stairwell that leads to the roof. I try not to get lost in memories, but that day is looming over me like a persistent storm cloud.

On that day, ten years ago, I ran into the house and grabbed as many finger sandwiches and brownies and cookies as I could carry. I nearly tripped over my own two feet in my rush to get back outside before the boys left me.

I handed them both the goods and stuffed a brownie in my own mouth so Gavin wouldn't feel like a charity case. In the brief time since my parents had died, I'd already had my fill of sympathy and I didn't like the bitter taste of it. At all. He and I were the same in that way, I could feel it. So I didn't ask, didn't say a word about why his clothes and hair were filthy, or why he was roaming around town alone in search of food.

We ate on the short walk to an abandoned lot where we proceeded to throw discarded beer bottles against a brick building until I couldn't lift my arm.

Each beautiful shattering explosion of glass brought me back to life, bringing to light the emotions I'd covered with a heavy black blanket. The world had turned gray the day our parents died, literally. It'd been rainy and gloomy in Texas every day since. But that release, "breaking shit," as Gavin put it, brought color back to my world like sun peeking through the clouds. It felt so good. Too good. Guilt for enjoying myself weighed on my nine-year-old brain.

"Fuuuckkk," I screamed out, just to release some of the pain and confusion.

Gavin stopped and stared at me. Dallas kept throwing bottles while I crumpled to the ground. Letting my long, tangled mess of curly hair provide a dark curtain between myself and the boys, I cried—really cried—for the first time since we'd gotten the news. At some point the sound of glass breaking ceased.

"Don't touch her." My brother's voice was frighteningly calm, but heavy with the threat of violence. "She's fine. You want to be friends? You don't *ever* touch her."

Lifting my head I saw Gavin approaching me. He'd been coming to comfort me, from the looks of it, but Dallas's warning had stopped him in his tracks. Gravel dug into my knees and the palms of my hands while I watched conflicting urges battle for control in the depths of the boy's mysterious eyes.

"Get up, Dixie Leigh," Dallas said, his voice softer than before. "It's time to go home."

Home. That was a joke. Home was a brick house in a suburb half an hour outside of Austin where we rode bikes and played with our friends. Home included our mom and dad, pancakes for breakfast, and Saturday morning cartoons. We were going to a rickety old shack with no TV and a dilapidated front porch on a dirt road in Amarillo to live with people we usually only saw on holidays.

Home had died with our parents. We weren't ever going home again.

As I burst out of the stairwell, metal door clanging behind me, I take in a deep lungful of damp air. It's cloudy in Texas today, just as it was on that day ten years ago.

Dallas and Gavin and I don't roam the back roads of Amarillo like a pack of strays anymore, but in a lot of ways, our lives are still the same. Except now we make our way across Texas in Emmylou, the used Chevy Express that hauls us and our equipment from gig to gig, playing music for anyone who will pay us to. Even though sometimes they just pay us in food and tips from a jar.

We started playing in our grandparents' shed when I was fifteen, but we didn't really decide to make it official until we placed third in a competition at the state fair when I was a senior and the boys had both graduated.

I play the fiddle in Leaving Amarillo and I'm good at it. Our opening act usually consists of me playing "Devil Went Down to Georgia" all by my lonesome to get the crowd's attention. Most of the time it works. Unfortunately, by the time we realized Leaving Amarillo might be more than just a hobby, I'd already accepted a scholarship to the most prestigious music school in Texas.

Last year I spent a semester and a half at Shepherd School of Music in Houston becoming a classically trained violinist headed straight for an orchestra pit. When our grandfather had a mild heart attack just before spring break, I was able to put my scholarship on hold and came home to help with his care. Once he'd made a close to full recovery, Dallas and Gavin let me join back up with Leaving Amarillo for a few shows. And then a few more. Now that we've gained some momentum, I'm hoping I'll never have to go back to wearing all black and being herded in and out of an orchestra pit again. But if a manager with legitimate connections doesn't sign us by the end of the summer, it's back to college for me in the fall.

Despite the many times I've told my brother that being in an orchestra pit makes it impossible for me to breathe, Dallas has made it clear that he won't allow me to throw away my scholarship in order to live cooped up in a van with him and Gavin while working for scraps. Other than music, a girl like me doesn't have too many more attractive career options. If I drop out of school and the band doesn't make it, I'll likely end up spending my days asking folks if they want pie with their coffee.

Looking out over downtown Amarillo and watching gray clouds roll quickly across the sky, I feel the weight of time passing, slipping through my fingers faster than I can hold on to it.

Tossing up a silent prayer to our parents or to anyone who's listening, I beg for a chance. For a break. For a shot at making it.

Please, please let us get to live our dream.

Chapter 2

"BIRDS GOT ANYTHING GOOD TO SAY TODAY?"

Gavin's voice pulls me from my deep contemplative moment on the roof. "Lots of gossip. Think I'm going to use it for lyrics to a somebody-done-me-wrong song." I turn and face him, leaning up against the retaining ledge.

He glances over the ledge quickly and winces before propping his elbows on it. He's always been slightly afraid of heights. But Gavin Garrison has never been the type to let fear stop him from staring the devil straight in the face.

"Yeah? Well, let me know when you're ready to lay them down."

My eyes travel up his heavily inked arms to his expansive chest. I let them drift up to his masculine neck and around the outline of his strong jaw. Dark tendrils of thick hair curl outward beneath the edges of the gray knit cap he's wearing. He has an almost imperceptible dimple in his chin that matches the shallow one in his left cheek when he grins. Lord the things that happen to my body when he grins and that dimple shows. My pulse quickens just thinking about it.

"Um, lay what down?" My mind scrambles to snag a coherent

thought. Unfortunately they all scattered upon Gavin's arrival on the roof.

When we're playing, it's electric. It flows perfectly and we complement each other in every way possible. But take away the music and the noise and my brick-wall barrier of a brother, and I am a mess of epic proportions.

"The lyrics," he says slowly, side-eyeing me warily.

"Oh, right. Yeah, I'll keep you posted."

He sighs loudly from beside me. "Look, I know you're upset about breaking it off with what's-his-ass, but trust me, guys like that—"

"I'm not upset about that. About Jaggerd."

The second the words leave my mouth, though, Gavin's dark eyebrows dip lower, and I kind of wish I'd gone with his incorrect assumption. It'd be a lot easier to explain.

"Oh. Well, that's good. You just seemed kind of distracted in there. And your brother was more on edge than usual."

"Papa's had a string of rough nights. And . . . it's been ten years, Gav," I say softly. I can tell by the crease in his forehead and the pinch of his lips pulling together that he doesn't know what I'm talking about. "Our parents. Ten years since they—"

"Oh God. I didn't realize . . . I'm an idiot." He looks so distraught that I forget my own pain in the overwhelming urge to comfort him. He gets *the Look,* as I've begun to think of it. The one that says *I'd really like to take your pain away, take you to bed and make it all better with my dick, but your brother would kill me so I'll just stand here awkwardly while trying to figure out what to do with my arms.*

"It's okay," I tell him, to ease his suffering. "Just weighing on me more than usual today."

Little does he know, *the Look* comforts me. Because even though he can't put his arms around me, can't whisper sweet comforting words in my ear, or soothe my pain with kisses or more, his eyes tell me that he wants to—or he's tempted to, at least. And for right now, it's enough. The knowing. I just don't know how long it will be enough.

Gavin pulls a soft pack of Marlboro reds from his pocket and deftly slips out a cigarette. I frown.

"Thought you quit?"

His eyes cloud over, his stormy gaze pressing against mine. "I can only deny myself so many things, Bluebird."

As irritated as I am at catching him smoking, the nickname he gave me when we were kids still sends a wave of warmth right through me.

Dallas and Gavin mowed lawns the summer I turned thirteen. Dallas was saving to buy a truck and Gavin was . . . well, I don't really know exactly. Probably hoping to make enough money to provide for himself so he wouldn't feel like Nana and Papa's charity case.

I was living smack in the middle of the in-between—mind of a child, budding body of a woman. Feeling very much both and neither all at once.

Nana sent me a few streets over to where they were mowing to let them know supper was ready. Fighting the urge to skip so as not to get all sticky and sweaty and gross in the Texas humidity before sitting across the dinner table from Gavin, I walked as calmly as I could manage, letting my hands dance on the breeze and trying not to get distracted by flowers I was tempted to pick.

When I arrived at Camilla Baker's family pond, where the boys were mowing, they were huddled together and staring at the ground. Thinking one of them had been hurt and might be bleeding or possibly could have lost a foot or some toes at the least to the mower, I broke into a sprint until I reached them.

"Shh," Dallas said, raising an arm that barred me from stepping on what they were staring at. "I think it's still alive."

"What's still alive?" I whispered, entranced by the stillness of two boys who I knew firsthand hardly remained still or reserved this type of reverence for much of anything.

"Look," Gavin said, nodding to the ground. "Its chest is moving. It's still breathing."

A thrill shot through me as I realized it might be a snake or something wildly unappealing, but I looked anyway. And there beside a patch of pond grass, monkey grass Nana called it, was a small, mostly round bird with midmorning-sky-blue feathers breathing rapidly but not moving. Instinctively I reached down to retrieve it.

"No," Gavin practically shouted at me. "Don't. You can't touch it."

"Why not? It needs help."

He shook his head and then looked at me with this hollow expression that haunted me for years afterward. "Because if it's a baby and too young to fend for itself, the mother won't have anything to do with it if she can smell your scent on it. She'll abandon it and it won't survive on its own."

Funny, the things we remember. I remember that we all debated for a long time, though I couldn't recall the words of our three-sided argument if my life depended on it. But I remember that look, I remember realizing for the first time, finally comprehending just how different Gavin's life was from mine and Dallas's.

We were orphans, sure. We'd gone from a cushy life in the suburbs to a much more meager existence. But after long summer days with Gavin, Dallas and I went home to love. To meals and music and hugs and warm, clean beds. Sometimes he stayed over and sometimes he didn't.

Even now I don't know exactly what Gavin went home to when he left us. But I knew then that it was vastly different from where I lived.

Finally, Dallas picked the bird up and cradled it close to his chest on the walk back to our house. The three of us hypothesized the many possible causes of the bird's state of distress.

Once we'd arrived home, Dallas moved his hand from his chest to allow us a peek at our wounded patient.

It was so small. And so very still.

A sob threatened to roll out of my throat and I nearly choked holding it in. Life was hard, Dallas constantly reminded me. You couldn't go crying at every little thing.

But the unfairness of it, of a small, harmless feathered creature's life ending with no rhyme or reason to it, hit my thirteen-year-old self hard. It was a reminder of death, of the inevitable and unpredictable ending that had stolen my parents and that loomed over us like a cloudy Texas sky. Just as tears formed in my eyes, the tiny bird opened his and shrieked out a loud, piercing chirp. Maybe a thank-you or maybe a startled cry of shock at finding itself captive in human hands. Before either of us said a word, it flew away, leaving us staring up at the sky after it. I felt like I'd witnessed a miracle.

Nana hollered for us to get in the house and we told her a story I suspect she probably thought the three of us concocted out of boredom.

After dinner, during my nightly piano lesson, I tried my hand at whistling like the bluebird had. I wasn't great at it. The boys mocked me profusely. Well, Dallas mostly. Gavin just smiled at his best friend's antics. When I'd finished my lesson and my attempts at whistling, we ate ice cream from paper bowls on the front porch.

Once we were finished, Gavin stood to leave. And because I'd seen his face, seen the hurt that flashed behind his eyes when he'd spoke of the bird's mother abandoning it, I didn't want him to go.

It was growing darker so Papa offered to drive him home. I stood there, trying to think of a way to make him stay. Once Nana had forced my brother inside to bathe and Papa had gone to grab the truck keys, I reached out for the boy standing solemnly on the porch and staring at the night sky. He stood just out of my reach, as he always tended to do.

"Don't go. Just . . . stay," I whispered, feeling my face heat with the words. "You could stay here." I meant forever, but I never asked if he understood the full implication of my offer.

He glanced over at me with sad eyes, but then he winked. "I'll be okay, Bluebird. You don't have to worry about me."

But I did. I still do.

Just like he stills calls me Bluebird. But only in private, and never in front of my brother.

Snapping back to the present, I snatch the unlit cigarette from his fingers and flick it over the edge of the rooftop. "Yeah, well, I think you can deny yourself cancer."

"What the hell?" He gapes at me and I shrug.

"Band wouldn't be the same without a drummer. Probably take us a little while to replace you."

His mouth quirks up but he narrows his eyes in what could pass for anger to an unknowing bystander. I can tell he's trying to be all broody and impenetrable, but that version of Gavin is for the public. The random girls who throw their red lace panties at him. But to me, he's Gav. The boy I've known most of my life. The one whose mom was so cracked out or high on whatever the hell most of the time, she couldn't be bothered to raise her son. *Raise* is too lofty a word for

Katrina Garrison. More like she couldn't be bothered to keep him alive. But thankfully Gavin is scrappy and tough and sure as shit never needed anyone like her.

When we were growing up, he was the one always keeping her alive, reminding her to eat and bathe. And she was too busy securing the means for her next hit to do the same for him. The Gavin I know has nearly fallen apart in front of us on multiple occasions when his worthless excuse for a mother nearly overdosed. So his tough-guy act is wasted on me.

"All right. You win." He reaches the hand holding the pack behind him as if to tuck them back into his pocket, but I hold mine out.

I twitch my fingers twice in a "gimme" motion and he scoffs at me.

"Jesus Christ, Dix. I won't smoke around you, okay? This pack cost me six bucks."

I raise my eyebrows, silently challenging him to keep arguing with me. It's pointless and his efforts to continue this are futile, which he should know by now.

After a minute-long stare-down, he rolls his eyes toward the sky in exasperation and places the pack in my outstretched palm. I promptly fling it over the side of the building.

"Well now you're just littering."

"Better than standing here getting secondhand cancer while watching you take years off your own life." I glare right back at him, because that's the thing about Gavin. The thing that infuriates me to no end. He will drop everything to take care of his deadbeat, drug-addicted mother. And if Dallas or I needed a kidney or something, he'd be first in line to donate. But when it comes to taking care of himself? The boy lives like he's trying to express-lane his own funeral sometimes.

"Aww, would you miss me?"

And just when I'm feeling good and sorry for him, he patronizes and antagonizes me. So sometimes I want to kick him in the shin. But then I'd be the one to drop to my knees and check to make sure he wasn't hurt. If I actually got on my knees in front of Gavin Garrison, there's no telling what kind of trouble I'd get into while I was down there. So I resist the urge to kick him for both our sakes.

"Yeah, I'd miss you, Gav," I answer through gritted teeth. "Because I'd be wondering where that giant pain in my a—"

"Ah, ah, ah. Language, sweet girl. What would your brother say if he heard you out here talking dirty to me?"

His eyes drop to my lips and I can feel what discussing dirty talk is doing to him. It's doing something to me, too. A couple of somethings.

"Okay," I relent, stepping even closer. "Tell you what. You keep your mouth clean, and I'll try to do the same. Deal?"

"Hm, I don't know. There is something awfully sexy about ugly words coming from such a pretty mouth."

I can't help but smirk. "The truth finally comes out. You think I'm sexy."

"You have no idea what I think." He winks but his tone is low, a warning. He turns to the side, resting his back and elbows on the ledge so that he's no longer facing me. I hate that I can't read his expression. The muscle in his jaw pops and his body is still rigid. He can't make up his mind about us. We've always had something. A connection. But the older we get, the more complicated it becomes.

"Whatever you say, Gav." I lift one shoulder noncommittally, as if I couldn't care less. But this close to him, my bravado melts and I'm seconds from becoming a quivering mess and begging him to tell me what he thinks about me. About us. Before my secret desire can get the best of me, I turn to walk back inside the building. But I am me and me is stubborn and I hate being the one to break first. So I turn and give him something to think about.

"Oh, and Gav?"

"Yeah?"

I make eye contact, making sure he hears me, that he feels the full weight of my words. "For the record, I don't make my decisions based on what my brother would say."

He cocks his head to the side and crosses both mouthwatering forearms over his chest. "That so?"

Yes. Unlike you.

The words are right there on the tip of my tongue, begging to be released. But I clench my teeth, trapping them inside.

I hold his gaze, fighting to remain grounded instead of tumbling headfirst into a stare that heats my blood hotter every time I see it.

"See you inside," I say softly before making my escape.

Okay, man. Yeah. Got it. And seriously, thanks. I mean it. There's anything I can do for you, holler. All right?"

Dallas disconnects the call and his shining blue eyes flicker first to me, where I'm standing applying rosin to my bow, then over to where Gavin has just joined us.

"That was Levi Eaton," he says without giving either of us time to inquire about the phone call that has him grinning almost maniacally. "His band is backing out of Austin MusicFest. His keyboard player slept with the lead singer's wife. Needless to say, they're taking a breather."

"Nice," Gavin says with a touch of sarcastic awe in his voice.

"Yeah," my brother says nodding as the door closes behind him;

he looks like he's announcing lottery winnings. "I mean, not that the dude nailed the guy's wife. But that means there's performance space available at the festival."

Austin MusicFest is a five-day music festival on Sixth Street, second in size only to South by Southwest. It doesn't pay much, but the exposure alone is worth more than we'd make in a year. Maybe even more than that.

We've signed up to be considered every year since we started playing seriously. But so far we haven't been able to get onto the lineup.

"So you think we can just show up and pretend to be Levi's band?" I set the rosin aside and join in the conversation.

"No." Dallas laughs as if I've said something funny. "We're in. As us. Levi even gave us his hotel room. Thank goodness, because otherwise we'd be sleeping in the van all week."

The air vacates my lungs as if Dallas popped them with his words. Maybe someone heard my rooftop prayer after all.

Up until now, we've mostly performed gigs close to home. Sure we've slept in the van from time to time when playing out of town, but never for more than one night at a time. And the boys always stay safely in the front seats and I crash on the bench seat in the back. When on the road we sleep in shifts and take turns driving the hunk of junk we lovingly named Emmylou after my infatuation with Emmylou Harris.

This will be different. Much different.

"There are over one hundred managers attending and at least as many booking agents and record label execs. This is it. This is our shot. Finally." My brother beams at us. "We'll leave tomorrow night." His eyes widen as they meet mine. "We're in. Holy shit, we're in."

The guys are fist-bumping and celebrating while I try to process what this means. My mouth is dry when my gaze makes its way over to the tattooed, tortured soul grinning from behind his drum kit.

I've done the best I can to keep my distance, to behave myself and not open my mouth and let my heart fall out. It would ruin everything.

One week. One hotel room. Our shot at finally making it.

I don't know if I can do this.

I just know that I have to.

Chapter 3

THE DRIVE TO AUSTIN TAKES A LITTLE OVER SEVEN HOURS. I SLEEP as much as one can in a moving vehicle in the backseat for most of the ride. During the few stretches where the three of us are all conscious at the same time, we discuss possible changes to the set list, ideas for reworking a few songs, and rough spots that need to be smoothed out in one of our newer ones.

When we pull into the parking lot at the Days Inn where Levi had booked the room he's letting us use, we're all a little road weary and yet keyed up with excitement and nerves.

Once we've checked in and been given access cards for our room, we head up to the third floor on an elevator that smells faintly of urine and stale beer. It's not the nicest hotel, but it's relatively affordable. Many of the musicians playing in the festival will likely be staying here as well.

As soon as we drop our bags in the small room with two beds and a cot, Dallas and Gavin begin unloading our belongings.

I lower myself onto the bed by the window and watch them.

Dallas frowns at the two beds and then moves the cot into the narrow space between them. "I'll take the cot."

Gavin stops drumming his sticks on the small table in the corner beside me. "I can take the cot. I've slept on worse."

My hearts lurches forward, yanking my stomach along with it. Trying to blink back the image of little boy Gavin sleeping on a filthy floor God knows where, I see my brother give Gavin a meaningful look that ends the conversation abruptly.

Relief loosens some of the tension I've carried since learning we'd be sharing a room. The thought of sleeping—or attempting to sleep—in a bedroom with Gavin is daunting, and playing at one of the largest music festivals in the South on no sleep was nerve-racking, to say the least. But with Dallas between us as he's always been, I'm probably less inclined to lie in bed wondering what it would be like to have Gavin in mine.

The truth is, while I don't need the fame and bright lights that my brother chases relentlessly, my desire to see the band become legitimate is just as strong. The alternative is a fate I try not to think about. I don't belong in an orchestra pit playing music that feels stifling and far too fancy for me. I belong here, with these two men I love in vastly different ways, playing the music I was raised on.

Once we're settled into the room and Dallas has spoken with Levi about a rehearsal space we'll be able to use during the week, I step outside to call Papa to let him know we've arrived safe and sound. He doesn't answer so I leave a message.

When I step back into the room both of the boys are already asleep. Chewing a barely warm, slightly spongy waffle leftover from our drive-through breakfast, I think about Papa. Since his heart attack—which he only refers to as an "episode"—I haven't been away from him for more than a night. He'll turn seventy-six this year and his hearing is nearly gone but his voice is still strong in my head.

The first time I picked up his fiddle he chuckled and said if I could tame it, it was mine. For weeks I pissed off the neighbors and every animal in hearing distance. And then he began to show me the basics. Major one, major four, and major five. Where to stroke the strings to get a richer sound, how to make it sing. "Amazing Grace" was the first song I ever played on it from start to finish. It was wobbly and rough, but Papa declared it officially mine that day.

When my parents died, it felt like everything good inside of me had been scooped out and thrown away. Memories hurt, any ideas about what my future might contain hurt. The strange looks from the kids at my new school made me want to turn myself inside out and hide. But playing Papa's fiddle filled me with something special, something magical. It gave me back something I'd lost with my mom and dad. Hope.

I ran home from school every day and woke up early in the mornings on weekends, itching to get my hands on Oz. Papa said I could name it, and I'd just seen *The Wizard of Oz*. Dorothy left behind her drab gray world and went somewhere magical and colorful and that's what playing was for me. Which is why I don't look over at Gavin's chiseled, tattooed body sprawled across the other bed in the room even though I want to.

I fall asleep thinking about song lyrics and pushing out of my head thoughts of how it would feel to have his hands on me and his lips on mine.

I woke up several times to see my brother sitting up and staring intently at song lyrics I know he's struggling with. But I was too tired to give any worthwhile input so I dozed off each time. I was still groggy when he roused Gavin and me so we could head out to rehearse our final set list at an empty storage space Levi had managed to procure for the week.

"Let's play 'Ring of Fire' before 'Whiskey Redemption,'" my brother commands. "We'll get their attention with covers then mix in our originals and try to keep the momentum upbeat throughout the entire set."

Gavin writes our set list down on a piece of hotel stationery he snagged from the room and raises his eyes to mine. "Dixie gonna play her opener?"

Dallas turns toward me wearing his worries plainly on his face. "You up for it? This is the real deal, Dix." Bright blue eyes just a shade darker than mine bore into me. I swallow hard and attempt a quick calculation of the odds of my getting distracted by some half-dressed, completely wasted groupie flashing Gavin. Wouldn't be the first time.

"I am. Promise." I give him my most confident grin and he gives me a taut smile in return. I don't bother commenting on his lack of confidence in me because the tension is already tight enough as it is.

"All right then." He nods at me before returning to his mark and strapping on his guitar. "Let's do this."

I am focused while we play, careful to concentrate on the nuances of each piece of music. Just as this is my ticket out of the orchestra pit, I know this is Dallas's shot to finally make a name for the band—to make us more than a little-known group that plays local gigs. Barely getting by makes him feel like a failure, like he isn't taking good care of me or giving me the life I deserve. I've overheard him telling Gavin that more than once.

"Take care of each other" was the last thing my father said to us before he and my mom found themselves directly in the path of a drunk who'd fallen asleep at the wheel. My brother took these words to mean so much more than I think my father probably intended.

Nana and Papa barely had two nickels to rub together when we moved in with them. They were simple folks living happily within their means. The funeral and burial ate up our parents' meager life insurance policies, and even the money from the state wasn't much. I can remember going to the thrift store for school clothes that the girls at school would only laugh at. Though not as much as they made fun of how I looked in my brother's hand-me-downs. Through it all, Dallas promised me over and over that it would get better.

He's still trying to make it better. Trying to keep a promise he never needed to make. I've told him a million times that I am okay. That I don't need expensive things or designer clothes to be happy. I didn't need them back then and I don't need them now. But Dallas feels like he failed Mom and Dad somehow and I've accepted that that's his cross to bear.

"Let's take five," Dallas calls out after we hit the halfway mark in our set.

We talk about changing my opener during the break. Dallas is nervous for me; I can tell by the worry lines creasing his forehead.

"It's not that I don't like it," he tells me. "I'm just not sure it's the right thing to open with."

"How about I play this one instead?" Tucking my chin down, I lift my bow and jump into Alabama's "If You're Gonna Play in Texas." The music carries me to a place where the stress and the pressure can't touch me.

When I finish, Dallas and Gavin are both grinning at me.

"That work?"

"Yeah, Dixie Leigh," Dallas says with a smirk of approval. "That'll do."

The rest of our set is a combination of songs we've written together interwoven throughout a stream of both contemporary and classic country songs. We play a few numbers by Johnny Cash with a rock-and-roll edge added to them, and then a few more recent hits with our own flavor. We've even countrified a few rap songs by Jay-Z and Bruno Mars just for fun, but strangely enough, those are the ones the audiences really seem to get into.

After a successful rehearsal, the tense lines on Dallas's face have smoothed and even Gavin seems more at ease.

"Can we grab some dinner? I'm starving," I tell them when we're finished.

"Let's just order pizza and have it delivered to the room. I want to work on our song some more. Try and get something workable down before tomorrow night." Dallas strides purposefully over to his guitar case and begins packing up.

We've been working on this song, the band's anthem my brother insists we need, for the better part of a year. If I have to go back to that room, where Dallas's worries are breathing up all the oxygen, I might wither and die. He isn't verbalizing them, but I can feel his concerns emanating from him, growing more intense every minute as we approach performance time. Maybe it's a sibling thing.

Gavin must be able to read my thoughts—a terrifying possibility, really—because he steps between my brother and me before I say anything.

"How about we go to that Italian place we passed on the way here? It's in walking distance. D, you can still get pizza and we can talk about the song without being stuck in that room."

I watch Dallas, waiting for his response. He rakes a hand through his hair before huffing out a loud breath and looking from me to Gavin and back to me again.

"I'd really just rather work, to be honest." He looks at each of us in turn again, frowning when he sees the disappointment on my face. "I know I'm being kind of slave driver lately, but I promise I have the band's best interest at the heart of my madness. Does that make me any less of a pain in the ass?"

I give my brother a gentle shoulder nudge of understanding. I know he means well, and Gavin knows, too. "It's okay, Dallas. We know that," I tell him. "It's just . . . sometimes—"

"Sometimes we throw darts at pictures of you for fun," Gavin breaks in.

Gavin's comment makes Dallas laugh out loud. The tension dissipates as if it never existed. This is why we work. Why Leaving Amarillo is still together. I love the music but hate the business side of it. Dallas lives for the business side of it. Meanwhile, Gavin keeps us from murdering each other with our instruments.

And this is why I'm afraid. If our dynamic changes, if I lose the thin white-knuckle hold I have on my feelings for Gavin, it will ruin everything. It will ruin us.

I don't know who I am without Leaving Amarillo. What's even more frightening is I don't know who Dallas or Gav are without it, either. Maybe in another life I'm a bank teller and they're construction workers or something. But in this life, we are this band. Each of us an integral part of something much bigger than us.

"Y'all go ahead," Dallas begins as we leave the empty warehouse. "I'll grab something at the hotel."

I frown at him. "Dallas—"

"Seriously. I've got half a dozen ideas about how to make this song work. I need to get on it before I lose the lyrics in my head." He opens the back of the van and puts his guitar inside, then reaches for my case. "Promise I'm good. I just want to get on this while it's fresh."

Gavin finishes loading his kit and slams the back door. "Dude, it's fine. We can come on back with you. We'll order pizza, like you said."

I sigh, because I know my brother has won and it's back to the room of doom we go. Between our luggage and equipment and the cot Gavin sleeps on, the overcrowded space is a cramped maze.

"Dixie looks like I just sentenced her to death," Dallas says with an eye roll in my direction.

I toss him a dirty look. "Or a life sentence in room 306 at the Days Inn, which is pretty much a fate worse than."

Just as Gavin turns to open the passenger door of the van for me, Dallas stops him. "Seriously. Go. Eat. I kind of need to be alone anyways. This song is kicking my ass and I'm sick and tired of it."

Gavin arches a brow, but I don't waste any time.

"You heard the man, Garrison. Let's go. Feed me."

"You sure?" Gavin asks, turning back to Dallas and prompting me to contemplate strangling him.

My brother reaches behind his head and rubs his neck. "Yeah, man. I'm sure. Just, uh, don't be too long. We all need our rest for tomorrow."

They exchange a look loaded with something I can't read from where I'm standing. But I can make an educated guess. Typically the three of us stay together. Gavin and I grabbing dinner alone, without my brother, shouldn't be a big deal. And yet, I see it. The warning in my brother's eyes any time Gavin and I do something without him chaperoning us. It says "sit across the table, don't let her have any alcohol, and keep your hands to your damn self."

Gavin nods at the unspoken agreement and we both call out to my brother that we'll see him later.

Walking the two blocks to the restaurant is an exercise in patience and restraint. Gavin walks close enough that I can feel the heat from his arm swinging next to mine. Just as I'm about to say to hell with it and link my arm with his like it's 1926 and we're strolling along the promenade instead of a cracked sidewalk on the run-down in-dustrial side of town, a horn blows and we both jump. Glancing over my shoulder I see my brother drive by and throw his hand out the window.

All I can think is, *the ass did that on purpose.* Gavin tosses my brother a quick two-fingered wave as the van pulls away toward the hotel. I cut my eyes to his profile. He's walking an extra foot away from me now and I already miss the warmth. The horn blast was a reminder: *Keep your distance.*

Chapter 4

GAVIN KEEPS AT LEAST AN ARM'S LENGTH BETWEEN US FOR THE rest of our walk to the restaurant. It leaves me more than slightly irritated with my brother.

Deep down I know that it's not that Dallas wants to hurt me, or that he wants me to be unhappy. Just like I can feel his constant anxiety about the band's future, I know that he hasn't missed my burgeoning feelings for Gavin. And I suspect he knows what could happen if I act on my feelings and get them crushed under the heel of Gavin's boot like so many other girls have.

My brother doesn't subscribe to the same belief system about love that I do. He seems to have very little faith in the magic ability of it to make everything better, or at least bearable. His high school girlfriend, Robyn, left for college at the University of Texas the summer after graduation and they did the long-distance thing for two years before calling it quits. From the bits and pieces I caught of their final days together, Robyn wanted to make it work. But for reasons my brother won't discuss, they broke it off. Robyn Breeland was gorgeous and funny and smart. And real. And most important, she was nice to me. Always. No matter what drama she and Dallas were dealing with, she was always there for me. She still checks in with me from time to time. She's like the big sister I never had.

Any time I've tried to pry my brother for information about what exactly happened between them, he has shrugged it off and grumbled some nonsense about long-distance relationships and priorities. But I was doing laundry the last time we were home and under his bed was a box Robyn had given him in high school. I glanced inside and my heart swelled when I saw the sweet pictures of them together. They looked so pretty and shiny in their homecoming and prom photos. The little notes she'd written him weren't covered in hearts, but I could tell they were private by how tightly they were folded, so I didn't read them. Just the fact that my brother still had the box nearly three years after their breakup told me that he still cared about her. He wasn't the type to hold on to things, ever. Even Mom and Dad's belongings hadn't held much sentimental value for him.

"What's keeping you so quiet tonight, Bluebird?"

Gavin's voice shakes me from my thoughts and I look over at him. His forehead is creased and he seems genuinely concerned. Still slightly peeved by his keeping his distance, I consider saying "nothing" and ignoring him. But those eyes have always pulled the truth right out of me.

"You think Dallas ever misses Robyn?"

His expression indicates he didn't see this particular question coming. "Breeland?"

"Did he date another Robyn I never met?"

He rolls his eyes and flicks the lighter I didn't notice before in his right hand. "No, smartass. I just didn't expect you to bring her up. What made you think of her?"

I shrug. "I don't know. Just seems sad to me. I liked her. A lot. I kind of hoped they'd get married one day."

Two more harsh flicks of the lighter and Gavin looks like he might be ill. "Married? He's only twenty-two for fuck's sakes."

"I didn't mean *soon*. I just meant one day. They were happy together. Not everyone can handle Dallas the way she did. In fact, I'm a little worried he won't ever be able to find anyone able to put up with his crazy self. I don't want him to end up alone and sleeping on my couch for the rest of his life."

Gavin chuckles and the musical sound tightens the muscles in my stomach.

There are a lot of different types of laughs in this world. Contagious ones, high-pitched ones, annoyingly out-of-control ones. But Gavin Garrison's laugh is low and deep, and so seldom heard that it slides into the cracks in my heart, filling them with the melodic sound like a habit-forming narcotic I can't get enough of.

Thankfully we reach Mangieri's and I have a few minutes to compose myself while we're seated and given menus. Perusing the menu covered with pictures of food that makes my stomach growl, I inhale the sweet, tangy scent of tomatoes and garlic.

"What are you gonna get, Blu—"

"Oh my gosh," a waitress standing beside our table exclaims before he can finish. "Y'all are in that band. Leaving Amarillo, right?"

Apparently the red-haired chick recognizes us, which is odd. But at least she got the name of the band right. We've been called everything from Loving Eldorado to Losing Armadillos. Score one point for her. I'm flattered and grateful that we actually have a fan. But when I glance up at her, she's fawning over Gavin in a way that makes me want to gouge out her big brown doe eyes.

"Yes ma'am," Gavin answers, his drawl a little more pronounced and his voice a little deeper than usual. I raise a brow but he doesn't notice. Because apparently I've turned invisible. "You've heard of us?"

A wide smile brightens her face and I have to admit she's not unattractive. She'd probably be even prettier if she washed off a good portion of the gaudy makeup she's wearing.

"I saw you at Beale Street last year and I pretty much stalk you online." Her cheeks darken with embarrassment and she lowers her head. "I mean, not *stalk,* but I have all the songs available on my iPod and, um, yeah. I'm a fan. Obviously. Wow, I am totally making an idiot out of myself."

Yes, you are. Now go away.

Gavin leans back in his chair and does elevator eyes on her and I have a sudden urge to throat-punch him. "We don't think any of our fans are idiots, darlin'. All five of you are wildly intelligent with excellent taste." He winks, and I swear, she nearly strips her clothes off right there.

In that moment, I'm extremely thankful that no one's brought us silverware yet because I'm feeling pretty stabby.

"I'm coming to see y'all at MusicFest this week. I was so excited to see that y'all had gotten added to the lineup. Me and my girlfriends could only get general admission tickets though. The VIP ones sold out superfast." She sticks out a pouty bottom lip, and I grip my own knee until it stings to force myself to remain silent.

"You got a pen?"

I tear my eyes from the exchange that's causing me more pain than it should. Swallowing the angry persistent lump forming in my throat, I stare at the red and black laminated menu as if there's going to be a test on it.

The jingle of the waitress's bracelets as she hands Gavin a pen grinds against my exposed nerves. I know in my logical mind that I'm on the verge of losing it for no real reason. But logic has never had much say when it comes to my feelings for Gavin.

It's when he takes her hand and slowly slides up the sleeve of her dress shirt so that he can write on her wrist that I lose my mind completely. The table rattles with the vibration of my suddenly jerking knee. I release it and exhale slowly, quietly, in an attempt to have my jungle-cat jealous-rage breakdown as discreetly as possible.

"That's my number . . ."

"Marissa," she offers helpfully.

"Marissa," he says slowly, giving her his trademark panty-dropping grin and gifting her a look at his stupid fucking dimple. "You just shoot me a text—or call so I can hear that pretty voice—when y'all get to the festival and I'll make sure you get a front-row spot when we go on."

I snort because we don't have that kind of control over the crowd. We barely even made it here. But then I feel sick because I'm sure he's giving her his number so he can give her a private show. Bile rises in my throat as they make let's-get-naked eyes at each other. The fist squeezing the heck out of my heart finally loosens its grip just as he releases her wrist so that she can get our drinks.

Gavin turns back to me like I haven't been sitting here for three and a half minutes plotting his gruesome death with flatware.

"So whatcha gettin'?"

My chest heaves with the effort it takes to sit still and breathe air instead of lunging across the table. I lower my menu and give setting him on fire with my glare a try.

"Bluebird? I asked what you were—" His words die in his throat when he meets my narrowed eyes. "Um, you okay?"

Focus, Dixie Leigh.

"You never touch me," I say evenly, surprised that I don't sound nearly as crazed as I feel.

"What?" He glances down at his menu as if it will contain an explanation of some sort.

"You never touch me. We've known each other for ten years and you don't casually sling your arm across my shoulders, or link arms with me, or hold my hand when we're walking together. You don't hug me or put your hand on the small of my back."

Gavin clears his throat and glances to the side like a cornered animal, probably looking for the nearest escape route. "Okay. So I don't touch you. So what? Can we order now?"

Reaching across the table I lower the menu he's holding up like a shield. "So you've known that waitress for five seconds and you caressed her arm like it was your dick. And yet we've known each other for forever and you never touch me."

I watch as his eyes widen and the knot in his throat rises and falls. "Please tell me you're joking. Do you seriously want to do this right now?"

"Just tell me why. Tell me why you have no problem putting your hands on a complete stranger and you avoid touching me as if I'm diseased, which I'm not, for the record."

"You know good and damn well I don't think you're *diseased.*" His expression hardens and I can't read it. It almost looks as if he thinks I'm playing dumb, like I already know the answer.

I scoff at him. "Don't blame it on Dallas. I hardly think he'd lose his mind just because you put your arm around me or something."

His hooded gaze gets even darker and I'm confused. The waitress returns with our drinks but Gavin doesn't look away from me to acknowledge her.

"Are y'all ready to—"

"We need a minute," Gavin practically growls at her.

Once she's gone, I take a sip of my water while maintaining eye contact with him. Whatever is happening between us, it's important. And I don't want to miss a single second of it.

"You act like I'm trying to lure you into bed. I'm not. I just want to know why you don't ever—"

"Listen to me, and listen close. You and me? We are not having this conversation. Not here, not now, and not ever. Is that clear?" His words, his tone, his penetrating glare—all of it—jump-starts my heart until it's a battering ram inside my chest.

I fold my arms over my chest. "Oh yeah? Well I say we are."

"Well you can have it with your fucking self then. I'll get my food to go." He shoves back from the table, scraping his chair roughly against the tile floor as he stands.

I flinch because he doesn't talk to me like this. Or at least he never has before. I both love it and hate it. It's hot and terrifying all at once.

"Gav, wait. Please. I'm sorry." I reach out and wrap my fingers around his wrist, which he jerks from my grasp as if I've electrocuted him. I fold my hands in my lap and stare up at him with pleading eyes.

He glares at me for what feels like ten lifetimes before he lowers himself back into his seat and trains his attention back on his menu. For the next few minutes I try to make eye contact, to bring him back to that place we were in moments ago when we were connected. But he's dead set on ignoring me.

"I'm torn between the pesto penne and Olivia's Alfredo," I say, to let him know he's off the hook. For now.

He cuts his eyes back to me, cautiously, as if testing to see if I've really let it go. I haven't, but I'm going to have to take it easier on him if I want actual answers.

"Order the pesto and I'll get the Alfredo. We'll split halfway," he relents.

I let the hint of a smile play on my lips and nod. When we were kids, I could never decide between chocolate and strawberry ice cream. Gavin always got chocolate and then traded me for my pink cone when I was ready. Even though Dallas gave him hell about it.

"Wipe that smirk off your face. I was going to get the Alfredo anyways."

"Mm-hm. Sure you were." My lips twitch and I'm about to remind him about the ice cream when the waitress returns.

"Y'all ready?"

Gavin gives her that freaking grin again. The one he never gives to me. "Yeah, darlin'. We're ready." He orders our pasta and hands her the menus. Once again my stomach tenses and turns.

"Put the claws away, baby. Let's just enjoy our dinner."

My face has betrayed me by putting my emotions on display. I contort it into a smile that he can probably tell is forced.

"I'll try. It'd help if you'd stop eye-fucking the waitress."

Both of his brows go up in surprise. His intrigued gaze drops to my mouth and I'm reminded of what he said about dirty words and clean mouths. I roll my lower lip between my teeth and lean forward.

"Gavin," I say, drawing his attention back to my eyes. "I'm not trying to piss you off. But we do need to talk. Soon."

"No," he says evenly, his eyes latching on to mine. "We don't."

"We're in a band together. We're about to spend a week practically living together. You can't just pretend there's nothing going on, that you don't feel it. I know that you do."

The tension rolls off him and crashes into me with the same kind of force he beats the hell out of his drums with. I know I'm pushing it, but if we don't at least acknowledge that there is something between us, then I am going to implode. And when I do, it won't be pretty. I'm afraid it will ruin everything. Ruin us, the band, everything good in my life—in all three of our lives. Maybe Gavin's content floating along in the river of denial, but I'm drowning in it.

He tilts his head from side to side, stretching his neck and then sighing. "Look, I'm a guy, and you're a girl, and yeah, there are moments when . . ." Gavin glances around as if there might be secret spies hired by my brother listening in on our conversation. "When things get a little intense," he finishes.

A little intense?

More like there are moments when I want to tear his clothes from his body and trace his intricate tattoos with my tongue. Moments I foresee coming this very week in which I will have to clutch my bedsheets with both hands to keep from reaching out for him in the middle of the night. Moments when I'm so overcome with a painful need I know only he can soothe that I might accidentally on purpose ravage him without bothering to care who's around.

A little intense is a gross understatement.

"And," I prompt.

He gives me a slight shake of his head. "And nothing. There's nothing we can do about it. Do I think you're beautiful? Of course I do. I have eyes. Every guy in this room is wishing he was me right now. But we're more than that. You and Dallas are all I have. Do you get that? Do you know what would happen if we . . . if we . . ." Another shake of his head and his gaze clouds over. "So do us all a favor and drop it. Okay?"

My head and heart are reeling from his admission. He thinks I'm beautiful, he's attracted to me, but he wants me to drop it because I mean too much to him. The waitress, on the other hand, apparently means just enough to him.

She returns with our food and lingers beside Gavin. After she sets our steaming plates in front of us she turns to him and slips the black leather padfolio into his hand. I suspect it contains more than just the check. I watch helplessly as their eyes meet.

"If you decide you want dessert," she says to him, her tone deepening and dripping with suggestion on the last word, "let me know and I'll take care of it for you."

I look down at my plate of pesto, suddenly not hungry at all. Gavin catches her wrist, and my heart leaps into my head and hammers out its anger inside my skull. Without even a glance in my direction, he pulls her to him and whispers something in her ear. She smiles and nods before walking away.

My feelings for Gavin have always been uncontrollable and pretty much impossible to identify by name or articulate. But right now, I hate him. I freaking hate him with every fiber of my being. My hands are trembling and I'm in danger of being blinded by rage.

Sucking in a breath as my vision blurs behind a red haze, I shake my head at him.

"You know," I begin on a shaky breath, "it's one thing if you don't want me. Or if you just don't want me *enough* to risk it. I can probably live with that. But watching you parade your conquests in front of me is too much. Even for me."

Gavin doesn't say a word as I stand and storm away from our table.

I just made a humiliating scene in front of the one person I've worked so hard to keep my cool in front of. But if I don't escape to the safety of the ladies' room in the next five seconds, I'm going to make an even bigger one.

Chapter 5

"OH, DON'T WORRY," I OVERHEAR THE WAITRESS TELLING SOME-one on the phone as soon as I step into the ladies' room. "I'm willing to do whatever it takes. We'll be in the VIP for sure." She laughs and I glare openly at her as she makes a crass joke about taking one for the team. "Hey, Stace, I'll call you back when I get off, okay?" Another harsh laugh and a pointed smirk at me. "Well, after I get off Gavin Garrison that is."

Her casual use of his name provokes a murderous rage inside of me. Her confident grin tells me she knows this. The lyrics to "Jolene" begin playing on a steady loop in my mind.

"Hey, you're the fiddle player, right? Have you and he ever, you know, before? Is he as yummy in bed as he looks?" She yanks her sleek red locks into a low ponytail and appraises her reflection in the mirror.

Yummy? Who uses such a childish word to describe sex? This chick, apparently. Well, now I just want to slap her on general principles.

A humorless laugh escapes my lips. "Guess you'll be finding out for yourself. Excuse me." Stepping around her, I brace my hands on the marble counter surrounding the sink. Determined not to have my breakdown in front of this random waitress, I take a deep breath and splash a few handfuls of icy water on my face. Straightening, I grab a paper towel and dry off. My mascara ran just a little so I dab it under my eyes until the smudges are gone.

Glancing over I see that she's applying lip gloss and leaving. Thankfully.

"I hope I'm not like encroaching on your territory or something." She smiles, but it's not genuine and doesn't reach her eyes. "I mean, I have a boyfriend and all. I just have a soft spot for musicians."

"I'm sure you've had plenty of musicians in your *soft spot*," I say without thinking.

Her eyes brighten and I can tell this is what she wants. A catfight. A confrontation. Half of the reason she wants him is probably because I had my defending-my-kill face on out there. Well to hell with both of them.

"Oh, aren't you precious. You've got a thing for him," she practically singsongs while squealing with delight. "How sweet. But, honey, that's a man out there. Bless your heart. You're just a kid, sweetie." She tosses me a falsely sympathetic head tilt on her way out.

I don't bother informing her that he's barely a year older than me. I'm pretty sure she's not talking about physical age anyway. I've lived in Texas my whole life. So I know when someone says, "Aren't you precious?" they mean, "God, you're stupid." And when a woman blesses someone's heart she's really telling him or her that they're too damn dumb to live.

Maybe she's right. My eyes narrow critically at my reflection. I'm tallish for a girl, five foot six and thin, but I have some shape to me. Enough that I haven't been mistaken for a boy since I was fourteen. My naturally curly hair is dark and has gotten far too long, nearly reaching my waist, but I haven't had time to get it cut since we've been on the road so much. It lightens a little in the summer, picking up tones of red when my pale ivory skin, reminiscent of my mom's tone, turns a light shade of golden brown. My eyes are large compared to the smaller features on my face and are a version of blue that looks like clear gray bordering on green in sunlight. But in the fluorescents of the restroom, I look washed out and faded.

I'm not hideous or anything, but I'm not a walking sex stick like Gavin Garrison, either. The waitress's words linger in my head. Maybe Gavin has had so many women he's tired of regular sex and is into cuffs and whips and God knows what else. And that's just not me. I sigh and watch as my shoulders drop.

I know what I am. I'm lace and daisies and a fiddle on my grandparents' back porch. Dirt roads and dandelions, like Papa says. Vinyl records in a world of digital downloads. Papa also used to say I had an old soul and that's why I had an appreciation for things before my time. But Gavin is the kind of man every type of woman wants. He's dangerous and daring where I'm sweet and safe. Hard where I'm soft, rough edges where I'm smooth.

We don't belong together and I'm an idiot for thinking I could ever have him. I feel foolish for daring to even dream that I could tame someone who's had every type of woman in his bed and never asked a single one of them back for round two.

Jaggerd McKinley was much more my speed. He works at his dad's body shop in Amarillo. He's a nine-to-five fella—a blue-collar guy with blue-collar dreams. He's right smack in the middle of my league. Heck, he's the epitome of my league.

I vow to myself then and there to let go of this lust-fueled need to have Gavin Garrison in any way other than as a friend, a bandmate. Maybe I should consider myself lucky to get to be a part of his life in any way. He's white-hot, burning flames licking up everything in his path. And I'm just a little bluebird flying dangerously close to the fire.

When I finally pull myself together and exit the women's restroom, I run smack into Gavin and his new friend. The redhead is wrapped around him like a vine, like the ivy that used to cling to Nana and Papa's oak trees. Papa used to tear it off and burn it—said it choked the life out of the trees.

I'm having a similar fantasy.

"Dixie, wait," Gavin says, extracting himself from the grasp of his company for tonight.

"I'm gonna catch a cab and head back to the hotel." I swallow the nauseating pride clogging my esophagus. "Enjoy your evening."

I've barely made it five steps when a tall, dark-haired man steps in front of me. "Your leftovers, Miss," he says, thrusting two heavy takeout boxes into my hands.

"Um, thanks." I take them and bolt out the door.

Gavin can get the check, if he hasn't already. It's the least he can do for twisting me up into this human pretzel of messy, ugly emotions.

As soon as I'm out the door I sling the boxes into the nearby Dumpster with all my might.

"What if I wasn't finished?"

The deep timbre of his voice comes from directly behind me. Close enough to cause me to freeze for an entire second before turning around.

"Then you should've gotten them yourself." I shoot a quick glare at him before sticking my arm out and hailing a cab.

"I wasn't talking about the food. I think you know that."

My fists clench at my sides. "You know what, Gav? If you weren't finished with your little cherry-haired dessert item, then you're free to take your happy ass right on back in there. Don't let me stop you. You never have before."

Gavin's hands fly up in exasperation. He so rarely loses his composure it rattles me even more than his yelling.

"What do you want from me? Tell me what I'm supposed to do, because for the life of me, I can't seem to stop pushing your buttons." His forehead is creased and he's looking at me like I'm a puzzle with missing pieces.

Oh, he pushes my buttons all right.

All my resolve to let this go evaporates instantly. I may never be able to have him, but I want him to know. I *need* him to know how I feel. And even more than that, I need to know whether or not he feels the same way I do, if he feels the pull, the connection between us. If I haunt his dreams the way he owns mine.

Mustering every once of courage I have, I take a step closer to him. When I open my mouth, my heart falls out.

"I want you to touch me. To take me, to own and possess me like you know you already do. I want *you*—all of you. The good, the bad, and that secret darkness inside that you never show anyone else. I want to be the one you spend your nights with, the one you wake up with, and the one you can't stop thinking about."

Everything about him suddenly seems harder. His eyes, his jaw, the set of his shoulders. "You're playing with fire, little Bluebird."

"I know," I say softly. "But I can't stop. I don't want to."

For a moment we are just two still beings, breathing and existing together in the same space on a busy street in the middle of the night.

A cab pulls up next to us and Gavin reaches around me to jerk the door open. "Get in," is all he says.

But I see the panic and determination swirling in his eyes and I'm afraid of which will win out. Afraid that if I get in, he'll slam the door and send me on my way.

"You go first," I barely manage to whisper.

"Get in the damn cab, Dixie. Now."

"Not until you promise me you're coming with me."

He scrubs a hand roughly over his face. "Get in the cab and go back to the hotel before I call your brother to come get you."

My eyes begin to sting. I told him how I felt, ripped back my carefully crafted exterior and bared my soul, and his grand response is to get me the hell away from him?

"Threatening me, Gav? You can't handle what I have to say so you're going to run and tell on me? I'm a big girl now. A simple 'thanks, but no thanks' would've sufficed." A choked sob reaches my throat and somehow finds its escape.

"Bluebi—"

"No. You know what? I'm going." I step forward, into where his arm is holding the cab door open. Turning, I tilt my face so it's only a hair's breadth from his. "But tonight, when you're with your random waitress, another one that you won't feel anything with, won't remember, and won't ever care if you ever see again, deep down we both know you'll be thinking of me. Good night, Gavin."

With that, I lower myself into the cab. I flinch when he slams the door shut. I don't miss that he does it much harder than necessary. It takes every single ounce of my self-control not to turn and look back at him as the cab pulls away.

Dallas isn't in the room when I get back, but just walking through the door strings me tight enough to snap. Gavin is everywhere I look. One of his vintage T-shirts is slung over a chair and his drumsticks are on the table. Dallas's cot is blocking the path to my suit-case. I stub my toe on it and it becomes the stupid *fucking* cot and all I can see is Gavin looking at that damn waitress.

Even blinking is infuriating me because every time I do, a flash of him flirting with her, his hands on her, that damn grin, every heart-battering touch—appears behind my eyes in a torturous montage.

My brother is going to have to get over the whole starving art-ists thing. We aren't rolling in cash by any means, and there have been times we've had to survive on week-old pizza, but enough is enough. From now on, I need my own room if we stay in a hotel overnight. I'll happily risk starvation for the sake of my sanity. But living in close quarters with Gavin is not going to work for me. I yank my suitcase up onto the bed and begin throwing my things into it. Once I've packed all my belongings, I grab the nearest pen and flip past Dallas's scribbled lyrics to an unused page of hotel stationery.

I scrawl out a quick note telling them, well, mostly telling Dallas because I'm pretty sure Gavin couldn't care less and won't be back to the room tonight, that I needed my own space and am getting a separate room. On my way down to the lobby, I take out my phone and text my brother in case he doesn't see my note.

Don't freak. I'm getting my own room. Need some space from all the testosterone.

By the time I've spoken with the front desk clerk and explained that I need a room as far from my previous one as possible, my phone chimes with a text notification. After I've been given the credit-card-style key to my sixty-five-dollar-a-night sanctuary, I read my broth-er's message.

What's going on? Just got back to the room. Where are you?

I'm so not in the mood to explain. Not that I could even if I wanted to. After I've settled into a room on the fifth floor on the opposite end of the hotel, I text him back.

Just need my own space, D. Female reasons. I had some extra cash put back. I'm in room 549. See y'all in the morning.

There. *Female reasons* is usually a surefire way to ensure my brother doesn't ask any more questions.

He texts back a single word. *Okay.*

God bless female reasons.

I unpack as much as I usually do, which isn't much at all. Then I flip through the television stations twice before shutting it off. Despite my best efforts, my mind won't let go of Gavin. Won't stop rewinding and replaying each painful second of our encounter. Won't stop falling into the gaping black holes wondering what he's doing right that moment. If he's with the waitress, if she's getting to see him, to touch him and feel him in a way that I never will.

Before I rocket off into complete self-propelled insanity, I take the hottest shower of my life. As if I could burn my need for him off my skin.

Slipping into the faded navy blue shorts I cut from sweatpants and a white tank top, I realize the one critical flaw in my hasty getaway. All the snacks and drinks are in the boys' room.

Damn.

I run a comb quickly through my still-soaked hair and step into my running shoes. Counting up a few bucks in change, I slide it off the nightstand and into my palm. Then I grab my room key and head to the door in search of sustenance. My stomach is painfully aware of the fact that my stupid heart made me miss dinner.

After unlatching the dead bolt, I pull the door open. The man standing there steals my breath and causes me to completely forget why I was leaving.

"What are you—"

"There is a reason," he says, staring at me as if I'm standing there stark naked instead of in pajamas he's seen a million times. "That I do not ever touch you."

"Oh-kay," I say slowly, because it's the only word that comes to mind. He's exuding visceral need and anger and something else I can't quite put my finger on. His tortured eyes meet mine and I'm adrift in a sea of want. "So tell me your reason."

My voice is barely above a whisper, but apparently he hears me because he grips my door frame and answers my question. Though it's practically through gritted teeth.

"If I ever touched you, ever let myself so much as lay a hand on you, I might not be able to stop."

I ache to test his theory, to touch him, to pull him to me and claim his mouth as mine. But the force of his confession and his fierce glare root me where I stand.

"W-what if I didn't want you to stop? Or what if I touch you, Gav? What will happen if I stop playing nice, stop worrying about controlling myself, about my brother, about the band, and give in to what I want for once?"

The truth is, it literally would be the first time I imposed my will, my wants and desires, on anyone. I've always taken life as it came, never manipulating the forces of the universe in any way. Somehow I've become a flower in the breeze, or maybe a stubborn weed, swaying gently whichever way I'm blown but remaining grounded. But now, in this moment, I want to rip up my roots and take. Take Gavin in the way I've only dreamt about.

His broad chest expands with the considerable effort he's making to breathe normally. Raking a hand through his hair, he glances over his shoulder.

"I don't know. But I think that would be about the worst thing you could do. For all of us."

My mind, heart, and body are suddenly at war with each other. I'm caught in the crossfire of their conflicting desires. It's like I'm plucking my own petals playing *He wants me, He wants me not,* with hands that don't know what they want the answer to be. Old insecurities creep up on me and come out victorious.

"Why?" I whisper. "Why don't you want me, Gavin? What is it about me that literally seems to repel you?"

For a long time I knew he only saw me as Dallas's little sister. I used to have frizzy hair and knobby knees and a chest as flat as both boys. But somewhere along the way, I changed. I'm having a hard time convincing myself that he really sees me for who I am now. Maybe he still sees knobby knees, frizzy hair, and freckles on my shoulders.

His eyes narrow and he shakes his head. *No.* "Don't. Don't do that to me. I just told you. You know why."

I frown involuntarily while swallowing the knot of emotion that's rising steadily in my throat. "How could I possibly know? You treat me like we're related most of the time. You put your hands on random waitresses right in front of me. You sleep with anything that moves. Except me. I tell you how I feel and you can't get rid of me fast enough."

Suddenly Gavin is a burning man, coming toward me with angry, gleaming eyes. He steps into the room, forcing me back against the wall. The door slams heavily behind him, and he braces his arms on either side of my head. I've only seen him this worked up when playing his drums. My heart morphs into a hummingbird inside my rib cage. It's trapped and wants to escape. Desperately.

His words come out with such force that they would shove me

backward if there were anywhere for me to go. "As flattering as your honest opinion of me is, how about you just tell me what the hell you want from me so we can both get on with our lives. You want to hold hands and go steady, Bluebird? Because I gotta say, you're not as smart as I thought you were if you're looking for that from me."

I jerk my chin upward, faking a confidence I don't have but refusing to let him intimidate me. "Did you sleep with that waitress? I want to know."

He snorts out a harsh, humorless laugh. "No you don't."

"I do. Tell me the truth." I look up into his eyes, praying the answer is no. Something about that specific waitress is really bothering me. Maybe because I saw their initial flirtation or maybe because of what she said to me in the ladies' room. I don't know. I'm well aware of the fact that he's been with countless women, but somehow this one feels different. More personal. Because this time, he knew how I felt and if he slept with her anyways, then he actively chose her over me. "Please," I add to my already pathetic plea.

He releases me from my forearm prison and shoves both of his hands into his hair. I inhale a much-needed breath and relax just a little. Until he slams a palm against the wall. I flinch, only because it startled me, but I can see in his wounded expression that he believes he scared me. As if I could ever be afraid of him.

"No, okay? No I didn't sleep with her. There, you happy now?"

"Well, you're obviously not. If you were going to be so upset about it, why didn't you just go ahead and do her?"

"You gotta be fucking kidding me," he says, raising his voice a few decibels shy of shouting. "Which is it? You want me to have screwed her or not?"

I'm all wound up, like the toys from my childhood. The ones with the knobs you turn and turn, winding so tight the spinny thing breaks and falls off. I'm confused and hurt and angry and turned the hell on in a way I can't even process. The combination is more than I can handle rationally. I take a page from his broody book and let my palm smack the wall behind me. It stings so I clench it shut. The pain distracts me and I blurt out the truth.

"No, I don't want you to have screwed her. I don't want you to screw *anyone!*"

His reaction is wide-eyed shock and disbelief. "*Anyone?* Christ, you want me to be celibate? Do you hate me or something?"

Licking my lips, I take several deep breaths in an attempt to calm down. It almost works. "I want you," I begin slowly before taking another deep breath. "To not engage in foreplay in front of my face."

He opens his mouth to respond—most likely to deny that he did that tonight—but I place my trembling fingers against his lips, firmly breaking our ten-year unspoken no-touching rule. I'd like to take a moment to enjoy the soft, full, sensuously masculine mouth of his, but there isn't time. I need to focus all cylinders of my brain on what I'm trying to say.

"I told you how I feel, what I want. And I get it. You don't feel the same way. Or you won't act on your feelings. But that doesn't mean I can switch mine right off for your convenience. And it doesn't mean that I'm not jealous, not hurt, and that I don't hate, *hate*, being in the presence of any woman who is going to have you in a way that I never will."

I'm breathing hard, tasting his anxiety and frustration in the air between us. Removing my fingers from his mouth and placing them on mine, I watch him go to war with himself.

His neck loosens, allowing his head to fall forward. Remaining completely still while he inhales the length of my neck, I swallow hard.

"Tell me I'll never have you that way. Tell me to move on and let this go," I whisper, needing to hear him say it and terrified that he actually will in equal measure.

"You're my best friend. Growing up, you were my safe place," he tells me on a ragged breath that seems to pull the life completely out of both of us. "I don't want to ruin you, Bluebird."

Before I can assure him that he won't ruin me, Gavin does the absolute last thing I expect him to.

In my mind's eye, I watch him grab me, kiss me, and we spend the entire night making love. But in the real world, where I unfortunately live, where parents die, and dreams don't usually come true, Gavin Garrison bites out his favorite curse, turns away from our intimate confrontation, and walks out on me.

Chapter 6

Austin MusicFest—Day 1

"ONE, TWO, ONE, TWO, THREE, FOUR!" GAVIN BEATS OUT THE count with his drumsticks and it feels like he's playing the drums on my temples.

After he left last night, I lay awake and tried to come up with some excuse for why I'd behaved the way I had. The memory of the humiliatingly honest truths I'd told made me want to turn back time, slap the me from yesterday, and shove a gag in her overactive mouth.

Could I tell him I'd felt sick and taken unnecessary cold medicine in order to avoid getting ill and screwing up MusicFest? Or maybe I could say that I had food poisoning and wasn't myself. Except he knew I hadn't really ever eaten.

My intro comes and I play my few lines in "Whiskey Redemption," a slow ballad Dallas wrote about a man who loses everything to a drinking problem. I usually love this song, love the harmony that Dallas and I play, but today it's grating on my sleep-deprived nerves.

Gavin Garrison riled me up and left me hanging and it's only now that I'm realizing how incited my pissed-off side is by him igniting a flame he couldn't—or wouldn't—stick around long enough to extinguish.

We finish up and play a few classic hits and then some up-tempo stuff. By the end of the set, the anger is ebbing and flowing, effectively draining me.

That's the funny thing about music. Part of the magic, I guess. Sometimes it replenishes me, like I'm feeding off its energy and it fills me. And other times, it pulls at my pain, weaves its way through the strands of my soul and wrecks it.

Between the man in "Whiskey Redemption" ending up homeless and dying alone, and Gavin refusing to so much as look at me, my emotional climate is dangerously unstable and the music is taking more from me than I have to give right now. Dallas is pleased, though, and says if we can just do that well tonight, he'll be a happy camper.

God. Tonight. The first night of Austin MusicFest.

I can't even stomach the thought of the redhead flinging herself all over Gavin. Or trying to play and listen for my intro cues while watching her executing her attack.

"Let's grab some food at Mae's and relax a little before sound check," Dallas suggests, giving me a nervous side-eye. His false assumption that I'm on my period, albeit one I led him to, keeps him from asking if I'm okay. But I see the worry even before he reaches out to put an arm around me. "Dix, you all right? Need a nap before the show?"

I nod. I'm too distracted by Gavin's steady avoidance to bother making up another excuse. "Yeah. Y'all go ahead and get some food or whatever. I'm going to head back to the hotel and rest for a bit."

Gavin just packs up his kit, keeping his head down and continuing his strategic efforts to ignore me.

Coward.

It is what it is, I guess. I lost the battle with myself and now I have to pay the price. Maybe it's for the best. If he's this avoidant because I was honest about what I wanted, I can only imagine how bad it would be if anything had actually happened.

"Seven o'clock sharp, Dixie Leigh. I'm serious. Do not be late. We'll have thirty minutes to warm up and that's it," my brother reminds me in his I-mean-business voice.

"Got it, sir. I'll report for duty at nineteen hundred hours, sir." I mock salute and turn to leave.

"I'm serious, Dixie," he hollers as I make my hasty retreat.

"I'll set an alarm on my phone," I promise him.

"Set two."

I shake my head as I make my way back to the hotel. It's only a few blocks from the warehouse we rehearse in but my feet are dragging. By the time I get back to my room, I'm beyond ready to crash out face-first on the bed—questionable body fluids on the comforter and all. But because I can't sleep with the possibility of disappointing Dallas prying my mind awake, I do as he requested and set two alarms on my phone. Both of them only five minutes apart so I'll actually get up when they go off.

For the first time in as long as I can remember, I don't think of Gavin as I drift into unconsciousness. I've lost him, pushed him away with the truth.

et the Drummer Kick" is playing loudly wherever I am. The crash of instruments pulls me from sleep.

Blinking myself awake, I see the bland décor of a hotel room. I sit up and glance over at my blaring phone.

Gavin's calling me. *Why is Gavin calling me?*

"Hello?" I say, pulling the phone to my ear with one hand and rubbing the remnants of sleep away with the other.

"Wake up, Bluebird. Your brother is flipping the fuck out."

His words soothe and panic me simultaneously. He called me Bluebird. Maybe I didn't ruin everything with my stupid confession. But holy shit, what time is it?

"What time is it, Gav?" I ask softly, becoming increasingly afraid of the answer.

"Sound check is in five minutes."

"Okay. See you in five." Even as I say the words, I know it's impossible. Even if I were completely ready to go, it'd still take ten minutes to get a cab and get to our stage. There's nothing in my stomach, so I have no idea why it feels like boulders are slamming around inside of it. Checking the alarms on my phone I see that I set them for a.m. instead of p.m.

Dropping my phone, I leap from the bed and strip out of my jeans and Lynyrd Skynyrd tee. I fling the top of my suitcase open and find the cleanest thing I can. Short black shorts and a white button-down dress shirt that might not even belong to me. There are some black sequined suspenders still attached to the shorts from the last time I wore them so I keep them to add a little shimmer to my outfit. My hair is a hopeless mess, so I throw a black hat over it. Slipping on black stilettos that I pray elongate my legs enough to help me get a cab quicker, I head to the door.

Glancing in the mirror on my way out, I realize I look a little like a slutty rockette, but there isn't time to do anything about it. My shirt might be buttoned wrong and of fucking course I'd be wearing a black bra under a white shirt on a night when it might rain.

My purse spills when I reached to grab it so I pick up a random tube of lip gloss and swipe some across my mouth. Mascara would be good, but I can't imagine Dallas would accept separating my lashes as a viable excuse for completely missing sound check.

Oz is still in his case so I lift it and my room key and literally run out the door. There's no time to wait on the elevator so I jog to the stairs and pray I don't break my neck in these damn shoes. The heels click like gunshots as I sprint across the lobby, where I collide with an elderly gentleman pushing a wobbly luggage cart filled with suitcases.

"Sorry. I'm so sorry, sir," I say, continuing toward the exit.

He gives me an appreciative smile and nods before adjusting his now-dilapidated pile of suitcases. Maybe he has a thing for slutty rockettes.

I've just hit the sidewalk when I slam into a solid mass. Gathering my bearings and catching my breath, I realize it's a man, well, a man-child with curly hair and a guitar case strapped to his back.

Jesus. Austin is crowded.

"Sorry," I say for the second time in two minutes.

He turns his twinkling gray eyes on me and raises a brow. "No need to apologize, beautiful."

Oh God. Okay, dude number two who appreciates slutty rock-ettes then.

"Right. Okay, then. Excuse me."

I go to step around him and hail a cab.

"You heading to MusicFest?"

Sighing as no cabs bother to stop, I turn and frown at my second innocent victim. "Yes. And I'm late for sound check."

He adjusts his guitar case strap and nods to the left of me. "So are we. Headed there I mean. Not late for sound check. Need a ride?"

A maniac on a bicycle tears past me, nearly knocking me into handsome man-child guitar player's arms. "Whoa."

"Careful, there. Austin's kind of crazy about fitness, apparently. That's the fourth person on a bike I've seen nearly take out a pedestrian. Today."

"Well this pedestrian is late and if she isn't on stage seven like ten minutes ago, her brother is going to murder her and stuff her body in a guitar case similar to yours. I'm sorry to be so rude, but I really have to go."

"We have a van and we know a shortcut," he informs me.

"A van?" I turn and see several guys around his age lugging equipment into a much nicer van than I'm used to traveling in. It probably even has air-conditioning. Which my frizzed-out hair is tempted by.

"Yeah. I'm sure we have room for one more, long as you don't mind being a little cramped."

Risk letting this guy and his friends gang-rape me and toss my body out on a back road, or face Dallas's wrath . . .

Sadly it takes me a full minute to decide.

"Um, thanks but I probably shouldn't—"

"Look, I get it. Random dudes in a van, not the safest bet. But we're All Grown Up, I promise."

"Yeah, we're all adults here. And while I appreciate the offer—"

His laughter cuts me off. "No, sweetheart. The band. We're the band *All Grown Up* and I'm pretty sure judging from the fiddle you're carrying and the fact that you're headed to stage seven, you're in the band that's opening up for us tonight."

I literally want to slap my own face.

"Oh my God. I know you. You're Afton Tate. Holy shit!"

The lead singer for All Grown Up was a child prodigy that the whole indie music world knows about. At only twenty-one, he's already turned down deals from several major record labels and his band is still one of the most requested and downloaded.

"Well that's a new reaction." He shrugs as we make our way to the van. "But yeah."

"I'm a fan. Wow. I can't even . . ."

He chuckles again as he holds the shiny black door of the van open for me. "You could give telling me your name a try. Since you're my opening act tonight and all."

"Um, yeah. My name. It's Dixie. Dixie Lark," I tell him, realizing I am obviously fangirling all over him now. Ugh. Now I'm the stupid swoony waitress whose eyes I still want to gouge.

A low wolf whistle rings out as I step into the van and sit beside a severely pierced-up guy that I'm pretty sure is Mikey Beam, their electric guitarist.

"Easy, fellas," Afton tells them as he gets into the driver's seat in the van. "This is Dixie Lark and she's in the band opening up for us tonight. She's in a bit of a hurry, so we're taking the shortcut."

A few of them nod at me, and Mikey steals my hat and puts it on his head.

"Hey, mister." I nudge his shoulder gently and he laughs. "My hair's a mess. I need that."

"I think it's more my style, what do you think?" He poses and readjusts it so it falls over one eye.

The guys whistle at him and I roll my eyes.

We're all jostled as the van hits a bump and I glance out the front windshield.

"Really, Afton?" The older man in the passenger seat who I hadn't noticed before asks. I assume he's some sort of handler since I know they don't have a manager yet.

"When a beautiful woman says she needs to get somewhere, you get her there," Afton replies, successfully heating my cheeks several degrees.

"Aww," Mikey coos. "Afton has a crush on you, pretty girl. I'll pass you a note asking you to go steady with him in a few minutes."

"That's real cute, asshole," Afton mutters, barely loud enough for me to hear.

As he speeds toward Sixth Street on a road that I'm pretty sure is closed for the festival, I examine him more closely. Dark curly mass of hair over a handsome yet boyish face. And yet.

He's no Gavin.

God I hate my subconscious sometimes.

Before I have time to check out him or any of the other muscled mounds of testosterone, we screech to a halt and Mikey slides the door open. Afton has literally driven me right up through the crowd to stage seven.

"Thanks for the ride, fellas," I call out as I hop down out of the van. My right ankle stings a little from the harsh impact but I don't have time to process the pain.

"Have a great show tonight," Afton calls out.

I've only made it a few steps when I glance up and see Dallas and Gavin both glaring at me from onstage.

I offer them each an apologetic smile and a small wave as I make my way to the stairs.

"Hey, opening act," someone calls out from behind me. "You forgot this."

Turning around, I see Afton holding my hat and grinning.

"Thanks." I reach for it but he pulls it back. "Have dinner with me."

"Um, what? You know I have sound check."

My back is searing with what I know will be my brother's infuriated glare.

"After the show, crazy girl. Have dinner with me after the show."

He's holding my hat just slightly out of my reach. Normally being taunted would piss me off. But somehow Afton Tate manages to be sweet about it. He's watching me with this nervous hopeful expression and I'm too busy dreading facing my brother to think about what his invitation really is.

"I'll think about it, okay? Kind of depends on whether or not my brother maims me for being late. The longer I stand here the more likely it is that I'll be on a Missing poster soon."

Afton grins and sets my hat sideways on my head. "Okay then. Since it's life and death and all. But find me after the show, okay?"

I nod, annoyed that I'm not more excited. He's Afton freaking Tate. Where are the butterflies, the flippy stomach? There isn't a teenage girl or her mom alive who doesn't drool all over him and his band. Instead I just feel flattered by the invitation and grateful for the ride.

Walking the death march up to the stage, where I'm sure Dallas is about to berate me, I ignore the reason I'm not jumping at the chance to go to dinner with Afton. The same way that reason ignored me earlier in rehearsal.

"Dallas, I'm sorry. I overslept. I set two alarms like you said and—"

"Just play, Dixie. I really don't want to hear it right now."

We play a few songs to warm up and make sure the acoustics are where we want them, and I am proving myself with every rake of my bow across the strings. Gavin breaks a drumstick at one point, glaring at me as if suddenly punctuality is so important to him as well. Neither of them even looks at me through sound check and as soon as it's over, I make one last attempt at begging for my brother's forgiveness.

"I screwed up. It won't happen again."

Dallas tells one of the MusicFest crew members that we're good to go and then whirls on me. "What were you doing with Afton Tate? I thought you were taking a nap, not gallivanting with—"

"Did you just seriously say gallivanting? I did take a nap, D. I was literally running out of the hotel and ran into him and he offered me a ride."

"So you just hopped into a van with a bunch of dudes, Dixie? What the hell? I thought you were smarter than that."

Shoving my bow into my case, I shake my head. "Just go ahead and say it. I'm irresponsible and immature. And you'd much rather I stay in college and tucked safely into an orchestra pit instead of being on the road with you."

He recoils at my accusation. "Dixie, I didn't mean—"

"No, you know what? I'm a big girl. I made a mistake. Hell, I've been making *a lot* of mistakes lately." My eyes shoot to Gavin, who's watching me warily from behind his kit. "But I've apologized, and frankly, I'm a human being. I'm not perfect. But I'm also an adult and a person who deserves the benefit of the doubt. All I can do is say I'm sorry and move on. If you can't, then that's you're problem."

Clutching Oz, I turn my back on them. I'm frustrated in more ways than I can count and unable to really do much about anything. Gavin doesn't want me, not like I want him, Dallas doesn't want me on the road, which is the only place where I feel truly at home, and a seriously talented musician just asked me out and I can't force myself to care.

"Dixie Leigh. That's not what I meant. I was just—"

I cut my brother off with a wave of my hand and start moving. I have to distance myself from both of them now.

The cracks that have been forming for years are widening beneath the surface. I feel each and every one of them. I've tried so hard for so long to keep it together. My whole life I've tried. Tried to accept my life as it is, to not complain, or live beyond my means, or want for more than I deserve. Tried not to let my welling ocean of grief from losing my parents overflow onto anyone else. I've tried to be what Dallas and Gavin needed, tried not to be any trouble as a kid and not upset grandparents who shouldn't have had to raise children in their golden years, tried my absolute damnedest to smother the fiery flames of desire that flare anytime Gavin so much as looks at me.

But doing all of that, holding everything back, has made a mess inside me, left me twisted up and hurting.

Holding my heart in check while I was in Houston was almost easy compared to this. Maybe that's why the thought of touring with the band seemed so appealing—why I never imagined there could be a downside. Knowing it will include a front-row seat to Gavin's parade of groupie conquests is like multiplying how I felt when he flirted with the waitress in front of me by infinity.

"Where are you going?" Dallas shouts from the edge of the stage.

"I just . . . need a few minutes. I'll be back in time for the show." My voice wavers and I wonder if either of them hears the tremor in it.

I won't be late. I just might not be whole, either.

Chapter 7

"SO I TAKE IT YOUR BROTHER WAS PRETTY PISSED?"

Afton's voice is sincere as he approaches me outside of a small bar where I'd sat alone at a round table. I'd been too busy cursing myself for not bringing my phone to notice him.

"Yeah, you could say that."

"Sorry. If I hadn't kept you talking outside the hotel—"

"I was already late. Not even remotely a possibility that any of this is your fault."

He ducks his head and peeks at me from under his eyelashes. "Can't blame a guy for trying."

I can't help but smile at him. "Thanks. It was a valiant effort."

"So, not that it's any of my business, but this looks pretty intense for being late to sound check."

Tracing the carved ivy pattern on the iron tabletop, I shrug. "Yeah. There's, um, other stuff."

Not that I plan to tell you any of it.

"I see," he says quietly. "Well, maybe we can talk about that tonight at dinner? There's a Mexican place on the other side of town that stays open late." I smile up at him but the ever-present gleam in his eye dims. "How many times can I ask you to dinner before I start to seem desperate?"

"If you've had to ask her more than once, she doesn't want to go. Bluebird never turns down free food." Gavin's voice startles us both.

And what the hell? He's never called me that in front of anyone. Ever.

Afton's eyes go wide and he puts his hands up. "My bad, man. She never mentioned having a boyfriend."

"That's because she doesn't have one," I inform him. I finally get it. Gavin can dish it out but he can't take it. Standing so that I'm level with both of them, I give Afton my full attention. "And I'd love to have dinner with you. Just find me after your show."

A wide smile breaks across his face. "Cool. Have a great show, Dixie Lark." With a wink, he disappears into the crowd, leaving me alone with Broody von Glareyface.

"What are you doing?"

"What are *you* doing?" I ask, folding my arms across my chest.

"Saving your ass so your brother doesn't kick you out of the band or take away your solo."

"Ah. It's time, I guess?"

"Yeah. It is." Without another word he turns and I follow him back to the stage. The crowd near the bars is thick, a sea of bodies we have to maneuver through. But as we get to the stage it's a bit sparser.

This is the trouble with being the opening act. Everyone is still sober and that makes for a much less forgiving audience. It's still dusk and not quite dark enough for the stage lights to work their magic. Dallas isn't completely wrong when he says we need to be perfect and not half-ass it. The sound guys are still working bugs out so there will be glitches during our show that we can't prevent.

For Dallas, this is unacceptable. For me, it's just part of it. The bumps and the bruises, the memories of everything gone wrong, of playing through the hiccups—that's part of what I love about it. Music is an experience. It's alive. Untamable. You can try to plan it out, pin it down, and bend it to your will, but it can't really be done.

I was born to be an opening act, to fly by the seat of my pants and make the best of it. But my brother is a headliner.

And Gavin . . . I don't know exactly what he is. The encore, maybe. The one nobody can get enough of.

As much of a train wreck as I am right now, I can't help but notice the way his black jeans are slung low across his hips, drumsticks sticking out of one pocket. And how taut his shirt is pulled across his broad back and the way his ink moves as the thick ropes of muscles shift in his arms.

When we reach the stage, Gavin goes straight to his drums. He's angry. At me, I think. I can feel it. I'm just not exactly sure why.

Sighing and retrieving Oz, I'm surprised when Dallas comes over to me.

"Dallas, I really am—"

I don't finish my millionth apology because my brother wraps his arms around me. His words are low in my ear as his hands thread through my hair.

"I know it's been ten years, and I know you miss them. I'm sorry, Dixie Leigh. I'm so damn sorry."

The shock of affection combined with the force of emotion weighing in his voice makes an impact the cracks beneath my surface nearly shatter under.

All I can do is nod against his warmth.

"It will be better. You will have a better life. I promise. No, I swear, Dix. I swear on their memory that you will have everything you deserve."

"Dallas," I say, clutching his shirt but pulling back to smile at him. "I already do. I have music and I have you. That's enough for me."

And I have Gavin, I almost say.

But you can't really *have* fire. You can't hold a flame in your hands without getting burned.

"You shouldn't have to settle for *enough*," Dallas says, his blue eyes meeting mine.

"Get to your mark, big brother," I tell him with a wink, because any more heavy heart-wrenching promises might break me. "Let's give these people a show."

He nods and moves over so that I can play my opener.

I don't look up until I'm done, but when I do, the crowd in front of us is significantly larger. And Afton and the members of his band are watching from beside the stage.

I don't know why, but Afton doesn't make eye contact with me through the entire performance. He keeps his eyes exactly where I wish mine could be. Where my heart is.

Firmly tied to Gavin Garrison.

So your drummer is kind of intense," Afton says as we walk to the restaurant after his show. A light breeze blows, cooling my still-overheated skin. The show went well, even by Dallas's standards, and the entire area around stage seven was packed to maximum capacity by the time we'd finished.

"Mm-hm." *Intense* is a pretty good adjective for Gavin. And drummer is an obvious descriptor. Though he's certainly not mine. I caught a glimpse of my least favorite waitress slithering up to him after our show.

"And, uh, he didn't seem thrilled about me taking you to dinner." Afton shoves his hands in his pockets and jerks his neck to move his hair out of his eyes. His curly hair is damp from playing out in the humid heat.

Gavin and Dallas stood like members of the Royal Guard, shoulders squared and effectively blocking me when Afton introduced himself after he'd performed.

Dallas had promised to hunt him down if I wasn't back at our hotel by midnight, because I'm Cinderella apparently. Gavin had glared with all his might but as I'd slipped past him to join my dinner date, I'd paused, giving him one last chance to say something. Anything.

Once I was certain he was just going to try to murder us with his eyes, I shrugged and took Afton's arm. At least one guy on the planet wasn't afraid to touch me in front of my brother.

"They're both just annoyingly overprotective," I assure him, sensing that Gavin has somehow really intimidated him with looks alone.

"Yeah, your brother maybe. But the drummer—that wasn't the overprotective brother vibe I was getting at all."

Even though we'd walked out of sight, I was still wearing Gavin's glare. It had penetrated my skin and clung to me as I tried to pretend I didn't care why he didn't want me having dinner with Afton Tate.

"And what vibe were you getting?" Baby butterflies flutter to life and I hate that this is the first time Afton has really piqued my interest. I am a terrible person. Worse, I'm a sick person obviously interested in masochism.

"He watches you while you're playing," Afton says thoughtfully, no trace of jealousy in his voice, as if he is simply making an observation. "Closely," he adds, lightly nudging my shoulder.

My throat constricts and the words are trapped beneath the knot that has formed in the middle of my esophagus.

Does Gavin watch me?

I can't see him when I'm actually playing. I don't see anyone really. I close my eyes and see the vibrant colors of the music I'm playing. The neon tendrils swirling in blackness. Sparks exploding from a midnight sky in brilliant flashes of light.

"Swear I'm not making it up. Why would I lie about that?" Afton's voice is gentle, as if his only intention is to observe this phenomenon and tell me about it. He's a genuinely nice guy. It seems unfair that I don't have anything to give him in return.

"No, I, um, I believe you. I was just thinking." I blow out a breath into the night as we reach the brightly colored funky blockish building he gestures to as our destination. "He's probably just watching to make sure I don't screw up and he doesn't have to cover for me or something."

Afton holds the door for me. A Hispanic woman wearing all black greets us. She stands there in stark contrast to the radiance of colors all around us. Sombreros adorn the walls and intricate blown-glass lanterns hang from the ceiling. The smells of salsa and fajitas entice my painfully empty stomach.

After we're given menus and seated at a small table in a back corner, a slightly more intimate setting than I'd prefer, Afton looks at me and then forces a tight smile.

"Whoa. Acting is out for you," I say, picking up my menu. "Change your mind about this date already? Better say something quick because I'm about to order the entire left side of the menu."

Afton lowers his menu and runs a hand through his hair.

"I'm kidding. I'm getting a chicken quesadilla. Relax."

I watch as he inhales deeply and leans forward. "I was impressed seeing you onstage. You're very talented. And beautiful. Obviously." He pauses to shake his head and I avert my eyes from this now very awkward situation I'm in. "I promise I have a point. I'm going to get to it here shortly."

I breathe an exaggerated sigh of relief. "Oh good. I was worried this was going to get uncomfortable before we even ordered appetizers."

Finally he grins, a boyish grin of amusement that brightens his entire face. "My bad. I'm usually better at this."

"I have to say, I don't think I've ever made a guy this nervous before."

"It's not you." He closes his eyes and smiles again. "I suck at this."

"Yeah you do. I think the 'it's not you, it's me' speech is supposed to come after dessert at least. Or maybe even after the sex."

Afton's eyes go so wide I almost laugh out loud.

"Y-you're planning to have sex with me? On the first date?"

There's an eagerness in his voice and also a fear.

"Well, I'm not going to *now* since you gave me the breakup line already." I can't hold back my grin and it gives me away.

"That's just mean. I'm starting to think maybe I should make *you* buy *me* dinner now."

"Oh, uh-uh. No way. You asked me to dinner, remember?"

Afton's lips twitch into a smirk.

A young man who looks barely old enough to drive interrupts long enough to greet us and set tortilla chips and a bowl of salsa on our table along with two glasses of water. I order my quesadilla and Afton orders steak fajitas. Once the waiter leaves I lift a chip from the bright red basket and return my attention to my date.

"So you were saying?"

His eyes meet mine and there's a heat under the playfulness. I triggered something when I mentioned sex earlier. I'm wondering if this works on all members of the male species.

"I was curious about why you agreed to come to dinner with me. Seemed to be a risky decision."

"Let me guess," I begin, pausing to take a sip of my water. "You got the 'we own her, you can look but don't touch' message from my brother and Gavin's behavior and now this is a severance dinner." I eat the chip and lick the crumbs from my lips. His eyes drop and I have to test my theory. "Unless . . ." I bite my lip while he watches and lean closer to him. "You're not as nice as you look, and you're willing to risk it."

Afton isn't just nice. He's smart, too. He catches on pretty quickly. And I'm not as sexy as I wish I could be.

He leans back with raised eyebrows. "Honestly? I'm not real big on risks."

"So I've heard," I say, dejected. This is why Gavin walked away. We both know I could never be what he needs. I'm not sexy enough, or experienced enough, and it must be written all over me if even someone I just met can dismiss my advances so easily.

"Meaning?"

"Meaning I've heard you've had lots of offers from major labels and big-name managers. Why turn them all down? Why not give one a shot?"

Afton's lips press into a line.

"I like my career how it is. I like my band how it is. The first thing those people do is tell you how great you are and then start changing everything that made you great to begin with."

"I see."

A flash of understanding pings through me. It makes me sad to think about Afton's band being stuck where they are. Even if they like it, they're amazing and they deserve better than being crammed in a van, playing for peanuts. The thought of never seeing them hit it big is depressing.

This must be how Dallas feels.

"Don't make that face. We have options. Right now this is what we want to do; if that changes, we'll start exploring those options."

I nod. It's none of my business anyway. "Right. Sorry to pry."

"I don't mind talking about it. And for the record, this is definitely not a severance dinner. I just like to know where I stand."

"In relation to what?" I swipe another chip through the salsa and toss it in my mouth.

"The drummer," Afton says evenly. "He's not watching you like he's worried you'll screw up. He's watching you like he's worried you'll disappear and take his heart with you."

"If I ever touched you, ever let myself so much as lay a hand on you, I might not be able to stop."

Gavin's words force themselves uninvited into my mind and I try to shove them out.

"Oh that's a good one. You should put that in a song."

He shrugs. "It's the truth. I saw him tonight, watching you like his life depended on you, and I felt like a dick for asking you out when there's clearly—"

"There's clearly nothing, okay? I don't have any idea what you're talking about and neither do you."

Afton arches an eyebrow at my outburst.

Fuck a rubber duck. Why does this keep happening? I'm going to starve to damn death if I can't stop having these Gavin-induced meltdowns at mealtimes.

"Look," I breathe, clenching and unclenching my hands just for something else to focus on. "It's not as complicated as it may seem. I guess I had a childhood crush on him but believe me, he's made it more than perfectly clear that we'll only ever be friends. Bandmates. That's all."

"We're more than that. You and Dallas are all I have. Do you get that?"

How has Gavin suddenly become the voice inside my head? Afton nods, watching me closely and opening his mouth as if he's going to say something else but the food arrives and it doesn't matter.

We both compliment the homemade tortillas. Afton tells me about a small, unsigned-artists tour he's trying to get his band added to. The conversation flows easily while we eat and I have a good time. But when the meal is over, all I am is thankful and ready to get back to the solitude of my room.

Gavin ruined my date and he wasn't even on it.

Chapter 8

I SAW HIM.

When Afton walked me to my hotel room, I saw Gavin. He must've heard us coming and turned the other way because all I saw was his back for a split second before he turned down a stairwell, but he was on my floor.

Why?

Part of me assumed he and Dallas were taking turns making sure I got back in time, but Afton's words had stirred an infectious hope inside of me. Maybe Gavin would one day want me badly enough to risk it. To risk Dallas's anger, the band's future, and our friendship.

I have to admit, it is an awfully big risk. The thought of risking those things, especially the possibility of having my brother's trust, the band, and Gavin's friendship all ripped away at once, was like standing over the gaping mouth of an endless chasm. Full of vipers.

"Thanks for dinner," I tell Afton as I open the door to my room. "Sorry I'm lame. I didn't realize how tired I was."

"You're the furthest thing from lame," he says, but his smile doesn't reach his eyes.

"And thanks again for the ride today. You really saved my ass."

Afton leans over, blatantly checking out my ass. "Oh well, thank goodness. It's a great ass," he tells me with a playful wink.

"Glad to have your approval." I reach my hand out to shake his and he lifts and kisses it, which makes me snort out a laugh. "Farewell, Mr. Tate. It was simply lovely to make your acquaintance. Best of luck in your future musical endeavors." I use my best British accent because this moment is so overly clichéd I can't imagine *not* using it.

"Same to you, Miss Lark. Perhaps our paths will cross again someday. Should the stars happen to align once again."

In that moment, when we're both using faking British accents and he's smiling so warmly at me, I sort of understand how Gavin can sleep with faceless randoms.

It's lonely on the road—lonelier now that I'm rooming alone, and the idea of comfort, even empty comfort that probably won't last long, is tempting. I could invite him in, let him press his lips to mine, tug at the waistband of his jeans and we'd probably get a great deal of simple pleasure and easy gratification from a night in bed together.

Except I can still see Gavin's tormented expression as I left, and I know exactly how many drumsticks he broke tonight. Five. Five drumsticks. The most I'd ever seen him break in one session. It's not exactly like we're playing heavy metal here.

So maybe he doesn't want me enough to grab on to me and jump into the abyss, but knowing I'm hurting him somehow by associating with Afton is enough to make me not want to.

"Perhaps," I say softly. "Good night, Afton."

"Good night, Dixie Lark," he says, accepting his dismissal and walking away like the gentleman that he is.

Once I'm in my room, I lean again the closed door.

Oz beckons me and I wonder if the people in the rooms beside me would complain if I played for a while.

It's too late to call Papa and I'm kicking myself. I always call him after every show to let him know how it went. But I know he'll be in bed at this hour so I sit with my fiddle and try to get down usable lyrics to an unfinished song I've been working on, until I can't hold my eyes open any longer.

I trust your minion reported back that I was tucked safely in almost a full hour before curfew last night," I say to Dallas the next morning in the hotel lobby.

"My what?" His brow wrinkles and his eyes land on Gavin making his way toward us looking like he just tumbled out of bed.

"Never mind," I say under my breath.

A heavy-eyed Gavin reaches us and in a husky voice that makes me instantly lust-drunk, bids us good morning.

"Morning," I say, tilting my head in an attempt to get him to meet my eyes.

"Where'd you run off to last night?" Dallas asks him. "Catch up with that redhead after all?"

Trying to mask my masochistic curiosity and the scowl that contorts my face at my brother's words, I turn away from both of them before Gavin answers.

It's better if I don't know. Even if he hooked up with Ginger, and even if I'd known he was going to, I wouldn't have done anything differently. Afton is a nice guy and I can't imagine ever being the type of person who could revenge-screw someone. So I swallow my hurt feelings and make my way outside into the harsh sunlight.

Squinting, I shield my eyes and spot the van parked in the lot.

"We walking or driving?" I ask no one in particular.

"Walking," Dallas answers. "Gavin's kit is already there and the place is crowded enough even though it's still early. If we leave now, we probably won't have a spot left to park when we get back."

I let them walk a few steps ahead of me, concentrating on keeping my eyes away from Gavin.

I need so very little to exist. Air. Water. Oz. Music. And for my heart to just beat. Just keep beating.

Just keep beating.

Breathe in. Breathe out.

Walk, Dixie Leigh. Focus.

But it's hard. The concrete beneath my feet is quicksand and my blood is syrupy-thick and threatening to smother my poor heart.

He's hurting. I can feel it. I don't know if it's because of Afton, or our dinner date, or something that has absolutely nothing to do with me. But his shoulders are slumped and the air of nonchalance he wears so effortlessly appears heavy on his back. His hands are in his pockets and his head is down. Something is wrong. Maybe he's hungover, or maybe he's angry. Maybe his mom called and asked for money for some bullshit that he knows is code for drugs. Maybe Ginger was so good in bed she kept him up all night and he's exhausted.

Whatever the cause, when Gavin's heart and soul are injured, it weighs on mine all the same.

I don't know when I became this pathetic mess so completely codependent on the happiness of someone who has told me in no uncertain terms that he will never cross the friendship line with me, but here I am. All alone on the in-love side.

We reach the street where the warehouse is and Dallas and Gavin jog across the empty intersection. My legs are heavy as I follow.

That year I spent attempting to become a classically trained violinist headed straight for an orchestra pit?

It wasn't just the music that didn't do it for me. It was being away from my family and from Gavin.

Away from Gavin's warmth and that damn dimpled smile, from my brother's understanding and his quiet laughter, without Papa's silent strength and constant encouragement, I began to change. Like a flower cast out into the darkness, I withered day by day, withdrawing into myself and into the girl I likely would've become if Gavin Garrison hadn't wandered up onto my grandparents' porch the day of my parents' funeral.

Everyone thought I was shy, and a few thought I was some sort of snob who believed herself to be above them. Nothing could have been further from the truth. When end-of-the-semester tryouts came, I made first chair without having any of the expensive schooling or training the rest of them did. No one was more surprised than me, but it didn't go over well.

When Dallas called to tell me about Papa's heart attack, I didn't hesitate. I took incompletes on my finals and hopped the first bus home. The scare with Papa reminded me how short life really is and by the time we got to bring him home from the hospital, I was ready to sprint to Gavin's house and tell him that I loved him and couldn't be away from him for a single second.

Dallas had taken all of that away with a few words.

Once we'd gotten our grandfather settled into bed that first night, my brother had stopped me in the kitchen. I told him that I'd spoken with my student advisor and since it was a family medical emergency and there were only a few weeks left in the semester, they'd hold my spot until fall and let me make up my exams.

"I can't say that I'm thrilled with you leaving school early, but I also can't say I'm not happy that you're home, Dix." Despite the exhaustion we both felt from a week in the hospital, excitement had shone like diamonds in his eyes. "I know we need to focus on Papa's recovery for the next few weeks, but I talked to a few owners of local venues. I can schedule Leaving Amarillo a dozen gigs next month."

"That's great, Dallas. Wow." Part of me was miffed at him for worrying about the band when Papa's health clearly needed to come first, but I couldn't deny that I was excited about playing with them again. It had been a long time since I'd looked forward to anything.

"And Dixie, don't say anything to him when you see him, but Gavin has been having a hard time. Without the band, he was just . . . kind of lost."

My heart clenches in my chest at the memory, the same way it did that day.

"W-what do you mean . . . lost?" I'd asked.

Dallas shrugged and averted his eyes, his tell that always revealed when he was keeping things from me. "Just . . . he really needs this, okay? We've played a few shows but it's not the same without you. He needs the band and he needs to keep busy. Otherwise . . ."

"Otherwise what, Dallas?" My white-knuckle grip wore quickly thin on my patience. "Tell me what you mean. Now."

Swallowing hard and clenching his jaw, my brother had informed me that when I'd left for school and he'd decided to stay with Papa instead of going to Nashville, causing the band to take a breather for the foreseeable future, Gavin had succumbed to the darkness, heading down a path dangerously close to that of his mother.

Shock had slapped any chance of hiding my emotions clear off my face, and I'd begged my brother to tell me what exactly had happened. But he'd said the details were none of my business—just that it had been bad. And only when Dallas had told him that I was returning to Amarillo, ironic considering the name of our band, and that he had gigs lined up for us, did Gavin step back into the light.

Which is why I have tried with all my might to keep my feelings for Gavin to myself. Until I had to watch him with that waitress and I suffered from a severe bout of temporary insanity.

Gavin needs the band to keep him from the darkness. Dallas has always dreamt of being onstage. My soul will starve if I can't play the music that nourishes it.

But if I can't hold my heart together, I am going to ruin everything. And everyone I love.

Because facing the truth—the one I can't deny while this close to him—is a hammer to all of my weakest places. The truth is, Gavin Garrison will never kiss me, or make love to me, or whisper my name in the quiet stillness of a darkened bedroom while holding me in his arms.

He walked out. Just turned around and left. That was his reaction to me admitting my feelings.

He will never say the words that I haven't heard since my parents died. Not to me. It's not worth the risk, not to him. And I understand why, I really do. But understanding and accepting are two very different things. My head understands what my heart can't accept.

It never bothered me that my grandparents didn't go overboard telling us. They just weren't vocal people. They believed in showing it instead of professing it all over the place. And I don't think Dallas ever even said it to Robyn, much less to me. I know my brother loves me just like I know how twitchy it would make him to have to say it out loud. But knowing that Gavin will never say those three words to me is splinters shoving themselves deeper into my heart every day. Knowing he doesn't want to hear them from me is fracturing it into a million pieces, creating a mosaic in my chest.

Because I need to say them. I have to get them out or I am going to go back to that withering flower of a girl and if the wind blows, those pieces of my heart will be like dandelion seeds scattering on the breeze.

I retrieve Oz from his case, keeping my back to Gavin and Dallas as they set up. They're joking around, talking about some of the girls they've seen in Austin. My brother makes a comment about appreciating that the heat of summer brings short skirts out of hibernation. Gavin's resounding laughter washes over me along with a wave of nausea. Dallas says something about a local hot spot where some girls want to meet up with them after tonight's show, but the ringing in my ears drowns out the details.

I wish they'd shut the hell up already and get on with it. I just want to play. Playing would be enough to hold me together. The music would wash away the hurt their jubilant exchange is causing. But neither one of them seems to be in a hurry to get started, and standing here listening to them making plans to go out and pick up girls I cannot do.

"I need to take five," I say, despite the fact that we haven't even started. I attempt to set Oz down carefully, but I hear my bow clatter to the ground on my way out.

Chapter 9

TEMPORARILY BLINDED BY SUNLIGHT GLARING IN MY EYES, I MAKE my way by memory to the alley beside the warehouse. Leaning over and bracing my hands on my knees, I do my best to pull the scattered pieces of myself together.

Dallas will be angry, and Gavin will likely be wondering if I've completely lost my mind.

"You okay, Bluebird?"

No.

For the first time in my life, I don't want to see him. I wish my brother had come to check on me instead. Because if he had, I could have fallen back on the female problems thing and laughed my outburst off, blamed it on hormones, and returned to rehearsal like nothing had ever happened. But those gray-green eyes are clouded with concern and all I can do is tell him the truth. I'm surrendering in the battle and handing over my heart. Along with the razor and the road map to the places where he can cut me the deepest.

I shake my head as he comes closer. Gavin blocks the glinting sun and it shines around him, creating an angelic effect around my tattooed tortured soul mate.

"I should've been honest. I should've told you sooner, no matter what Dallas said." A small sound escapes and I rush on. "Then maybe I wouldn't be coming apart at the seams during the most important week of our lives. I guess it's true what they say about hindsight."

He stares at me as if I've launched into a foreign language he doesn't speak. "I don't know what you're—"

"I came home for Papa, everyone knows that. I came home to help take care of him so that Dallas wouldn't have to deal with everything alone. But there's more to it than that." Taking a deep breath, I tell him the gut-twisting truth. "I came home for you, too, Gav."

He's going to walk away again, just like last night. I can already see his plans for retreat forming behind his eyes. But I have to get it out, consequences be damned.

"I hated my life in Houston. Being away from you . . . It felt—*I* felt like there was this magnetic *pull*. Like you needed me, or we needed each other. But this is even harder than being away. Being so close when I can't . . ." My words are becoming raspy, choking me on their way out. "I don't know if I can do this anymore. I've tried so hard to just deal with it alone. Everything is suddenly happening for us and I know I should just be grateful that we're here and that this is my chance to escape the orchestra pit, but spending the rest of my life like this—on the road together but . . ." I can't even put it into words, because it's impossible to articulate what I need. And I'm running out of oxygen.

I can't help wishing I had a beer bottle to throw against the wall about now.

His gaze darkens as his surprise-widened eyes meet mine. My head is still shaking back and forth, my body telling me to shut up, to keep it all in, but there's no stopping the outpouring of honesty now that I've broken the dam. Everything I've worked so hard to hold in comes tumbling out faster than I can even process what I'm revealing.

"I know you don't feel the same way, and that it will wreck everything we've worked so hard for, but I lo—"

Gavin's lips land roughly on my partially open mouth and steal the words about to slip out. Light flashes behind my eyes and my hands instinctually fly to the back of his head as if I could permanently seal him to me.

His fingers press into the flesh beneath my bottom as he grips me tightly, never once pulling his mouth from mine, and lifting me to his waist. My back hits the brick wall behind me but I barely register the impact.

He breathes into me, filling me, and I take his offering greedily, pulling his tongue and lips into my mouth harder than is appropriate for a first kiss. His teeth graze my bottom lip and I tug at his, thrusting against him uncontrollably. I need to be closer, even though it's physically impossible.

Maybe it's pity, maybe it's lust, or maybe this kiss is just to shut me up. But I know this may very well be all I ever get so I am taking ravenously until he stops or one of us passes out from lack of oxygen.

The world spins faster, fading from view as his lips slow their assault, and I try to follow his lead. I want to memorize every intake of breath, savor each small groan of pleasure that falls from his mouth into mine but his intoxicating flavor is making me too drunk to concentrate. I want him to etch himself onto the tiny crevices in my lips, make it sting and sear so that I can remember every fraction of every second.

When our tongues lash against one another a white-hot flash tears through my body, awakening every cell that makes up my being. A soft moan escapes my mouth and I shudder against the sheer force. The taste of him is more than I can handle while standing upright. Thank goodness he's supporting my weight. It's heartbreaking knowing I've lived my whole life without this.

A deeper cry slips from my lips, and Gavin lets go so abruptly he almost drops me on my ass. As soon as he sees I'm steady on my feet, dazed, but steady, he rakes his hands through his hair and takes a step backward. And then another. But the real distance between us, that mile-wide chasm that separates us, isn't in that few inches, it's in his eyes.

He's pulling away. Already. Too soon. I take a step toward him, desperate to bring him back to me, to those few seconds of perfection that have been unquestionably the best ones of my life.

But he matches me with a step backward. Taking another one, he's cleared a foot between us.

"Oh God. *No.* Dixie. *Oh God.* I shouldn't have. *Oh fuck.* I'm sorry, I—"

"Don't you dare." The anger burns like acid in my chest. "Don't you fucking dare try and take that back, Gavin Garrison."

His mouth opens and closes. He's wavering between consoling me and berating himself and he's ruining our moment.

"Don't say anything else. Don't apologize or make excuses. Please. Please leave it. Okay?"

I meet his tumultuous stare, and he nods. "Are you okay? I lost control and I'm so sor—" My narrowed eyes clip his apology. "Did I hurt you?"

Not yet.

I shake my head no. But we both know he's about to destroy me, to decimate my battered heart once and for all. Because as much as I wouldn't trade anything for that kiss, it's worse now. I've had a taste, a taste of the glorious, luxurious bliss that is being kissed by him. And now all that fills my mouth is his bitter regret.

"Y'all coming, or what?" Dallas hollers, his voice alerting us that he's approaching the open door beside us.

The smoldering stare of the man across from me lifts to my eyes and I take a soul-soothing breath. I'm okay. For now.

I don't look at my brother as I make my way back into the warehouse and lift Oz onto my shoulder, murmuring an apology for treating him so carelessly. My tongue darts out and runs along my swollen, thoroughly kissed lips.

I've taken the first hit and already I'm addicted. This will have to hold me over, will have to patch the dam I nearly destroyed.

I play better than I ever have. I'm alive and on fire from the brief memory of Gavin's mouth on mine. Dallas asks what has gotten into me and my face heats as I shrug and replay the kiss a thousand times in my mind.

I tell myself that I can do this. Can feed off this. I have to. For four more nights at least.

As for how I can survive touring with a man I love and can't have, I have a plan. One that will either allow me to work in close proximity to Gavin for the foreseeable future or set fire to the world as we know it.

Chapter 10

Austin MusicFest—Day 2

THE SECOND NIGHT OF AUSTIN MUSICFEST IS EVEN MORE INTENSE than the first. Thankfully I didn't have to throw myself together in two seconds and hitch a ride this time. Tonight I've donned my carefully selected leather and lace-layered top. My jeans are well worn and torn in all the right places. It's cooler tonight; the breeze holds the promise of rain. I breathe it in, closing my eyes and playing my fiddle the way Gavin kissed me only hours ago. Passionate. Hungry. Desperate.

The crowd is larger. The sun sets slightly earlier, granting us—the opening act—that blessed darkness that somehow makes music more magical and mysterious.

Tonight we're on stage eleven, which is farther from the main strip. The band we're opening up for hasn't arrived and the coordinating crew members keep signaling to Dallas to keep going. We're four songs past our set list and reaching the point of making it up as we go when the headliner finally shows up.

"Living a Past Life" is a Christian rock band with a huge fan base.

Their manager is explaining to the crowd about being stuck in traffic as we exit the stage. We're swept off with a soundtrack of ardent applause. Whether it's for us or the band taking the stage, I have no idea.

"I'm going to hang around, talk to their manager a bit," Dallas tells Gavin and me with a nod toward the stage we just left, once we've packed our equipment into the van. "Y'all can take the van back to the hotel if you want."

If I thought for one second that Gavin would come to my room, I'd take Dallas right up on that. But judging from how hard he's been working to avoid close contact with me, I'm betting he'd lock himself safely in their room without so much as a good night.

"It's a nice night. Think I'll walk around the strip a bit before heading back." I don't wait for permission from either of them before turning to leave. "See you later, boys."

I almost smile to myself. No way in hell either of them will let me walk around Sixth Street alone. It's chaos. Everyone's thoroughly inebriated. Most people are looking to hook up. For once, I'm most people.

"Wait up, Bluebird," Gavin calls out from behind me.

Turning around slowly, I see him coming toward me with an amused smile on his lips. My heart sings.

"You really think Dallas would let you loose out here without a chaperone?"

I smirk because we both know he wouldn't.

"Ah. So you do know how to manipulate men after all. And here I thought innocence was part of your charm."

"Maybe I did learn something in college after all. How about that."

He grins and shakes his head. My fingers twitch at my sides, aching to reach up and plow through his hair, bringing his lips back to mine, where they belong.

"So . . ." Gavin says softly, jamming his hands into his pockets as we walk farther into the crush of the crowd.

"So," I repeat.

"We should probably talk, I guess."

"You guess?"

"Jesus, Dixie." He huffs out an annoyed breath. "You a mocking-bird now?"

"You kissed me, Gavin. Mr. I-Will-Never-Touch-You. Guess that plan is pretty much shot to hell. So now what?"

"I think I preferred it when you were just repeating what I said."

Leaning gently against him, I nudge his shoulder with mine. That kiss has opened a door, a door to a place where I'm allowed to touch him. It's delicious and reckless and I can't get enough.

"Are you going to tell me why?"

"Why what?" He arches a curious brow at me but he's frowning.

"Why you changed your mind. About me. About kissing. About us."

The lights from the bars are bright all around us as we make our way through the crowded street, but as I wait for his answer, we might as well be alone in stark darkness.

"I didn't *change my mind* exactly."

Oh God. My heart sinks into the hollow pit that is my stomach.

"Okay," I say slowly, dragging out my response to give myself time between his verbal blows. "So what then? You slipped and fell on my mouth? Just before *accidentally* picking me up and ramming me into a building while you—"

"Enough." Gavin stops abruptly and faces me. He's a burning man, lit up from the inside out and glaring at me with a look of sheer warning. I'd back up for my own safety but apparently I don't much value self-preservation. "That's enough," he says, appearing mildly calmer than before. "It was a mistake. Like I told you before, there are moments when things between us get . . . difficult to control. This time I screwed up and gave in, that's all. It won't happen again."

The noise that escapes me sounds like laughter, but I imagine this is how a house pet must feel when kicked unexpectedly.

"You know what, Gavin? If that's true, then I'm just disappointed. When did you turn into this guy?" I keep walking as if I'm completely unconcerned with whether or not he's following.

"What are you talking about? What guy?" He's beside me again, easily keeping my pace.

"The one who lies—to me and to himself. The one who *apologizes* like a damn coward for finally taking something he wanted. Something that he knows he *enjoyed*."

He opens his mouth to argue but I put my hand up.

"Ugh. Don't bother. Guess I misjudged you. I'll just take my one hot kiss, hold the lame-ass apology and bullshit, please."

My view of Sixth Street changes abruptly. Gavin is gripping me by my shoulders and has slung me around to face him.

"What guy do you want me to be? One who lies to his best friend and screws his little sister behind his back?"

Now it's my turn to gape with wide eyes. Once I've lifted my chin from the ground and regained the ability to speak, I take a deep breath and meet his penetrating glare.

"No. That's not who I want you to be at all." I let my hands rest on his hips and pull him in just until my chest is lightly brushing against his. "I want you to be the guy who kisses me because he wants to, because he's can't *not* kiss me for another second. I don't want you to screw me behind Dallas's back. I want you to spend time with me because you want to, because we have a connection that we can only deny for so long, and because the thought of never having me is more than you can stand."

"Oh, is that all?"

I smile up at him. "Is it really that much to ask? I know we can't jump headfirst into anything and I get that it wouldn't be good for the band right now. But you feel it, this thing between us. I know you do because you poured it into that kiss today."

The moment he kissed me, we were connected on a level that far surpassed the physical contact. No matter what he does or doesn't believe himself to be capable of, I felt it, the way he gave himself over to me, every feeling that emptied out of him when that wall between us finally came down.

Our kiss gave life to an idea that I hope will work—one I have no idea how to proposition him with. My mind continues to hammer down the specifics of what I need him to agree to in order to make him see that he is capable of so much more than he is allowing himself to have.

"Dixie. Listen to me." Gavin's face is a hard plane of determination. "I don't do more than one-night stands. I don't make promises about the future and forever and all of that nonsensical bullshit because it doesn't apply to me. I could never give *anyone* that."

He's wrong. I can feel it. I felt it.

Gavin Garrison is capable of love, and I am going to prove it.

He closes his eyes briefly and shakes his head. My fingers tighten their hold on his hips before he can pull away. Music from the surrounding stages pulses and throbs against us as we stand in the sea of bodies coming and going.

"I have a plan," I say just before a breeze whips a strand of hair across my mouth. I'm afraid to relinquish my hold on him to move it for fear he'll back away from me. I don't have to debate on those odds for long before he moves the hair for me, sending a shiver down my spine as he teases my lips with his fingers.

"A plan, huh?"

I nod. "I'm not asking for a commitment or a label, or even that we tell Dallas. Not right now while he's so stressed-out, anyway. I'm nineteen, Gav. I'm not going to start shopping for rings or making lifelong-commitment demands. Obviously I won't turn into a crazed maniac and stalk you like some of your other groupies have. Pretty sure I know where to find you most hours of the day."

His lips press together in a speculative look of contemplation. So far so good. "So what exactly are you asking for, Bluebird?"

I swallow hard, pulling in a lungful of cool night Texas air and all the courage I can gather with it. This is it, my shot to make him see why my plan is a good idea.

"After MusicFest ends, I want one night. Me and you. Alone. We have things to discuss and . . . and well, if something else were to happen, we can figure it out from there. But I can't keep hiding behind my brother and neither can you."

Gavin fingers a strand of my hair, twirling it between his fingers and giving it a gentle tug while I wait for his response.

Looking up at him, I see that love-starved little boy I met ten years ago. Gavin Garrison the man is tough. Hardened by a rough life full of unfairness, he's intimidating to the naked eye. But I see so much more than that. I see how closely he guards his fragile heart and how rarely he lets his actual feelings show.

"I was right about touching you," he says absently, still eyeing the curl entwined loosely around his finger. "Now that I started, I can't stop."

"I don't want you to stop." My confession is barely loud enough to be heard over the bedlam around us.

He clears his throat and glances around. I know he's checking for Dallas and I try not to let it upset me. "One night?"

I nod.

His brows dip inward as he contemplates my request. "And what are you expecting from this one night?"

The images of what I'm expecting form so quickly I'm afraid there's a slide show presentation showing an erotic montage in my eyes. *For you to see that you can love and be loved.* There's no way I can admit this. So I give him the only answer that I can.

"Nothing. No expectations. Just us, being honest with each other. No outbursts or brothers or meltdowns or waitresses in the way."

"Why? Why is this suddenly such an issue?"

"Why did you wait for me to get home from my date last night?" I ask without thinking.

His eyebrows lift and then lower, drawing together as his gaze grows darker. "I needed to know that you were safe."

"How very brotherly of you. But, Gavin, today, outside the ware-house, that wasn't brotherly. At all." My skin begins to tingle as a pulsating ache throbs between my thighs at the memory.

His hand reaches up to cup the back of his neck. I wait for him to call it a mistake again and crush every ounce of hope that his kiss gave life to.

"I'll agree to your one night on one condition. Tell me why, Dixie. Why are you pushing all of this now?"

Because if we find our way into the spotlight, I'm afraid everyone will see what I've tried so hard to hide.

My hearts trips over itself and lapses into an erratic rhythm.

"Because . . . I need us to . . . to address this *thing* before I implode and destroy everything. I won't always be able to get my own hotel room."

I can tell by the way he's pressing his lips together he still doesn't completely understand. I have the fleeting thought of just being honest, of telling him I want one night of him giving me everything, one night where I can pretend we have a future together as more than bandmates, so that I can put it in my internal memory box along with the few cherished moments I have left of my parents. If I can't make him see that he is both capable and worthy of love, that memory will have to be enough for me, even if it's all I'll ever have.

"Okay," he says, finally relenting, causing my heart to give a little squeeze. "But maybe we should just keep our distance for the next few days, okay?"

My mouth forms an involuntarily pout when he pulls out of reach and he smirks down at me.

"Friday night I'll tell your brother I met someone, because, technically, that isn't a lie. We did meet at some point. I'll crash in your room if that's really what you want. Not sure it'll solve any problems, though."

It will solve one. Because if everything goes according to plan, after Friday night I will know exactly how Gavin feels about me. And how it feels to have him inside of me.

He couldn't hold anything back when we kissed. I'm betting my whole heart on the hope that making love will be as powerful in releasing his emotions as that kiss was, if not more so.

The sound of meaty fists slamming into bone interrupts our moment just as it begins to rain. Two sweat-slick guys beside us trade punches, startling me and sending several people careening into us.

"Let's get you back to the hotel and safely tucked into bed," he says, draping an arm indulgently around me. *"Alone,"* Gavin clarifies, ruining my hopeful mood as he steers me away from the circle forming around the brawl. "Before your brother sees us and does something that makes *that* look like a friendly handshake."

When we get to my room, Gavin takes a step backward and shoves his hands into his pockets, making it clear that he won't be coming inside. He doesn't give me another earth-shattering, spine-jolting, tingle-inducing kiss, either, but he does rest his chin on my head and say, "Sweet dreams, Bluebird," in a way that I suspect will ensure I actually have them.

Beggars can't be choosers, I suppose.

After he leaves and I'm all alone in my room, I notice it's not quite as late as I thought, so I pick up my phone.

Four rings later, still no answer.

"Hi, Papa. It's me," I tell his voice mail once the automated message finishes informing me that the person I'm trying to reach is not available at this time. "We've had a few late nights and I haven't been able to reach you." Sighing, I kick my shoes off and let them drop heavily onto the floor as I settle onto my bed. "I hope you're doing well. Both shows have gone great and the audience here is the most enthusiastic I think I've ever seen."

Searching for the words to wrap up the call, I realize that I'm getting anxious. I always call Papa after every show and tell him how it went. It's a mutually beneficial situation because I need to hear that he's all right and he lives vicariously through the band. If he would've answered I'd have told him about the van ride right up to the stage yesterday and the fistfight I witnessed tonight. Then he'd regale me with similar stories from his brief time in a band when he was my age.

He's told me one version or another of every memory he has about his days in his band. "I was in a band once," his stories always began, as if we didn't know from being told dozens of times over the years. "We thought we were really something," he'd say, his kind eyes crinkling in the corners. "We broke up after a few years, though."

"How come?" I'd always ask, just to keep the stories going.

"We didn't make more than change. Played for free mostly," he'd grumble, turning frustrated about the topic. "That was no kind of life for a man looking for a wife."

The day he gave me Oz was the first time he told me the story of how Nana's parents didn't want her to marry him, a broke musician without a cent to his name. He'd joined the navy to get their approval and to save up to buy her a ring and a house, but even after he came home from his deployment, Nana's parents still said no. They had their heart set on a banker who was a son of friends of theirs. No matter how many times I heard the story of their courtship and how they finally eloped, I felt the tingles of longing and pride each time. Such rebels, my grandparents were.

Years later, when Dallas and Gavin and I became more than just three kids messing around with used instruments from Papa's old shed and from pawnshops, Papa became our biggest fan. He'd sit outside on a lawn chair and listen to us rehearse in that same shed where we'd stumbled across his bass guitar and drum kit. It was then that I'd catch a glimpse of that version of him I'd only seen in a yellowing photograph from before my time. Even now, if I don't call him and tell him about nearly every show, he gets grouchy with me about it.

We're the same that way, Papa and I. Both of us gravitate toward music the way a plant turns toward the sun.

While much to my brother's constant dismay, I don't dream of selling out stadiums or touring Europe, I do live and breathe music.

The purity and the sanctity of it. I need it like I need air to breathe. I can't even imagine what my life would be like without it.

Tracing the pattern on the hotel bedspread absently, I say my goodbye. "I miss you. I'll try and reach you again tomorrow." I know I'm running out of time on my one-sided conversation so I hastily add, "Love you."

I disconnect the call, feeling slightly mollified by the fact that there is at least one man who will always be happy to hear that I love him.

Chapter 11

Austin MusicFest—Day 3

ON DAY THREE OF THE MUSIC FESTIVAL, THE AIR IS SO THICK WITH lung-sucking humidity I don't even bother with makeup. It'd just melt off anyway.

I wake up to a text from Dallas informing me that he's having breakfast with a manager he met the night before, Mandy Lantram, one of our first choices, who has a client list full of some of the hottest country artists currently topping the charts.

As much as I complain about Dallas being kind of a drill sergeant when it comes to the band, he has a knack for knowing how to make things happen. If anyone can land us a manager, it's him and for that I am grateful.

Since I'm pretty sure Gavin isn't going to change ten years' worth of strictly enforced distance and come watch a movie in my room, I decide to call and check in on Papa again since I haven't gotten in touch with him yet this week. When he hasn't answered on my third try, I begin to worry.

Mrs. Lawson next door usually checks in on him when we have to be gone overnight, but I dread calling her because if I'm not careful, I'll have to listen to an hour's worth of stories about her ungrateful children and their offspring and a complete sermon on the spiritual healing powers of her cats.

But by noon, I'm panicking and pacing and Dallas isn't answering his phone, either. I guess his breakfast meeting ran long, which I hope is a good thing.

Unlike my grandfather, Mrs. Lawson picks up on the first ring.

"Hi, Mrs. Lawson. This is Dixie. From next door," I say loud enough for her to hear.

"Pardon? There's a what next door?"

Dear God. Lowering myself onto my bed and bracing myself for a nice long chat, I repeat my greeting.

"Well, little Dixie Leigh. You hang up this phone and bring yourself right on over here this instant. I've already got tea made."

"Um, yes, ma'am, I would. But I'm not next door at the moment. I'm in Austin."

"What in the Sam Hill are you doing in Boston?"

"Austin, Mrs. Lawson. I'm in Austin, Texas. For a . . . never mind. I'm just out of town. Can you do me a big ol' favor and check on my granddad next door? He's not answering his phone."

"Well I'm not surprised. You know your granddaddy's deaf as an oak tree."

"Yes, ma'am," I say, smiling.

"Just last week I saw him at the mailbox and I hollered over at him, and that man didn't hear a word I said. He just went right on back inside."

Papa has a hearing aid. I'm betting he was playing possum on poor Mrs. Lawson. Her husband had to go stay in an assisted living facility after his last stroke and Papa said Mr. Lawson was probably just faking the paralysis so he could get away from the motormouth of the South.

"I'm sorry he didn't hear you, Mrs. Lawson. I guess he isn't hearing his phone, either. Do you mind going over and knocking just to make sure he's alive and kicking in there? I'm getting worried."

Lord help, she'll probably chat him up for over an hour. That's what he gets for not answering the phone Dallas and I bought him. Bet he'll be sure and get it next time I call.

"Sure thing, doll. I'll head over now. You want me to call you back after I check on the old goat? Tootie Lou and Mr. Darcy have been extremely in sync with the spirits lately and I could have them read your tea leaves over the phone."

"Gee, Mrs. Lawson, that sounds . . . educational. But um, if you could just have my granddad call me, I'd really appreciate that so much."

"Sweet girl, missing your granddaddy. I tell you, my kids couldn't care less. I could've been over here rotting all month long and wouldn't see hide nor hair of either of them."

"I'm sure that's not true, Mrs. Lawson. You're just such a strong, independent woman. They probably figure you don't want them meddlin' in your business."

A huffy sound comes through the phone and I shake my head even though she can't see me.

"Tell you what, you go check on Papa for me, and I'll make sure we have a nice, long visit next time I'm in town, okay?"

The things I do for that man. First thing I'm doing when I get home is changing his ringtone to "22" by Taylor Swift and turning the ringer up to sonic boom.

"All right, darlin'. I'm a-headin' over there now. I'll tell that stubborn old cuss to call you." I hear the creak of her screen door opening and sigh with relief.

"Thank you so much, Mrs. Lawson. Kiss Tootie Lou and Mr. Darcy for me."

"Will do. Best of luck with whatever you're doing in Boston, sweetie." Once she hangs up I jump in the shower. I figure it will be at least an hour before she leaves him be and he calls to bless me out for sending her over.

I've just finished towel-drying my damp hair and stepping into a simple, short black dress for the show tonight when my phone rings.

Assuming it's Dallas calling to remind me that I have to be in the lobby an hour earlier because Ms. Lantram wants us to meet her for dinner, I answer without checking the caller ID.

"Dixie Leigh, what have I told you about siccing that damned woman on me?" My grandfather is exactly as angry as I expected him to be. And he sounds healthy as a horse so I feel like I can finally breathe.

"Papa, we got you the phone so we could check in. You worry me sick when you don't answer it. You don't answer, I send Mrs. Lawson. *Capisce?*"

"She spent forty-five minutes talking about those caterwauling felines. I was trying to listen to the Rangers game. Missed the last inning and the final score thanks to her yammering."

"Sorry. But you know I worry." I balance on one foot and slip on a black leather ankle boot while holding the phone to my ear. "You taking your pills like Dr. Rogers told you to? Are you using that case I got you that has the days of the week on it?"

"Yeah, yeah," he grumbles. "Y'all behaving in Austin? You keeping an eye on those boys?"

"Yes, sir," I promise him. "Funny thing is, they think they're keeping an eye on me."

He chuckles softly. "Well now, they'd have to have two sets of eyes each to keep up with you, wouldn't they?" He asks how the shows have gone and I recount the past few in vivid detail.

Papa played bass guitar with a group called the Harmless Gangsters. They had a tagline; something about the only thing they stole was hearts. I saw a picture of them in his old things out in the shed once, a discolored black-and-white shot of four guys leaning leisurely against a classic car.

I'd let out a low whistle and handed it to him. Papa had smiled and set the photo aside. Later I'd wished I'd taken it. It was probably packed away or half moth-eaten by now.

My chest aches with missing him. "I miss you. Dallas has a few things lined up after this festival, but then we're coming home for a bit, okay? I'll make you that meat loaf you like so much. Like Nana's."

He's quiet for a moment and I wonder if I've lost his attention to his talk radio broadcast blaring in the background. It's been over two years since she passed away, but Papa holds on to his pain the same way that I do.

"I'd like that, Dixie Leigh. Nobody could make it like she did, but yours is pretty close I 'spose."

"Thanks, Papa. I try." My throat constricts and I begin to wonder if I'm going to pay for my lie to Dallas by actually starting my period soon. My emotions are running away with me and I can hardly keep up. "I'll, um, play that piece you like on the Wurlitzer, too. That one by Glass that she used to play."

He grunts out a sound of approval then lingers a moment, as if he just wants to stay on the line a little longer, but I note the time on the alarm clock on the nightstand and tell him that I need to go.

We say our goodbyes and I sit on my bed and stare at myself in the mirror across from it.

It's odd, the things we remember and the things we forget. My memories of my parents are like a whimsical montage that plays at the press of an unseen button in my mind. The images of them holding hands in the car, swinging me by the arms, my mom putting on earrings and glancing at me in the mirror with a smile and a promise about getting my ears pierced one day, her musical chiming laughter when my father made a joke, her smiling up at his handsome face before they would kiss. It's always behind a thick, gauzy haze that feels more like I watched a movie about them than actually lived that life. But memories of Nana and Papa are sharp and well defined—all of them.

Even though I'm staring at the reflection of a woman who looks a great deal like my mother, I can't help but think of Nana and how when she was alive, our house was full of music. It was what helped me to moved past the devastation of losing my parents.

She taught us everything she knew about playing the piano—about timing and feeling. She showed me how to pour my pain into the keys.

Music might not have fixed what was broken inside me when my parents died, but it was the balm that soothed the wounds.

When I meet the guys in the lobby to head to the meeting with Ms. Lantram, neither of them hides his reaction to me very well.

It's not like I usually perform in sweatpants or anything, but I'm dressed a little more provocatively than usual. My dress is short, my heels are high, and I worked for half an hour on getting this smoky eye done right. The black dress with tiny white skulls looks more like a shirt with a belt than an actual dress and the McQueen ankle boots with skull zippers I bought at a yard sale are much racier than my usual flats or boots.

Dallas is on his phone and frowns his disapproval but says nothing to me, causing me to once again be grateful that he thinks I'm in a highly hormonal state.

Gavin's reaction is more what I was going for. Because I don't want him to just *agree* to our one night, I want him to look forward to it. To be counting the time, measuring the moments and heartbeats until we're alone, just as I am.

The frustration rolls off him in waves as I step between him and my brother. His hands are fisted at his sides and I watch him swallow three times more than is necessary.

Finally. He finally sees me. He glances down, his eyes meeting mine and reflecting the painful need I've shouldered alone for so long.

"You didn't bring Oz?" Dallas finally says after he's ended his call.

I force my eyes reluctantly away from Gavin's. "Are we not going to have time to come back here after the meeting?"

Dallas sighs as if I have asked the world's dumbest question. "I don't know, Dix. But I'd prefer to be prepared just in case."

So much for having it together for a change.

"I'll grab him," Gavin volunteers, reaching his hand out for my key. "I left my extra set of sticks, too."

I'm not sure if he's just trying to make me feel better or what, but there's no way in hell he's going to my room right now. Though I do appreciate that he called Oz a *him* and not an *it*.

"Um, actually I need to grab a few things if we're not coming back here. I'll hurry."

The lyrics I've been working on are out in plain sight and they're about him. My bras and underwear are strewn around the room—

though that last one shouldn't matter so much if I'm going to let him see everything Friday night anyways. Anticipation rolls over my stomach at the thought and threatens to pull me under.

"Grab what you need and let's get moving. I don't want to be late."

Gavin and I nod at my brother's command. The two of us head to the elevator and I avoid looking at him because, once again, Dallas has reduced me to the kid sister who forgets and needs reprimanding.

Gavin presses the button for the elevator and I catch myself watching his hand, his fingers long and masculine and graceful. They gripped me so hard when we kissed that I should've checked for bruises on the back of my thighs.

Dear God in Heaven, give me strength.

I want him to bruise me in a passionate lovemaking, fingers-denting-flesh-hard-enough-to-hurt-while-I-scream-his-name sort of way.

There's a ding and we wait for a few guys in reggae getup to exit the elevator before we step inside. Alone. Our arms brush and this is so the wrong time to be fantasizing about Gavin holding me hard enough to hurt.

His shoulders are rigid and I'm wondering if I am somehow conveying my thoughts via mental telepathy. He seems to know exactly what's going on in my head and it seems to be making him angry and uncomfortable. I hit the three for him and the five for me, keeping my eyes fiercely trained on the glowing round buttons.

The third floor comes and the doors open. I start to tell him I'll see him in a few minutes, but he doesn't move. The doors close and we continue our ascent. I raise my eyebrows at him and he cuts his eyes to mine.

"What are you doing?" I whisper.

"Isn't this what you want?"

Yes.

"Um, what?"

His eyes meet mine and he's sneering at me. "Me to fuck you real quick in your room so you can check that off your list?"

My body recoils at the maliciousness in his tone. "Excuse me?"

Gavin slams his hand on the stop button, jerking the car to a halt, and braces his arms beside my head.

"You wore *my shirt* on your dinner date with that boy-band kid, then you said those . . . *things*. Now you're making me agree to one night alone with you and wearing this goddamn dress. I may not have gone to college, but I'm not fucking brain dead, either."

The rush of conflicting feelings floods my brain. I love him. I hate him. I want to slap his face and kiss him until I'm drunk and dizzy.

What in the hell is wrong with me?

My chest heaves between us as I work to breathe normally. "For one, I didn't know that was *your* shirt. Secondly, I was honest yesterday. Finally. For once, I was completely honest and I'm not taking back a single thing I said or did. Thirdly, there is nothing wrong with my dress," I bite out through clenched teeth. "And for the record, I didn't *make* you agree to anything. You want to say no? Then say no, Gavin."

I cross my arms in defiance, meeting his icy glare with one of my own and daring him to back out on our one night even though it will break me apart when he does. I've been holding on to that one night like a lifeline.

The heat in his glare burns into my icy one, but he doesn't say it. Not yet.

"Gavin? The words, I need the words. Either you're in or you're out."

An intruding buzzer sounds, making me flinch, and he steps out of my space. He hits the emergency stop again and we ride in silence to my floor.

My heart hammers in my ears as I walk on unsteady legs to my room with him close behind. Retrieving my key card from my bra makes me self-conscious and my fingers tremble. I drop the slender piece of plastic twice and mutter a curse under my breath when I pick it up the second time.

Gavin's breath is hot against my neck as he reaches around and takes the card from my inept fingers.

"Let me," he says low in my ear, sending a shiver across my shoulders and down my arms.

I slide my tongue across my lips in an attempt to moisten them so that I can speak. He opens my door easily and I step inside on the wobbly legs of a newborn foal.

"Gavin, I need the words. I—" I'm ashamed at how my voice breaks.

I have no idea what else was about to come out of my mouth. But it doesn't matter because his lips press against my neck and I am rendered immediately speechless. Tilting my head to allow him better access, my intense appreciation for what he's doing to me slips out of my mouth in a moan.

"I'm in, Bluebird," he whispers in my ear. "But I think you already knew that, didn't you?"

"Y-you know what you're saying? Do you understand what I want?"

He presses against my backside and I feel something I have only ever imagined in my wildest fantasies, the thick ridge of Gavin's arousal. A guttural sound escapes and I should be embarrassed but I can't recall what that would feel like. All I can feel is his mouth on my neck, his hands on my hips, and the promises of what's to come—literally—against my backside.

"I think I have a pretty good idea. And I think we both know what it could cost us. You okay with that? Risking it all for one night?"

All I can do with his body this close is nod. *Yes.*

"Hmm. I am not happy about anyone else seeing you in this dress. Not happy at all."

His blatant desire gives me courage. "And what do you plan to do about it?"

His tongue flicks against my earlobe and I shudder. "Let's just say if you get what you want on Friday, you probably won't be able to walk anywhere on Saturday."

My knees go weak and his arm wraps my waist to support me as if he anticipated the effect he'd have on me. "Do we have to go to this meeting?"

A low, dark laugh tickles my ear and reverberates through my body. "I think so." He places one last kiss against my neck and pulls back.

When I turn around, knowing I'm flushed and mussed from his assault, I'm annoyed at how calm and collected he appears.

"Planning to seduce me, were you, Bluebird?" His half smile is infused with infuriating arrogance, but I'm still quivering so I'm in no position to be upset that he figured me out.

"Maybe," I say, retrieving my bow from the bed and placing it alongside Oz in the case. "But I meant what I said about talking and being honest, too, Gav. I need . . ." I pull in a breath and he steps closer to me.

"I know what you need. I just don't think I'm worthy of giving it to you." All vestiges of his smug façade have evaporated and he is that boy again. That fragile boy with a heart of glass.

"You are. I know that you are." Reaching my fingertips up to his jaw, I stroke the stubble gently. "You always have been."

"I have a condition," he tells me. "Well, an additional one besides your brother never finding out." His jaw flexes beneath the tension.

"Okay," I say as I wait for him to reveal the restrictions he's going to place on our one night together.

He swallows hard and rubs his nose against mine. "Don't fall in love with me. It's one night because that's all I can give you. Sometimes women confuse really great sex with love. I can give you great sex. I have every intention of making it a night you'll never forget. But love isn't something I'm capable of and you of all people know why."

His mom enters my mind immediately. She never loved him—or at least I never saw any evidence that she did. She never hugged or kissed him or held his hand. My heart clenches in my chest and a small piece breaks off inside me, the debris gathering in my throat.

Gavin doesn't know how to love. And oh, *oh,* I want so badly to teach him. But I can see from the pained expression on his face that he doesn't want that—not from me or from anyone.

"I promise I won't fall in love with you just because we sleep together," I assure him while gently raking my fingers through his hair.

Because I have been in love with you from the very first day we met.

Chapter 12

MANDY LANTRAM LOOKS LIKE A LONG-LOST KARDASHIAN SISTER. She's got flawless mocha skin and raven hair that flows down to the middle of her back. Her navy blue dress fits like a second skin over her voluptuous figure and I feel like a little kid playing dress-up when she stands to greet us at dinner.

When we walk onto the back patio at a barbecue place overlooking Austin, Dallas introduces us in turn.

"Please, call me Mandy. It's nice to meet you both," she says, smiling warmly at Gavin and me. "As I told Dallas when we spoke yesterday after the show, the three of you have made quite a name for yourselves around the great state of Texas."

I don't miss the way her eyes linger on Gavin as he leans back in his chair.

"You could say that, I guess," I interject. "We play mostly for free, though, so that doesn't hurt."

Everyone chuckles good-naturedly even though I was being completely serious.

"Well, I'd like to change that," Mandy says with a pointed look at each of us. "I think you're worth so much more than that."

It feels so good to hear. Someone finally believes in us—someone with legitimate connections and knowledge of the industry. I want to hug the woman I hope will help my brother to see that this is where I belong instead of back in Houston.

Gavin surprises me by clearing his throat loudly. "Yeah, well, as you know, getting gigs isn't the easiest thing in the world and we're not the typical country trio. We play multiple genres and have been told by several managers that country radio isn't ready for our sound."

Part of me wants to kick him under the table.

But Mandy nods as if this is exactly what she expected him to say. "Yes, the fiddle and the R&B remixes are certainly unconventional." She waits for one of us to interrupt but no one does. "That being said, I think it's time for the three of you to make some hard and fast decisions. The reality is, you can play covers and revamped rap or bluegrass or both for all I care in festivals like this one. But when I get you into a showcase, you'll have to streamline your sound. Play the songs that best represent what you're capable of, the ones that sound a bit more like the hits topping the charts today."

I don't miss that she says *when* and not *if* I get you a showcase. Hope grows wild inside of me, unfurling in my chest and spreading like wildfire. I can practically see myself sprouting wings and flying right out of stringent music theory classes. A showcase would be huge. It would put us in front of managers and record labels. I know this because for years now Dallas has been saying how important they are for getting record deals.

"I think I speak for everyone when I say that we understand about sacrifice and compromise when it comes to this business," Dallas says. "And we know that as we start out, we'll have to do whatever it takes."

"That being said," Gavin interrupts bravely as I watch this conversation unfold. "We're not going to pretend to be something we're not. It won't do us any good to get a deal based on something we aren't capable of or happy doing."

"The last thing I want is for you to be unhappy," Mandy says. "Or unsatisfied. Music is very . . . personal. And I plan to make it my personal goal that you are very satisfied with everything we do together."

There's excessive warmth in her tone and it's a little unsettling, but her smile is genuine. I have a nagging sensation of female intuition trying to alert me to something, but I have no idea what.

Mandy's eyes might linger on Dallas a little longer than they do on Gavin or me, but I assume that's from their established familiarity. And in a way, if she's interested in either of the guys, I'd prefer it be Dallas anyway. Gavin's groupies are one thing, but working with a manager who was attracted to him would be my worst nightmare.

Before I can analyze the situation any further, a waiter appears and takes our order. I haven't even looked at the menu so I just ask for whatever pasta they have and a water. Gavin gets a burger and so does Dallas. Mandy orders a salad.

Once we're alone again Mandy asks about the details of our story, how we came to be a band and how the guys managed when I was at school in Houston.

"They called me crying a lot and begging me to come home," I say with mock seriousness.

"We mostly just played shows where we could meet halfway between Houston and Amarillo when Dixie wasn't too swamped with school," Dallas tells her with an eye roll in my direction. "Gavin and I played a few local shows on our own."

"And you're prepared to give up a prestigious scholarship for this? For life on the road with these two?" Mandy looks almost confused by this.

I nod without hesitation. "I realize that a career with a nationally recognized orchestra is a dream for a lot of people. It's just not mine. I didn't belong there." The last part sort of snuck out of me and I feel embarrassed by revealing so much, but Mandy nods as if taking it all in thoughtfully.

After that she inquires about our social media presence, what bands we've opened for, and other managers we've previously spoken with. Social media management is my department, my contribution to the band. I keep our pages up to date and post pictures on our blog. We actually have a surprising number of followers.

Our food arrives and the conversation is temporarily halted. My nerves are too tightly wound in my stomach to enjoy eating.

Mandy is the picture of sleek sophistication and while I can't tell yet how she feels about me, I feel certain that all of my hopes and dreams are pinned on her. Whether or not she signs us will determine what my plans are come fall. I'm slightly tempted to throw myself at her feet and beg if that's what it takes to seal the deal, but that probably isn't the best strategy. So I eat quietly and nod and smile each time she shares information with us about how she's helped her clients' careers.

Once we're finished eating and the plates have been cleared, Dallas leans toward us. "Mandy has the same vision for our future that I do. Y'all have always trusted me to make these types of decisions and she knows of an opening in a major showcase that she can get us into the day after this festival. If it doesn't work out, then we'll know. But I think we should give her a chance to show us what she can do for the band."

I take a deep breath and let my eyes slide briefly over to Gavin before returning to my brother's expectant stare.

"I trust you, Dallas," I tell him quietly. I do trust him, and I think he is capable of making good decisions for the band. But I'm about to do something behind his back that he isn't going to like at all. And then we are going to play our very first showcase the very next day. "If you think this is what's best then I'm in."

Mandy smiles brightly at me and I return the gesture.

"Me, too," Gavin says, side-eyeing me. "But I'd rather not sign anything until after the showcase. Let's see what happens; if we get some interest, we can have Mandy help us out if she's still on board after our performance."

"I will be," Mandy pipes up. "And the issue won't be whether or not you get any interest, it will be trying to sort through the many offers coming your way."

The budding sprout of hope grows to a full bloom at the confidence shining in her eyes.

Goodbye, orchestra pit.

M andy accompanies us to Sixth Street and hangs around while we warm up. Once we're ready, we play to a decent-sized crowd outside one of the most popular bars on Sixth Street. I'm able to glance backward a few times and watch Gavin play, his beautifully inked body bathed in the blue of neon lights from the surrounding signs as he takes out his aggression on his kit.

My brother is wholeheartedly giving this show his all, strutting around the stage like an overly confident peacock. I have a feeling the extra ass shaking and crowd eye-screwing has to do with the woman in the front row, but I'll be keeping my opinions to myself. Opportunity has knocked and thy name is Mandy.

I let go of my fears about not being enough for Gavin, sweep aside my concerns about whether or not we'll end up signing with Mandy Lantram, and ignore my brother's strutting across the stage, and just play. I am the music.

None of that matters as I stroke my bow across the strings. All that matters in this moment is the melody, this experience we're creating.

When it's over, we bow to applause and wish the audience a good night. I follow my brother offstage and we make our way to where Mandy is standing texting on her phone.

"Great news," she says once we've stepped far enough from where the next band has taken the stage and begun to play. "The *Indie Music Review* is doing a human interest piece on bands playing in the festival. A reporter will be by to interview the three of you tomorrow."

"Wow, that's amazing." The high from performing still has me barely touching the ground. "Whatever you did to make that happen, thank you."

Dallas gives us the specific time to be at rehearsal for the interview, and then bursts my hyped-up bubble by telling us we're going to head back to the hotel so we can get plenty of sleep tonight.

Gavin and I lag a few steps behind Mandy and my brother while they discuss possible interview questions.

Leaning down until his mouth is level with my ear, he says, "Looks like we aren't the only ones considering crossing some lines." His arms grazes softly against mine, sending a trail of warmth sparking down it.

I glance over and see Mandy smiling her toothpaste commercial smile at my brother. Dallas is grinning and nodding and using his hands to tell her an animated story about a show we performed recently where the stage was behind a Plexiglas wall due to the fact that the patrons tended to throw things. Not necessarily the tale I'd be regaling her with if I wanted to impress her, but Dallas was so proud that we were the only act that night that didn't have to dodge beer bottles.

I grin and return my attention to Gavin, vaguely aware that the bottom of my stomach drops out when his eyes meet mine.

"Is that all we're doing? *Considering* crossing them?"

Before he answers, Dallas tells us to get a move on. The conversation remains behind us.

Chapter 13

"LICK," I SAY WHEN HE OPENS HIS DOOR.

Gavin's eyes widen. "What?"

"Lick," I repeat, peering past him into the boys' slovenly room and enjoying the way his pupils widen, an ethereal glow illuminating them as his heated eyes latch on to mine. "The ice cream place. I want to go there."

After our show I changed into jeans and a plain white tank top because as cute as my boots were, my ankles were in serious danger of snapping. But I couldn't just sit restlessly in my room.

Gavin checks the leather cuff that contains his watch. "Okay. Should we wait for Dallas?"

We both turn toward where he stands below us in the parking lot discussing the plans for tomorrow and the showcase with Mandy. I don't really think my brother would *actually* cross any lines with her because he's always been a business-first type. But I'm glad they have chemistry and that she's taking us seriously.

"Um, I think he's probably going to be busy for a while." I send up a silent prayer that we don't screw it up this time, that Gavin and I can manage getting dessert without turning it into an argument and ruining our plans for Friday night. "We could ask them to join us."

Gavin calls out and asks if they want to come with us, but they wave us off.

"Don't be out too late," my brother cautions.

"Yes, Dad. We'll be back by curfew," I say before turning to smile at Mandy. "It was fantastic meeting you. I hope you enjoyed the show."

"I did," she says, nodding. "I'll be here the rest of the week checking out a few bands but I'll see you three tomorrow at the interview."

"Sounds good," Gavin says with an odd lilt to his voice. "You ready, Dixie?"

I nod, knowing that Gavin is probably nervous about the interview. Public speaking of any kind has never been his thing.

"Gav?" I say after a few minutes of walking in silence because the high from performing hasn't worn off yet and I can't just keep quiet.

He turns toward me. "Yeah?"

"Are you worried about the interview?"

He's quiet for a long string of seconds, then he shrugs. "Nah. No reason to be. Why? Are you?"

"I just have this feeling that this is bigger than the fair, bigger than anything we've done before. I think things are about to change. The band, us, everything."

He slows long enough to give me a questioning glance. "You've always known Dallas wanted to go to Nashville. Is that scaring you now that it seems like a real possibility?"

I shake my head. "No. I'm thrilled about that. This is my dream, too, you know. I might not pursue it as aggressively as my brother, but it is."

Gavin nods. "I get that. It's mine, too, I guess. I just never thought of it as a dream—more like the only thing I'm good at."

"That's not true," I tell him quietly.

He shrugs. "Not all changes are good, Bluebird. You want to rethink the whole one-night thing?"

Hell no.

"Do you?"

He stares straight ahead, his profile revealing nothing as we walk. He doesn't speak again until I feel like I'm going to scream. The tension strung tightly between us feels like it's wrapping around my neck.

"I agreed to it. So I'd think the answer to that would be obvious."

The relief whooshes through me and I can't contain my smile.

He cuts his eyes to me and grins. "I'm almost nervous when you look at me like that. What have you got in store for me, little Bluebird? Some *Fifty Shades* fantasy you can't wait to play out with a willing participant?"

My heart quickens its pace at his naughty suggestion. "Gavin Garrison, have you been reading mommy porn?"

He chuckles and holds the door open for me. I walk inside the vibrantly colored and brightly lit ice cream parlor and glance over my shoulder at him. Part of me feels like every moment with him is a dream, something I'm lying in bed alone and imagining, instead of an experience I'm actually living.

Holding fire, I realize as we get in line. This is my brief time to hold the flames that will destroy me, burn me to ash, and scatter my soul in the wind. It's that split second when the heat first hits, mercifully numbing the nerves before they alert the brain to the pain.

Several high-school-aged girls in front of us suddenly can't concentrate on the flavors before them. They're too busy giggling and glancing back at Gavin. He's tall, dark, and still slightly sweat soaked from performing. His eyes are bright under the lights and his ink is alive with each movement of his arms. I can't blame them. I look up at him and he doesn't even notice. His eyes are focused on the display of flavors.

My mind slips back in time to the first time we had ice cream together. It was Gavin's first time to ever have it and he swore it was heaven in his mouth. I'd bought it from the ice cream truck with change I'd saved up from my lunch money and shared with him. His eyes had closed and I'd fallen in love with him a little more that day. The boy who knew and understood the importance of savoring something sweet—because pleasure like that was rare—the same way that I did. My heart had broken wide open knowing that he'd lived twelve years and no one had ever given him ice cream. He'd moved into that broken place in my heart and remained there ever since.

"If I get sweet cream and strawberry, will you get—"

"Yeah, yeah," he says. "You know I will."

Gavin places a hand on the small of my back, and I'm smiling so hard at the guy taking our order he probably thinks I live for ice cream. Or I need to lower my dose.

We order and pay and walk out into the street with our desserts. I take a bite and sigh as the cool sweetness melts on my tongue and slides down my throat.

"So do you think Mandy will make an official offer?"

Gavin swallows his ice cream. "Seems like a distinct possibility."

"Seems like an awfully big risk."

Gavin gives me a questioning look and I hear what he doesn't say. I've been an advocate of risks lately.

"Forget it," I mutter, digging back into my two scoops. We come to a crosswalk and wait for the signal to change.

"No, I hear you. Any decisions we make that affect the band will affect all of us. Life is one big risk. You can't really avoid them. No matter how hard you try."

Once we've made it safely to the other side of the street, I slow my pace. "Am I supposed to be listening between the lines?"

Gavin tilts his head as if trying to determine what I mean. Understanding hoods his gaze and he silences me with unspoken words.

Shaking his head, he picks up speed. "If you're this worried about how wrong everything can go, why do you want to do this?"

"*This* meaning the music or you?"

"Both."

I take my time letting my ice cream melt in my mouth and then lick my lips. He watches me closely and I'm suddenly very aware that we're not alone. The streets are busy, people still enjoying Austin nightlife.

"I guess," I begin, lowering my voice and leaning toward him, "I expect it to be worth it."

My words hang heavily in the air between us.

"Ready to switch?" Gavin says, straightening his back and handing his cup of chocolate over to me when we enter the hotel lobby.

"Sure." I give him mine, our fingers grazing as he takes the cup. The electricity from the charged connection zaps my mind blank and all I can focus on is the need building inside of me. Somehow we've reached the elevator, but I don't want to walk away yet.

Surely our one night will cure me of this. It has to. Because nothing could be worse than wanting and not knowing exactly what it is that I want.

"You're going to have to stop it with those looks or whether or not Mandy Lantram signs us is going to be the least of our problems."

"What looks?"

Gavin is staring intently at me with careful restraint in his eyes. Has he been talking to me and I missed it?

He takes a huge bite and I have to wait for him to finish it before he answers me. He shifts his body weight forward, leaning into my space as we wait for the elevator.

"You give me these looks sometimes—like that one," he points his spoon at me. "Your eyes go dark and right now, without Dallas or anyone else around to stop me, all I can think is how good this ice cream would taste if I was licking it off your body instead of this plastic spoon."

He shrugs like he didn't just send me up in a flaming inferno of need. I flew too close, got burned, and now I want more.

The elevator opens and I walk inside and jab the button displaying the number of my floor. Just mine, not his. He watches me, the surprise evident on his face.

He stands with confusion pulling his features inward. "Dixie, what are you—"

I will make it impossible for him to say no, somehow. I have five floors on the elevator to figure it out. My heart rises into my throat as we make our way upward.

Taking his hand without permission, I pull him from the car the second the doors open. I let go long enough to retrieve my key card from my bra and slam it into the slot on the door. Thankfully it co-operates, and we enter my darkened room. The curtains are open and the streetlamps provide enough of a glow that I can see my way to the bed.

I place my ice cream on the bedside table and lift my tank top slowly over my head. Facing Gavin in my jeans and strapless black satin bra, I sit down tentatively on the edge of the mattress. I'm waiting for him to grab me, to hand my shirt back to me, and tell me to stop this nonsense right this instant. But he doesn't. His eyes are lit from somewhere inside of him, shining brightly with desire, and he's staring intently in a way that I would mistake for anger, but he's still here. He's not running or storming out.

"You know what I love about music, Gavin?" I say softly, leaning back slightly on my elbows.

He says nothing, but his eyes meet mine and I force myself not to shrink away from the fevered stare engulfing me.

"I love that you can't pin it down, can't control it. Music is free. It's unpredictable and alive. You can't own it or buy it or sell it. Not really. No matter how hard people try. It belongs to no one."

"Like you," he says evenly.

"Like us," I answer. "No one can control us, Gavin. No one can stop us if this is what we want. If you want to eat ice cream off my body, then you damn well should. Life is short. Ask my parents."

The mention of my parents breaks his impenetrable barrier and his mouth gapes open when I lie down on the bed. He stands above me and I see the fleeting thoughts of retreat flickering in his eyes.

So I let my head fall back as I close my eyes, and I wait.

Ice-cold ribbons scorch a pattern onto my bare flesh when he lets the mostly melted ice cream drizzle onto my stomach. My back arches off the bed and I allow a tiny shocked whimper to escape my lips. When my eyes fly open I see him standing above me, watching me writhe beneath him.

"Gavin."

"Cold, Bluebird?"

He kneels between my thighs and I take advantage of the opportunity to drive my fingers through his hair. His tongue is liquid fire lapping up his—well, technically my—dessert as I shiver beneath him. Pressing his warm palms against my hips, a tortured moan escapes the back of his throat. My eyes want to slam shut but I wrench them open so that I can watch Gavin's beautiful body moving between mine. His hands slide lower, his fingers pressing hard into my thighs as if he's holding me down, denting deeper with each stroke of his tongue.

All I can think is, *Gavin's mouth is on my stomach.* Where do we even go from here?

Before I can ask, he unbuttons my jeans and uses a hand to drag them down my hips. As if he can't wait the two seconds it would take to remove them completely, he presses his lips to the fabric of my panties.

A moan that sounds like pleasure mixed with an attempt at his name breaks free. I've never had anyone's mouth *there*.

"Want me to stop?" His eyes lift to mine and I shake my head. *No.*

The ache between my legs becomes more insistent, turning to a steady pulsating throb as he removes my panties and drops them to the floor with my jeans. My body jerks forward when his tongue parts my folded flesh. Gavin growls against my sensitive skin and I gasp.

"You taste even better than ice cream, Bluebird." Scorching circles of wet heat blank my mind of any fears or insecurities of concerns I might have had about him being so intimately acquainted with my body. By the time he dips his tongue into my opening all I want is more. All I can think about is how to get him closer, deeper.

I'm thrusting against his mouth and moaning in pleasure when I feel it. The pressure has reached its peak and I need him inside. Now.

"Gavin. *Oh,*" I bite out when he pulls my clit into his mouth. The room spins around us and I can't slow it down.

"Yeah, baby?"

"I need you. I need you inside me," I tell him breathlessly. "Please."

"Soon," he promises, sliding a finger into my slick opening.

"*Oh God. Oh my God. Don't stop.*" I'm both desperate and demanding. When he thrusts another finger into me I lose my grip on my sanity and am flung over the edge of oblivion.

I can hear myself crying out but my words are unintelligible.

I'm covered in a thin sheen of perspiration and writhing on the bed like a woman possessed as Gavin continues to lick me down from my orgasm.

Slowly I become aware of the parts of my body I'd assumed had drifted into outer space. Gavin pulls back from the apex of my thighs and I see it, the rabid lust and determination. This is it. He's going to make love to me—or maybe something much more intense that I have no name for—right now.

A sudden persistent knock peppers the door to my room like gunshots to my chest. "Dixie? You in there? Open up."

My brother's voice effectively murders the moment and threatens to give me a heart attack. Gavin mutters a curse under his breath and I sit up.

Using the blanket on the bed to wipe the sticky ice cream remnants from my stomach, I pull my shirt back over my head and try not to die while yanking my jeans up my legs.

"Maybe you should, um, hide?" Panic scatters my thoughts around the room and I can't seem to grab hold of a single one that tells me what to do next.

"I don't hide. Not even from Dallas." Gavin stands and strides confidently toward the door. How he's so calm is beyond me. I keep forgetting to breathe and my lungs are exceptionally pissed about it.

"What are we going to—"

"We're just hanging out. Eating ice cream. I think he can handle it."

Yeah, but I can't seem to. Eating ice cream now has a whole new blush-inducing meaning.

"Okay." I nod and try to arrange myself casually on my bed, folding my legs beneath me. My entire body pulsates as if my heart had quadrupled in size and is pounding so hard it's reverberating through my core.

I nearly fall over snatching the television remote and clicking the on button before Dallas walks in. The preview channel shouts that for 19.95 we can subscribe to the adult movie channel for a full twenty-four hours. I'm changing it as quickly as I can, barely landing on a country music video channel, when my brother charges into the room.

"What's going on in here?" The blue of the screen glows against his hardened features.

Gavin stands calmly behind him, as if all he was really doing was hanging out eating ice cream.

"Looked like you might have some company tonight," Gavin says, propping on the wall beside the bathroom door. "Figured we'd give you some privacy."

"Company?" He looks utterly perplexed at the suggestion.

"You seemed to be in a deep discussion with Mandy," I clarify.

My brother sighs and drops down heavily on my bed, grabbing the remote to lower the sound. "Speaking of Mandy, we need to talk."

Gavin folds his arms over his chest. "What's the word on the showcase?"

Dallas is silent, which never happens unless something is up. His gaze swings from Gavin and back to me again before his chin drops forward. "About that . . ."

"What about it?"

Dallas's forehead is creased as he tries to look at the both of us simultaneously. His expression reminds me of pictures I've seen of my dad when he was younger—both of them intense and rugged in the same handsome way. Not that I'd ever tell him that. He's cocky enough as it is.

"The only way she can get us into Saturday's showcase is if we sign with her. She pulled all the strings she can, but we'd have to sign something with her first."

My surprise and subsequent irritation must show plainly on my face.

"She said we could do something short term, give her a trial run and see how things go. If after six months we're unhappy or she just can't make anything happen for us, we walk away unscathed. No hard feelings."

Gavin snorts out an angry sound that surprises me and from the looks of his expression, Dallas, too.

"What is it with you two thinking you're untouchable? Six months or one year or one night or however the hell long, making a commitment to someone like this has an impact. Maybe the effects will be short term or long term, but let's go ahead and scratch escaping unscathed and unaffected off the fucking list here."

Dallas begins lining out the many artists Mandy has launched careers for. It's an impressive list for someone who is only twenty-seven, and I agree, but I can't take my eyes off Gavin. He's visibly upset, whether it's about the new stipulation from Mandy, the one-night arrangement with me, or the fact that my brother interrupted some seriously intense foreplay, isn't clear. But the fact that he's immensely aggravated is.

When Gavin's eyes finally meet mine, and I make a concentrated effort to convey silently to him that I know our one night will have an effect on me. I do. I'm just willing to do what it takes to survive the fallout because I know it will be worth it. Whatever pain comes after will be worth knowing how it feels to be that close to him, to be connected to him in that way. For him, it's one night. One he might even forget within a week's worth of one-night stands. But I know I will keep that one night with me forever. It's the memory that will become the final piece in my mental treasured-experiences box where I keep the most important moments of my life.

"So we're okay with this then? Signing the short-term contract with her and seeing what she can do?"

Gavin stares at my brother intently. "You think this chick is the real deal? If you believe she'll make the right decisions for the band and you trust her, then I think you know I'm in. But if you're not sure, or you doubt her intentions at all, then slow your roll, man. We're not in a race here and I'd rather wait as long as it takes to find the right manager than rushing to sign a bad one just to say we have one."

Dallas turns from Gavin to me and lifts his eyebrows, indicating it's my turn to speak, so I shrug.

"If you think signing with her is the right decision, then I'm with you."

With you, but still planning to lie to you because hell will freeze over and grant underprivileged orphans free admission to the ice rink before I tell you about Gavin and me.

My brother nods. "I do. I wouldn't be here right now if I didn't. You both know the band is my whole world. I'd never risk doing anything that could ruin what we have."

The silence hangs heavy in the air as Gavin and I take turns avoiding eye contact with each other. When I can't take it anymore, I hold my stare steadily on him until he returns it.

"So we're doing this then." Maybe it should be a question but somehow it isn't.

His eyes darken and I know that we've crossed our moment of impasse. It's time for him to lay it on the line and jump into the abyss with me or bail out while he still can. "Yeah. Yeah we are," Gavin says quietly as if my brother isn't even there.

Dallas claps his hands together. "Then it's settled." He grins at us, and I do my best to look excited about this decision despite an entire universe of things that could go wrong teeming to life in my mind. "We'll get out of here and let you get some rest, Dix."

I walk him and Gavin to my door, freezing solid where I stand when Dallas turns to us and asks, "So how was the ice cream?"

My mouth drops open but can't seem to form any words, but Gavin looks my brother right in the eyes when he answers.

"Best I ever had."

Chapter 14

Austin MusicFest—Day 4

GAVIN'S PHONE RINGS ELEVEN TIMES DURING OUR INTERVIEW with Scott Levinson, a hipster thirty-something from the *Indie Music Review*. Scott adjusts his rectangular black-framed glasses frequently while he asks about everything from how we developed our unique sound to Emmylou.

Dallas is midway through explaining our sound to Scott when another one of Gavin's attempts at silencing his ringer before we hear it fails. Mandy gives him an icy glare. She has an authoritative presence about her that makes me feel even younger than I am. I keep waiting for her to confiscate Gavin's phone the way teachers did in high school.

"Everything okay?" I mouth silently to Gavin over my shoulder after we finish the interview and prepare to play a few numbers for Scott and Mandy. He gives me a slight nod but averts his gaze and focuses on his drums.

Dallas said Mandy suggested we ditch some of our reworked editions of classic hits and replace them with acoustic versions of billboard chart toppers. Right now I don't really care what we play. I just want to know what's going on that has Gavin's phone blowing up.

I stare at him until Dallas plays the opening cords to our new show closer.

The sound of Gavin's cymbals shattering the silence sends a delicious shiver down my spine. I watch him tap the snare lightly, and notice the line between his brows. Playing is usually an outlet for Gavin, always has been. But right now he's working through something and I have no idea what it could be. Guilt prickles at the edge of my awareness because it's possible that his frustration has something to do with our one night, and yet I have a persistent intuition that whatever is bothering him has to do with his relentless caller.

We've just finished a slightly modified set when the sound of Gavin's phone buzzing interrupts Scott telling us when the edition with our article will run.

After Scott and Mandy say their goodbyes, Dallas shakes his head while yanking a cord free from our amplifier. "Take five. And Gavin, answer your fucking phone and tell that chick to move the hell on."

Dallas jogs out of the warehouse, chasing Mandy down to apologize, I suspect.

"Gav? Something going on?"

"It's nothing," he answers quickly without looking at me. "I'll turn my phone off."

But he doesn't.

My stomach curls painfully inward. Could be one of his randoms calling like Dallas suggested. Though I don't think I've ever known one to be quite this tenacious. The thing about Gavin is that he's always honest with them. He doesn't pretend to want more and they know this going in. Just as I do.

"Maybe you should just answer it." As if conjured to life by my words, the phone buzzes in his hand. He must've turned the ringer off but not the phone. He closes his eyes as it continues to vibrate. Whoever is calling is upsetting him. A lot. "Okay. I'll answer it then."

I'm impulsive enough to snatch it before he can stop me.

"Hello?"

An automated voice answers me. "You have a collect call from an inmate at the Potter County Women's Detention Center. Say yes to accept. Say no or simply hang up to decline."

My mouth drops open but no words come out.

The robotic female voice begins detailing the instructions that I should follow if I no longer wish to receive calls from this number, but Gavin snatches the phone from my hand and presses the disconnect button before she's finished.

"What are you going to do?" I'm barely able to harness my heartbreak for Gavin and my murderous rage for Katrina Garrison. It has to be her. He's bailed her out more times than I can count on one hand. Nobody deserves this kind of mother, and the injustice of Gavin being stuck with her has my blood pressure rising steadily.

"What can I do?" He gives me a half shrug as if the weight of the world on his shoulders is too much to allow a whole one.

"Don't go," I whisper, knowing better. I've never known him not to bail her out. Ever.

His tormented gaze meets mine and I know. He's going.

I do some quick calculations in my head. When my mental math gets to be too much, I begin working it out aloud.

"Potter County is about eight hours from here, seven the way you drive. There's still no way you could make it there and back before tonight's show, obviously. We could leave right after we get offstage tonight. But then you figure they probably won't open for visitors or bail until eight tomorrow morning. And then it'd probably take an hour or so for the paperwork, but if we didn't stop for food or to use the restroom too often we could make it back in time for—"

"Stop. Just stop." He shakes his head, looking at me as if I've just rattled off my thoughts in a foreign language he doesn't comprehend.

"Gavin, look at me."

He complies and I can see from the way his hazel eyes have dimmed that he's switched over to autopilot. "What makes you so sure I'm going to go?"

"The fact that you always do."

Tension ripples along his jaw, but he doesn't argue with me.

"I know you're going to go get her, and I know you'd probably prefer to go alone, but think about how much time you'd save if we could drive in shifts. Straight there and straight back."

The thought of him going alone hits me like a fist. If he goes alone, gets sucked into his mother's dark, depraved bullshit, I fear I'll never see him again. Dallas never told me the full extent of the details, but I know that during my time in Houston—the year we stopped performing together as frequently—Gavin sank like a rock in a black sea. I can't lose him again. I won't. There's no way in hell I'm letting him go home alone.

He swallows hard, the thick knot in his throat bobbing as a piece of his unruly dark hair drops over his forehead. He needs a haircut, but now is not the time.

"Tomorrow's the last day of the festival," I remind him. "Dallas said Mandy's boss would be here to check out our show. He's the one who determines whether or not she can actually sign us. Imagine screwing that up because you were too stubborn to let me come with you."

"No," he answers abruptly, not even bothering to pretend he considered my offer.

It stings, but I continue making my case in this one-sided debate. "You'll have to sleep. Like it or not. And you won't make it back in time. Even if you're a superhuman machine that doesn't need sleep to live, what if your phone dies? Or the van breaks down, or bikers swarm you on a deserted road and decide to have their way with you?"

He closes his eyes as a short huff of amused breath escapes his chest. A tiny smile teases at one corner of his mouth, allowing me to finally exhale.

"You gonna protect me from the big, bad bikers, Bluebird?"

"If need be." We're joking now, but the protectiveness I feel for him surges in my chest. I want so badly to keep him safe, to keep him away from anything or anyone that would cause him pain. His mother included. His mother first and foremost.

"Your brother would never go for it."

I lower my voice, even though Dallas and Mandy are likely too caught up in their own conversation to pay attention to us. "I wasn't planning on *telling* my brother. Or asking him for permission. Maybe you haven't noticed, but I'm a big girl now." I force a smile and wink, even though I'd prefer to take him by the shoulders and shake. Hard.

His eyelids lift and he scans me slowly from head to toe. "I noticed. Believe me, I noticed."

If I had even the slightest hope that I could convince him not to run off to his mom's rescue, then I would. But at this point, I know it'd just be a waste of time. Years of watching him drop everything for someone who wouldn't spit if he was on fire has erased any ability I had to think that maybe one day he'd just walk away from her.

"Then it's settled. Meet me at the van as soon as we're done tonight."

I don't know how this impromptu trip is going to affect our deal for tomorrow night, but for as much as he protested, there is obvious relief smoothing the lines of concern on Gavin's face once it's decided that I'm going. Which I am. Whether he likes it or not. And for me, knowing that I've eased even a fraction of his pain is enough. For now.

O f all the people who could screw up my plan to ride to Potter County with Gavin tonight, Afton Tate is the last one I expect to actually do it. And yet, here he is. Standing next to the stage as soon as we step off it. We opened for his band again and he looks entirely too happy to see me considering our "breakup."

"I'm so glad I caught you," he greets me while smiling warmly.

"She's not a fish," I barely hear Gavin mutter from behind me.

It doesn't appear that Afton heard him, because he continues with exactly as much gusto in his voice as he started with. "There's a party after the shows tonight. At Crave. A lot of the big-timers will be there. We got invited and I'd love for you to come as my date."

Crave, Lick, what is it with Austin and their one-word verb-titled food places? There's something to be said for getting straight to the point, I suppose.

I sigh and try to let him down easy. "Um, I don't think I—"

"She'd love to," my brother chimes in unexpectedly. Turning to me he grins like he's giving me some great gift. "Dix, this will be such a great opportunity for you to meet other people in the business. Have a great time." With a wink he turns and walks off with Mandy, leaving me to glare at his retreating figure. I told him to back off a little before we came to Austin and he thinks this is what I meant.

A quick glance at Gavin reveals that he isn't quite as thrilled with this new development but isn't going to do anything to prevent it from happening. His stare stays straight ahead as he calls something I can't make out to my brother and makes his way toward the van. He didn't say goodbye to me. Didn't ask me if I needed a ride back to the hotel.

"Yeah, um, I guess I'll see you after your show," I say to Afton while simultaneously formulating a plan in my head.

"Cool." Afton smiles and I almost feel guilty. But it's not like it's a date, it's just an after party and I'm not using him for his connections. I couldn't care less about that, which my brother would be sorely disappointed to know. "I'll pick you up at your hotel around eleven. I'll text you when we're done and I head that way."

"Sounds good. Have a great show." With a hurried smile, I wait until he's heading up onto the stage before I turn and practically sprint in the direction of where the van is parked. Luckily it's not far.

Gavin slams the back doors and heads around to the driver's side. I'm in the passenger seat by the time he's in and has pulled his door closed.

His eyes widen when he sees me already seated next to him. "Jesus, Dixie. Give a guy a heart attack."

I can't help but grin. "My bad."

"You didn't want to stay? Watch your boy play before your big date?"

I lift an eyebrow that he doesn't turn to see while he cranks the engine. "I didn't realize I had a boy. Or a big date."

"Tate seems pretty persistent. And honestly, maybe he's the one you should be—"

"Be what, Gavin? Interested in? Attracted to?" Okay, now I actually am annoyed. This conversation just took a left turn right into Piss Me Off Town. "Because I can honestly say, I like Afton. I do. He's a nice guy and someone I could learn a lot from and would like to be friends with. But my friendship with him has very little, no, wait, *nothing* to do with our . . . arrangement."

With a shake of his head, Gavin drives into the back parking lot of the hotel. "I was going to say, maybe he's the one you should spend this evening with and let me make the trip to Potter County on my own."

Oh God. My entire body heats from the inside out. "I see. Well, about that. I have a plan."

"You and your plans," Gavin mutters under his breath. I ignore him and continue.

"So Crave is a sushi place, I think. I'm going to leave early, say I'm not feeling well. Then I'll text Dallas and tell him I can't make rehearsal tomorrow because I have food poisoning and I want to rest up for the show."

Gavin parks the van and shuts the engine off. "I don't quite get how fake food poisoning helps me—us."

I try not to grin like a crazed psychopath at hearing him include me. "It buys us time, Gav. So we don't have to be back until sound check tomorrow. You can text him that you're holding my hair back all day. Making sure I'm drinking plenty of fluids or whatever. It will free him up to be with his lady friend and we won't have to break the speed limit and risk getting a ticket in every town between here and Amarillo."

My smile is smug because I can tell he's impressed. There's no denying I'm feeling pretty proud of myself for thinking so quickly on my feet.

"You always think of everything." He sighs and leans toward me until I shift in my seat. "But baby, I have news for you."

My eyebrows are probably in my hairline as I stare openly at his handsome face, surprised at how close he is. "And what's that?"

He leans even closer to me and my lips begin to tingle in anticipa-tion. My hands clutch the weathered leather upholstery of my seat to keep from reaching out and grabbing his face and dragging his mouth to mine.

"There are some things you can't control, can't plan for."

I fold my arms over my chest in an attempt to hide the serious effort I'm making to breathe while this close to him. "Such as?"

Amusement slides across his features as he licks his lips but it is almost immediately replaced with a scowl.

"Nothing. Forget it." Pulling back from our intimate moment, he extracts himself roughly from the van and slams the door, causing me to jump.

What the hell?

I follow his lead and practically tear the door off the hinges as I make my escape. "I'm sorry," I call out sarcastically to his back. "Was I supposed to take a mind-reading class at some point? Be-cause I must have skipped that one."

"Just go on your damn date, Dixie. I can handle this shit on my own." I'm gaining on him, close enough to hear when he mumbles "been doing it my whole life" under his breath.

"Just because you can and you have doesn't mean you should. You shouldn't have to be alone in this. You *aren't* alone."

He ignores me and continues walking toward the side entrance to the hotel, pulling out his key card to open the door as if he didn't hear me.

"Damn you, Gavin Garrison. Wait a second." I reach him just as he pulls the door open. "You know you don't have to do this alone. Dallas will even come along if you want him to. In a heartbeat."

Turning, he gives me his broodiest squint-eyed glare. "I know that. I also know that if he knew what my intentions for tomorrow night were, he'd probably kick my ass and kick me right out of the band." Raking a hand hard through his hair in a way that makes me ache to do the same, he frowns at me. "Look, there's just a lot of shit I have to deal with. And honestly, I'm used to dealing with it alone. I *like* dealing with it alone. It's no one's problem but mine. I'm leaving in a few minutes. I appreciate the offer, I do. But honestly, I got this."

Giving up on reasoning with him, I reach out and grip his arm with my hand. Holy muscle. I swallow hard and ignore the urge to run my hands up his arms and across his chest, because now is so not the time.

"If nothing else, you're my friend. And I like to think I'm yours. Friends are there for each other when shit goes sideways. I want to go. The sushi excuse will give you more time to get back tomorrow." I shove my pride down my throat and resort to begging when his cold stare meets my pleading one. "Wait for me tonight, Gavin. Please?"

He glances at my hand on his arm, then back to my face. "Why? Why do you want to tag along on the road trip from hell? This isn't going to be beef jerky and Big Gulps and mixtapes, Bluebird." So gently it breaks my heart, he removes my hand from his arm.

Because I want to be where you are. Because I want to protect you from her. Because I won't be able to sleep or think a coherent thought until you're back safe and sound. Because when you leave, it's like you take my soul with you. Because it hurts like hell when we're apart.

I can't say any of the actual reasons and I can't lie to his face, so I tell a half-truth.

"Because I want to check on Papa. Even if it's just long enough to give him a quick hug and remind him to take his pills."

Gavin frowns, but finally relents. "I can't guarantee there will be time for that, but we can try. I'm leaving at midnight. With you or without you. That will put me there as soon as the jail opens so I can pay her bail and get her home in time to get back here for sound check."

"Midnight. Got it. I'll be here."

"Don't waste time coming back here. I'll be outside of Crave. But I'm not messing around. Midnight."

"Yes, fairy godmother. Midnight or I turn into a pumpkin."

"Yeah, okay." He scratches his head and looks at me as if I've lost my mind, then goes inside.

Gavin probably doesn't know about Cinderella. Not all the specifics, anyway. I don't know why I thought he would, other than I assume every child would have at some point. But no one ever would've read it to him or taken him to see the movie. He probably doesn't know many fairy tales. How this has escaped me all these years is beyond me. I add reading him the best of the Brothers Grimm and a Disney movie marathon to my list of things to do.

Chapter 15

AFTON TEXTS ME AT A QUARTER TO ELEVEN TO LET ME KNOW HIS show has ended and he's heading over to pick me up for the party.

I glance at my reflection in the mirror and hold my hair up with one hand, trying to decide if up or down is the way to go. I paired my favorite black leather secondhand McQueens with the nicest thing I own, a short red halter dress I wore to my senior homecoming dance. Up seems more sophisticated so I grab a few bobby pins and tuck them tightly into my updo. Smearing on some red lip stain and applying a thick coat of mascara, I notice that my hands are trembling. I don't know if I'm nervous about this party with Afton or what's coming after—lying to Dallas, leaving with Gavin.

What if he leaves without me?

Fighting off a panic attack and the urge to text Afton and tell him I can't make it, I toss a change of clothes, my toothbrush, and clean underwear into my black faux leather shoulder bag. A bag of plain potato chips and a granola bar from the vending machine are on the small desk in my room so I toss those in too for good measure.

I can only imagine what Afton would think if he glimpsed the contents of my purse. Probably that I planned on spending the night with him and possibly that I had low blood sugar. Whatever.

I'm standing outside at the front of the hotel when Afton pulls up in a cab. I don't know if I was expecting his band's van or what, but he catches me off guard in his dark blue button-down and black slacks. Cleaned-up Afton looks a lot older and more sophisticated and metropolitan than young, scruffy musician Afton.

"You look nice," I say as I make my way toward him.

"Thank you. You look . . . hazardous to my health."

I can't help but grin. "What's that supposed to mean?"

He doesn't clarify, just holds the cab door open and climbs in behind me.

"So this party . . . bigwigs, huh?"

He shrugs in the back of the darkened cab as the driver takes off. I figure Afton already gave him our final destination. "Sort of. It's a small gathering. A record label executive interested in All Grown Up invited me. Probably just wants to flash his bling and entice me to sign with them."

"This happen a lot?" I ask while watching the electric rainbow of neon lights blurring by us before returning my attention to him.

"Occasionally." His eyes slide over me and I feel every place they land. My mouth. My chest. My bare legs.

His attention makes me squirm and I hope he doesn't notice. "Can I ask why you invited me? Specifically?"

Even with the absence of light, I can tell he's blushing at being caught ogling me. I'm flattered, but it barely registers over my nerves about tonight.

"Um, honestly, I hate these things. I hate anything social really.

It's awkward as hell and people come up and introduce themselves like you're supposed to recognize them and give a shit." He sighs. "God, I sound like a pretentious prick."

"Nah. Just a slightly antisocial prick."

He chuckles softly. "It's just not my scene is all. But I invited you because we had a good time the other night—"

"Despite the awkward 'it's not you it's me' part," I interrupt.

"Yes, aside from that," he agrees with a grin. "But I was hoping to bring someone I actually enjoyed talking to so that this night wouldn't be an entire waste."

"Wow. I feel so special. I'll try to be particularly witty this evening."

"Thanks. I'd appreciate it." He winks at me and surprising warmth spreads through me. "If you know any good jokes or how to tie a cherry stem with your tongue, tonight would be an excellent time to showcase those abilities."

"Good to know," I say with mock seriousness.

He elbows me lightly in the side. "I promise I'm kidding. But you'll see, it gets really lame really quick and you start hoping someone chokes on an hors d'oeuvre just to relieve the monotony."

"So why even go?"

His entire body goes rigid beside me. When he answers, it's practically through gritted teeth. "Can't really be avoided. Julian would cut us off if I weren't at least trying to get officially *into the business,* so to speak. In his eyes, everything we do is pointless unless we get a major deal with a legit label."

Sounded a lot like Dallas's perspective. I could relate. "Julian?"

"Our financial backer. He was sitting up front with me when I drove you to the stage the other night."

Ah. I'd wondered who that guy was. "I see. So he pulls all the strings?"

"All the ones not attached to instruments, yeah, pretty much."

Afton's voice is so much tighter than usual, I search my brain for ways to change the subject but come up empty.

"That seems . . . complicated."

He sighs. "It can be. He's also my uncle and pretty much the only person in my family who supports my decision to be a musician—or squander my potential and quash every dream my father has ever had for me, if you ask my parents—so yeah, it gets tense and messy from time to time. But that's what keeps life interesting, right?"

Thankfully we've arrived at the restaurant before I have to answer. Afton pays the cabdriver, tipping way more than I would have, and the man practically leaps out and hurdles the hood in order to open the door for us. He gives Afton a card and tells him he can call him directly and he'll pick us up when we're ready.

Stepping aside, I raise my eyebrows at my date. "So this is how the other half lives? Good to know."

"Other half?" He gives me a questioning smirk and I laugh.

"I don't think I've ever had a cabdriver offer to come back and get me. Or open my door. One almost ran me over when I didn't get out fast enough."

"You must not have been wearing that dress. Pretty sure that's why he offered." Afton winks at me and I shake my head.

Now I'm the one blushing, probably as deeply as the shade of red I'm wearing. He offers his arm and I take it. Walking in the back entrance into a private dining room, I feel a bit like a celebrity. And like a big fat phony. I'm a jeans and Chucks and ponytail walks into a greasy diner kind of girl. Not a designer shoes, sexy dress, updo using a private entrance to a swanky restaurant chick.

Tonight, I think as both my chin and my shoulders lift a bit higher than usual, *maybe I'm both.*

Immediately upon entering Crave, I find myself in a sleek room with mahogany ceilings, marble floors, and a fireplace in the corner. People of all ages are clustered into groups and scattered around the room.

The conversation is so boisterous and loud it fills the space in the private dining room. Waiters deliver sushi to the people seated at round tables covered in slate-gray material that probably costs more than my dress did its first time around. Afton takes me by the hand and we migrate between the high standing tables where mostly men are drinking liquor in short squat glasses and discussing people by names and labels. I don't recognize many, but I'd bet a year's worth of tips that Dallas would.

After my date says a few obligatory hellos and makes the necessary introductions, calling me "the Very Beautiful and Talented Dixie Lark" as if they're supposed to know or care who I am enough times that I want to jump out one of the ceiling to floor-length windows that make up one wall of the room, we make our way to the bar and Afton orders himself a scotch before turning to me.

"Um, sweet tea is fine."

He grins. "Trust me, another hour of this and you're going to wish you'd ordered something much stronger."

Little does he know, I don't plan on staying another hour. He orders me a Long Island iced tea instead and I go with it.

Turns out, he was right about things getting pretty bland pretty fast. After hearing him have the same conversation with four different groups of people, I'm ready to tell the bartender to line up shots on the bar and keep them coming.

I sip my second Long Island iced tea and pick at the spicy tuna roll with my chopsticks. Thank goodness I have a toothbrush in my bag. Several times throughout the evening I check my phone, as if I expect Gavin to be texting me a countdown. *T-minus twenty-six minutes until Operation Free Deadbeat Mom commences.*

He doesn't, and I'm annoyed at myself for expecting him to and being disappointed. That's not his style and he made it clear this wasn't something he wanted me along for.

Hope is a funny thing, though. It continues to build in my chest even after being deflated time and time again. So maybe it's a stupid brain-dead thing that refuses to learn from experience.

At a quarter to midnight, I excuse myself to the ladies' room to empty my bladder and brush my teeth before the top-secret road trip to Potter County. Afton stands as I leave and I can't help but think that one day, he is going to make some girl very happy. He's charming, sweet, attentive, polite, and not overly full of himself even if he has every reason to be. But try as I may, my heart remains utterly unaffected unless in the presence of a certain drummer who will be here in a few short minutes.

I can't contain the smile that fills my face as I walk to the ladies' room. I'm still smiling when I step out of the stall and am caught like a deer in headlights in front of my own reflection. My eyes widen and my mouth opens slightly, as does the woman's in the mirror. But I barely recognize her.

Her skin is glowing and her eyes are gleaming brightly under the merciless glare of the lights. Her cheeks are flushed and her hair is nearly perfect, a few loose strands falling beside her face in a way that looks effortlessly intentional.

She looks so much older and wiser than I feel. So much so that I want to ask her what the future holds. If Gavin will ever see her this way. If this trip is doomed, if the band is, if I'm going to ruin every-thing. But before I can, two women enter the small room practically holding each other up as their laughter bounces off the walls and into me.

They appear oblivious to my presence as each of them takes a place at the available sinks and begin touching up their makeup. I wash my hands slowly, knowing I need to brush my teeth but real-izing it will be an odd thing to do in front of them.

It's not until I hear a familiar name that I actually pay attention to what they're saying.

"Have you seen the catch Lantram reeled in? I mean, my God. Who even cares if he can sing? I'd sign him to the label just to watch him shake his ass in my office." The busty blonde in the black dress that fits like it was custom made for her body applies a thick layer of gloss and smacks her lips loudly together.

My stomach roils, catching on quicker than my mind does.

Dallas. She's talking about Dallas.

"Right? No wonder she isn't here tonight. Probably tied up. Liter-ally." The brunette tousles her hair back and forth then gives each of her cheeks a slight pinch. "You know she does them all. Hello, why do you think all of her most successful clients are twenty-something and male? Woman knows what she wants, I'll give her that."

"Can't say I—" The blonde stops talking midsentence and glares at me. "Can we help you?"

Oh shit. I've been staring openly at them. My mind races; thank-fully I'm good on my feet. "God, sorry. I didn't mean to stalker stare. I was trying to figure out what kind of gloss that was. Your lips look *ah-mazing*. I can never find a good plumper and collagen only lasts so long, you know?"

I have no idea how long it lasts but I can tell that she does.

Her glare eases and she gives me a glassy-eyed smile, flashing pearly white veneers. "Right? It really is the best. It's Lust for Life by Marc Jacobs. *So good.*" There's enough of a slur to her words that I'm thankful her buzz is helping me out of a very awkward situation.

"Well it looks gorgeous on you. I'll have to pick some up next time I'm out," I say, even though I doubt they carry it at the CVS where I buy what little bit of makeup I wear.

"Here, put some on. It will look killer with that dress." She digs it out of the clutch she's just dropped it into and hands it to me.

"Oh. Um, okay. Thanks." I take it, feeling extremely awkward about using a stranger's lip gloss but knowing it will be even more awkward if I reject her offer after staring like a creeper. Oh well. You only live once.

I slide on some gloss then return it to her. They leave giggling and discussing which plastic surgeons have done the best jobs on their lips. My attention returns to my reflection and damn. Now I wish I'd never even put the stuff on because it really does make my lips looks fuller.

I use my fingertip to smear toothpaste inside my mouth instead of brushing because I am now in love with this sinfully perfect lip gloss that in a million years I'll never be able to afford. Rinsing and spitting carefully, I roll my eyes at my own stupidity.

Somewhere in the hazy fog of three Long Island ice teas and the adrenaline rush from my encounter in the ladies' room, I know that there is an analogy in here someplace. Gavin is kind of like this lip gloss. Even kissing him the other day changed everything. No one will ever kiss me like that again, will be able to affect me the way he did, turning everything from muted blue to a bright, blinding shade of red.

Damn him. And this designer gloss.

I check my phone while I'm walking out of the restroom and see that I now have only eight minutes to make my escape. Just as I look up from the glowing numbers, I narrowly avoid smacking straight into Afton's chest.

"I was getting worried. You okay?"

It couldn't have been a more perfect opening if I'd planned it. Though the genuine concern on his face makes me feel like a complete ass for lying to him. Part of me considers just telling him the truth and making him swear on his guitar not to tell my brother. But this isn't my secret to tell—it's Gavin's. And that makes it a precious one that I'll keep no matter the cost.

"Yeah, um, actually I'm not feeling so hot. Maybe I should've taken it easy on the spicy tuna. Would you hate me if I bailed and headed back to my hotel?"

"No, but I'd hate myself if I let you take a cab back alone. I'll call our guy. He can come pick us up. I'm pretty much done here anyway."

Well there's a complication I forgot to plan for.

"Afton . . ." I look into his eyes and try to be as honest as I can without sharing Gavin's personal business. "I kind of already texted someone to pick me up. I didn't want to ruin your night."

"Your brother?" There's a hopeful tone in his voice and the guilt begins to shove my chin and shoulders back down where they belong. "Because if Dallas is coming, he should come on inside and have a drink first. There are a few people here he should probably talk to. I could introduce him around and—"

"Not Dallas," I interrupt gently, feeling like the human equivalent of pond scum.

"Ah," he says, shoving his hands in his pockets and rocking back on his heels. "The drummer, then."

I start to bite my bottom lip, then stop, remembering the gloss that is bliss on my lips.

"Yeah, and he's probably outside waiting for me as we speak. My brother is out with Mandy Lantram, as he has been pretty much every night. I guess we're signing with her and I didn't want to interrupt his night, either."

Several emotions flicker across Afton's face too quickly for me to identify before he settles on one.

Concerned.

"Mandy Lantram is a pretty big deal, I suppose." He clears his throat and steps aside so a few women can get to the ladies' room entrance. "She's got quite the reputation around town, and as much of a tool as this is going to make me sound like, I have to tell you something."

"I've heard, actually. A little about her, I mean. Recently." As in five seconds ago. I'm still clearing the debris from the bombs that were inadvertently dropped on me.

Afton glances around as if she might be nearby. That would be a plot twist I just couldn't handle at the moment.

"She approached me last year when the band starting getting some attention. Told me I could ditch my bandmates, go solo, and change the face of music, blah, blah, blah."

That familiar sinking feeling from the ladies' room assaults my stomach once more. "Let me guess. She loved the band, loved the sound, but loved you the most?"

He nods and now I'm not faking anymore. I actually feel sick. The room tilts and I don't think it's from the Long Island ice teas.

"I hope she's not selling my brother that same song and dance."

"Think he'd buy it if she did?"

"I hope not." I shrug. "We're signing with her as a band, far as I know. So I can't be sure."

"Just . . . be careful, Dixie. She's got real connections so she can make or break you if she wants. If he's really set on signing with her, then play nice. Otherwise, I'd encourage the three of you to explore your options a bit more. I've heard you play; you definitely have options."

I make a note to talk to my brother about this before any legal agreements are signed. "Thanks for the heads-up. And thanks for bringing me tonight. Believe it or not, I had a good time and I hate that I didn't get to spend more time actually just hanging out with you."

"Well I am pretty good company. Some girls even think I'm decent to look at, if you can believe that." He grins and keeps the pace beside me as I begin making my way toward the exit. "Though I suspect I wasn't your first choice tonight."

"Afton . . ."

"Please don't. Let me keep my dignity since I'm the one who already gave the 'it's not you it's me' speech."

A smile tugs at my lips once we've reached the door. "Okay then. I'll try and pick up the pieces and move on. Somehow."

"It won't be easy," he says with a wink.

"Of course not. It will be excruciating and there will be several gallons of ice cream involved."

I give him a quick one-armed neck hug and a peck on the cheek. A tiny shimmer from my borrowed gloss remains behind as trace evidence.

"Hey, Opening Act?" he calls out as I step past the door he's holding open for me.

"Yeah?"

"In the future, if you aren't interested in a guy, do him a favor and don't wear that dress, okay?"

I nod, embarrassed at how his words make me feel.

I feel . . . pretty. Maybe even sexy. My skin flashes hot everywhere and I know I'm grinning, probably maniacally enough to be scary instead of sexy.

The self-congratulatory smirk I'm wearing fades quickly, though, once I turn toward the street and see no signs of our van anywhere. Extracting my phone from my overstuffed purse, I check the time and nearly cry out. It's 12:02.

Gavin's words repeat in my mind.

"I'm leaving at midnight. With you or without you."

A four-door silver Honda and a late-model white Ford pickup are parked on the curb. But that's it. Emmylou isn't anywhere to be seen.

Disappointment gathers in my throat and seeps into my chest. Not only does he probably think I stood him up or that I'm a flighty moron who lost track of time—which, in a way, I guess I am—but now I either have to call a cab and risk Afton seeing and being unnecessarily hurt, or go back inside and tell Afton that Gavin didn't show and I need a ride.

Once when we were kids, the boys left me behind and went camping. I'd been upstairs packing my sleeping bag and dreaming of roasting marshmallows by the campfire. When I bounded down the stairs my grandparents sat in the living room wearing matching masks of sympathy.

"Dixie Leigh," Papa had said softly, "sometimes boys just need time to be boys."

Nana nodded. "You don't want to be around when they start

acting foolish and passing gas in the tent anyway. Let's go into the kitchen and see if we can't have some fun of our own."

That night my grandparents and I had had an indoor campout. We'd made s'mores over the stove and had a sing-along at the piano. Despite how the boys had broken my heart, and abandoned me, that night had turned out to be one of my most favorite memories.

I had a feeling that this time I wouldn't remember being left behind quite as fondly.

Chapter 16

JUST AS I'M CONTEMPLATING HITCHHIKING BACK TO THE HOTEL for lack of a better option, a cherry red '67 Camaro SS with black racing stripes rumbles into the alley where I'm standing. My time dating Jaggerd taught me to recognize a muscle car when I saw one. I step backward as it rolls to a stop beside me. The driver leans over and swings the door open in invitation. Just as I'm about to politely decline this very intriguing yet unexpected offer, I catch a glimpse of a very familiar arm.

The rope is what I see first. It's detailed and intricate and I know for a fact that it morphs into a serpent farther up his bicep. I've fantasized about tracing it with everything from my fingers to my tongue enough times that I could draw it blindfolded in the dark. The sheet music across his knuckles ripples as his hand returns to his side of the vehicle.

"Nice wheels," I say, sliding onto the black leather bench seat beside him.

"Nice dress," he says back even though I have yet to see him actually look at me.

Crave is barely out of the rearview before the silence and the tension get to be too much for me. "So . . . you boost this hot rod or what?"

The tiniest twitch at the corner of his mouth is the only response I get for several seconds. "Something like that," he finally says.

"I see. We planning to rob a bank later, too? I've only got one change of clothes, but we could grab some disguises at the Quickie Mart unless we're going to knock it over, too."

"You brought a change of clothes?"

I laugh and relax back into the seat, enjoying the powerful vibration beneath me. "That would be the part you paid attention to." I turn my neck so that I'm facing his profile as he shifts gears and merges onto the interstate. My eyes travel the most indulgent route up his ink-sleeved arms and across his chest before they trace the outline of his profile.

"You were late," he says softly, finally turning his turbulent gaze to mine.

"So were you."

"That was my second time around the block." He returns to facing forward and I'm grateful.

Maybe it's because he waited for me, or because we're alone in a darkened muscle car that is practically seducing me with its motor, but I am two seconds from telling him to pull over and please, pretty please touch me before I implode.

"Sorry," I whisper. "I didn't want to be rude and just bail without an explanation."

I watch his fingers flex on the shiny black steering wheel. "You really don't have to do this, you know. Seriously. I can handle it. Bikers and all."

I smile and scoot a little closer to him. Even over the powerful scent of leather and what I'm pretty sure is Armor All, I can smell his cologne, the kind I bought him and I'm in danger of sniffing until either it gets embarrassingly obvious or I pass out.

"I know. I told you, I wanted to come. And I'm here now and we're on our way so you can give the disclaimer a rest already." I sigh and resist the urge to lean my head over on his shoulder. "Besides, if I'd have known you were driving this, you wouldn't have been able to talk me out of it anyway. I have to admit, I am insanely curious about this car and how you got it."

He slides his hands lower on the wheel. "Borrowed it from a friend who owed me a favor."

"I didn't realize you had friends in Austin."

"She's not from Austin, just happened to be in town for Music-Fest."

"Ah. Convenient." *She.* My stomach clenches and I scoot back to my side of the seat and stare out the window.

"Has anyone ever told you that you have an excellent poker face?"

"No," I answer shortly without tearing my gaze from the window.

Gavin lets out a low, seductive ripple of laughter. "And they probably never will."

"You're hilarious."

I peek over just in time to catch a glimpse of the dimple in his right cheek. "Her name is Janie Ledford and trust me, she'd be much more interested in you than me. Especially right now."

"Why right now?" I shift my body so that's it's turned completely in his direction.

His eyes dart over to me then back to the road. He clears his throat and I am suddenly very aware of how small the space we currently occupy is.

"I wasn't being a smartass about that dress. It's nice . . . Does things for you."

"I see." I slip my shoes off, letting them fall gently in the floor-board, and tuck my legs beneath me. "What kinds of things?"

His tongue snakes out and slides enticingly along his lush lower lip. It's all I can do not to steal a taste of that lower lip myself.

"Things that are going to make this a very long drive." He shifts uncomfortably in his seat and I can't help but smile—he's right, I have no poker face whatsoever.

"Good to know." Mentally I'm cataloging everything I own. Gavin likes dresses. I wonder if I can pull off wearing one every day for the rest of my life.

A low rumble that I'm pretty sure isn't the car interrupts my silent plotting.

"Gav? You hungry?"

He shrugs. "Skipped dinner. Trying to save money since I don't know how much her bail will be. Chances are I'll have to pay a bonds-man ten percent to get her out and I didn't want to risk being short."

His words pull me out of the car and back in time. He was always hungry, always going without.

"Gavin . . ."

"Relax, Bluebird. I'll survive."

Before I get caught up in my painful memories of our child-hood, I remember that I came prepared. Pulling the chips and gra-nola bar from my bag like rabbits from a magician's hat, I present them to him.

"Sweet or salty?"

He side-eyes me and sighs. "Salty I guess."

I open the bag of chips and hand them over. He places the bag between his legs and I force myself not to check out the bulge in his jeans.

Classy, Dixie. Real classy.

"Um, shoot. I didn't think about something to drink." I look down to see that there's a cup holder in the middle console but it's empty.

"That part I do have covered. There's a cooler in the back floor-board. Just Mountain Dew and a few bottles of water, feel free to help yourself."

"You want a soda? Caffeine might be good for the drive."

"Sure."

Without thinking, I turn around and lean over the seat, stretching as far as my arm will allow to flip open the white lid of the cooler. My fingers encircle the damp plastic wrapper of his drink and then I reach for a bottle of water for myself.

"Jesus Christ. Sit the hell down! Forget the fucking soda. I'll get it when we stop."

The urgency in Gavin's voice jump-starts my heart and I immediately picture us slamming into an eighteen-wheeler. Whipping my body around and back into my seat, I gape at him wide-eyed when I see that there is no threat of an immediately impending accident.

"What the hell? You scared me to death."

"Yeah, well. You almost got us killed." He's gripping the steering wheel so hard his knuckles are turning white.

"Um, okay. Did I bump the wheel or something?"

He lets out a loud breath and shakes his head. "No. You flashed me your ass in the rearview and I nearly took us off the damn road."

I fold my lips inward to keep from bursting out laughing. He is clearly upset.

"My ass distracted you?"

"Not half as much as the black lace thong did."

Oh dear God. I want to curl up and hide. He's not kidding. I am wearing a black lace thong.

"No need to be embarrassed now. I've already seen it. You got some sweatpants or something you could put on?"

"I didn't know sweatpants would be required road trip attire. I have jeans I can put on if you're serious."

"I am dead fucking serious."

"Ugh. Fine. Here." I hand over the green bottle containing his beverage and climb over into the backseat, careful not to flash him this time. Much.

"Thank you," he says through gritted teeth. I don't know if he means for the drink or for putting pants on, but I can't resist.

"I'm changing. Don't peek." I meet his hazel stare in the rearview and wink. "Or do."

He shakes his head but even from behind him I can see the telltale dimple showing in his profile. "When did my sweet little Dixie Lark turn into . . ."

"Into what?" I ask, mildly offended that he called me little. Taking my time slipping out of my dress in the backseat, I wait for him to answer.

"Into my worst nightmare."

A hurt noise pops out of my throat as soon as I get my dress over my head. "Ouch, Gav. That's kind of harsh."

"Truth hurts," he answers quietly before meeting my eyes again. There's no trace of teasing in them, just blatant honesty. I want to hide my face and turn invisible like the game we played as kids.

The pain swells in my chest until it's consuming me completely. My bag with my clothes in it is still in the front of the car and I'm afraid my voice will break if I ask him to hand it to me.

I focus on folding my dress into a small neat square, wishing I could do the same with my stupid heart.

"Because of who you are," he adds gently. "You're the one person that's supposed to be off-limits. I made a promise. One I intended to keep."

A breath escapes my lips, taking a tiny bit of tension with it. "Some promises are made to be broken. I don't think anyone has the right to decide that for us. Not even—"

"I know." His stare leaves mine and returns to the road. "It's just complicated. There are things you don't know. Things that happened while you were in Houston."

This much I do know. But Dallas never would share the details. Just that it was bad.

"So then tell me."

I watch the back of his head shake back and forth.

"Trust me, it's better if I don't. You're better off not knowing."

I'm not, though. That's the part he doesn't get. I want to know everything. I want to know what his life was like before we met as kids, I want to know if anyone ever read him fairy tales, or made him pancakes, or cuddled him in a blanket fort. I want to know if he was upset last year because of the band or because of his mom or because of me. I want to know what he did to try to fill the void. And mostly I want to know if there is any chance at all that our one night could be more.

Before I can find my voice, rain begins to pelt the roof and the windshield with a hellacious vengeance.

"Shit, I can't see a thing."

I'd make a joke about him peeking but the noise from the downpour would just drown it out. "If you really can't see, you should pull over."

I lean over the seat to grab my bag from the front and he hits the brakes suddenly to avoid hitting bright red taillights that have only become visible that instant. My head hits something solid—the window maybe—and the back tires spin angrily in an attempt to find some traction. We skid to a stop and a horn honks loud and long behind us.

"Fuck!" Gavin bites out before pulling over into the emergency lane. "You okay?"

I rub my hand soothingly across the bump on my head and fall back into the backseat, no longer caring about my lack of clothing. "Yeah, I'm okay."

Gavin eases us beneath the safety of an overpass and I can see the car in front of us doing the same while a few brave souls soldier on despite the monsoon.

He shuts the engine off and turns to me with worry deepening each line in his face. "I'm so sorry. I didn't see them. Christ. That could've been so bad."

I witness the exact moment he starts to lose it. Something terrifying flashing like lightning in his eyes and his gaze goes somewhere far away from me and from this car.

"If anything had happened to you, if you'd been hurt . . . if I'd hit them, you would've went through the goddamn windshield." He's shaking. "I could've killed you," he whispers and the words wrap my heart and squeeze. He never once says anything about my brother or what my brother would do to him. Because he's not worried about him. He's worried about me. Only me.

Before I can think of any other way to comfort him, I'm over the seat and straddling his lap.

"Look at me," I say, locking my fingers behind his neck and staring down into his eyes. "I'm fine. It's fine. You stopped in plenty of time. I'm okay. We're okay."

So slowly I wonder if I'm imagining the sensation, his warm hands slide up the outside of my bare thighs. As if he can't believe it himself, he watches his fingers move across my skin.

"You're okay? You're sure? What about your head?"

"I'm tougher than I look," I say quietly. I want him to understand this. Badly. Our one night together is not going to break me.

"You have no idea what it would do to me if something happened to you, if I hurt you." He squeezes my thighs hard and my body rocks involuntarily against him. "I never want to hurt you. Do you get that? Why I never touch you? I'll only hurt you."

I shake my head, because, God, he does not get it. At all.

"Sometimes . . . sometimes pain is a good thing, Gavin." His eyes widen and I lower myself onto him, relieved that he's as turned on as I am right now. "Sometimes it's the only way to make sure that you're still alive."

When Gavin lifts his hands to my waist and yanks me against him, I am alive. When he crushes his mouth to mine, I am having an out-of-body near-death experience.

For a moment I hover above us, seeing myself half naked and pressed against him in a car beneath a steadily cascading force of nature. He drags me slowly back down to earth, kissing my mouth as if he plans to devour me. My tongue slides against his and he licks it gently before sucking my bottom lip hard enough to bruise.

There was this piano piece I played once, one of the first ones Nana taught me. It was a classical piece by a famous composer whose name I can't recall this very second. But I remember learning it and feeling like my fingers were battling for control of the keys. That is us right this minute, each of us desperate to be closer, deeper. Fighting for more. I want more so bad I can taste it, can touch it like a tangible thing.

Hearing the sound of my own whimpers and breathy pleas makes me realize we've steamed up the inside of the car. Rain or no, Gavin could take me any way he wanted right here, right now. I'm about to tell him so, writhing against him as his hands roam everywhere at once, across my back, down into the waistband of my panties, gripping my hips, when he stops suddenly.

"Damn it, Dixie. What are you doing to me?" His question startles me and my body begins to retreat, but his hands hold me firmly in place. "I used to have all this control. All these years I've done so well. Now . . . I got nothing."

Leaning forward, I let my lips brush gently against his, pulling in his air with my breath. "You've got me," I say quietly into the stillness.

He leans his head back against the seat and I take advantage of the opportunity to lick a path up his neck. A low groan escapes the back of his throat and vibrates against my tongue. I suck at the sensitive skin beneath his ear, savoring his warm male flavor. He even tastes like rain.

"You tryin' to mark me, Bluebird?"

I smile, letting my bared teeth graze against his throat. "Mmm. Now that you mention it . . ." I suck harder and he struggles beneath me, pulling me backward with both hands.

"And how would I explain that?"

"Not my problem." I attack his neck again and his warm chuckle fills me with so much happiness I feel as if I could burst. "I love when you laugh."

We both go statue still. The L-word. I forgot that he doesn't want to hear it. The damn thing just slipped out on me.

He gets that broody look again and I roll my eyes. "Relax. It wasn't a marriage proposal. I just like your laugh. Always have."

He tilts his head and grins at me. "Oh yeah? What else have you always liked?"

"Your tattoos," I whisper, cranking up the intensity sparking between us and ruining our teasing moment. "I have pretty much been aching to touch every single one since you started getting them."

"That so?" His eyes drift down my body and my mind goes immediately to one of mine that I know I have to keep hidden. For now at least. If he sees it, there's probably no way in hell tomorrow night is happening. "Speaking of tattoos. You have a few more than I knew about."

"That's because you never bothered to look."

"It stopped raining," Gavin says evenly without responding to my complaint. "We should get back on the road."

I nod, feeling painfully exposed. "Yeah. We should."

Swallowing hard, I start to move off of him as gracefully as I can in hopes that my dignity doesn't fall to the floor. Pretty sure it's somewhere around my ankles.

A firm hand lands on my outer thigh with a light slap, effectively stopping my lateral motion. "Wait."

"For?"

Confidence and pure male bravado exude from him along with his intoxicating scent. "This," he says, sliding a hand between my thighs.

I should say something. Come back with a witty retort, but I can't. Not with his warm fingers sliding beneath my previously offensive black lace panties.

"I fucking love these," he says, stroking the thin scrap of fabric barely covering my most sensitive area.

"You can borrow them sometime." His mouth swallows my self-congratulatory smile and his fingers slide slowly through the slippery folds between my legs. The combination of what he's doing causes the remaining brain cells necessary for playful comebacks to explode on impact.

Once he feels my surrender in the form of every bone in my body liquefying against him, Gavin lets a deep sound of animalistic content roll through his throat and into my ear. "My sweet, wet girl. If this car were more accommodating, I'd spread you out and taste every single inch of you."

"*Gavin.*" I'm dying—writhing against his hand in hopes his thick fingers will stop teasing and slip inside. Preferably before I burn to death with the heat of needing him. The incessant throbbing inside me seeks his attention so badly I'm willing to outright beg for it.

"Tell me what you need, sweetness. What can I do to make it better?" His index finger traces the outline of my labia before repeating the same languorous circuit around my clit.

Too many things to list. "Gavin, *please.*" My voice breaks. It's too much to handle all at once. And yet I still want more.

"Since you said please." Freeing me from the delicious imprisonment of his teasing fingertips, Gavin dips his entire middle finger straight into my pulsating opening. Thrusting rhythmically while using his thumb to massage the throbbing bundle of nerves between us, he whispers dirty promises in my ear until I plummet headfirst past the point of no return. Clutching his shoulder for stability, I press myself upright.

And that's when I hear it.

Whoop whoop. The unmistakable warning of a police siren.

Gavin practically tosses me off his lap and into the passenger seat. "Get your clothes and seat belt on. Now," he barks at me.

My fingers are clumsy and uncooperative as I rifle through my bag. "I packed a T-shirt. I know I did."

"I have a black duffel in the back. There are probably a few in there. Grab one. Quickly."

Turning in a position that sadly doesn't affect him at all anymore, I lift his bag from the back and pull the first shirt I find out of it. The blue lights from the officer's car are creating a strobe effect against the darkness. Out the back window I see the uniformed man getting out of his car. My heart rate triples at the sight.

I examine the shirt so that I don't put it on inside out or backward. "I bought you this one," I say, holding up an army-gray short-sleeved shirt that says *Always be yourself. Unless you can be a drummer. Then always be a drummer.*

"Yeah. You did. For my birthday a few years ago I think. Put it on, please. Before you get arrested for public indecency."

I pull it over my head and try to be discreet about inhaling his scent like a coke fiend taking their last hit. I've just yanked my jeans on and snapped my seat belt across my lap when the knock comes at my window. I don't know why I expected him to go to Gavin's, but I did. After recovering from a near stroke at the shock, I roll the window down and offer the uniformed gentleman a smile.

"Hi, Officer."

"Evening, kids. Out kind of late. Car trouble?"

"No, sir," Gavin answers, leaning over to look at the stockily built guy. "Had some trouble with my windshield wipers during the downpour, but I got it handled."

He got something handled, but it sure wasn't the windshield wipers.

The office makes a grunting noise. "I see. This a '67?"

Gavin nods and his lips curve upward, but I can still see the way he's barely breathing. "Yes, sir."

I don't know if it's the cop or Gavin's obvious tension that's rattling my nerves, but I feel jittery, like I've drank a dozen cups of coffee and have caffeine surging in my veins. Even my legs are trembling, but that might be from previous events.

"It's nice. Well cared for. Tell me, where are you two heading?"

"Amarillo," I say just as Gavin says, "Potter County."

The officer frowns, then glances over the top of the car at the traffic speeding past. "Listen, this rain could come and go all night. You kids get where you're going safe, all right?"

"Yes, sir," we answer in unison like a pair of ten-year-olds being reprimanded.

"Have a good night." With that, he walks back to his car. Once he pulls away, I finally feel like I can breathe.

Gavin cranks the key in the ignition, bringing the rumbling, thunderous engine to life. He's paled at least two shades since I was sitting on his lap.

"You okay? I've never seen you get so twitchy about cops before."

He nods without looking at me. "I'm fine. He just surprised me is all. You should get some rest. It's a long drive."

The roads are rain-slicked as we drive and Gavin keeps his eyes closely on them. I'm sitting silently buckled in tight as he requested and contemplating turning up the Civil Wars song playing on the radio when he breaks the quiet tension blazing between us.

"You look good in my shirt," I hear him say. His words hang in the air between us until I fall asleep.

Chapter 17

Austin MusicFest—Day 5

"WAKE UP, BLUEBIRD." I HEAR THE FAMILIAR VOICE COMING FROM far away but I don't quite recognize it. "Rise and shine. We're here."

My head throbs hard and my hand is on it before my eyes open.

"Mmph."

"Good morning to you, too. Head still hurt?"

Gavin. I'm waking up with a skull-splitting headache and with Gavin. I blink my eyes into focus. Apparently I'm also waking up in a car. My eyes scan our surroundings. A nondescript brown building with American and Texas state flags flying side by side greet me. Gavin hands me a Styrofoam cup of coffee through the open car window.

A black and white sign declares this the Potter County Women's Detention Center and my memories come rushing back all at once.

"Oh God. Gavin. I slept the whole way." That's what a raging orgasm will do to a girl. It's cloudy and overcast, but still bright enough that I have to squint up at him. "Crap. I am so sorry. I'll do the driving on the way back to Austin. Promise."

He opens my door for me. "Not a big deal. Roads were too wet last night for you to drive anyway."

"What time is it?"

"About five minutes after eight. I was here when they opened."

"So . . . have you talked to the cops or a bondsman or anyone yet?" I stretch and yawn loudly once I'm out of the car.

"I talked to the magistrate and if there's only the one charge, her bail isn't as high as I thought it would be. I can swing it without a bondsman."

I sip my coffee, black with about a pound of sugar—just how I like it.

"When you say swing it, you mean—"

"It's all I've got, but it's enough."

I can't help but sigh my frustration. Watching him hand over every cent he has to his name for someone who couldn't honestly give a single shit about him makes my heart sick. "Have you ever considered not bailing her out? Just letting her pay the price and face the consequences of her actions?"

Gavin eyes me over his steaming cup. "Easy, Bluebird. It's a little too early for this conversation."

"I'm serious," I say, taking a step toward where he's leaning against the hood of the car. "What if you just told her she is a grown woman and that if she is going to break the law, she'll have to deal with the fallout?"

I'm about to suggest he change his number when he gives me the strangest look. "So you mean I should encourage her to be an honest, upstanding citizen or prepare to deal with the consequences of her actions, whatever they may be?"

"Well . . . yeah. I mean, that's how life works in the real world. Maybe it's time she started living in it." *Instead of in her blitzed-out drug bubble,* I think, but don't say out loud.

"Ah. I see. So people who lie or cheat or say, go behind their best friend's back and kidnap their sister while plotting to do unspeakable things to her body, should own up and pay for it, right? Should be punished?"

Of course he would go there. I narrow my eyes at him. "We're not breaking the law, last I checked. Although I've been doing some Internet research and there are a few positions I want to try that might be illegal in some states."

Gavin shakes his head. "Only you could make a crack like that when you've only been awake for five minutes."

"What can I say? I'm pretty damn special."

"If that's what they're calling it these days." Gavin gives me a hint of a grin before motioning to the building before us. "You don't have to go in, but I need to fill out some paperwork and help her get her personal belongings."

I huff out my annoyance. I didn't ride all this way to sit in the car. "I'm coming with you. Surprisingly, this is my first trip to a jail."

Gavin rubs his neck, and I notice the exhaustion ringing his eyes for the first time. "Considering some of the crap we pulled as kids, that actually is surprising."

I nudge him gently in the side as we make our way to the front door. "Well, Clyde, I always knew we'd end up here someday."

His shoulders stiffen but then he winks at me. "You're not bad company to have, Bonnie. I'm almost glad you came along."

Bailing someone out of jail is a lot more complicated than it sounds. And when it's someone who truly doesn't deserve the time and effort involved, it's that much more frustrating.

I think I always assumed you walked up to a teller's window like at the bank and handed over your money in exchange for the inmate of your choosing. I couldn't have been more wrong.

"Katrina with a *K* and Garrison with two *R*'s," Gavin tells the lady in the uniform at the front desk. "She was picked up the day before yesterday."

"Charge?" The woman says without glancing up from the computer.

"Solicitation, I think. I'm not entirely sure of the specifics," Gavin mutters.

Sliding my fingers between his, I give his hand a squeeze. He doesn't return it, but he doesn't pull away, either.

The raven-haired middle-aged woman with a pixie cut taps away on the keyboard for several minutes before letting out a low sound that reminds me of one my Nana used to make. I'm pretty sure it's the equivalent of her calling Gavin's mom a two-bit hussy. Which she is, but still . . . this is her son standing here.

With an overly exaggerated sigh, she rubs her eyes before giving us an exasperated look as if she's bored with our presence already. Her impassive gaze meets Gavin's and I can see the pity and the slight disgust in it. I have no doubt that he can, too.

"There are several charges against her," she tells us. "She solicited a police officer, Mr. . . ."

"Garrison," Gavin supplies. "She's my mother."

The woman cringes and I want to slap her. What is it, her first day? Even I can manage to contain my feelings better than she is.

"Well, I'm sure your mother would love to see you, but unfortunately visiting hours are on Sunday only."

"I'm not here to visit. I'm here to bail her out," Gavin snaps.

Tugging gently on his hand, I pull him back enough for him to take a breath.

"Ma'am," I say, leaning over the desk a little. "We've driven a really long way and we have to turn around and get back to Austin as soon as possible. If we need to contact a bondsman or whatever, we'd need to do that as soon as possible."

"It's ten grand to get her out today, but honestly, her court date is Monday morning. I can see that she's had warrants out before for failing to appear. If I were you, I'd leave her here." She shrugs and the movement tremors through Gavin's body as if she punched him in the chest.

Ten grand. Holy hell.

"Well you're not me." Gavin's eyes are blazing. "And I'm here, and she's going home. You got a bondsman you can recommend?"

The woman shakes her head as if Gavin is too stupid to waste any more time on. "Here," she says, handing him a business card with plain black print on it. "Good luck, kid."

"Gav?" I tilt my head indicating I need a quick sidebar. "A moment, please?"

We step over to a plain gray seating area and Gavin turns his phone over and over in his hand while waiting for me to make my case. I'm rooting for the wrong team this time and I don't know how he's going to react.

"Look, it's none of my business, but I mean, it's three more nights. I think she'll be okay."

His eyes harden against my imploring gaze, turning to granite and effectively shutting me out. "You're right. It's none of your business."

His anger thumps me hard in the chest. Okay then. I take a deep breath and speak as calmly as I can. I've watched enough courtroom dramas on television to know he's risking an awful lot for someone who doesn't deserve it.

"Fine. But just so you know, if you do get a bondsman to post bail and then she doesn't show in court, you'll be the one paying that money back. Good luck with that."

I turn on my heel intending to leave the stubborn jackass on his own to deal with his mama drama but he stops me in my tracks. Not by grabbing me—or even reaching for me—but with his words.

"I'm sorry. I shouldn't have snapped at you. Especially not after you rode all this way with me."

And after what we did mere hours ago, I think to myself. Turning back to him, I take a deep breath and ask him a question I've wondered about for half my life.

"Why do you do this to yourself? No, wait. Why do you let *her* do this to you?"

She's never made him a priority. At least not in the years I've known him. And yet, he would move hell and earth to help her.

"It's complicated." He gives me a halfhearted shrug. "She had a rough childhood—one that makes mine look like a trip to Disney World. Closed-in spaces . . . they just . . . They really upset her. And I . . . I owe her this. Okay?"

I swallow the emotions threatening to cut this conversation short. "Okay . . . Well, maybe she should see someone about that. Like a therapist. But Gavin, none of that is your fault and she's not your responsibility. You don't owe her shit."

His eyes darken and I worry I've gone too far, or that I seem cold-hearted because I'm not accepting the excuses he's making for her.

"There's more. Events that transpired while you were gone that I don't have the time or energy to explain right now. I'm not just going to leave her here. Period. You didn't have to come, you know. And if you rode all this way just to talk me out of it, that was a huge waste of fucking time."

"That's not why I came and you know it." My eyes narrow on his back while he walks over to the small lobby area that contains two vending machines and a few chairs and makes a call.

I sit while he tells someone on the other end that his mother has been picked up for solicitation and needs someone to post bail.

"Yes, ma'am," I hear him say while I watch his jaw clench. I wish he'd put it on speakerphone so I could hear both ends of the conversation. "No, ma'am, I don't." He's leaning forward and facing the floor so I can't read his face. "Yes, ma'am, she has."

Between every response is a long pause and the adrenaline rush from our mini-argument is still coursing through me. This is frustrating the hell out of me. I stand up and stretch my legs.

"I'm going to find the restroom," I tell him quietly. Gavin nods and I make my way to a water fountain and some elevators. Beside them is a sign for the bathrooms and I glance back before stepping into the ladies' room. Gavin is already dialing another number on his phone so I assume that one turned him down.

Despite the severely pressing need to relieve my bladder, I can't look away. He looks so alone. And lost. My frustration and anger evaporate, and I finally get it.

The random waitresses and fangirls don't see this part. They aren't there the morning after, they don't know about his mom, or his childhood. For them, Gavin is one-dimensional. A hot tatted-up drummer who can give them a good time. This is why he doesn't want to cross that line with me. Because he needs me for this part, for the ugly un-fun parts of life. I wish I could make him see that I want to be both. I want to be everything. Burning bright nights and dark cloudy days. Before I take off running and throw myself in his arms like an overly emotional idiot, I escape into the restroom and pee before I burst.

Even in the ladies' room everything is gray, utilitarian. The tile on the floor, the concrete walls. The paper towel dispenser is even gray and has a hand crank. After I've washed and dried my hands, I glance at my reflection.

Oh my holy sweet baby Jesus, I look like an extra on *The Walking Dead*. My skin is pale under the harsh fluorescents and my hair is a certifiable mess. I splash some cold water on my face then take my hair down and plow my fingers through it in the most comblike manner I can manage before pulling it into a high ponytail. Thankful for the toothbrush I packed in my purse, I use it and feel marginally less like a rumpled pile of dirty laundry.

Gavin's shirt is a size too big on me and I know I'm still a hot mess, but when I walk out of the restroom, his eyes land on me and he doesn't appear to be the least bit concerned about how I look. He looks happy to see me so I smile. I'm glad to be here for him. Even though I know our one night is a thing of the past, a fantasy that will have to remain just that. Swallowing the pain and regret, I make my way toward him.

"Find someone?" I lower myself into the seat beside him.

"I did." He breathes deep, like it's the first breath he's taken in days. "The first two said they couldn't do it because she's failed to appear in court in the past. But the third guy said he just charges a higher rate in cases like hers."

"So . . ."

"So I have to come up with fifteen hundred bucks like now. He'll be here in an hour."

I glance at the digital display on my phone. It's almost nine. If we get out of here by ten and stop by to see Papa, we can be on the road by eleven and we'll make sound check by the skin of our teeth.

"I have three hundred dollars to my name. It's yours if you need it." The regret flashes in his eyes and I see the shame there. So I place my hand on his knee and squeeze. "You can pay me back later. It's not a big deal. You'd do it for me."

He stares at me so intently I have to look away.

"I mean, if Papa gets picked up for murdering all of crazy Mrs. Lawson's cats, you're going to help me pay for his defense attorney, right?"

Gavin finally cracks a smile and the tension eases in my chest. "Of course. That puts us at eight hundred. I'm still short seven hundred bucks and the car needs gas." He scrolls through his phone for several minutes before standing. "I'm going to step outside and make a few calls. You okay in here alone?"

"I'm basically surrounded by cops and security guards. I think I'll be all right."

His eyes shift as if this makes him uncomfortable for some reason, but he nods and heads toward the same doors we entered.

Watching him walk outside, I can't help but wonder who he's calling. I try not to concern myself too much because if he wanted me to know he would've told me, but there are so many gaps in my knowledge about Gavin I can hardly stand it. The year I was in Houston, we didn't keep in touch and Dallas's vague comments have turned that year into a mysterious back hole that I fear I'll never get answers about.

There aren't any magazines or anything, so I just curl up on the chair and close my eyes. There's really nothing else I can do. And I need to rest if I'm driving us back to Austin in a few hours.

Chapter 18

THE BONDSMAN IS LATE. IT'S NEARLY ELEVEN BY THE TIME HE shows.

Gavin is pacing all over hell and back and it's as if he's holding a piece of twine rapped around my insides while he walks.

"Fuck. We're never going to make it back in time." He's been cussing at his phone for the past half hour.

I've texted Dallas a few times and he seems to buy my dying-from-bad-seafood story.

"We don't have to stop and see Papa, Gav. I'll live. We'll get your mom home and we'll hit the interstate. I'll drive ten over the limit all the way to Austin. We'll be fine."

Before he can say anything, the bondsman, a short, stocky black-haired man with a military-style buzz cut and slight paunch over his belt, named Arnie, strides purposefully out of the metal doors and tells us everything is handled and that Gavin's mom will be out in about fifteen minutes after she signs some paperwork for her belongings.

He and Gavin shake hands and he leaves us to wait some more.

"Do I even want to know how you came up with seven hundred dollars on such short notice?"

Gavin closes his eyes and shakes his head. "No, babe. You don't."

I do, actually, but now is not the time. I use the ladies' room one more time, eat the granola bar in my purse after offering to split it with Gavin, who shakes his head, and follow him out to the car, where we enjoy our last few minutes of freedom from the inside of the Camaro.

If I thought I looked rough, Katrina Garrison gives the word a whole new meaning. Her hair is greasy, black roots showing several inches above the bleach-blond dried-out strands. and the bags under her eyes are deeper and darker than I remembered. I'm not sure how I expected her to greet her son but I know a slap to the face wasn't what I'd pictured.

He doesn't even flinch. He was expecting it, even if I wasn't.

"Two fucking days, you ungrateful little bastard. You left me in that godforsaken place for two whole fucking days. Do you know what it was like in there? No, of course you don't. You have no idea of the disgusting conditions I just suffered through."

Her yellowing teeth show as she sneers at him, and I see how thin her lips have become. "Meth mouth," my friend Cassidy and I used to call it when we'd see crackheads hanging out around Jaggerd's dad's garage.

I'm still reeling from the sting of the slap that might as well have landed on my own face, when he opens the back door and tells her to get in the damn car.

Katrina is shaking and so am I, though hers is likely from amphetamine withdrawal and my rattled nerves are from caging the urge to throttle the living life out of her.

"Breathe, Dixie Leigh," Gavin whispers as he opens my door next. "I'm okay."

"I'm not," I choke out. "Gavin, why did she do that? You have got to stop letting her do this to you. I mean it."

"I'm sorry you had to see that. Get in the car please. We need to get on the road."

I do as he says, because he sounds so desperate and because I know Dallas will be flipping out if we're late.

The second Gavin is inside, Katrina starts in on him but her tone has changed completely—from enraged to whiny. "I need twenty bucks, baby. I owe someone ten and I have no food in the house."

"I just gave everything I had and then some to a bondsman to get you out of there, Mom. I don't have twenty bucks. I'll barely even have enough gas in this car to get it back to its owner." He snorts out a harsh sound. "And I grew up in that house, remember? I know good and well you don't give two shits about keeping food in it."

My soul splits open at the reminder of how neglected he was. How Nana made him stay for dinner and a bath every night because she knew he wouldn't get either at home. I can hardly breathe for the fist barreling through my chest.

"Um . . . are you holding? Or do you have anything we could take to Lippy's?"

Lippy's is the pawnshop in Amarillo and I know from overhearing him and Dallas that she's hocked everything from their television set to the bicycle Papa bought Gavin for his twelfth birthday to pay her dealer. But holding? I don't know much about drugs, but in my heart I know that's what she's referring to. Why in the hell would Gavin have drugs?

My eyes are wide when they meet his narrowed ones as he glares at her over his shoulder.

"No. To both. Say another word, Katrina, and I will put your ass out on this road and you can fucking walk home."

"Does *she* have anything?" she asks, nodding to me but not actually addressing me directly.

"Do not fucking look at her or talk to her or go anywhere near her. Ever," he barks in her face.

She makes an irritated sound in the back of her throat. "That's no way to talk to your mother. Don't forget, I'm the one who bailed you—"

"One more motherfucking word, I swear on everything holy and unholy, I will remove you from this car and you will walk your ass home."

I flinch back from the weight of the hatred and venom-laced anger in his voice. My mind can't reconcile it with his constantly rescuing her.

We ride the rest of the way to his house suffocating in tension and silence. I swallow hard as we pull up to their trailer, a run-down one off the highway that makes where I grew up look like a mansion. I've always known where he lived but I've never been inside. The gravel complains under the tires as we pull in and I relocate myself to the driver's seat while he walks his mother to the door.

She's screaming at him, waving her arms wildly and I can see how thin she's becoming beneath her oversized white T-shirt and faded black skinny jeans. How this woman gave birth to something as beautiful as the broad, healthy man across from her is beyond my abilities of comprehension.

The scowl on his face turns to surprise when he walks away from her and sees me sitting in the driver's seat. I meet his stare with defiance through the windshield, daring him to argue. He needs rest so badly he looks like he could fall facedown in the driveway and sleep for days.

Shaking his head, he walks around and slides into the passenger side.

"You know the way?"

I nod and shift the car into reverse. "I put it into the GPS on my phone. Two lefts and a right. We'll be there in no time."

My heart aches as if it's being pulled when we pass the road that leads to Papa's but I know there's no time so I don't say anything. It wasn't the best idea since this is a covert operation as it is.

"I'm sorry we didn't get to see him," Gavin says quietly.

It hurts too much to discuss so I change the subject. "You should get in the back and lie down. Get some real rest before tonight."

"You sure? I can navigate."

I hold my phone up. "I got it. Promise. At least try to sleep, Gav. Please. For me."

He acquiesces, and climbs over the seat. I barely even check out his ass as it goes past me.

I lean forward to turn the radio on but stop, because there is something I have to say first or I'm going to scream.

"Gavin?"

"Yeah?" My eyes rise to the rearview mirror and meet his while he packs his duffel beneath his head.

"We are going to talk later about why your mom asked you if you were holding. And you will explain her comment about bailing you out. But more importantly, if I ever see her lay a hand on you again, I will slap her the fuck back. Hard."

"Dixie—"

"Go to sleep, now. I just had to get that out."

I focus on the road for the next eight hours. We'll be late, but I know I look like someone who actually has food poisoning. It's a hell of a lot more believable than the truth.

Gavin didn't get as much sleep as I would've liked. His phone rang half a dozen times. Two calls were from people who he had to promise he'd get their money to within twenty-four hours. I know from the tidbits I could hear that he's already promised the cash from a month's worth of gigs to cover money he borrowed to get his mom out of jail.

Before I can open my mouth to ask once again why in the world he does this for her, his phone rings again and he tells the caller her car will be parked at our hotel. He laughs a little and says, "No, nothing like that. It's . . . a lot more important than that." His eyes drift over to me, and my face heats for some reason. Is he talking about me?

After we stop for gas at the halfway mark, he takes over the driving despite my protests. We've been driving only a few hours when his phone rings again.

"Son of a bitch," he mumbles before taking this one. "Hey, Dallas."

My stomach tenses. I've been texting my brother, but apparently that wasn't enough.

"Yeah, man, she's a trouper. We'll be at sound check." His hand tightens on the wheel and I notice that it's sprinkling outside.

"You did? Shit. I didn't hear you knock. She was probably asleep. I ran to a gas station to grab her some Gatorade. They didn't have any in the vending machines."

He's lying. And doing it alarmingly well. Panic wells inside of me, rising to my throat like bile as I realize what my brother is saying. Dallas came to my room. We didn't answer because we weren't there.

"Yeah, man, I remember," he says, barely loud enough for me to hear. "Got it. Look, I promise I'll get her there in time. I'm not at the hotel right now. I have to meet up with a friend first but we'll be at sound check on time come hell or high water."

High water is an honest possibility at this point. The rain that ushered us out of Austin is now welcoming us back.

He says a few more things to my brother but I can barely hear them over the sound of the clouds pouring a year's worth of tears upon us. Gavin drops his phone into the console and turns to me.

"You won't have time to shower, but from the looks of the oncoming downpour, it won't matter anyway."

"Did he believe you?" I bite my thumbnail and watch the flashing red warnings of the brake lights in front of us. We slow practically to a stop. At this rate he lied about more than Gatorade. We're not going to make sound check at all if traffic doesn't move.

"Guess we'll find out tonight. I'll deal with him if not. Don't worry about it." He sighs and frowns at the cars in front of us.

"I bet you twenty bucks you can get us there in time." My mind flickers to Afton. "We could always just drive right up to the stage."

Gavin lets out a low ripple of laughter. "Too bad neither of us has twenty bucks."

I laugh because life sure has a sick sense of humor sometimes. We literally have nothing to our name, aside from a change of clothes. And yet . . . in this moment, alone with him, breathing in his sharp, clean scent in a borrowed car under a turbulent sky, I feel richer than I ever have.

"Gavin?"

"Yeah?" He cranes his neck in an attempt to see around the traffic.

My subconscious has been scolding me for the majority of this drive.

Let him go. Tell him he doesn't have to stay with you tonight. He has enough to deal with. It's on the tip of my tongue.

"Nothing. Never mind." I shake my head, not ready to talk about this right now.

"You hungry? I was kidding about not having twenty bucks. I didn't tell my mom because I learned a long time ago that you don't give addicts money, ever, but I have some cash left from what I put aside for gas."

I shrug, thankful that he can't read my mind. "I could eat. If we have time."

"We'll make time." Gavin pulls off and parks in front of Gibson's bar. We walk up to Luke's Inside Out food truck and he orders us each a cheeseburger combo.

He hands me a bag that smells like heaven, and while I should be starving, my stomach is too busy working its way through a gymnastics routine to digest food. I eat slowly as Gavin pulls back into traffic, and notice that the clock on the dash says five fifteen, the same thing it said the last time I looked. Over an hour ago.

"Um, Gavin?" I say through a mouthful of french fries. "Does that clock work?" I swallow and take a sip of Diet Coke before pulling out my phone.

"Fuck me," he mutters under his breath. "No, apparently it doesn't."

According to my phone it's ten minutes until seven. "It's six fifty," I whisper, afraid voicing it too loudly will make it real. "How far are we from Sixth Street?"

"'Bout fifteen or twenty minutes give or take," Gavin tells me. "Damn it." He swerves roughly around two cars and speeds through an intersection, nearly giving me a heart attack.

"It won't do us any good if we're dead before we get there."

"Sorry." Gavin rakes his fingers through his hair, then slams his hand against the steering wheel. "Fuck it. I'm going to have to call a buddy of mine and see if he can help Dallas set up my kit. We're going to be late."

"Eat, Gavin. Finish your food. I'm done. I'll text him." I take his phone and type out a quick message to my brother that I hope sounds Gavin-ish. The response comes instantly. "He's already got it handled. He said just come to the stage and hurry."

I drain my drink and toss the empty cup in my bag, which I set aside, and then pull out my purse. Thankfully I folded my dress instead of wadding it up.

My jeans are halfway down my legs when Gavin nearly chokes on his burger. "What the hell are you doing?"

"Changing. We don't have time to go to the hotel and I can't very well perform in this."

"Right. Okay." He nods and stares straight ahead, his flexing forearms and flinching jawline the only indicators that my impromptu wardrobe change is making him uncomfortable.

I try to be discreet, pulling the dress up under his shirt before I take it off. I let my hair down, knowing it's going to get soaked anyway so a ponytail crease is the least of my concerns.

Once I'm done, he finally turns and asks me to text his friend Janie and tells her the car will be parked as close as he can get it to the stage where we're performing. I do, and then I'm putting my jeans in my bag when I see the access key card to my hotel room that I still haven't worked up the courage to give him.

Later. I'll give it to him later.

Chapter 19

"No more sushi for you, little sister," Dallas tells me after Gavin and I sprint from the car to the stage in the rain.

"Trust me, I have no interest in . . . sushi."

I try hard not to smile at the smirk on Gavin's face. I'm pretty sure he'll be referring to Afton as "Sushi" from here on out.

"Well I'm glad you're feeling better. Looks like they're going to delay sound checks for opening acts another half hour due to the weather."

If I let a laugh out right now, it will cross quickly over into hysteria. We nearly got killed rushing to get here. We broke every traffic law known to man. I ran my ass off in stiletto-heeled boots in the pouring rain, narrowly avoiding busting it on slick cement. And we still have a half hour until we can plug in our equipment. I nod and glance at Gavin, who's shaking the water out of his drenched hair like a wet mutt. His mouth threatens to smile at me and I shake my head.

The three of us step under the blue awning of a nearby bar and huddle together like everyone else is doing.

"Where's Mandy?" I ask my brother, just to make conversation.

"She's staying at her hotel tonight getting the paperwork together for us. Said she'd catch up with us later."

I take advantage of the privacy, still disturbed about what I overheard in the ladies' room and what Afton told me. "And we're sure about this? About signing with her?"

"What's up, Dix? Something you want to tell me?"

I shrug. "Afton just mentioned that we might want to explore our options a little more."

Dallas pulls a mockingly introspective face at me. "Ah. We're consulting Afton for business advice now? This the same Afton who refuses to work with managers and labels?"

"Funny. You didn't seemed concerned about that when you were all 'she'd love to go' and 'Dix, this will be such a great opportunity for you to meet other people in the business.'"

My brother smirks at my mocking him and I feel like I'm fourteen again.

"Rain's letting up," Gavin announces suddenly. "We can probably go ahead and start setting up now."

In other words, to your separate corners, kids.

Tamping down my annoyance, I step out into the rain and let it wash the exhaustion of the last twenty-four hours from my body. There's something cleansing and renewing about just getting bone-drenched soaked by rain. I stretch my arms out and tilt my face skyward.

While the guys start carrying our equipment from inside the bar it's been temporarily stored in, I open my mouth and let the drops fall on my tongue. Breathing the damp air in deep, I find things that have been so completely muddled becoming blindingly clear.

The rules I thought I could place on myself, on Gavin, on everything, they're just me kidding myself. Gavin's right, I can't escape unscathed. Not from him, or this band, or this life. And I can't force him to feel something for me that he doesn't even believe himself to be capable of.

"Gavin?" I call out to his back as he walks toward the stage with my brother.

He stop and turns, watching me walk toward him. As soon as I reach him, I hand him something I knew I'd have to give him eventually. But the words accompanying it aren't at all what I'd originally planned.

"Here," I begin, placing the plastic key card in his hand. "I changed my mind about . . . about everything."

He looks down at my room key then back at me. Confusion turns his eyes the color of the ocean sky clouding over before a storm.

"I can't be just one more person making demands on you. You have enough to deal with. Dallas, your mom, your friends, whoever the hell else it was blowing your phone up all day." I shake my head, knowing tonight I'll lie in bed alone regretting every word I'm saying. "Forget what I said about one night, about expectations, about everything."

His brows pull inward and he looks as me intently as if I'm one of those magic images where if you stare hard enough the jumbled mess of shapes will become one clear picture. "I'm not sure I'm following you, Bluebird. You hit your head really hard last night."

I'd smile if my mouth would cooperate. I nod at the key still sitting patiently in his open palm. "If you want to come tonight, to my room, then do. But not for me. Not because I asked you to. Come because you want to." I take in the deepest breath that I can. "And if you don't want to, because of Dallas or the band or you're tired or just not interested, then don't. No hard feelings and nothing between us will change. I thought I needed something more from you . . . but I don't."

"You don't?" he says slowly, as if still processing the words I've piled up between us like bricks.

I shake my head. "As crazy as the past twenty-four hours have been, I think adding more insanity to it might be the worst thing I could do. You had a condition, one that I said I could uphold. I lied. Expecting you to . . . um, you know, whatever, with me, and then pretending it didn't matter or didn't change anything, would be the definition of denial. So this is your out."

My brother says something to us and Gavin nods his understanding over at him before returning his full attention to me. "My condition had nothing to do with not expecting it to matter." He leans down and taps one finger under my chin. "Everything we do together matters, Bluebird. Everything."

He's right. And I think that's why I'm willing to forgo our one night. I wanted to be closer to him and after today, after everything I saw, mostly the parts he didn't want me to see, I know that I am probably closer to him than anyone has ever been. I walk in a daze behind him toward the stage.

"And Dixie?"

My attention snaps into focus. "Yeah?"

"I never said I wanted an out." His eyes don't leave mine as he slips my room key into his back pocket.

Lightning stops everything as soon as sound check is over. People are milling around like disoriented cattle as coordinators try to herd them into bars.

"Stage nine, you're going into Bourbon Girl. Let's go," a man in a black T-shirt and matching ball cap turned backward hollers at us.

We follow his directions into Bourbon Girl, a bar we've played in before. Seeing the familiar lit-up American flag onstage comforts me and also makes me want to burst into "The Star-Spangled Banner."

Dallas and Gavin set up our damp equipment while wiping it all down with towels the bar has generously provided. My hair hangs wet and heavy down my back as I retrieve Oz from his nice dry case. I missed him.

Some musicians look at their equipment as a way to earn money. And I guess mine does that for me, but there are so many memories connected to this fiddle, some that aren't even mine, that I could almost swear he comes to life and speaks to me when we play. Sure, he's dented and scratched and has a few nicks here and there, but those things are part of what makes him so special. After a few paying gigs, Dallas encouraged me to buy a new one, but I couldn't even fathom the idea. It felt like cheating or selling out. New strings are about all I can handle. I'll play Oz until he crumbles in my hands.

Dallas is texting on his phone off to the side of the stage when I look up and realize that the bar is full.

"Um, D?" I call out. "Think maybe we should play some music or something?"

Dallas looks up from his phone and grins at the crowd. "Or something. You ready, Garrison?"

"Let's do this," Gavin answers, lowering himself onto his stool. He taps out the count and I play my opener. A montage of this past week plays behind my eyes. The waitress at Mangieri's, Gavin blowing into my room like a tornado, the kiss outside of the storage space, him licking ice cream from my stomach, straddling him in his friend's car, his mom slapping him, the look in his eye when he slipped my extra room key into his pocket.

I pour everything I'm feeling into Oz—the confusion, the lust, the pain, the need, and the excitement that is beyond anything I have ever felt before. I'm alive. I'm so alive in this moment that I'm almost outside of myself looking in.

It's times like this, times when I'm on, giving it my all as my bow dances across the strings like it has a mind of its own, that I feel like I can fly. Leave this stage, this crowd, this world even, and ascend to a higher plane.

The deafening kick of Gavin's drums beats steadily along with my pounding heart while Dallas's guitar strums a rhythmic river flooding my veins and carrying me across the stage. The sound lifts and holds me while I play my heart out. The music flows around us and into me, lighting every single cell my body is composed of on fire from my toes to my head until I am blazing with the heat of it.

The section of the audience that my eyes can reach is cast in a neon blue glow with hues of red streaking on the periphery. The colors are as vibrant as I feel and would be distracting if I weren't playing, but I am focused. I am one with my instrument and its rich sound is so much a part of me it's as if it's coming from inside my soul instead of from the fiddle on my shoulder.

We take the audience on a fever-dream roller coaster of emotions with our sound. Dallas likes to begin and end on fast-paced songs and weave the slower ones through the middle. "Whiskey Redemption" comes just after a string of reworked R&B hits that had everyone singing along. We play "Ring of Fire" and then my favorite Adele hit. All three of us chime in on the vocals for our version of "Love Runs Out," playing it like a game of round-robin.

My favorite song is up next and I feel electric and on fire while we play it. It's a mash-up of a song called "Whataya Want from Me" and another called "Beneath Your Beautiful." It's our most downloaded cover online. Took me forever to get Dallas to agree to it and even longer for the three of us to get the timing right. But the hard work was worth it. I can see it on the faces in the crowd.

We play Dallas's favorite drinking song, one he wrote himself, and then our set ends with our updated version of "When You Leave Amarillo." The applause is so loud it vibrates through to my core and the sensation is electrifying. It's a serious struggle to catch my breath. We bow and thank the largest, most enthusiastic crowd we've ever played for and escape backstage. I'm not even sure if my feet are touching the ground as we step off the stage.

My brother is immediately swept into a darkened corner by some suit chatting him up, a potential manager probably. But Gavin is right behind me. He's so close I can practically taste his adrenaline high as acutely as my own.

"That was amazing," I breathe, turning to face him. "I think it might've been better than sex."

He stops tapping his drumsticks on his knee and pins me with his stare. His hazel gaze darkens as he backs me into the hallway and out of my brother's line of sight. "That was amazing because *you* were amazing."

The dim lights backstage are reflected in his pupils, making him look almost possessed, otherworldly. Somewhere the next act is being introduced and my brother is shaking hands and making a deal that will change the course of the rest of our lives. But here, where I am right now, Gavin Garrison is making love to me with his eyes. And I don't want him to stop. Ever.

Lowering his head enough that his lips are almost touching mine, he says the words that send my already racing heart into overdrive and halt my ability to form coherent thoughts. "But if you think that was anywhere near better than sex, those pretty boys you've been screwing around with have been doing it all wrong."

Chapter 20

"Let's go," Dallas calls out, pulling Gavin back with his words. "Mandy is having a drink with some of her associates over in the Warehouse District. I told her we'd meet her after the show."

The band playing after us, one I haven't heard of before and that plays harder stuff than we do, has already begun playing loud enough to make my entire body throb along with the bass.

"Who were you talking to just now?" Gavin asks my brother as we follow him out of the heavily crowded bar.

"Dave Lenard. He's kind of like Mandy's boss. He's the CEO of Red Light. He said he enjoyed the show, wanted to make sure we were on board."

After loading all of our equipment into the van, I take one last look at Austin. The bright lights glowing against the night. I breathe in rain-drenched air and look at the turbulent sky. Heat lightning dances across the blackness like strobe lights in a club.

Things are on the verge of changing irrevocably. I can feel it with everything I am. We have a manager now, a showcase tomorrow night, and who knows what will come after.

My hand slides against Gavin's as he takes Oz's case from me and places him gently inside the back of the van. That same spark, the one I've felt since we were kids, since the first time his hand touched mine, snakes up my arm and down my spine. Our gazes finally meet on the collision course I feel like we've been on forever. There's a flicker, a brief flash in his eyes like he's going to say something, but he looks away.

I want to ask him—no, I want to *demand* that he tell me if he's coming to my room tonight or not. But Dallas is still going on and on about meeting up with Mandy.

"Hey, Dix, you look pretty beat. Why don't you sit this one out?"

"Um," I begin, unsure as to whether I should go or just head to the hotel. I wish I could say that Dallas needs to let Gavin get some sleep, because he's had even less than I have, but I can't. So I just lift one shoulder noncommittally. "Okay. I can take a cab or—"

"Naw, we'll take one from the hotel. I want to make sure you get safely to your room before we head out." Dallas smiles warmly at me and my heart swells a little in my chest. I love my brother, overprotective ass and all. But I really wish he wasn't dragging Gavin out on the town tonight. "And I'm going to set half a dozen alarms on your phone."

"Well . . . thanks, I guess."

Once we're in the van, Dallas in the driver's seat and Gavin beside him while I sit in the back, my brother details our agenda for the next twenty-four hours.

"So it's a twelve-hour drive to Nashville tomorrow. The showcase runs through Monday but all Mandy can get us is a nine o'clock slot tomorrow night. There was a last-minute cancellation. If we leave at six we'll have plenty of time even with traffic. Sucks that we don't have a demo to hand out but I have that recording you made us,

Gavin. The one with 'Whiskey Redemption' and the encore medley on it."

I take it all in, feeling wearier with each word, as if they're weights my brother is handing me to hold.

"I have a cleaner copy on the laptop. Want me to burn another one and bring it tonight?"

My eyes trace Gavin's profile while he and Dallas hash out the details. Even exhausted, he's beautiful. And he's going out tonight. *Out* out from the sounds of it.

"Nah. We might be out late tonight so just do it tomorrow on the way to Nashville."

The word "late" pulls me from my greedy perusal of Gavin's face. They're going out and staying out. Dallas says something about sleeping in shifts and taking turns driving Emmylou to Nashville, but I'm still distracted by what they're doing tonight.

The entire ride to the hotel I'm waiting. Waiting for Gavin to say he doesn't want to go out, that he's tired, or has other plans. Something. But he just keeps up the conversation with Dallas about rearranging a few songs and suggestions for tomorrow night as if I'm not even here.

Somehow in the four blocks to the hotel, anger has ignited inside of me and I'm fiercely pissed-off by the time we pull into the parking lot. Exhaustion has given way to frustration and I'm not even sure what exactly I'm so upset over—the cryptic comment he made about not wanting an out or the fact that I know he might meet someone else while out with my brother.

Dallas pulls into a parking spot and we all shuffle out of the van. Gavin leans against it and I force myself not to even look at him.

"I'm fine, Dallas. You were right. I'm beat. I'm just going to head in and crash. No need to walk me. I'm a big girl."

"You sure?" My brother pulls out his phone, to dial a cab I assume.

"Yep. I'm good. Just tired."

"All right. Text me and let me know you're in safe, okay?"

"Sure." I nod and adjust my purse containing the evidence from my road trip with Gavin. "Have a good night, boys."

"Night." Dallas nods and lifts his phone to his ear. Because I'm weak, my eyes drift over to Gavin as I turn to walk into the hotel lobby.

"Sweet dreams, Bluebird," he says barely loud enough for me to hear.

With an obvious huff of annoyance and disappointment, I shake my head and keep walking.

I gave him an out. My brother gave him another one.

Seems he's taking them both.

Sitting alone in my room while Gavin and my brother go out on the town is not an option. Unless I want to drive myself insane.

Dallas would have a come-apart if he knew what I was doing right now. I went to my room and texted my brother that I was inside safely, before promptly turning around and walking right back out of it. The rain has eased to a drizzle and it's barely even dampened my hair by the time I get to the Driskill hotel. We played a wedding reception here once and I know the bar has a piano. It's been a while since I've played one, but the moment I lay eyes on it, it calls to me.

The room is mostly empty with the exception of a few business-men sitting in the bar. I make my way over and lower myself onto the bench at the baby grand.

Nana used to make me play a few warm-ups before launching into a complex piece, to keep my fingers from cramping, she said. But tonight I don't have the luxury of taking my time. The bar isn't open much longer and if I don't lose myself in the melody I'm going to lose my mind in the abyss that is wondering what Gavin is doing right now.

Placing my hands on the keys and rounding my fingertips instinctively as I've been taught, I fall into a familiar hymn Papa likes before transitioning into a faster-paced classical number it took me years to master. Metamorphosis takes all of my focus and concentration. When I finish part one, I keep going. No one has come to kick me out by the time I finish Metamorphosis Two so I still have time to keep playing. There's still a swirling hurt inside of me, the feelings I have for Gavin still ache to break free. Thankfully there are three more extremely complex parts to play. God bless Philip Glass.

Catching my breath and inhaling the sound, I let it pour out of the piano and into me. My fingers play of their own accord, and it's not perfect, but it's not terrible, either. Anything is better than crying.

Part four is the most haunting and the most difficult. It always has been for me so I shove my pain aside and focus on the keys and the timing.

Timing is the most important part, Nana used to say. You can play all the notes correctly, but if you screw up the timing, the piece is ruined. Timing couldn't be taught, she also used to say. It had to be felt. Closing my eyes, I do my best to feel it as it is intended to be felt.

Part five is reminiscent of part one and by the time I finish, I feel as if I've come full circle. My fingers and back both ache but my soul feels whole again—or at the very least—patched in the sorest places.

I stand and am startled when my small audience applauds politely. A few gentlemen raise a glass in my direction and I bow before

I leave, ducking my head so they don't see how flushed my cheeks are. I completely forgot they were there.

And that's why I don't just love music. I'm not in a relationship with it. If I were, it would be a dangerously codependent one. I don't think about whether or not I enjoy playing any more than I take the time to savor the flavor of oxygen. I play because I have to, because when everything falls apart and the walls of my world try to cave in around me, it's music that holds me up. Right now it's the only thing keeping all the parts of me together.

The rain was falling harder when I made my way back to my hotel so the first thing I did was remove my drenched clothing and get into the shower. Scalding water sluicing the bone-deep rain-induced chill from my body felt too good for me to do anything other than enjoy it. I might have even moaned a time or two.

But now, alone in my room, while combing through my wet hair and looking at my two vastly different options of pajamas, I am hollowed out and cold once again.

Plain white tank and faded-out boy shorts or the sexy black lace nightie and panties I'd hoped to wear for Gavin. They lie side by side on my bed, the two parts of me, the girl I am versus the woman I wish I could be. Stepping into the lace underwear, I nearly laugh at myself. Who am I kidding? He isn't coming. He practically breathed a sigh of relief when my brother ordered me to my room.

Throwing the remaining clothes on my bed onto the floor, I hold on to the fading sounds of my impromptu piano concert and slide into the shirt of Gavin's that was still in my bag from our trip. I didn't even take it on purpose, just forgot to put it back in his bag. But tonight I'm glad I have it. It's a small thing, but a part of him I can wrap around myself.

Drowning out Glass, Bonnie Raitt's "I Can't Make You Love Me" plays in my head on a steady loop as I climb into bed. Tonight I can wallow in my self-pity but tomorrow I'll have to put my game face back on and deal. Turning on my side, I curl around my pillow and mourn the loss of something I never had, until I fall asleep.

Chapter 21

THE FACT THAT IT'S STILL DARK OUTSIDE AND THE ONLY LIGHT IS from the soft golden glow of the lamp I left on before I feel asleep are the first things I become aware of when I wake up. The second thing is that I'm not alone. Someone else is in my room.

I remain on my side with my head turned toward him as I blink his figure into focus. He's sitting in the chair with one elbow propped on the small round table beside it. His chin rests on the fisted hand covering most of his mouth but his eyes are open. He's still wearing the jeans he performed in, the well-worn faded ones I love and his cobalt-colored T-shirt with "I'd Hit That" above the picture of a drum kit.

"You're here," I say quietly, my voice coming out rough, as if I'd smoked a carton of cigarettes before going to bed.

Suddenly joining the party, my heart begins slamming into my chest, singing as it realizes that he came. For whatever reason, he came. He's here.

"I am," he answers evenly, but his voice is heavy with exhaustion. "Mostly."

"How long has it been since you've slept, Gavin?" I sit up and run a hand through my messy hair. The last thing I remember is taking a shower, so I must've fallen asleep with it soaking wet. Which means it looks like I was mauled by rabid squirrels then. Great. Very sexy.

"A while. I'm okay. I wanted to make sure you were okay." He lowers the ankle he had crossed over one knee and leans toward me. "That was a good-sized lump on your head, Bluebird. We should've had it checked out."

"So that's why you're here? Checking to see if I've got a concussion?"

My shoulders fall noticeably. I hate myself for getting my hopes up. I should've known better.

He shakes his head slowly, his eyes meeting mine. *No.*

"Then why—"

The searing heat in his stare as he takes in his shirt covering my body stops me from finishing.

Oh. *Oh. Oh God.*

This is it. He's here. This is our night, for better or worse.

I shove down every insecurity, silence every doubt, and stand before him. "I'm glad you came," I whisper.

"I'm glad you're wearing my shirt," he says evenly, leaning back in the chair as his chin lifts slightly. "Now take it off."

My legs tremble beneath me as I make my way to him. I reach him in three steps and lift the hem of his shirt over my head before dropping it to the floor.

His warm hands encircle my rib cage as he pulls me onto his lap.

"Gavin," I whisper, but his name is lost in our kiss. His lower lip teases my mouth, brushing gently against me before his tongue thrusts violently into me. My hands tug at his shirt as I lower my hips onto his. I need skin. I need him. I need more. Always more.

We pull apart only long enough for his shirt to pass between us and then are drawn back together like uncontrollable magnets. My hands run greedily over his ink-covered muscles.

"I love the way you taste, baby. I haven't been able to get it out of my head, haven't been able to cure the craving since our little road trip."

His words come out laced with desperation and bare honesty. I smile against him as they fall into my mouth.

"How do I taste, Gavin?"

"Like forbidden fruit I'll never be able to get enough of." I bite his lower lip and he growls. "You can bite me as hard as you want to. I like for it to hurt."

"Me, too," I whisper against his lips. "The way you grabbed me outside the warehouse made me so hot I've had to touch myself every time I thought of it."

A deep, tortured moan escapes his throat and I drink it in.

"Show me. Show me how you touch yourself when you think of me."

"I will," I say standing, using all the self-control I have to pull away from his hands. "But I want to taste you first."

His eyes widen as I drop to my knees before him.

"Dixie, you don't have—"

"I want to. Let me, Gavin." I've wanted to do this since our road trip. "Let me." I wait eagerly, looking up at him as confusion and lust mingle in his eyes and lower his brow. "Please? Pretty please?" I thrust my lip out in a pout and reach for his zipper.

He shakes his head and assists me with opening his jeans. "You're going to be the death of me. You know that, right?"

I lick my lips in anticipation. My heart pounds harder at the sight of his erection springing free in front of me. We work together removing his Calvin Klein boxer briefs and jeans from his hips and down his legs.

He's big, which I assumed he would be after feeling his arousal against me the other night. But he's thicker than I expected. It's going to hurt going in and I can hardly wait. Part of me, a part in the southern region mostly, wants to climb back onto him and let him fill me. But I know I need to pace myself. This is our one night. I want everything. Want him everywhere. I want this night imprinted in our skin like our tattoos.

My fingers slide up his inner thighs and I stare at them as if they belong to someone else.

"Baby. Wait. You don't have to do this. Have you ever—"

"No. I haven't. You're the first," I say before I lean forward and take him into my mouth.

Tasting him is perfect oblivion. I close my eyes and my mind explodes in blues and blacks. The world around us disappears and we exist in nothingness. Just him and me.

His hands thread my hair and pull enough to hurt. It adds red to the blue and black swirling behind my eyes. I want more.

Licking up the underneath makes him squirm, sucking the tip makes him moan, and hollowing my cheeks to pull his full length to the back of my throat tears a sound from him I want to hear every day for the rest of my life.

Having this power, this kind of control of him, rattling the calm that seems to never leave him, makes me slick and needy between my legs. His warm arousal is sweet with a salty tang and I know I'm the one who's going to have an incurable craving from now on. I'm throbbing so hard it's tempting to touch myself, even if just to apply pressure for some relief. But I don't because the aching for him is necessary, delicious torture.

"Christ. Enough," he growls when I shove him hard to the back of my throat.

Before I can ask if I've done something wrong, I'm airborne as he lifts me from the ground and tosses me effortlessly onto the bed.

I giggle at the fierce expression he wears while glaring down at me.

"Think you're funny do you?" His dimple dents his cheek when he smiles and I grin lazily up at him.

"Now we both have a craving."

The moment burns between us, a lit fuse taking its time.

"Lie back," he commands, and all the playfulness is gone. "Spread your legs apart."

I do as I'm told, swallowing hard and struggling to breathe as my entire body is exposed to him.

"Tell me about this." He crawls onto the bed, hovering above me and his fingers graze lightly over the wild vine on my right side.

"Us," I say softly. "The band."

It's a fairly large but simple display—three flowers on a vine that wraps from my hip to my rib cage. A blue thriving bloom in the center for Dallas, a pink succulent with tattered petals for me just above my hip, and closest to my heart, a black rose growing amid thorns.

"This me?" The pad of his thumb rubs across the rose just below my breast, creating delicious friction on my skin.

I nod.

"Why the thorns?"

I bite my lip and take a much-needed breath. "Because you survived the harshest conditions. You're the strongest."

I can't read the emotions on his face, but they're powerful.

"I'm not," he chokes out while shaking his head, his eyes retreating from mine. "If I was, I wouldn't be here."

Sitting up, I use both hands to pull his face back to mine. "Gavin. Look at me." His eyes meet mine and I rub my nose against his. "You are the strongest person I know. Being here tonight isn't about being strong or weak. It isn't about breaking promises you never should've made. It's about us. Come back to me. It's just us."

My lips brush against his once, twice, and a third time before he finally kisses me back.

"And these?" he asks, catching my wrist on the side of his face.

"My parents," I answer, nodding at the two larger swallows taking flight inked in black on my wrist. "Me and D," I add, when he moves to the smaller ones left behind.

I shiver as he places a kiss on them before lowering my back onto the mattress.

His grins up at me, a mischievous gleam in his eyes as he dips his fingers beneath the waist of my panties. "What are you thinking about, beautiful girl?"

"Ice cream," I answer immediately.

"Was I the first? To—"

"Yes."

"Fuck. It's killing me knowing I was the first one to taste you. Give me a second." He closes his eyes and takes a steadying breath. I know he can probably feel my body trembling beneath him, but I can't do much to stop it.

His fingers press hard into my sides as he holds me down. I whimper loudly when he takes my right nipple into his mouth and sucks. My body bucks hard against him when he repeats his torment on the left.

"Feel good, baby?"

"Mm-hm," is all I can manage.

His mouth continues placing erratic kisses down my stomach

until he reaches what I knew might end up being our deal breaker. His fingers lower the top edge of my underwear and he stares openly, his eyes darting back and forth from my face to my tattoo.

"What's this?" I can't tell if he's angry or not. Mostly all I can identify is shock.

"A bluebird," I whisper. It's small, on a low enough branch on the vine that it's hidden even in a skimpy bathing suit. Its body is a treble clef and music notes fly from its wings.

"Why do you have this?"

Because I love you.

"It's a part of who I am, Gavin. The part of me I don't know if I would've found if I'd never met you. The part that throws glass bottles just to hear them shatter, the part that runs outside and screams when she's frustrated, plays music to feel, and the part that will strangle your mother with a smile on her face if she ever hurts you again."

This is going so wrong. So very wrong. This never happens in the movies. Sex scenes aren't supposed to be like this. I want to scream and cry and kiss him so hard it draws blood. I want to get back to the dreamlike buzz-inducing foreplay that had me practically levitating off the bed without dragging us down into the harsh pit of reality.

"What are you doing to me?" There's such obvious anguish in his eyes and I don't know why this hurts him so badly but it does.

"You're a part of me," I say quietly. "You always have been."

He doesn't say anything at first. Just glares as if making up his mind. I can practically hear the fight-or-flight argument he's having with himself in his head.

His eyes stay on my tattoo for what feels like eternity before they meet mine. And I see it. He knows.

"I don't deserve to be a part of you," he rasps out as if he's in pain. "You're good, too good for me and I can't . . . I told you not to fall in love with me."

"You told me ten years too late," I answer, crashing my mouth to his before he can argue his point any further.

The exploration of my tattoos ends, thank God, and he's with me again. Consuming me with his mouth and his broad muscular form above me. I feel tiny beneath him, but I hold my own as we fight for control of our kisses. We are breaths and moans and pleas in the darkness. Flesh on flesh. Tongues and fingers finding each other again and again. Battling for more, like the composition I still remember. I rake my nails across his back when his hard length brushes against the most sensitive part of me. I'm ready. I'm so ready it hurts in a place I can't reach.

"We have to slow down, Bluebird," he says, pulling back. The way his mouth quirks tells me that whether or not he's willing to admit it to me or himself, my tattoo makes him happy.

My body practically convulses as he slides down it. His fingertips touch my chest and my heart leaps to meet them.

"I'm ready, Gavin. I'm past ready. Please."

"I know, baby. We'll get there. I promise." He kisses each of my hip bones before dropping his hands to my inner thighs and easing them apart.

I can't breathe. Can't think. Can't grab on to a single substantial thought.

"Just your scent is making me insane. I want to beat on my chest, open the window, and tell every motherfucker in hearing distance that this is mine. That you're mine."

"Yes, yours," I pant.

His head dips lower, his tongue parting my swollen folds, and I scream. Actually scream. I hear it in my ears as if it came from someone else.

"Why do you have to taste so fucking good? I'm ruined. Damn it." His fingers squeeze my thighs tightly. "Your scent is driving me out of my fucking mind."

I want to answer him, say something as hot as the words falling from his lips, but I can't. I try and it comes out a garbled moan. I tear at the bedsheets when he sinks a finger inside me and tongues my throbbing center.

"Gavin. Oh *God.*"

His tongue swirls around my pulsating bundle of nerves and a slew of incomprehensible words fly out of my mouth. I don't know how my body is remaining on the bed—feels like it should be well on its way to outer space. Pleasure spirals out of control, wrapping its powerful tendrils around me and tearing me in two.

"Say it again. I want to hear it when you come for me."

"W-what?"

His tongue laps up my wetness just before he suckles my clit between his lips and it's too much. My legs try to close, their pathetic attempt at escaping the mind-blowing pleasure overloading my senses.

"My name. I want to hear my name in that sexy fucking mouth of yours. Say it, baby." He attempts to add another finger but my insides clench shut, trapping one and denying the other. He pulls out and drags them slowly through my slick heat before trying again.

"Gavin," I bite out as he forces his fingers inside. "Oh my God. Oh God. *Please.*"

"Fuck me, you're so damn tight. Open for me, sweetness."

I'm trying. God, I'm trying.

I don't even know what I'm begging for, but he seems to. His fingers plunge in and out rhythmically while he tongue-kisses my clit.

I feel the pressure build, feel it breaking through the dam and spilling over, drowning me, submerging us both, as I climb higher and higher into ecstasy.

Gavin curls a finger inside me, his mouth devouring me like a starving man, and I'm gone. Engulfed in flames and held under to burn slowly to death. Black and red and blue turn to blinding white as I'm flung over the edge into oblivion.

"That's it, baby. Come for me."

I do, good Lord, I do. I writhe and twist and moan as the pleasure overtakes me. For what feels like endless hours.

"Damn it to hell and back, your tight little pussy is going to break my dick off when you come with me inside you." Gavin's words yank me back to the present as he pulls his fingers out and licks them, *sucks them* actually, into his mouth, smiling as if they taste like manna from heaven. I could probably come again right this instant at that sight alone.

There was more? More than this? I was going to have more of this? It seemed too good to be true, like an intense fever dream I could only have once.

The questions must be evident on my face because when Gavin lifts his eyes to mine, he grins. "Oh, my sweet little Bluebird. Did you think we were done?" His voice is gleefully sympathetic. "That was just to take the edge off, sweetheart. We're just getting started."

He leans down and rains passion-filled kisses down on my mouth. I taste myself and a quiver breaks through at the obscene amount of pleasure I take in our intimacy.

Gavin has tasted me. *I* have tasted me on Gavin. No matter what happens, we will always have this. I will treasure it the way I knew that I would. The night I held fire.

Chapter 22

"I'M NOT GOING TO LIE TO YOU. EVEN AS WET AS YOU ARE RIGHT now, it's going to hurt at first. You're tight as hell." Gavin leans over and reaches for his pants, extracting a square-shaped foil packet. I watch his fingers as they open it and roll the latex deftly over his length.

"I'm on the pill," I say quietly. "And, um, I don't have any diseases or anything."

He nods. "We've been on the road together, baby. I know you're on the pill. And I get tested and always use protection. But I've known guys who've ended up daddies swearing the girl never missed a dose. It happens. Nothing is fail-safe. I want to be careful with you, baby." His fingers stroke my face and my eyes fall shut momentarily. "Do you even know how precious you are to me?"

The urge to cry hits me unexpectedly. I blink the tears back and stare up at him. I want to tell him that I love him—that I'm in love with him and always have been. But I know he doesn't want to hear those professions right now so I just nod and keep my mouth clamped shut until the urge passes and I can speak coherently.

"Show me, then. Show me how precious I am to you."

"Yes, ma'am," he says with a wink, dragging his hard length through the center of me.

My back arches off the bed, bowing toward him as he lowers onto me. A satisfied whimper escapes and he catches it with his mouth.

"I wish I could've taken you someplace nicer than this. You deserve so much better than this."

I reach between us and cover his lips with my fingertips. "I only wanted you, Gavin. I don't care when or where or how. I just want you."

"You have me," he says, parting my folds with the thick head of his erection.

For tonight at least, I think to myself just before I decide to banish any more bitterness from this night.

I feel him at my entrance and my entire body goes rigid.

"Breathe, baby," he whispers in my ear. "I promise to take it slow."

The hunger inside me grows, building with each slide of his skin against mine, his bare chest teasing my nipples until they're hard against him. I don't know if I want him to take it slow. I'm about to tell him he can take me however he wants to, plunge inside and pound out all of his pent-up emotions all night long if need be, when he presses inside and the sensation whips every coherent thought from my mind.

My fingers clutch his shoulders tight enough to tear his skin, but he only groans in a way that sounds like he's enjoying it.

There's a pinch and more pressure as he ventures deeper inside and then I'm pierced by his fullness. My walls begin to tense around him, gripping and releasing him as I throb in an attempt to accept the intrusion.

"Oh. *Oh God.* Gavin. You're so . . . it's so . . ."

"It's so what, baby?" His voice is low and gravelly, successfully heating my already burning blood to a dangerous temperature inside my veins.

"Full. You fill me so perfectly."

He groans and his hips grind against mine. "Easy, sweetness. Too much talk like that and this will be over a lot sooner than I'd like."

I spread my legs a little wider, my muscles finally accepting the invasion and easing slightly as he begins to move inside me. "I can't wait. God, Gavin. I can't wait to feel you come inside me."

"Please. *Fuck*. Please stop talking." The raw vulnerability only makes me want to talk more.

"I wanted this for so long. Wanted you. It's even better than I imagined." I moan loudly when he buries himself as deep as my body will allow, then again when he presses even further, passing a barrier I didn't expect him to. "You feel so good, Gavin. So big and thick inside me. So deep."

His hands fly to my wrists and pin them on either side of my head. His scorching glare sears my eyes as he hisses out a command. "Stop. Fucking. Talking."

"Or what?" I meet his sweltering stare with torrid desire of my own flashing in my eyes.

"Or I will cover your mouth with my hand and fuck you a hell of a lot harder than you're ready for."

Yes, please.

My walls pulsate furiously around him and my mouth curves into a smile. "Fuck me harder, Gavin. I can take it harder. I want it."

His hips pound savagely against me, slamming him inside even deeper and I cry out for mercy.

"See, baby? See what happens when you don't do what I say?" He leans down and kisses me roughly, ravaging my mouth and leaving his moisture on my still-searching lips. "Now be a good girl or I will spank your pretty little perfect ass."

"A spanking sounds like a surprisingly good idea." I clench down and constrict my walls around him as if I'm trying to push him out, even though that's the last thing I want.

"Christ, baby. Okay, ease up. You're so tight I can't fucking breathe."

His words flare a competitive streak I only have when it comes to him. I want to be the best. I *have* to be the best. I want to be the one he can't forget, can't get enough of. Won't walk away from.

I squeeze even tighter, then I rise up and lick a path up his chest and neck. He returns the favor by leaning down and teasing my nipples with his tongue.

"I want to touch you," I breathe out, jerking my hands that are still trapped in his viselike grip above my head.

"Say please."

"Please," I cry out on a ragged breath when he pulls himself nearly all the way out of my body.

He releases my wrists, allowing me to wrap my arms around his back and neck. My legs wrap instinctively around him, driving him deeper inside where he belongs.

It's building again, that delicious pressure that means I'm close. The tension coils in my lower stomach and strokes all the way down to where he's sliding against my core.

"I feel you tensing, trying to hold it back. Let go, baby."

I don't know how he knows, but he's seemingly tuned in to my every need. He slows his rhythm, changing from the punishing thrusts to an intense grind that puts him right where I need him.

"Gavin." His name drops like a prayer from my lips. "I want to wait. I want to feel you come with me."

"I'm close, baby. So fucking close."

"Kiss me, please."

His mouth curves in a smile before landing on mine. I pull him in, sucking his lips in the same way my internal walls are suctioning around him.

A throaty groan reverberates into my mouth and I'm lost in a turbulent sea of untamable pleasure. The instant I feel him jerk and throb inside me, I fall—losing the last ounce of control I was clinging on to with my fingernails.

His body rocks hard against mine, bucking his hips into mine with enough force to bruise. I let loose an animalistic sound that I couldn't re-create if someone held a gun to my head. My legs drop from his waist, shooting out straight and stiff until the first wave rolls over me. He moves relentlessly inside of me and a second wave hits.

I'm confused and overcome. My mind tries to divide itself to accommodate the sensations. I had sex but I've never felt anything like this before. Never-ending orgasms and tremulous aftershocks are new to me. Gavin brings his hand between us, pressing his thumb to my clit, and I scream. This wave is slower, taking over my body in languid strokes of ecstasy.

I'm going to die. These are my last glorious moments on earth. I couldn't have picked a better way to go.

"Ohmygodohmygodohmygod," slips from my mouth in an endless stream.

I feel the damp heat of the whispers in my ear before I can make out what he's saying.

"So beautiful, so motherfucking perfect and beautiful," are the first words I comprehend.

And then a deep breath and one more declaration.

"You've wrecked me, Bluebird. I. Am. Wrecked," whispered just before he collapses on top of me.

Chapter 23

I'M DREAMING. AT LEAST, I THINK I AM.

I fell from a cliff into the ocean where a current held me down. I've been under for too long, much too long. I know I can't breathe this long underwater. I start to panic but my screams are lost in the water. Until the music begins to play.

It pulls me to shore, the glorious sound of the violin being played masterfully. I have to see who this master musician is up close. He saved my life, after all.

I run, my bare feet struggling to find purchase in the sand. But then I see him. His back is to me and he's not playing a violin at all, but making love to a woman.

Gavin. My beautiful Gavin. His tattoo-covered muscles flex and strain as he moves, and she's crying out in pleasure or pain, I can't tell. But her cries are music to my ears and I see her face.

It's me. She has my face.

They're on fire, it's all around them, and I want to help them but I'm frozen where I stand. Helpless.

Water begins to fill my mouth and lungs again and I try to scream, to ask them if they see me, to tell them they're on fire, but my cries are muffled by more water.

"Dixie?" Gavin stops moving above her and gapes at me. "Blue-bird? Are you okay?"

He does see me.

My eyes fly open and I'm in his arms panting for breath. In a hotel room. Not drowning. I'm not drowning.

"Dixie? Baby, are you okay?"

I nod frantically while trying to catch my breath. "Bad dream. Weird dream."

"Holy fuck, you scared me to death."

"Sorry," I say easing back into his arms. "I was on the beach. We were together, but then I was separate. I was drowning."

His arms tighten around me. "We must've passed out. I woke up to you making a strange noise, like you were choking to death."

My head settles against his chest and his heartbeat lulls me into a calmer, much more peaceful state. "Yeah. It was crazy." I shake my head against his warm skin. "It was like I knew I was dreaming, but it was so real at the same time."

"Well, I promise, you're awake now. And so am I. You damn near gave me a heart attack."

"Hmm . . ." My hand slides down his chiseled stomach. We're still naked. I find his thick fullness with my fingers and wrap around him. He jerks in my grasp and is hard almost instantly. "Maybe we should make sure. You know, just so I know we're really awake."

"About that," he murmurs into my hair. "We got kind of messy in my half-ass, half-conscious attempt to dispose of the condom. Shower with me?"

Now there's an offer I can't refuse.

Our bodies seem to have magnetized during our lovemaking, or fucking, or whatever that glorious experience should be called. We remain connected in one way or another as we make our way to the bathroom—his arm around my waist, a hand on my back, my face to his chest, his fingers in my hair, and finally I get brave and press my lips to his when he stands from leaning over to turn on the shower.

"You taste like rain . . . and like me," I tell him when we eventually pull apart.

He grins at me, the seductive heat of want returning to the gleam in his eye. "Oh yeah? Well, I must taste fucking amazing then. Because I can honestly say, until tonight that strawberry ice cream I licked off your stomach was my favorite, but now . . ." He pauses and glances over my head in the mirror. "Now I can honestly say, you, Dixie Leigh Lark, are my favorite flavor."

Turning to see what has caught his eye, I stare at our naked figures in the mirror before the thick steam covers it.

"We look good together," I whisper.

Gavin meets my gaze in the mirror and nods his agreement almost imperceptibly. With his arms covered in ink and my shoulders and waist decorated as well, we look like an erotic oil painting. I watch our conjoined reflection as his hand snakes around my waist, dipping lower in a way that causes my bones to liquefy.

His other arm wraps around me higher and his hand massages my breasts gently.

I let out a throaty approval of his ministrations. "God, Gavin. I don't want you to stop touching me. Please never stop touching me." I mean ever, as in, *ever,* but he doesn't seem to need or want clarification.

His mouth meets me ear and I can't tear my eyes away from the glass.

"Spread your legs for me," he says low in my ear, causing me to quiver noticeably in his arms. "Please," he adds when I don't comply immediately.

"Since you said please," I answer, doing as he requested.

"That's it, baby. Just like that." My nipples harden from his praise and unwavering stare. Gavin's expert fingers find my most sensitive spot immediately as he slides through my center, dipping in and out of my opening. "My sweet, wet girl." The mirror shows me his muscular forearms flexing at his efforts and I could come again already.

"I might not be able to stand up in the shower if you keep going."

His hand stills between my legs and his arousal strokes my bare ass. "You want me to stop?"

I shake my head, still held captive in his gaze like prey locked in a predator's in the mirror. "I just want to make sure you're okay with holding me up and bathing me."

"Anytime, Bluebird. Anytime." Gavin grins and quirks an eyebrow before breaking our bonded stares to dip his head and place a searing kiss against the sensitive skin on my neck.

My whimpered moans escalate to pleading cries as he strokes my heat more intently.

"Gavin, *oh God.*" My voice is strained, as is my entire body. I buck hard against him, and he tightens his hold on me.

"Please," I beg, but I can't get anything else out of my mouth that makes sense.

If feels so good, so amazingly, mind-blowingly good that I'd be afraid if I didn't trust Gavin implicitly.

The realization hits me almost as hard as my orgasm does. This is why it's so different, so amazingly consuming and overwhelming, and so much better than anything with anyone else ever was or ever could have been. I trust Gavin. I trust him and I love him. With all my heart.

I've given myself over to him completely.

Once I come back to earth, I meet Gavin's livid stare in the mirror. He has this look on his face and I can almost read his mind.

"Trying to decide if we should shower or if you should bend me over this sink and fuck me until I speak in tongues?"

His mouth curves wickedly. "I did love the hell out of watching you come like this and the idea of watching your beautiful face while I take you from behind is pretty much all I need to die a happy man."

I lean back against his body, my boneless legs struggling to support me. His arm around my waist is doing a better job of keeping me upright than they are.

"But I think our time is running out on how much longer you can stand upright." He winks at me.

"Shower it is, then."

Gavin pulls me inside the steam-filled shower, rinsing my hair as if I'm a delicate doll he's afraid of breaking. I trace the ink on his chest with my fingers while he lathers shampoo into my scalp.

"I remember this one," I say, pointing to the lightning bolt/music note hybrid on his chest. "You got it when I got back from Houston."

"At Black Lotus, I remember."

I close my eyes as he moves to let the steady stream of water remove the thick, soapy lather from my hair.

"I always wondered why we went downtown that night. I thought you got your tattoos done at Jinxed Ink. I never asked why you switched for this one."

Gavin is mid-shrug when I open my eyes. "I go where Xander goes. He does all my ink. He was freelancing at BL that night."

Xander Erikson did my ink, too, actually. He's the only one Gavin trusts, for whatever reason. But I was nervous and had seen him do a few of Gav's, so when I was ready, I went to him. He did Dallas's, too, our last name in script on his right inner forearm and the guitar on his left.

"He did mine, too. I had to make him take a blood oath before he did my bluebird."

"I'll be kicking his ass when we get home."

"You love it," I say with an impish grin.

Gavin doesn't answer. He places a hand on my chest and presses gently until I step backward, putting my back flush against the shower wall.

I open my mouth to ask if he's seriously mad about the tattoo, but before a single sound comes out, my attention moves south and I see his erection straining proudly between us. Liquid desire spreads instantly to my core, flooding me with overwhelming need.

"Gavin," I begin in a breathy plea.

"I do. I do love it," he says, taking a step closer to me and dropping to his knees. "So fucking much."

My head falls back the second he puts his open mouth on the tattoo below my hip. I suck in a breath and slide my fingers into his hair. For a second I think I know where this is going. He did this in bed, placed his mouth where no man's mouth had been before. But then he pulls back and brushes a finger over my little bluebird.

"So beautiful," he says reverently. "So fucking beautiful."

I try to breathe normally. "Yeah. Um, Xander did a great job."

He looks up at me and smirks like I'm missing something. "Did you take your pants off for this?"

I shake my head, heady feelings of gratitude filling me at the sight of his jealousy. "No. I just unbuttoned my jeans and pulled them down a little. I had to move my panties for him, but he was a perfect gentleman."

"I'm kicking his ass either way."

"Then who will do your ink?"

He tilts his head to the side. "You think I need more ink?"

"You need my name across your ass, so yeah. And then one above your dick that says 'Dixieland Delight.' I mean, the second one is optional but it would be a nice touch."

A low chuckle begins in his throat and ends on my pelvic bone as he presses his lips to me. "You gonna get one for me, then?"

His warm breath tickles my center and I moan even though he hasn't actually touched me anywhere other than my hip yet.

"I already have one for you," I whisper, because even though he knows my secret, knows about the tattoo and what I taste like and how I feel on the inside, I'm still a little embarrassed. I'm busted. Between the black rose and the bluebird, I feel like I FUCKING LOVE YOU, GAVIN GARRISON is inked permanently across my forehead.

"Hmm. Apparently you do. Guess I owe you one then, Bluebird. Maybe even more than one."

Before I can answer, he licks me hard and fast right between my legs. I cry out in shocked ecstasy, my moans stretching like a seamless instrumental into one long pleasure-filled ballad while he swipes his tongue through my throbbing center, around my clit, and back again.

"Oh God, Gavin. Oh God."

He sucks my clit hard and releases it with a wet sound that nearly breaks me apart then and there.

"After tonight, you can't say the words 'Oh God' and my name ever again. Got it?"

"W-what?" I'm aching to the point of pain for more and I'd gladly agree to sell a kidney on Craigslist if he'll just finish what he started.

"Those words. You can't say them after tonight. Ever."

"Why?" *Please touch me. Stop talking. Please touch me.*

"Because," he says evenly as if I'm not melting into a puddle and about to disappear down the drain with the water. "Every time I hear them, this is what I'll think of. And me thinking of this, after tonight, will be very dangerous and detrimental to our agreement."

Our agreement. One night.

"Screw our agreement, Gavin. Right now, if you don't finish what you just started, I'm going to say 'Oh God, Gavin' every single time I see you. I might even whisper it to you in church."

An enticing grin dances across his tempting mouth.

"You know what? Never mind, drummer boy. I can't handle it." Without giving him an opportunity to stop me, I dip my hand between my legs and stroke myself.

I keep my gaze trained on his until he looks away to watch my fingers finishing what he started.

"Feel good, baby?" He arches an eyebrow up at me.

"Not as good as your mouth and nowhere near as good as your big, thick . . . fingers," I say with a teasing wink. "But I know how I like it. Years of wanting you to touch me have given me an extremely vivid imagination."

I see it the moment the need blooms wild and bright in his darkening eyes. He's crossed over from sweet and teasing to animalistic and dangerous. The way he did in the car when he lost it on his mom. I push the memory aside and let my instincts take over. Dipping my fingers inside my inviting heat, I move them until they're slick and covered in my wetness before placing them against his lips.

"I love when you taste me, Gavin. How do I taste?"

He opens his mouth and sucks my fingers inside. Hard. He closes his eyes and I feel the throaty growl all the way to my insides.

I've barely blinked when he returns his mouth to the needy apex of my thighs. It was sweet in the bed, to take the edge off like he told me. But this is different. This is about gratification and pure, unadulterated need. His teeth graze over my sensitized flesh and I cry out his name.

Two of his fingers thrust into me, blanking my mind of any logical thoughts.

I hear my cries, the praise I'm raining down on him like water, the pleas for more. I'm outright begging him not to stop when I feel my body falling over into the abyss. It's a rush, like spending years climbing a rocky mountain ridge only to rappel off it bungee-style when I get to the top.

I'm mid-release when he stands abruptly and slams his bare cock into me. A hiss slips through his teeth and falls onto my lips.

"Harder, Gav. I want you harder. Oh my—Yes, *oh God*, Gavin."

He complies, lifting me, impaling me on his velvet-encased steel and slamming me into the slippery back wall over and over until there's a rhythmic beat to it. He's inside me without a condom but his eyes are animal-kingdom gone. He's too wrapped up in us to remember, and it feels so good that I can't bring myself to care about things like consequences.

My legs wrap around his soaking wet waist and I cling to his powerful body for dear life. If we fall in here, we will get seriously injured and there will be no way to explain it. But I'm pretty sure I'd happily endure a body cast for this degree of pleasure.

He fucks like he drums. Putting everything he is into the intensity, giving himself over to it one hundred percent. His mouth covers mine, drinking it in greedily, swallowing my moans and breathy pleas. My release has become too intense to contain quietly and I claw at his back while his pounding forces noises of surrender from deep inside me. Once the pleasure has rolled over me, I'm weak, going limp in his arms.

I feel him losing himself and his grip on me, but as soon as I'm aware of it, he makes it clear that it's intentional. Gavin lowers me to my feet, keeping an arm around my waist as if to make sure I'm capable of standing. I am—barely.

He grips my waist and whirls me around so that my back is to him. The curtain whips open, letting cooler air inside. My eyes land on the reflection of us in the mirror. Gavin stands behind me looking like he could devour me in one bite. I lean back against his body, covering his hand with mine as it roams my stomach and breasts.

"You nearly broke me with that comment about bending you over the sink." Gavin squeezes my hip and I spread my legs without having to be asked this time.

The moment I'm open enough for him, he thrusts upward and into me in one delicious stroke.

My head drops back onto his chest when his expert fingers begin massaging circles around the outside of my sex while his dick does the same to the inside of me.

His shoulder nudges the back of my head. "Eyes open, Bluebird," he says, leaning down to breathe his command into my ear. "I want you to watch. Watch how hard you make me come."

My eyes are liquid fire from his words as I watch the reflection of him taking me from behind. Seeing us in this erotic pose, fully bared and completely connected, even in the mist-covered mirror, is so earth-shatteringly hot that I know it's an image that will be burned into my mind for the rest of my life.

"I have to pull out, baby. I'm sorry. I went in without—"

"Don't," I say, gripping his hands tightly and clenching my internal muscles down on him. "I want to feel you, Gavin. I want you to still be inside of me even when this is over."

His body tightens against mine, so I squeeze and bear down, clamping myself tighter around him until I'm using every ounce of strength I have left. If all I get with him in my entire lifetime is this one night, then there is no time for shy and cute and coy. Or safe.

"Damn it," his hisses in my ear. "Goddamn it."

"Spill in me, Gavin. Fill me with you. I want you inside me in every way I can have you."

He swells inside me and I watch the veins in his neck bulge and strain; his groans come out through gritted teeth and for a second my feet leave the wet floor.

My arms remain wrapped around his neck, stretched to their fullest capacity as his fingers dent deep into my stomach and hip while he fills me with the hot, scorching bursts of his release. Somehow in the midst of his madness, he finds my clit again and strokes me exactly how I need it until I'm writhing and coming right along with him. It's too much. My body strains against itself, wanting to push away from him and meld to him permanently at the same time.

It's burning hot inside me as I feel my soul tear into two equal pieces. One half accepting that this is all we'll ever have and the other hissing and gnashing its teeth angrily, refusing to settle, demanding more. Always more.

His eyes meet mine in the mirror and I see the same greedy demon whispering to him.

"I've never—" He interrupts himself to kiss my shoulder. "It's never been like that for me." He kisses my neck, wrapping his arms around me tighter. "You okay, Dixie Leigh? I didn't hurt you, did I?"

My logical mind is still shattered and doesn't fully understand his words but my body and soul do.

"You set me on fire, Gavin," I whisper. "I'm nothing but ashes now."

The first conscious thought I have is that he tucked me in. My exhausted sex-and-sleep-muddled mind has a vague recollection of him taking care of me in the shower, getting on his knees with a washcloth and washing me gently between my legs. I'd nearly blacked out and he'd rinsed me and carried me to bed wrapped in a towel, which it feels like I am still wearing. Partially, anyway.

Gavin's solid muscled chest is beneath me and his heat is making me sweat. I lie still for a few minutes, absorbing the moment, memorizing it and listening to his even breaths.

Our night together has been a lot of things, but we haven't spoken about what comes next. If anything. Propping up on one elbow, I stare at Gavin's sleeping form, admiring his masculine profile and perfect mouth. A familiar ache rakes across my chest, reminding me that no matter what happened between us tonight, he is not mine. He's not anyone's. Gavin has always been a lone wolf, he just decided to allow Dallas and me to join at his flanks temporarily from time to time.

Watching him breathe, and feeling a heck of a lot like a creeper, my mind recalls the first time I ever got the chance to watch him like this. It was our second summer living in Amarillo. Nana and Papa had ordered pizza and let us eat outside. After dinner, Dallas had been doing something in Papa's shed, restringing the guitar Papa had bought him at a secondhand store most likely, and Gavin and I had sat on the ground, sated from dinner but hungry to make the day last longer. Lightning bugs, as I called what he and Dallas called fireflies, had begun to dance in the yard as darkness fell, calling to each other with flashing glows of neon green in the night. It was hot, and despite the breeze, I still felt the sting of the day's summer sun on my skin.

Leaning back on his arms stretched out behind him, Gavin stared up at the stars unabashedly. My eyes trailed his long black shorts, pants he'd cut off at the knee either because he'd outgrown them or because it was hot as Satan's balls outside according to the boys. His iron-flat abs rippled and flexed when he spoke about the Big and Little Dipper, but I barely heard him.

Sitting with him, watching him look at the expanse of stars in the broad Texas sky, I realized something that night, something it had taken me this long to actually learn, to absorb and fully understand.

Heartbreak is an actual physical thing.

Falling in love with Gavin Garrison happened without my permission; as inevitable as a Popsicle melting down my chin in the middle of a heat wave, Gavin cracked my heart open and seeped into me slowly and all at once. My feelings for him consumed me, worked their way into my genetic makeup, and became an intrinsic part of who I was without my actually realizing it. Even when I was dating Jaggerd, it was there. Even if I grew up and got married to someone else and had children that I loved with all my heart, my love for Gavin Garrison would still be there. Like my blue eyes, my brown hair, and the freckle to the left of my nose, it was a permanent part of me.

I can't even fight it or try to hide it like I have been. Even if this didn't work and he doesn't feel what I do, or believe himself to be capable of feeling it, I can't pretend anymore. Not after this.

"I love you, Gavin," I whisper against his chest. His breathing remains even, but his arm tightens around me. Glancing up I see his thick eyelashes flutter. I can't help but wonder what he's dreaming of, if he's ever dreamt of me. "With my whole heart," I add before drifting off to sleep against him. "Always."

Chapter 24

"WAKE UP, SLEEPY GIRL," A LOW VOICE SAYS FROM ABOVE ME. "Time to go."

I stretch my legs, feeling the soreness down to my toes, before I open my eyes.

"Morning, Bluebird," Gavin says with a smug grin. "How are you feeling?"

"Sore," I admit honestly, eliciting an even wider grin from his mouth. "You?"

"Proud of myself mostly. Especially when that's the answer to how you're feeling."

"I can tell." I sit up and pull my towel around my still-naked body. "Mostly?"

He shrugs and glances down at his phone. "I told him I crashed with a friend last night and that I would come wake you up."

There's no need to clarify who *him* is, so I don't ask. "How much time do we have?"

His eyes widen before landing on my bare chest when I let my towel drop.

"Not enough," he practically growls at me.

I bite back an intrigued grin. "I meant how much time do I have to get myself together before we hit the road. But if there's time for—"

"There's not. Get dressed." He hands me a pair of jeans from my suitcase and a white sleeveless shirt with Adele's face on it. It's pretty much the last clean one I have left. "Dallas is downstairs waiting in the lobby."

And that's that. Last night was *last night* and now we're back to business as usual. Doing my best to ignore the lethal claws digging a jagged pit into my stomach, I pull my clothes over my body and watch him lace up his boots. Glancing at the clock, I see that he's right. It's seven already. Dallas wanted to leave at six thirty.

But I can't make myself button my jeans, or slip on my shoes. I can't imagine walking out of this room and back into a world where he doesn't touch me. Where I can't kiss him when I want to. Where the sun will glare its uninvited light onto us. I want to stay here, in this cocoon where the room is bathed in the safe blue hues that protect our secrets.

Time passed too quickly and I'm not ready to let go. I'm not prepared to lock our memory away yet.

Walking over to Gavin feels like a funeral march. My legs are heavy, weighed down with our goodbye.

He finishes lacing his second boot and looks up at me. My waist is level with his face.

"Baby . . ."

My voice comes out as a whisper, as if I'm giving away my biggest secret even though he already knows them all. "I'll tell him I had to take a shower."

Those are the last words I say before my lips return to Gavin's, where they belong. Last night, or in the early hours of this morning, he fucked me, had sex with me. Thoroughly and wonderfully. But this morning we make slow sweet love. Despite the time, we don't hurry.

My clothes come off and end up on the floor along with his. He sits back down in the chair and I lower myself onto him without words. His hands welcome me like old friends wrapping me in their warmth as I move over him.

His mouth never leaves mine. There aren't words, no banter, dirty or otherwise. No promises or declarations.

There is only us.

W e'll have to drive like hell since Dixie thought it was vital to wash her hair. If there's traffic we're screwed." Dallas is still complaining about the delay I caused when we load into the van, but I'm still somewhere in the strange in-between where even he can't touch me. But my brother has never been the type to just let it go.

"I mean, Christ, Dix. You think we can just show up when we feel like it? This is it, little sister. Our shot. This is it."

"I'm sorry," I answer, but I'm not really. I'm not sorry and I'm not really in this van on the way to Nashville. I'm still in a hotel room in Austin with Gavin.

Dallas slams on the horn when a maroon Acadia pulls out in front of us. "Damn it."

"We'll get there, D. I checked my GPS and it's only—"

Dallas looks away from the windshield long enough to throw a pissed-off look of barely leashed fury at me.

"Oh, your GPS? Because your phone knows the traffic conditions on the interstate? Or it has an app for telling the future? That a new model? You get an upgrade I wasn't aware of?"

I smirk at him in the rearview mirror, feeling bad that I put us behind. But if this is the price for my last time with Gavin, I'll pay it happily.

"No," I say, tucking my legs up on the bench seat beneath me. "I was just saying that—"

He huffs out an exasperated sigh. "Well don't just say, okay? You saying we'll get there on time doesn't mean that we will."

"Neither will your bitching about it," Gavin breaks in, the fierce undercurrent of violence flowing in his words. "So give it a goddamn rest already."

Dallas turns his attention to Gavin and I swallow the urge to smile. He's always been the peacemaker, but he never takes sides. The look he's pummeling my brother with says this time he has. And it's mine.

"Easy," Dallas warns, the tension in the confined cab of the van growing heavier among the three of us. But then my brother laughs. "Dude. I thought you got laid last night. No luck?"

Oh no. Every cell in my body goes on high alert. Dallas is grinning good-naturedly, but Gavin looks like he wants to jump out of the van and into oncoming traffic.

"None of your business, *dude.*"

"My bad." My brother laughs as he weaves into the fast lane. "You said you were crashing with a friend, so I just assumed—"

"Lark, I'm dead serious. Shut it the fuck down."

I swallow hard, pulling my arms around my knees and trying to pretend they're talking about something else. *Someone* else.

"All right, all right. Shutting." My brother shakes his head. "Guess this one actually meant something for a change. I've never seen you so worked up over a one-nighter. Any chance I'll get to meet her? Or you too afraid she might actually have taste and ditch you for me?"

Holy disgusting incest, Batman. Shut up.

Despite my urge to plug them, my ears perk, both anxious and dreading Gavin's response.

Gavin ignores him. "I'm taking a nap. Wake me up if you want me to drive."

I can see from the space between the seat and the window that he's shoving his duffel against the glass and using it as a pillow. My voice leaps into my throat to tell him we can switch places and he can sleep on the bench seat, but he's practically radiating anger and frustration and I'm still too wound up and raw to risk being snapped at by him.

It doesn't take long before I'm dozing in that murky area between sleep and reality. I'm vaguely aware when the boys change places somewhere between Little Rock and Memphis. They hand me a bag of drive-through food that gets cold before I eat it.

Somewhere in strange daylight hours that feel oddly bright for almost dinnertime, we're stopped when I'm roused from restless napping and I see Dallas practically hurdling Gavin to switch seats with him once again.

Sitting up, I blink myself awake just in time to see a uniformed police officer walking to where Dallas is now sitting. I sit upright and try to look like a willing participant in the van instead of a kidnapped hostage. Pretty sure my bedhead in the middle of the day isn't helping. The officer leaves with Dallas's license and proof of insurance.

I glance out the windshield but all I can see is the highway and trees. "Where are we?"

" 'Bout ten minutes outside of Nashville." Dallas gives Gavin a strange look and mumbles something under his breath that I can't make out.

"No shit," Gavin responds. My gaze travels over him. He's shifting uncomfortably, drumming his thumbs on his right knee.

"Why the quick change? You got warrants out, Garrison?" I'm kidding, but when he glances over his shoulder at me his expression is wary.

"Something like that."

I'm about to demand that they both tell me what the hell is going on when the cop returns.

Dallas gets a speeding ticket for going ten over the limit. Both the guys grumble about the guy being a dick as we pull back onto the highway.

"What do you mean, 'something like that'?"

"Nothing," Gavin says without looking at me.

"*Nothing* wouldn't have sent the two of you sprawling across each other to switch seats."

"Now's not the time," Dallas says, giving me a warning glance.

"I'm not moving from this van until one of you tells me what is going on." This combined with Gavin's weird-out when the officer stopped to check on us on our way to Potter County has me convinced that what happened while I was in Houston was much more significant an event than the two of them have made it out to be.

My body feels like it's made of wet cement anyhow. But whatever they're hiding is big if they've kept it from me. My time in Houston has become a window of time that they've both turned into a black hole I know very little about.

I watch from behind as the two of them exchange a look. Gavin's shoulders go stiff for a second before he angles around to look at me.

"I got into a little trouble after you left for school last year. Started screwing around with stuff I should not have been screwing around with and some unpleasant shit went down. It's over with and I'm handling it."

I narrow my eyes at him. "Which is it? Is it over with or are you handling it?"

"We're here," my brother announces loudly, cutting off my inquisition.

Great. My eyelids are swollen and heavy and my mouth tastes like the inside of a Dumpster. Minus the blinding neon lights lighting up the street, it's growing dark already. A day in a van will seriously mess with a girl's concept of time.

Dallas continues on, giving our marching orders as he parks the van. "We have less than an hour to get cleaned up and get to the venue where the showcase is being held. Mandy booked us a room here at her hotel."

Knowing that tonight I'll be sharing a room with Gavin and my brother has my head spinning as I crack my neck. I stretch my legs and groan a little at the ache unfurling inside them.

Dallas gets out to start unloading our equipment and Gavin twists in his seat to glare at me.

"You have to stop that."

My arms freeze mid-stretch and I glance down at my protruding chest. "Stretching?" I frown and lower my arms when he doesn't answer. "I'm going to have to stretch every now and then."

"Not that," he says, his eyes darkening in a way that I feel down to my stomach. "The noises. Don't make those fucking noises around me. Ever."

A tiny snort of amusement escapes me before I rein it in. He looks like he might want to hurt someone. "Don't call them *fucking noises* if you don't want me to laugh."

He shuts me out by closing his eyes. I reach a hand out and touch his jaw, which has hardened to granite with his anger. His eyes open and I am paralyzed by what I see in them. If I thought there was heat in his gaze before, I was wrong. Every look he has ever given me is like lukewarm bathwater compared to the molten white-hot lava burning into me now.

"I can still smell you, can still taste you. It's fucking killing me, Bluebird." My stomach twists at the obviously excruciating agony he's experiencing trying to articulate our situation. "What we did, it's not just something—"

Gavin doesn't get to finish because Dallas yanks open the back doors.

"Let's get moving. Time's not exactly on our side right now."

Jerking out of my reach, Gavin gets out the van without another word. I'm more than a little affected by what he's told me and slightly frustrated that I didn't get to say what I felt, too.

I can still feel you, Gavin. I can still taste you, too.

There's a difference, though, the same difference that has always divided our feelings for one another.

"You're the one person that's supposed to be off-limits. I made a promise. One I intended to keep."

His words from our conversation in a borrowed car repeat in my head. The truth is, I'm glad I still have part of him inside me. I'm savoring the taste of him for as long as I possibly can. But now there is something else inside me.

A sharp-edged fear that he regrets it—that he regrets me.

Mandy is waiting for us when we walk into the hotel. The second my perusal of the expansive lobby lands on her, she smiles a toothpaste-commercial smile at the three of us, stopping when she reaches me.

"Hi, guys," she says, practically beaming at us. "You're all checked in and here's your key." She passes the plastic card to Dallas before turning her attention to me. "There are some major players here tonight and I've been talking the band up to everyone who would listen."

"That's very . . . kind of you," I say because I don't know what else to say. We signed the preliminary contract Dallas had with him this morning, so she's our manager now. But I honestly don't feel like I even know her. She looks like she just stepped off the runway and I look like . . . like I just spent twelve hours in a van.

"It's my job," she says. "But Dixie, I could only get one room so I told your brother I'd be happy to let you room with me."

Well that's . . . unexpected.

"That's a great idea," my brother announces before I can say anything. "Especially since we all need to get changed and to the Palace."

She turns to me and I give her the best look of gratitude I can muster. I'm having an out-of-body experience, watching myself being herded like cattle into the elevator.

I resemble a fish out of water, gaping between her and Dallas as they detail the plans for the next few hours. We'll get ready, our van will be driven to the venue by Mandy's assistant Randall, we'll take a town car with Mandy to the Palace, meet and greet the executives in attendance, then perform. I focus on the last word. I need to play, need to work out the craziness of the last week and get off the emotional roller coaster I've been on for the last few days. Mandy tells us that there will be record label execs and Grammy-winning producers, along with promoters, music publishers, and booking agents, oh my!

Every word she says lands on my brother like a precious gift. They feel heavy to me. Like pressure. Expectations. The possibility of screwing up and letting him down or damaging our chances at obtaining a record deal.

"You okay?" Gavin whispers from beside me.

I nod because I can't open my mouth for fear the truth would fall out. Or the drive-through dinner we had somewhere between Memphis and Nashville.

"This is you, boys," Mandy says when the door opens on the eighth floor. "See you downstairs in twenty."

As soon as they're gone and the doors close, she turns her attention to me. Either I'm really wiped from the past week and hallucinating, or she has multiple personality disorder. My vote is on the second one. Her once bright, gleaming eyes that greeted us in the lobby are now dark and menacing.

"Now, Daisy May, what are we going to do with you?"

"Um, hopefully not murder me and pay someone to toss my body in a Dumpster." I smirk, despite feeling a little afraid and a whole lot intimidated by her but refusing to let it show. "And it's Dixie Leigh. Not Daisy May."

She laughs, cackles actually, which I didn't know was a real thing until this moment. It's dawning on me that perhaps my initial assumptions weren't all that far off after all.

"Oh, I'm just teasing. I'm super-excited to see what you're going to play on your little fiddle tonight."

I arch a brow because one: no one calls Oz my little fiddle. And two: she may have my brother and Gavin convinced, but I'm not buying it. Clearly she isn't even trying to sell it to me anyway now that we're alone. A sickening truth settles onto my shoulders. Afton was right.

"I ran across a friend of yours in Austin."

She purses her lips as the elevator comes to a stop on the twelfth floor. "Oh yeah? Who might that be?"

"Afton Tate," I say, gesturing for her to step out of the elevator before me. I have no clue where our room is anyway.

"And what did Afton have to say?" I can see her fighting the urge to roll her eyes.

"He suggested we continue exploring our options. Any idea why that might be?"

We reach a room and I glance at the number for future reference. Eight twenty-nine. She opens the door and we step inside a luxury suite that I'm guessing is a lot nicer than what Gavin and Dallas have.

"Well, to be honest, Afton was still really young and new to the business when our paths crossed." She opens her closet while I set my bag down. "He couldn't see the big picture, couldn't grasp that not everyone plays fair."

"I didn't realize it was a game," I mumble under my breath.

"Everything is a game, Dixie." Suddenly she whirls on me, her expression inscrutable. "In every aspect of life, there are players and moves to be made. There are winners and there are losers."

"That's an interesting way to look at it, I suppose." I open my suitcase, underwhelmed at the wrinkled mess I find inside.

"It's the only way to look at it," she says haughtily. "Speaking of looking at things, some of the men here are going to make their decisions about Leaving Amarillo based on how much they enjoy looking at you. So let's make sure you're worth looking at, shall we?"

"Excuse me?"

"Here," she says, thrusting two dresses at me, one a black one with silver embellishments that looks as if it would barely fit my left leg and the other a champagne-colored sequined bodice top with a short ruffled, belted skirt that would be fine if it were four inches longer. "Try these on. Either look will work for tonight."

"I didn't realize playing dress-up was a part of this."

She shakes her head and gives me a sardonic smile. "I'll leave you to get changed. See you downstairs."

I hear it, the words she places the most emphasis on, causing them to echo around the room once I'm alone.

Get changed.

I stare at my road-weary self in the mirror. The ruffled dress is cute, kind of innocent and pretty. Well suited to the old me. After my night with Gavin, I feel like I have changed. So I shove my body into the black one, holding my breath as I force it on like a second skin.

Turning in the mirror I see someone else standing there. The dress is a few centimeters more fabric than lingerie and glimpsing the tops of my breasts and narrow valley between them, a part of me I don't show to the general public, ever, I flash hot all over. If I spread my legs too far apart even my inner thighs will be part of the show.

Oh-kay. Mandy Lantram is either high out of her mind or a madam trying to recruit me for a prostitution ring.

I turn and look over my shoulder to see how it looks from the back and gasp out loud.

There is no back. My ass is the only thing covered by the expensive-feeling fabric. My ink is on display and I feel proud of it for once, instead of the need to hide it. Taking a deep breath, I commit to this dress. I can do this. I can play and perform and . . . and who the hell am I kidding? I dig in my bag and find a black leather blazer-style jacket. Pulling it on, I feel a lot better. Hot and a little sweaty, but less exposed.

My hair is a lost cause as usual so I stick a few bobby pins in to pull the sides and front out of my face. Putting on some mascara and a shiny lip gloss, I decide this is the best it's going to get.

My favorite black boots with the skull zippers await me and I slide them on and repeat the method that I still believe brought us here to begin with.

I send up a silent prayer that this is it, for the band, for Dallas and Gavin and myself—the chance to stop living behind the shadows of a painful past and start living our dream.

Chapter 25

AFTER I'VE GOTTEN COMPLETELY READY, I CALL PAPA TO TELL him about the showcase. Once again I get his voice mail and contemplate sending Mrs. Larson over. But it's nearing his bedtime so I picture him dozing in his favorite chair listening to his talk radio station while I give his voice mail a brief rundown that includes Mandy and the interview with the *Indie Music Review* and the showcase.

When I step off the elevator, I see that the lobby is crowded with people congregating in small groups. I make my way down wishing that I'd gotten Oz out of the van instead of letting a stranger drive him to the showcase. Too late to worry about that now, though.

"There she is," Mandy calls out from across the room where she stands with Dallas and Gavin. Dallas is wearing jeans I don't recognize but suspect she bought him and a sleek black sport jacket. My brother is much more of a T-shirt and flannel with cowboy hat kind of guy so I'm almost as taken back by him as Gavin seems to be by me. "Gang's all here."

Gavin's doing his glarey, broody stare, which I now know is his *I-hate-that-I-want-to-fuck-you* face. He looks almost as uncomfortable in his all-black attire as I feel.

"Is that a tie you're wearing, Mr. Garrison?" I say, giving the skinny black tie a tug as we fall in behind Mandy and Dallas and head to the car.

"I don't know," he bites out at me. "Is that underwear you're wearing, Miss Lark?"

"Actually I'm not wearing any," I whisper conspiratorially to him. "There wasn't any room for them under this dress."

His eyes darken and the world around us falls away. He stalks past me without another word.

Well now he's just hurting my feelings.

I don't speak to anyone on the drive to the venue. I just watch out the window as the busy streets of Nashville blur by. Mandy makes a comment about my jacket but I don't bother engaging. Whatever her game is, I'm not playing.

This is a big night and it's not about me, or her, or even Gavin. It's bigger than each of us as individuals, more powerful than we could ever be on our own. This is about the band, about everything we've put in to the success of Leaving Amarillo. The sacrifices and the time and the dedication. Blood and sweat and tears and nights and days in vans and rehearsing for hours on end. Not just us, but Nana and Papa gave everything they had to support our dream, too. Playing helped heal us when we were three broken kids and I'm not letting anyone get into my head and get in the way of what we've worked so hard for.

I glance over at Gavin and watch him drum his thumbs hard against his knees. My gaze lingers on his hands and for a brief second I remember how they felt on me. But when he feels my stare and turns my way, I resume staring out the window.

No, nothing is going to get in the way tonight. Not even my stupid heart.

The Palace is a fairly large venue. It's half bar and restaurant, half stage and it's full of men and women in everything from expensive suits to country western attire. A band called Black Revolver is leaving the stage and thanking the audience. Mandy ushers us to a sign-in table as another band called Cold September introduces themselves and begins to play. Their sound is more alternative than what I expected at a showcase in Nashville but it's decidedly unique and I find myself paying more attention to them than Mandy's instructions.

"Dixie, did you hear me?" she says, her voice equal parts exasperated and annoyed.

"Um, no. Sorry." I have to shout a little over the music the closer we get to the stage. "What was that?"

"I said, you have ten minutes to mingle and introduce yourselves. Then you need to be ready to play your opener."

I nod. "Got it."

Dallas looks eagerly at all of us. "Same set list as last night, okay?" He looks like he wants us to put our hands in and do one of those sports huddle cheers but Gavin is just listening and nodding passively and I'm still partially distracted by the band that's playing. "Guys? We good?"

"Yeah, D. We got this," I say, reaching over and giving his hand a reassuring squeeze.

He smiles at me, and Mandy nudges him. "You're going to be amazing. You always are." She means him, not the band. Just him. It's obvious by the way she edges Gavin and me out with her shoulders, but I don't even care. His smile widens and I'm happy that he's happy.

"Okay, then," he says, clapping his hands together. "Let's get out there and meet some folks, shall we?"

I walk behind them, Gavin close beside me as if we're silently competing for who gets to stand farthest in the back of our little group.

The first table Mandy stops at holds two men in suits and an attractive woman in a jacket similar to mine. Mandy says their names and the label they're with, one with initials that I'm not familiar with. Dallas turns on the charm instantly, introducing each of us and giving them a short rundown on our band and the places we've played. I smile when they nod at me, but this is so not my area.

When I see that the woman at the table has returned her attention to the band onstage, I assume it's okay to do the same. They're older. These guys are probably in their forties or so. Before they finish their set, we follow Mandy to two men standing at a high-top table drinking liquor in short glasses.

"Brian Eades and Lowell Kirkowitz, meet Dallas and Dixie Lark and Gavin Garrison—or Leaving Amarillo. My newest clients." Mandy winks and flirts as they chat with us about our band, how we came to be and where we've played. Dallas fields most of the questions while Gavin and I nod along like puppets whose strings he's pulling.

Just as we start to walk away, moving on to another table, the one she called Brian, the younger of the two, catches my elbow. "Dixie, is it?"

I nod, looking over to Dallas, who doesn't notice I've been held up. "Um, yeah."

"I had a question for you. If you can spare a few minutes."

I look over to my group once more and see that only Gavin has noticed my absence. He says something to my brother and I give them both a little wave. Mandy gives me a thumbs-up, which I assume means Brian Eades moonlights as a serial killer.

"Sure. I guess I do."

He smiles and waits patiently for me to give him my full attention. After widening my eyes at Gavin, who looks as if he might like to set this entire bar on fire, I turn to Brian and lean close to hear what he's asking.

"Is there a difference?" is all I hear.

"I'm sorry," I call over the beat of bass and drums. "A difference between what?"

His blue eyes twinkle as if he's teasing me and I've missed the punch line. "The violin and the fiddle. Mandy said you played the fiddle and I was wondering if there was a difference between the two."

"Ah." I smile because this is a question I can actually answer. "Well, my grandpa used to say there was only one real difference."

"And what's that?" he says, leaning in to hear.

"You don't spill beer on a violin," I answer with a wink.

His laughs, a low rumble vibrating between us, and his blond stubbled jaw catches my attention. He's got a grown-up Justin Timberlake thing going for him and after Gavin slamming my dress, it feels nice to have someone be interested in actually having a conversation with me.

"But fiddles are beer-proof?"

Since he seems genuinely interested, I give him a real answer.

"I think what he really meant was, violins need to be kept in pristine condition. But with the type of music played on fiddles, it's the dents and the dings in the wood that give it a unique sound." He nods appreciatively so I continue my tutorial. "The main thing that makes them different is the type of music that's played on them. Classical music is played on the violin whereas when you're playing something more folksy, it's considered a fiddle." We step closer together so that I can speak without shouting. "Both have four strings, though there are differences in the setup—meaning the changeable parts, like tuners and the bridge. I like my bridge flatter, for instance, than most of the traditional violinists did at the school I attended in Houston."

"A flat bridge, got it," he says cheekily.

"It'd be easier to explain if I had Oz with me and could show you exactly what I'm talking about."

Brian side-eyes me. "Oz?" He takes a sip of beer and I grin.

"My fiddle. Yes, I named him. And no, you better not spill beer on him."

I tense a little in anticipation of his asking me why I named him Oz. I really don't want to go into detail about my parents and how playing brought color back to my world, but I don't want to lie or be rude, either.

Turns out, Brian doesn't get the chance to ask any more about Oz or even Houston, because strong fingers wrap my upper arms and tug before he says another word.

"Time to go." Glancing up at the livid expression on Gavin's face, I assume I've messed up and lost track of time. Looking over at the stage, however, I see that Cold September is still playing.

"Excuse me a moment," I say to Brian before Gavin practically drags me over to the darkened area beside the stage. I nearly trip over chairs in my path as his momentum propels me forward. Over Gavin's shoulder I see Dallas and Mandy chatting animatedly with an older gentleman who reminds me a little of Papa. Or maybe I'm just homesick.

Once we're out of sight of the audience, I jerk out of Gavin's grasp.

"What the hell, Gav? That felt a lot like a possessive boyfriend move and since you're neither possessive nor my boyfriend, care to tell me why you just pulled me away from an adult conversation like I was an errant child?"

"Adult conversations don't involve staring at your tits. And believe me, he was doing a hell of a lot more of that than listening to what you had to say."

"You're something else," I say with a shake of my head. "If I had ever in my life dared interrupt you with one of your groupies, I can only imagine how pissed you would've been."

Gavin scoffs as if I've said something inane. "I wouldn't have been pissed at all."

"How in the ever-loving hell would I possibly know that?" I don't know why this conversation is making me so angry, but it is. The hot lights above feel like laser beams melting my jacket to my skin. "I mean, last night I finally got it—what's so great that you feel the need to share it with the women who come asking for it. But Jesus, Gavin. How many of them have been paraded in front of me and I never said a word? That was a strictly professional conversation you just interrupted to act like a crazed caveman."

"Exactly. You never said a word," he says, tugging at the collar of his shirt. "And you know as well as I do that last night wasn't . . . wasn't like . . . . whatever."

"Oh, yeah? Well that clears it up. Glad we had this talk." I start to turn around and walk away because the last thing any record label executive wants to see at a talent showcase is band members arguing, but Gavin catches my wrist and pulls me to him.

"Wait a damn second. I need you to hear me, okay?"

I nod, rendered effectively speechless by the intoxicating combination of his smoldering stare and the needful lilt to his voice.

"Last night wasn't how it normally is for me. Neither was this morning. In fact, this morning, well, I don't even have a name for that."

Lovemaking, I think but don't say.

Gavin rakes a hand through his hair and continues. "And I care about you more than I have ever cared about any other woman, and it pisses me off that you don't seem to get that. The reason we never did any of . . . of *those things* before was because you mean more to me than that."

"And because of Dallas," I say, because I know it's true even if I don't know why exactly.

He nods. "Yeah. That, too."

My brain is processing his words at the speed of churning molasses but my heart and lungs seem to grasp them immediately. My chest swells between us, grazing his with the considerable effort it's taking to breathe normally.

"Bluebird," he begins, lowering his face to mine so that our noses are almost touching. "Seeing you in this dress is killing me because I know how other men are thinking about you when they see you in it. For instance, that Brian guy was practically salivating."

"He wasn't—"

"He was. He still is." Before I can check over my shoulder, Gavin lowers a hand to my hip and speaks low into my ear. "Give me a break, baby. I know we had our night and that's that, but you haven't even showered my scent off you yet. So forgive me for still maintaining an alpha male sense of ownership over your body. You're going to have to give me a little more time before I can stand idly by and watch another man wish he had what I did last night."

"And this morning," I add with a sly grin.

"And this morning." For a moment we're just sharing a secret smile, locked in a mutual memory I'm ready to relive as soon as humanly possible.

"Everything okay?" Dallas says, his voice bursting the lust bubble that had formed around Gavin and me.

"Yep," I say, taking a step backward as Gavin releases me. "Just going over the last-minute details."

"We straight, Garrison?" he asks Gavin without looking at me.

"As an arrow, Lark. Time to go on?" We look up to see Cold September starting their last number.

"Almost. Let's head backstage," Dallas says, casting a wary gaze that lingers over the two of us.

"Lead the way, big brother," I say, anxious to get this over with.

Sweat rolls down my back and I decide to play without the jacket. Once we're backstage, I remove it and set it on a chair. Mandy's eyes meet mine knowingly. She shifts her smug gaze to Gavin and lifts her chin.

Damn it. She knows.

A full-blown panic attack looms on the horizon as Dallas runs through the set list with us one more time.

She's been paying closer attention than Dallas has and now the one person I don't trust knows my biggest secret. She sits back like an ominous voyeur as we prepare to set up. I start to wonder how much she's seen, how long she's been watching. My stomach twists and turns while it sinks it that she has something on me—on me and Gavin, really.

"In every aspect of life, there are players and moves to be made. There are winners and there are losers."

I finally understand exactly what she means. She's the player with the advantage now. That advantage being knowledge of something I never intended for my brother to find out.

Question is, what will she do with it?

I don't have to wait long to find out how Mandy plans to use her leverage. We have twenty-five minutes from the time Dallas says, "Welcome, y'all. We're Leaving Amarillo, managed by Mandy Lantram. Thank you for having us," into the microphone until we sing "When You Leave Amarillo," an obscure song from long before our time that Dallas found on YouTube and had us put our unique twist on.

The butterflies come to life in my belly in perfect time with the tingling that begins in my toes and ends at my head. I tame the fluttering creatures with my notes, finding my peace on stage when they begin to dance to the music I'm creating instead of slamming around wildly.

The audience seems divided, more of them perking up and paying attention when we play "Whiskey Redemption" while several of them return to texting or chatting with the person next to them during our covers. I stop noticing them and focus on playing, on putting the passion Gavin poured into me into Oz. I live between the strings, playing as though my soul is trapped there and the only way to set it free is to play every note perfectly.

I almost miss a cue because Dallas notices that the standard country covers aren't holding anyone's attention and throws in a few more originals and a reworked R&B hit we've only rehearsed a few times. By the time it ends, I can't breathe. I've been so caught up, I don't know if we blew the room away or fucked it up completely.

Dallas thanks the audience and carries his guitar offstage. Gavin is behind me when we exit stage left, drumsticks tapping out my anxiety on one another. I want to grab them and throw them. I'm placing Oz in his case when Mandy meets us backstage.

"That was a decent show, guys," she says, giving my brother a pointed look. "It could've been better. I think I saw better than that in Austin, which is unfortunate since this is the show that actually matters."

"All of our shows matter," Gavin says evenly.

"Right, of course." Mandy stops in front of Dallas. "Thankfully each band gets to play an encore. So hopefully that will go a little smoother. I'd like to chat briefly about song choice for that one. But first, Dixie, can we talk?" She steps around my brother, gently placing a hand on his forearm. "Private girl chat, you understand," she says to Dallas and Gavin, dismissing them. I don't bother giving either one of them pathetic please-don't-leave-me eyes because there's no point. Gavin catches my gaze and I nod that I can handle her.

Once they're gone, I fold my arms over my chest and level her with an even stare. "What can I do for you, Ms. Lantram?"

"I don't think I need to point out that you were a little off out there." She smirks at me, making it clear that this goes without saying. "What I do want to say is that Dallas is an amazing talent, and it's about time you stepped aside and let him shine, don't you think?" She admires her reflection in the floor-to-ceiling mirror I didn't even realize was next to me, as if I'm no longer standing there.

"Or what?" I already know the answer, but for some sick reason I need to hear it out loud. From someone else.

"You know, it's funny. I asked your brother about you and Gavin when I first reached out to him in Austin."

I do my best to keep my expression placid, but I hate the sound of Gavin's name in her mouth. She runs her perfectly manicured fingers over Oz's case and I have the sudden urge to smack her hand the way Nana used to do mine when I reached for a cookie on the stovetop before they'd cooled.

"Want to know what he said?" She turns her full attention to me, and I shrug.

"Pretty sure you're going to tell me whether I want to hear it or not." Her plump red lips curve. "He said, and I quote, 'We're like family, the three of us. Gavin is like a brother to me and Dixie both. Always has been.' "

I arch a brow because in some ways, this is true. Gavin looks out for me, does his best to keep me safe, even from myself. "Your point?"

"My point is I'm pretty sure there's nothing incestuous happening between you and Dallas."

My face contorts in disgust. "Seriously?"

"But I see it, the way you and he look at each other. The drummer, I mean."

"I know what you mean. And frankly, it's none of your business."

"Isn't it?" Mandy places a finger over her mouth, mulling over whatever crazy game she's playing with me. Contemplating her next move, I suppose. "You know, if I saw a potential *situation* that could be hazardous to the well-being of my clients, part of my job is to bring it to their attention so that we can prevent it from affecting their performance or the future of their career."

Every word she says, every carefully veiled threat and insinuation, begins to deflate the fight right out of me.

"So what? You're saying that you noticed my gaze tends to linger on Gavin from time to time so you think it's vital you bring this up to my brother? Wouldn't that just be an added distraction at a crucial point in his career? And aren't Gavin and I technically your clients, too?"

"That can be amended easily enough. I'm starting to think that if band members are sneaking around behind his back, perhaps your brother would fare a bit better as a solo act."

My heart falters in my chest. "So you want me to quit my own band?"

"I would never suggest that. I would, however, suggest that you sit the encore out tonight. You seem a bit . . . *distracted* this evening. This venue is a bit more significant than the honky-tonks and back-alley bars you're likely used to."

My hands tremble at my sides. But not for the reason a bystander might expect if they'd witnessed our little dispute. The idea of not playing the encore number with my band causes me physical pain. The knowledge that Mandy has caught on to whatever it is that's happening between Gavin and me is unsettling. The possibility of her telling my brother and causing him and Gavin to get in a fight at the worst possible time is downright terrifying.

"You and Dallas are all I have. Do you get that?"

The band is all Gavin has. He needs Leaving Amarillo to be successful for his own reasons, just as Dallas and I do. But Gavin needs it to keep the darkness at bay, to keep him from sinking and submitting to it again. I can't help but wonder if I'll ever truly know what happened when I was gone. What I do know is that I won't be the one to hold the band back, and I won't be what causes my brother and Gavin to have an altercation before what might be the biggest night of our lives.

"Okay," I say more to myself than to her.

"Okay?" This time her surprise is genuine.

It's just one song, I tell myself. *We'll deal with everything else after the showcase.*

When I don't respond, Mandy nods and turns on her heel to leave. "Dixie?" she calls over her shoulder before leaving me alone to wallow in my decision.

"Yeah?"

The look she gives me is almost apologetic, or would be if it weren't marred by her self-satisfied arrogance. "For what it's worth, I think you're doing the right thing."

It feels like someone has my skull in a vise. The dull throbbing between my eyes is now unrelenting pressure at my temples.

"For who?" I ask softly after she's already walked away.

Chapter 26

I'M SEARCHING FOR DALLAS AND GAVIN, HOPING TO DISCUSS WITH them my sitting out the encore before Mandy drops the bomb about it, when I hear my brother's voice near a secluded corner behind the bar. The anger sharpening it surprises me.

"I have to find her. I'll talk to her and get this handled. This isn't a fucking game of musical chairs where one of us just can sit out every now and then."

"She isn't feeling well. She looked a little panicked up onstage, Dallas. As your manager, I have to advise you not to get into a dis-agreement with a band member in front of a room full of people who could make your career. If she wants to sit out the encore, you should respect that," Mandy purrs.

Bile rises in my throat and I'm just about to barge in on their moment and announce that I won't be sitting the encore out after all when Mandy continues.

"Look, I promised to be honest with you and I'm sorry if the truth hurts. But this might be for the best." Her voice has grown distant, as if she couldn't care less what he decides at this point. "You have the talent and the marketability to make it, to *really* make it. But how many major acts have you seen opening with a fiddle solo by Daisy Duke?" She answers before he can. "None. That's how many. None, Dallas." Her voice softens a bit but her words remain sharp, jagged-edged daggers stabbing me in my most sensitive places. "Your sister seems lovely and I can tell that you mean a great deal to each other. But she's holding you back. Plain and simple."

I gasp out loud, and then take an immediate step back in case they heard me.

"She's holding you back. Plain and simple."

I've been holding Dallas back. I'm the reason we've been passed on time and time again by managers and recording labels.

There it is—the cold, hard truth spoken out loud by an industry professional. Maybe I don't like her very much, but Dallas respects her and her opinion. It's not like she's saying these things to hurt me—she has no idea that I'm listening.

The bright neon dream I've held on to for so long, an image of Leaving Amarillo playing together, making a life of touring and playing the kind of music that was so prominent it was a physical presence in the home we grew up in, fades until it has evaporated completely.

The seeds of doubt planted long ago by curious bystanders paying amused attention to my opening act begin to grow and bloom in my stomach, sending a nauseating excess of fluid up from my throat. My head swims and I know, I know in that moment that she's right. And that I am going to vomit.

I've made it to the back of the building and placed my hands on my knees before I yak all over the place. Thankfully I haven't eaten so it's only dry heaves and not anything too substantial.

"Bluebird?"

Oh God. Of course. Of course he'd be the one to find me. A thousand tingling pinpricks dance across my skin. A slick sheen of sweat spreads across my forehead and down my neck as I stand.

"H-hey." I raise my head and see him crushing a cigarette with the heel of his boot. His tie and button-down shirt are undone. Beneath them he's wearing his "drummers hit it harder" T-shirt and I don't know whether to comment on the smoking or the shirt first.

"I thought you quit?"

"Correction. I quit smoking around *you.*"

"Well, that's hardly helpful since you've been mostly avoiding me since we got here." Except for the macho man scene he made with Brian, that is. I wipe my mouth with the back of my hand while working to regain my equilibrium. "I've never known you to be the type to duck and hide."

He gestures to where I'm standing. "And I've never known you to get nervous before a show. What's wrong?"

"Do you think I'm holding you back, Gav? You and Dallas, I mean." I can tell by his mildly offended expression that he has no idea what I'm talking about.

"What are you—"

"The band, Gav. Do you think the band would have made it by now if I wasn't a part of it?"

His forehead creases and his mouth angles downward. "Where the hell is this coming from? Somebody say something to you?"

I can't help but notice that he didn't answer my question. I shake my head, unable to voice the lie out loud. Traitorous tears gather in my eyes and give me away.

"Hey," he says softly. "Don't do that, Bluebird. Whatever it is that's psyching you out, let it go."

Suddenly everything I've held in all this time channels itself into a powerful cyclone of deep-seated frustrations aimed right at Gavin Garrison. Grief and guilt and loss intertwine, gaining momentum by the second. Narrowing my eyes, I shake my head.

"I wish it was that simple for me. It's not like I really have any other choice, though. Not really."

His dark brows thread inward as he takes two steps and closes the distance between us. "We still talking about the band, or am I missing something?"

"Do not play dumb with me, Gavin Garrison. We're past that and you know it." I lean back against the brick building and watch him process what I've said through my haze of hurt and anger.

"This is why I didn't want to do what we did." He pauses to point an accusatory finger at me. "*This* right here. You're pissed, and for reasons I'm not entirely sure of. Which only seems to be pissing you off more."

The lump of tears to come in my throat swells, constricting my airway. A sound halfway between a scream and a sob narrowly escapes my throat. Either that came from me or a wounded animal is nearby.

I didn't want to do what we did repeats a thousand times in my mind.

It hurts, it hurts so bad it takes all my strength to remain upright. A shard of glass carving out my heart would feel better. Would be a welcome relief. My breath comes in gasps.

"Sorry I forced you to do something you didn't want to do," I spit out at him. My hands shoot forward, my palms striking him against his broad chest. "I fucking hate that shirt."

He grabs my wrists with one hand and wrenches them into the tight space between our bodies while bracing his other one beside my head. I'm a willing hostage between brick and Gavin's solid body.

"You didn't force me to do shit." His breath tickles the side of my face. "And don't hate on the shirt. Especially now that you know it's telling the truth."

My pulse races at the reminder, not that I could've possibly forgotten. The memory of last night has played on repeat behind my eyes nearly every second since.

Shoving myself against him in a weak attempt at pushing him away, I try my best not to inhale his intoxicating scent. Masculine soap, a faint hint of tobacco, and undertones from the cologne I bought him for his birthday.

"You're an asshole."

"True, but completely beside the point at the moment. How about you tell me what's really got you so upset and we go from there?"

My chest rises and falls between us, barely grazing his as I pull in much-needed breaths.

"I-I don't even know how to explain it exactly."

"Try." The force of the command in his voice is only half as harsh as the punishing glare in his gaze.

"Okay." I recall what Mandy said about band members not needing to fight in front of the influential audience members inside. I don't want to lie to him, but the last thing I need is Gavin defending my worth to Dallas or arguing publicly with Mandy. Settling on a lie of omission, I pause to lick my lips and lift my chin. "I overheard someone saying the band would be better off if I wasn't a part of it. Not just anyone, either. Someone who would know—someone who matters."

"Dixie. Listen to me." He leans closer and I feel the anger from where I stand. "Whoever said that is a fucking moron. You are what makes this band. You are why people stop drinking or texting or whatever the hell it is they're doing and pay attention. Don't ever let me hear you say that we would be better off without you again. Understood?"

I hear myself let out a breathless sound and then a whimpered, "Okay," while still locked in his stare.

"Do not make those noises. Unless you want our second time to be in this alley."

We're so close that his lips brush mine as he speaks and I can't help but smile against them. "Technically it would be our fourth time. Our second time was in the shower. The third time was in that chair by the window. Try and keep up."

His hands fall to my backside and his fingers press into my flesh. I'm not sure if I rock my hips forward or he does, but the part of me that's throbbing with need brushes against his obvious arousal.

"You're going to get us into trouble, Dixie Leigh."

I shiver when his head drops onto my shoulder and his teeth graze my neck. "I think maybe I like trouble," I whisper. "A lot."

It feels like home in his arms, safe and warm, protected from the judging eyes of an unfamiliar audience and Mandy's painfully honest observations. The deep cadence from Gavin's rumble of low laughter tickles me behind the ear and I squirm. Turning my head when a metal door clangs shut I see that we're no longer alone.

Straightening myself upright immediately, I watch Gavin take a necessary but excruciating step backward. Dallas's horrified anger is obvious enough to be a tangible thing even from five feet away. His fists are clenched at his sides when he stalks over to us. The sickening fear that those fists might be about to slam into his best friend's face sends my body into panic mode.

"What in the ever-loving fuck is going on out here?"

I barely hear him over the pounding of my heart. An inferno of fiery rage flares in his face and heats my skin with the shame of being caught like this.

"Nothing," I answer quickly, ignoring Gavin's entreating gaze. "I wasn't feeling well. I got sick and was upset about . . . about what I heard Mandy tell you. Gavin was comforting me."

Dallas's rage is somewhat diluted by guilt. His eyes soften, cooling a few degrees when they land on me. "Dix, she didn't mean that. I talked to her, explained. She—"

"She said I was holding you back, Dallas. Maybe she's right." I shrug, despite the soul-stinging pain of knowing she might be.

"What happened to her getting us, D? I thought she liked our sound. Dixie is damn sure a part of that sound." Gavin's stance has changed and now he has clenched fists, too.

I realize that I just inadvertently revealed that Mandy was the one who'd upset me a second too late.

"It's more complicated than that. Dixie only heard part of the conversation." Dallas shoots a fleeting look of sympathy at me before turning a hardened glare on Gavin. "Speaking of complicated, in the future, if *my little sister* is upset, you tell her to come talk to me. And from now on, you comfort her from arm's fucking length."

"I don't take orders—not even from you, Dallas. And right now, I'm not real happy about the way you let your new friend run her mouth about *your little sister*. And for the record, she's not anybody's little anything and she's standing right here so how about not talking about her like she isn't."

My brother squares his shoulders and steps right into Gavin's personal space without apology. "You got something to say to me, Garrison? Because I thought we'd already talked about this. I thought I was pretty clear the first time, but maybe you need clarification."

Gavin gives my brother a smirk that morphs seamlessly into a sneer. "Don't bow up on me, D. You know how I feel about that shit. Or maybe you're the one who needs a reminder."

Oh God. I'm not sure what they're referring to specifically—half of what they've said makes absolutely no sense to me—but my female intuition is on high alert. This is about to go so wrong so fast. I'm practically being forced backward by the surge of testosterone flowing violently between them. I can't be sure if I'm holding Dallas or the band back musically, but causing fights between him and Gavin will definitely send all three of us crashing down in blazing flames of failure.

"Stop. Just stop." I move to stand between them. "It was nothing. I got my feelings hurt and I really don't feel well. I'm going to sit the encore out, D. You do your thing and if anyone is interested in us, we'll discuss whether or not I still need to be a part of this band. Maybe I'll be your opener when you're on your worldwide tour." I nudge my brother in hopes of softening him before he and Gavin come to blows.

His gaze lowers to mine and he shakes his head, continuing as if I haven't spoken. "You're a part of this band, Dixie Leigh. You always have been and you always will be. And it's time for us to go on. So let's go."

Gavin is flicking his lighter at his side and I know it means he needs to channel his angry energy, needs to pound out his frustration on his drums instead of on my brother's face. I'm holding them up—holding them back.

"I'm serious, Dallas. Let's not make this some big, dramatic thing. It's one song. Go. I'll be cheering y'all on in the audience." I nod encouragingly, trying to convey to my brother that I'm really okay. And I am. Mostly. The truth is, even though sitting out the encore causes my chest to ache as if it's been hollowed out like a woodwind instrument, I need to know. I need them to do the encore without me. If this is their big break, I can't stand the thought of being what keeps them from getting discovered. So I'm going to step aside and give them a shot to do this on their own.

"Guys? It's time." Mandy's head pokes out of the metal door and she waves a hurried hand at us. "Let's go."

"Dixie?" My brother looks wounded, as if I'm hurting him instead of helping him.

"Go, Dallas. I promise, I'm okay. I think I let my dinner sit too long and it just isn't settling well. Y'all go ahead."

His eyes narrow as he takes in what I know is probably my less than stellar appearance. I'm not being entirely honest, but Mandy's words did make me feel ill.

Watching the uneasy acceptance of my decision in Dallas's eyes causes my mind to drift back in time to when I was eleven and Dallas and Gavin were going climbing at a quarry outside of town. There was a man-made lake and they planned to climb the highest cliff and jump. I was terrified—heights were never really my thing either. But I went along to make sure neither of them broke their neck. In the end, they both jumped, fist pumping and acting like they'd conquered the world afterward. I'd sat on the sidelines, rolling my eyes and acting as if I weren't impressed even though I was. Just as I was about to tell Dallas I was going to jump after all, having finally worked up the courage, the boys announced that they were ready to go home and that was that. We left, my moment had passed. And just like back then, it passes again.

"Gavin?" My brother asks with a slight tilt of his head, having moved on from scrutinizing me. "We doing this or what?"

Gavin pauses beside me. "I need a minute." My brother hits him with a hard look of disapproval. "I said I need a minute," he says through gritted teeth.

His words form a fist that grips my heart and squeezes it tightly.

Once Dallas has left, shaking his head and muttering curses under his breath, Gavin turns to me.

"Why are you doing this? Is it really because of what that ma-nipulative bitch said or because of me? Because of us?"

"Can there really ever be an us, Gavin? Kind of sounded like you and my brother have already decided against it. Guess I didn't get a vote."

Regret and sorrow are etched into his features when I reach up to smooth them. He says nothing, but I can see it. Being with me is a betrayal of my brother. I don't know why exactly, I just know that it is. I can't ask that of either of them, but I can't deny my feelings anymore, either. I can't keep doing this with them, being a ticking time bomb waiting to explode all over their dreams and destroying their future.

"I wish I could explain—" he begins but I cut him off by placing my fingers against his full firm lips.

"I can't go back," I whisper softly, praying my voice is loud enough for him to hear because this is all I've got left. I can hardly believe what an idiot I was to think I could channel ten years' worth of feelings into one night. My need blurred my vision until I was able to lie to myself I guess. "Thank you . . . for our night together. I know that's all it was for you, and I will never regret it. But right now, Dallas needs you and I need to let him have his shot without stand-ing in the way or complicating things with his drummer. He needs you to have his back out there."

"Come with me. We'll do this last song like we normally do. Everything else we can figure out later." His warm hand slips into mine, lacing our fingers together, and I'm tempted. But I saw what almost happened between them and I heard what Mandy said loud and clear and I know I have to take a step back. For now at least.

"I've already figured it out. Go. I'm fine. I promise." Lifting onto the tips of my toes, I place the whisper of a kiss on his cheek. "Knock 'em dead, drummer boy."

"After the show, we're going to talk. And then we're going to talk to your brother and our new manager." Disdain hardens his voice on the last word.

"Gavin, I—"

"No, Bluebird. Don't. Don't talk yourself out of what you want. Right now I couldn't give a shit about what Mandy Lantram or anyone else says. You always think of everyone else. I want you to decide what *you* want during this show. If you want to be in the band or not, I want you to decide for you, only for you and not for anyone else. Understood?"

I nod, knowing full well what I want. The band is everything, and without it, I feel lost.

The metal door clangs open again, startling me. "You coming or what?" My brother's voice is razor sharp as his eyes zero in on Gavin's hand in mine.

"Coming." Gavin nods and once my brother is back inside, he pulls me in close. "After the encore, wait for me. Okay?"

I nod again, but when he lets go of my hand and his fingertips graze my palm, pulling away from mine, I know I'm letting him go in more ways than one.

Chapter 27

THE STAGE LIGHTS ARE STILL DOWN WHEN I FIND AN EMPTY SEAT on the edge of a front aisle. I don't even know what song Dallas finally chose so I have no idea what to expect. The woman next to me is smiling at something on her phone when the gentle sound of Gavin's cymbal sends shivers across my skin. Dallas plays a few chords and I recognize the song immediately. It's called "The End" and it's fitting since they're the last act to play.

The lights come up and I see them on the stage, the two men I love more than anyone else in the world—with the exception of Papa. In this moment, I am that girl again. The one sitting on the ledge wishing she'd jumped instead of chickening out. But at least this way I will know if I'm holding the band back from making it big.

Over the past year we've speculated a lot about possible issues. Our love of the classics, our refusal to conform or play pop music, even our look has come under Dallas's scrutiny when it came time to discuss possible changes. But it was never even suggested that Oz and I could be the cause. We seem like the obvious answer now.

Emotion swells like soaked cotton balls in my throat and my vision blurs behind moisture as I watch Dallas play the guitar solo.

His voice is different from the original lead singer's and he goes with it, making it his own instead of trying to emulate someone he could never be.

I'm filled with pride and love to the point of tearing right in half when I see how the audience's demeanor has changed. Nearly every single member is sitting upright, focusing their rapt attention on the stage, captivated by the energy and the uniqueness of Dallas and Gavin.

And as happy as I am for them, not being a part of it feels like having an appendage ripped brutally from my body. The hollow ache in my chest is so acute, I half expect to see a gaping bloody wound where my heart should be.

My gaze lands on Gavin, and the sight of him playing his heart out, completely focused and in the moment, leaves me gasping for breath. Now that I've allowed myself to look at him, I couldn't tear my gaze away from him for all the money in the world. My heart pounds out a rhythm identical to the one he's playing. It doesn't even seem possible, but somehow, getting to really watch him like this, I am falling even more in love with him. Surrounded by a room full of strangers, I am lost in the memory of him making love to me, my senses re-creating our night together in gloriously vivid details.

He is alive out there, behind his drum kit, the man behind the beat. He's the heart of the band, beating steadily, needing this to survive. I silently shame myself for daring to do anything that could take this away from him.

Dallas sings the last few lyrics a cappella and I feel them all the way down to my soul. I see us, as kids, the three of us so lost and yet somehow not alone because we held each other together—the bonds we formed became our home, our safe place.

When they finish, there is applause, but I'm not a part of it. My hands are otherwise occupied, one over my mouth to keep me from screaming wildly for them and the other over my heart because it's so completely broken.

I reach in my bag to grab my phone so that I can snap a quick picture of them onstage, something I normally can't do since I'm up there with them. Ignoring my notifications, but noticing that there are several I need to check later, I take a picture of them as Dallas tells the crowd good night. I'm about to head backstage to tell them how amazing they were, when a hand lands unexpectedly on my lower back.

"That was great, but it would've been better had you been up there with them." The voice in my ear belongs to the owner of the hand. It's male and low and far more intimate than the moment warrants.

I turn to see Brian Eades giving me a sympathetic smile.

"Yeah, um, I wasn't feeling well. Decided to sit this one out." I try to step out of his reach but he walks with me toward the stage.

"Their loss," he says, winking as if we share a secret.

"Nah. They did great without me." My lips attempt a grin but only half my heart is in it.

"Hey, Bluebird. You ready?"

Tingles explode across my skin the moment I see the fierce glint in Gavin's eyes. He's pissing on me a little, marking his territory in a way he shouldn't, but I can't even muster up any fake feelings about being offended. I give Brian a parting smile and make my way to Gavin.

My brother is standing farther away from us but not out of my line of sight. He's shaking hands with the man Mandy introduced us to along with Brian.

I follow Gavin outside, feeling much more at ease when I can feel his warmth.

The driver steps out but I wave him off because I just need some fresh air right now.

"I know what you did back there, and I saw your face when we were done."

I don't respond. There's no use in lying and I don't have the words to explain what it felt like sitting there watching them perform without me.

"I don't care what anyone says. You aren't sitting out ever again."

My chest heaves noticeably either from my pounding heart or the effort it takes to breath over the pain threatening to surface.

"Damn it, Dixie. Say something. I *saw* you. What that did to you. Look at me."

My eyes move upward to meet his gaze. "Y-you did wonderful. Both of you. The encore was amazing."

"The encore was fucking *wrong*."

I shake my head. "It wasn't. The two of you were electric up there. You had the entire room captivated."

Gavin frowns at me. "I didn't notice. The only person I could see was you."

It feels so good to hear, so much better than the pain of not performing with them that I lift up on my toes and kiss him without thinking.

Firm hands grip my shoulders and move me backward a step. "We can't do this, Bluebird. You know that we can't." His voice is a barely coherent groan, but his eyes say something completely different. I drop my bag on the ground and let my hands slide into his hair.

"I know. You're right. I know." Those are the last words out of my mouth before I lift up to kiss him again.

What begins as a sweet gesture of love and understanding— maybe even of apology—quickly turns into the wettest, dirtiest most intense kiss I've ever experienced. We are lips and tongues and teeth fighting to get closer, to mark and claim. When he growls into my mouth and lifts me onto his waist, my legs wrap around him and I'm ready—ready for him to open the back door and take me in the backseat in more ways than one.

"Gavin," I whisper when his mouth descends on my neck.

"Fuck me," he says more in surrender than in demand. His tongue traces the outer shell of my ear before his teeth graze the sensitive skin below it as if he's contemplating taking a bite. "Why do you have to taste so damn good?"

I shiver in his arms, and he sets me down.

He's shaking his head softly side to side even as he rests his forehead on mine. I wrap my arms around his waist, attempting to pull him closer using his deliciously defined hip bones but he steps back.

He's breathing hard and still shaking his head when he steps up onto the curb. "I promised him. I fucking promised."

I look up at him from beneath my lashes. "Gavin, life is not black-and-white, right and wrong. *Nothing* about what we did is wrong. At least it didn't feel wrong to me . . . It still doesn't." My heart begs me to shut up, to stop this before I put it in a vulnerable position it isn't prepared for. It's still reeling from watching them play without me and hasn't had time to suit back up for round two. "Do you regret it? Do you regret me?"

Sitting out the encore has taught me about the sting of regret, about the weight of finality that settles onto your chest when you realize there's nothing you can do to change what did or didn't happen. You just have to accept it and try to move forward carrying whatever scars it left on you. I'm terrified he's about to give me another one I don't have room for or the strength to carry.

His brow dips as he glares hard enough to cause me to spontaneously combust where I stand, but he says nothing.

"Just tell me," I demand, my voice rising uncontrollably. "Fucking tell me. Do. You. Regret. Me?"

Lust deepens in his gaze, giving way to anger. When he finally speaks, it's through a clenched jaw.

"Remember what you said? About being the one I fall asleep needing, the one I want to wake up with, and the one I can't stop thinking about?"

I nod because it's all I can do when he steps closer and scrambles my brain.

"You are, Bluebird. You already fucking are. You always have been."

My entire world shifts at his confession. The band, the pressure, my brother, even the music fades, breaking every bond I've ever made to this world. There is only Gavin, only us. Illusions of grandeur are blinding as they come to life behind my eyes. What we have is so much stronger now that I know I'm not alone in this.

He's still glaring down at me, his eyes memorizing me as if seeing me for the first time. I pull my lower lip between my teeth and watch him watching me. We have everything to lose, but somehow that doesn't mean what it once did.

I reach for him, to hold him, to kiss and console him, to tell him everything. That I am in love with him, that I'll never sit out again, that he is so much more to me than he realizes. But I don't get the chance.

"Garrison! What the fuck, man?" My brother's voice lands on both of us like a sledgehammer shattering our perfect moment.

Gavin whirls around to where Mandy and Dallas are charging

toward us. His hands go up and he takes a step away from me. "Easy, Dallas. It doesn't mean what you think it does."

It doesn't mean what you think it does?

What does he think it means? What does it mean? The questions sting my mind like angry hornets. The neon lights blur on the darkened street before me.

"You two bailed on me in there. We should be meeting people and introducing ourselves. Not hiding outside."

"If Dixie was feeling so ill she couldn't perform, I think it's time to call it a night." Gavin stands like a proper doorman ignoring my brother's obvious annoyance.

Mandy goes first and Dallas follows. I wait a beat, picking up my previously discarded purse and allowing my eyes to meet his with an unspoken uncertainty.

Once we're all in the car and Mandy gives the driver the address to our hotel, I feel my purse vibrating and remember the notifications I meant to check earlier. Both of the guys are sitting with clenched jaws staring out the windows. Mandy is smiling to herself and I'm pretty sure she's checking her makeup in the driver's rearview mirror.

Pulling out my phone I see several missed calls from Mrs. Lawson's number. Probably more updates on her cats, but she left a few voice mails so I press the button to listen to them anyway.

The first one is so shrill and panicked that I can barely understand it. But the second one is crystal clear.

Papa had a heart attack. She found him in the front yard early this morning, and he's at St. Anthony's in critical condition.

"We have to go home," I say, feeling the phone slip from my grasp. "Now."

Chapter 28

THE DRIVE FROM NASHVILLE WAS A BLUR. I DON'T THINK I SPOKE A single word. After the initial chaos of deciding if the three of us could afford a flight and realizing none of them left until eight the next morning anyway, we loaded into Emmylou and hit the interstate. I think they might have tried to get me to eat and I know I took a drink of someone's gas station Big Gulp at some point, but that's about all I can remember.

I was hurt and upset but I can't remember why. I can't remember anything. Nothing feels consequential enough to matter.

My thoughts are muddled in a foggy tunnel of fear and uncertainty.

The intensive care unit waiting room is bathed in the grayish blue of the cloudy afternoon. Faint hints of human waste and the overpowering sting of strong antiseptic hit me hard, like running into a wall. We made it a few hours earlier than we should've arrived had we been obeying traffic laws. Dallas finds a nurse in charge and we're told that a doctor will be in to speak with us during afternoon rounds, until then, all we can do is sit by Papa's bed and watch machines breathe for him and drip fluid into him. They beep out a rhythm but for the first time, I don't hear music. I hear finality. I hear time passing.

Moments and breaths measured, rushing us toward the end and reminding me that there isn't a promise of tomorrow. We assume so much—take so much for granted. If I could break out from beneath the heavy weight of the shock, I'd launch myself into Gavin's arms. I'd announce to my brother and anyone who would listen that I love him today, I loved him yesterday, and I will love him until machines count out my last heartbeats. But right now, with Papa looking frail and ten years older than I remember beneath a thin white sheet, it all feels selfish and indulgent. Loving, having love, being loved. Like any energy I spend on something as mundane as showering or eating is wasted when I could be focusing it on willing him to be okay.

So we sit, Dallas, Gavin, and I, in a lopsided triangle around Papa's hospital bed with the beeping and CNN playing with black-and-white captions at the bottom of the flat-screen television in the corner of the ceiling because no one has bothered to change it or turn up the volume. There are only supposed to be two visitors at a time, but somehow Gavin works his charm and is allowed to stay, for which I am grateful. Nurses come in and nurses go out, asking us our names, introducing themselves, and taking Papa's never-changing vitals.

Lunchtime comes and goes and no one comes to explain what's going on. Dallas calls Mrs. Lawson and she cries and carries on about her cats and how they predicted a tragedy was coming.

"She found him near the mailbox, said he was on his back and gurgling fluids but nonresponsive. She called 911 and they tried to instruct her on how to perform CPR but she couldn't clear the foam from his mouth."

Dallas is relaying their conversation and I'm nodding because it's all I can manage. He might as well be punching me in the stomach. It wouldn't feel much different.

"It took the ambulance about twenty minutes to get there and the paramedics were still working on him when they pulled away. Mrs. Lawson said to keep her posted."

More nodding.

I'm fighting off unconsciousness when a tired-looking blond man in a white coat steps into the already overcrowded room. Dallas has nodded off with his head on his fist and Gavin is slumped in his chair.

"Miss Lark?"

I stand, snapping to attention like a soldier caught napping on post. "Yes, sir."

"Are you his daughter?"

"Granddaughter. He raised my brother and me after our parents died in a car accident." I gesture to Dallas. I have no idea why I just blurted all of that out, but I'm functioning on autopilot, recalling information and reciting it on command.

He shakes my hand firmly and I notice his eyes are shot through with red and lined with heavy rings even though he's probably only thirty or so "Dr. Paulsen. I wasn't here when your grandfather was brought in—Dr. Rasheed was—but I oversaw all of his tests."

"Tests?"

"Scans mostly. Your grandfather suffered a heart attack. We found a ninety percent blockage, and after several scans it appears that he currently has little to no brain activity. A neurologist will be in tomorrow to speak with you about the specifics of his results."

That's supposed to mean something—something permanent, but my sleep-deprived mind can't determine what that is right away. I'm waiting to hear the part where he tells me the solution, the procedure or surgery or whatever that's going to fix it, fix him.

Dr. Paulsen gives me a sympathetic smile that I'm too tired to return. A lump forms in my throat and drives tears to my eyes.

"So it's bad?" My voice barely makes it out.

"It was a severe heart attack, and frankly, there's no way to know for sure how long he went without oxygen."

"Meaning?"

"Meaning even if he wakes up, he will most likely remain brain dead."

My mind immediately rejects this. I look over at my granddad and decide that he's just tired, just sleeping extremely heavily. This man is wrong, and anyway, he never said that he was sorry and isn't that what people say if something is really this bad?

Papa's chest heaves up and down and I ignore the knowledge that the machine over his nose and mouth is forcing this to happen. He's breathing. He's alive. He's not brain dead. The last conversation we had on the phone is not the last one we will ever have.

"I was supposed to make him meat loaf," I choke out before the man marks some things on his chart and slides it loudly into the plastic slot at the foot of Papa's bed.

The doctor continues, oblivious to my meltdown. "We'll keep an eye on his vitals and move him to avoid bedsores, but I have to be honest because it's my job. There are some hard decisions in your future. For instance, you may have nurses asking you about a DNR and you may want to consider signing it."

"I don't even know what that is."

"A DNR is a Do Not Resuscitate order. If you sign it, they'll place a purple bracelet on him and a note in his chart so that should he go into cardiac arrest—as many patients in this condition do—they won't put his body through the trauma of trying to bring him back. We'll simply let him go."

We'll simply let him go. The words ring out in my mind as if he'd shouted them, when in reality he's barely speaking above a whisper.

"I was supposed to make him meat loaf," I say again, because I am stuck now, like a broken record with a hitch on the last conversation we had.

"Yes, well, I'll let you speak with your family and if you or your brother have any questions, I'll come by again tomorrow during morning rounds." Another weary attempt at a smile and the universal head tilt of sympathy and he's gone, leaving me alone to try to remember everything he just said and how to relay it to Dallas.

"I'm sorry," Gavin says, startling me because I thought everyone was asleep.

"Not your fault," I say, lowering myself into the chair I was practically becoming one with before the doctor came in.

"Get some sleep now, Bluebird. I heard enough to get the gist. I'll explain it to Dallas when he wakes up."

A tiny hopeful part of my brain, one that still believes in happily ever after despite a lifetime's worth of evidence to the contrary, tells me that I'm already asleep. That this is a horrible nightmare I'm having and when I wake up, this will have all been my mind playing tricks on me and Papa is fine. So I let that part push me over the edge into unconsciousness where everything is okay.

M orning," I hear someone say as I blink myself awake. My attempt at returning the sentiment comes out muffled. Sunlight streams into a gray room with a white bed. An empty white bed.

"Where is he?" I'd stand but my legs are cramped and sore from being tucked beneath me.

"They took him down for some tests," Dallas informs me. He looks as exhausted as I feel.

Gavin's chair is empty. "Where's—"

"I sent him to the house to check on things. I told him to man the fort and we'd call if we needed anything."

I nod and attempt to swallow the desert that has taken up residence in my mouth.

"A neurologist whose name I couldn't pronounce came in this morning. He told me what Gavin said the doctor told you yesterday, about the EEG."

I see it, the severity of these results, in my brother's slumped shoulders and slightly bowed head, but I'm not ready to discuss it.

"How long have I been asleep?"

"Nearly sixteen hours. Dixie, you were past exhaustion. I know our schedule has been rough lately and maybe I've been pushing too hard. I was—"

"Stop. I'm fine. Tell me what else the doctor said. Anything new?"

Dallas leans forward in his chair, angling closer to me and giving me the same look Dr. Paulsen did. "Dix, I know this is hard and believe me, if anyone knows what a fighter Papa is, it's me. But I think we need to discuss—"

"You want to sign the DNR," I say, cutting him off because I knew he would think that was best the moment the doctor mentioned it.

The stubble-covered knot in the center of my brother's neck jerks upward as he swallows. "I think Papa would hate this, hate having people turning him and wiping his ass. Seeing him lying there like that, knowing he'll never be the same again, knowing the rest of his life will be like this, I can't imagine why we'd want to prolong this. I think it's what he would want."

"He'll be a marked man, Dallas. They'll put this let-him-die bracelet on him and it just feels . . . wrong—like we're giving up on him." The words barely make it out over my raw throat and the boulder of emotion wedged in it.

Dallas's eyes shine like the surface of a lake in the sun. I can't remember ever seeing him cry. He won't now, but if he blinked hard enough the tears would fall. "Okay. We won't sign it then. Not until you're ready."

My brother doesn't argue with me, which I appreciate because I don't have the strength for a debate right now. And I know he's right—Papa would be so angry knowing we'd let him lie there undignified this way. *"I'm a veteran, for God's sake,"* he would tell us if he could. Dallas comes over and wraps his arms around me, holding me and whispering how much he loves me and how sorry he is that this happened over and over.

"I was supposed to make him meat loaf," I say, because it's all I can say. It's all I have left, the hope that he'll wake up and I'll get to make him meat loaf and life will continue on as it is supposed to.

Four days pass before Dallas puts his foot down and tells me to go the hell home or he is checking me into the psych ward. He's not kidding. I heard him telling Gavin he has twenty-four hours to figure out a way to get me home or he's scheduling an evaluation here at the hospital.

I haven't really eaten anything substantial and I haven't showered. I look like the scary movie version of myself and I know it—I see it in the mirror when I use the tiny bathroom attached to Papa's room.

"Just for one night, Bluebird. Come home, take a shower, eat an actual meal, and get a good night's rest in your own bed. Then I'll bring you right back here," Gavin promises me day after day.

He and Dallas have been rotating shifts, and seeing how desperate they both seem to get me home, I realize they haven't been coming to watch over Papa. They've been coming to keep an eye on me.

I've brushed his thinning silver hair, trimmed his fingernails, and shaved his jaw. Papa's eyelids flicker from time to time, mostly when I'm telling him about Austin, and when we're alone, about Gavin. Aside from that, not much has changed. I've played Oz twice and so far no one in the hospital has complained. After the first time, I thought Papa squeezed my hand but the doctors both said that was just a muscle reflex and didn't mean anything.

When a nurse comes in and begins asking me all kinds of questions about myself—have I eaten, can she get me something to eat, do I ever think about hurting myself—I know she isn't just making conversation. Dallas is worried about me and he finally consulted a professional.

When she leaves, I look over at Gavin, who is the current watchdog on shift. He's snoring softly in the chair beside me. I lean on his shoulder, letting my head fall onto it and wrapping my arms around his. He slides his hand in mine and gives me a gentle squeeze.

"Okay," I tell him quietly. "Let's go home."

Chapter 29

FOR SOME REASON, I EXPECTED THE HOUSE TO BE MUSTY, LAYERS of dust accumulating on coffee tables and furniture like the abandoned ones you see in movies. But it isn't. The pale yellow curtains are open and even the weathered wooden floors are swept. The house is neat and tidy. Warm. Lived in. Dallas and Gavin have been taking good care of it.

I run my hand along the edge of the buttercream and blue floral-patterned couch, stirring memories of my childhood. That couch has been so many things to the three of us over the years. A protective shield during hide-and-seek, a safe base during games of tag, and where I sat tucked between my grandparents while we played board games in the years before we finally begged enough until they bought a television set.

It's been someone's bed recently. There is a blanket and pillow stacked neatly on one end of it. Gavin, I assume. Dallas would probably sleep in his old room, but Gavin always slept on the couch when he spent the night.

I hear Gavin turn on the shower and assume it's for him, but while I stand staring at the old Wurlitzer where Nana taught me and

Dallas to play, Gavin reappears in the doorway. My fingers drift over a few keys just heavily enough to make faint sounds. C, D, E. The first three notes I learned to play. I can still hear Nana's voice.

"C, D, E, Dixie Leigh. One, two, three."

"Shower's ready for you, babe. Hand me those clothes and I'll throw them in the wash."

Looking down, I realize I don't even remember putting on the jeans and T-shirt I'm wearing. Without argument or putting up a fight about being a grown woman, I strip my clothes off and hand them over. Gavin disappears down the hall and I make my way to the bathroom. The room is filled with steam from the steady rush of hot water. I'm grateful that I can't see my reflection through the thick layer of condensation gathered on the mirror.

Bracing my arms against the wall once I've stepped inside, I let the water sear the past few weeks from my skin. I've been carrying it all for so long and I can't anymore. I wash quickly, thinking about the many things I'll say to Papa if he wakes up. For one, I'm never leaving again. I can get a job in town and settle for playing music on the back porch for him every night. For two, I'm going to yell at him for not taking better care of himself. And then I'm going to sit and listen until he has told me every single thing he knows about music and life. Every day with him was a lesson, and there was so much more I wanted to learn.

Some tiny section in the landscape of my mind realizes that if Papa passes, he'll finally be with Nana, which is where he's wanted to be all along. He won't have to sit alone in this house anymore, missing her. They were quite a pair—a team, they used to say. There's no denying he's been half the man he used to be since she died.

I step out of the shower and wrap the towel around me that Gavin must have set out. Sweeping the moisture from the mirror with my hand, I stare at my reflection. Papa would be ashamed of me, wasting away, grieving as if he were already gone.

He didn't let Dallas or me spend a single moment moping when we found out Nana was sick. He sat us down and told us to make sure every single day of the rest of her life was filled with laughter and happiness—that we didn't mope or cry or feel sorry for ourselves. We did the best we could—holding our tears until we were allowed to release them at her funeral six months later. Even Papa couldn't deny us that. His eyes were wet as well that day and he didn't meet me outside for my lesson for a month. But I kept going out there, same as always, until one morning he joined me after his coffee.

"You're pretty like a flower and tough like a weed, Dixie-girl," he said before imparting a few pointers about relaxing my hands during a piece I was learning to play by Pachelbel.

Looking in the mirror, I don't know about the flower part, but tough I can definitely work with. I owe it to him to be tougher than I have been.

After I slip into a clean pair of well-worn striped pajama pants and a tank top, I run a comb through my wet hair and meet Gavin in the kitchen.

Seeing him standing there, making macaroni and cheese on the stovetop from a blue box—my favorite—I'm torn between wanting to kiss him and wanting to kick him out. Dallas had to cancel two shows already this week and I know Gavin needs the money. I can take care of Papa. They should go. The words form on my tongue but I don't say them, not yet. Instead I smile and sit at the table, where he hands me a heaping plate of macaroni and a glass of sweet tea.

"There's no way I can eat all of this. Is this the whole box?"

"Nah, just half." Gavin sits across from me with his own plate, dousing it in hot sauce before he digs in.

For a moment, all I do is watch him, sipping my tea and appreciating that he's here with me.

"Shit. My bad. We're at your grandparents' house. Did you want to say a blessing?"

I can't help it. I start laughing. Gavin looks seriously concerned as he swallows a mouthful of pasta.

"I think we'll be okay. God knows I'm a little distracted."

Gavin grins back and points his fork at me. "Okay, then. Eat."

I do as I'm told, and we laugh about Nana and how mad she'd get if one of us snuck a bite before the blessing.

"Swear I thought that woman had a direct line to the Lord. I told her once that God had no use for me and I was damned anyway since my parents weren't married when I was born and my mom didn't even know who my father was."

I stab another forkful of cheesy noodles. "Oh yeah? What'd she say to that?"

Gavin swallows and wipes his mouth with a paper towel before answering. "She said, 'Noah was a drunk, Jacob was a liar, Moses had a stutter, and Lazarus was dead. God can use whoever he wants to use—bastards and all.'"

I stifle a burst of shocked laughter by covering my mouth, because that was such a Nana thing to say. "She had an answer for everything."

"Reminds me of someone else I know."

I drop my fork on my plate and point to myself. "Me?"

Gavin arches his eyebrows and cocks his head to the side. "Yeah, you."

"I wish," I mutter under my breath before returning my attention to my food. I don't have an answer for anything. I don't have an answer for how to make Papa better, or what to do about the band while we're dealing with this, or even how to tell my brother that I am deeply in love with his best friend and I always have been.

"Tired?" Gavin asks when I stand to rinse my plate and yawn.

"A little. Think I'll turn in early so that we can get back to the hospital first thing in the morning. Thanks for dinner."

"Good night, Bluebird," Gavin says softly, taking my plate from my hands and lowering it into the sink.

There's a flash of something, a heated flare that flickers between us only for a moment. But then he turns back to the sink and I go to bed alone.

The last thing I remember is staring at dancing shadows on the ceiling made by wind-rustled leaves moving behind my half-open blinds. I must've fallen asleep, though because the next thing I know, I'm awake in my bed and it's still dark outside. I stumble to the bathroom in a stupor and reality doesn't seep through until after I've washed my hands. Why I'm home, why I'm here in this house. Once I get back into my room, I text Dallas for an update on Papa but figure he's asleep when I don't get a response in several minutes.

Restless and unable to fall back asleep, I make my way to the living room in hopes of playing Nana's old Wurlitzer for comfort. I'd thought Gavin might sleep in Dallas's room but nope, he's right there on the couch. His bare chest rises and falls with steady breaths and I watch him in his peaceful state for a few precious moments before taking several steps backward into the hall.

My room feels suffocating so I don't shut the door all the way. It's warm since the house only has window unit air conditioners in the kitchen and in Papa's room. After kicking off my pajama pants, I curl onto my side, hugging my pillow to my chest and trying not to think about how many times Papa tucked me in, how, at some point, I outgrew that bedtime tradition and he stopped.

My pillow is damp and I'm lying there wondering if I was crying or drooling or both in my sleep when my bedroom door opens the rest of the way, letting in a thick slice of light from the hallway. He doesn't say anything, doesn't ask if I'm okay or if I need anything; he just walks over to my bed and slides in beside me.

"I woke you," I say softly. "I'm sorry."

Gavin shh's me and pulls me in tightly to his bare chest. "I wasn't asleep. And even if I was, you could've played the piano all night if you needed to."

The rumble of his voice vibrates against my cheek on his chest and I become acutely aware of just how close our bodies are. Me in an old threadbare tank top and panties, and him in boxer briefs. It doesn't make sense, going from drowning in grief to seeking warmth and comfort in Gavin's arms in mere seconds, and yet my body has shifted gears before my heart and mind can catch up.

"Gavin, I need . . ." I don't know what I need, but I feel like someone has poured ice water into my veins and the only way to alleviate the bone-deep chill is to press myself closer to him.

"Take whatever you need. Anything I have, it's yours. Tell me how to make it better." He speaks into my hair and I drape my leg over his waist and pull him closer.

"I need you," I whisper, because even though we're alone it still feels like a forbidden secret we share.

"You have me, Bluebird. You've always had me."

Sitting up, I lift my shirt over my head and toss it aside. Watching me with his eyes flashing sparks into the darkness, Gavin remains completely still when I climb onto him. My hair covers us both like a protective curtain as I lean down and press my lips to his. He raises up to cradle my face in his hands and kisses me back, his tongue sliding past the seam of my lips into my welcoming mouth.

"I need you inside, Gavin."

Wordlessly, he strips us both of our underwear and places me above his straining erection within a matter of seconds.

Just before I lower myself onto him, he stills as if remembering something vital.

"Wait. Are you sure? I don't have anything with me."

"I'm sure," I say, easing down slowly until I can't anymore and whimpering at the fullness.

It's completely inappropriate to have this kind of pleasure during a tragedy, kind of like experiencing mind-shattering joy at the throwing of glass bottles against a brick building the day of your parents' funeral, but Gavin gives me this. This release, this reminder that I am alive in the midst of so much grief. He fills me, letting me work out my pain and overcome the numbness, taking me to the edge and over, again and again until I am too exhausted to move before he gives in to his own body's need for release.

"I didn't come in here for this," he says while I'm catching my breath on his sweat-dampened chest. "To take advantage of you or anything. I just—"

"I know." My lips press against his searing skin and I trace the hardened planes of his body. "Good night, Gavin."

"Good night, Bluebird." His arms wrap around me and he gathers my hair in his hand. I settle the side of my face just below his shoulder and let the steady beat of his heart lull me to sleep.

Chapter 30

My grandfather died on my birthday.

I hadn't even realized it was my birthday and I don't think Dallas or Gavin had, either. I only remembered because Robyn texted me Happy Birthday and asked how Papa was doing. Bad news traveled fast in a small town. I was returning from a quick coffee run when I made it to Papa's room and saw Dallas standing outside of it. He was waiting for me with this look on his face. This deeply sorrowful and sincerely apologetic look that made him appear years older and much more world-weary than he actually was. I knew the moment our eyes met that Papa was no longer with us.

It's a strange thing when someone dies on the day you were born. For the rest of my life my birthday will not only mark another year that I've lived through, but another year that he's been gone.

I'm still processing this as Dallas drives me home from the hospital. He's already on the phone with the funeral director and discussing our appointment to pick out flowers and a casket for Papa's funeral. Just like when we were kids, Dallas steps in and saves the day, protects me from having to handle the painful details. He reaches over and squeezes my hand while he continues his call.

The words he's saying barely penetrate my grief-stricken haze.

Staring out the window while the rain trickles crisscrossed paths down into my line of sight, I see the field of dandelions surrounding the pond past Baker's Point. Most of the bluebonnets are gone by now, but the dandelions live on.

"Dandelions are tougher than they look," Papa told me one afternoon when I was making magical wishes on them, much to my heart's content. "Dandelions can thrive almost anywhere, Dixie Leigh. They don't get to choose where they grow."

Something had made him sad when he'd spoken to me that afternoon. I always remembered the frown lines around his eyes but I never understood why he'd looked that way until now.

He'd heard me. The last wish I'd made before he spoke was for my parents back—for me and Dallas to get to go home. My heart aches so deeply, I have to place my hand over it to keep it from bursting apart.

Dandelions didn't get to choose where they grew and neither did I.

I'd been blown from my pretty little life into a completely different world. One that was much less polished and a hell of a lot humbler.

Had I been raised in my mother's home I would've gotten piano lessons from the most expensive teacher she could find—probably some stuffy tie-wearer who didn't know bluegrass from rhythm and blues. As it was, Nana taught Dallas and me both on Saturday afternoons and then made us practice what we'd learned all week long, an hour after dinner every night.

My mom would've sent me to some artsy school when I showed interest in the violin, probably would've signed me up for cello lessons, too. But in Amarillo, I woke up at the crack of dawn while Papa was still having his morning coffee and perched my happy ass on a cracked concrete garden bench in the backyard and waited. He'd amble out when he was finished with his second cup. I got a few instructions and a firm pat on the head before he went back inside and I spent the rest of the day practicing and making all the dogs in the neighborhood wish they'd been born deaf.

A sob catches in my throat and my breath hitches loudly. Tears are coming down faster than the rain and I don't know if it's because I feel guilty that Papa died alone or because at some point I stopped wishing for my parents back.

"Dix? You all right?"

Removing the evidence of my meltdown with both hands, I turn and force a smile for my brother. I hadn't even realized he was no longer on the phone.

"Yeah, I'm good. It's just . . ." I glance out the window once more, swallowing the heartache gathering in my throat before I can finish. "You ever wonder how our lives might have turned out differently if Mom and Dad hadn't . . ." Another swallow and I can almost breathe normally. "You know."

Dallas is quiet for a beat before answering me. "No. I don't. Not really. No point in that line of thinking. They died. Nana and Papa raised us. That's just how it was."

"Right. Yeah, I know that. I was just thinking that I like our life, our memories. It makes me sad to think we might not have ever learned to play if we hadn't stumbled across Papa's old instruments out in that shed. Kind of makes me feel guilty, like maybe I should've missed mom and dad more or—"

"You were a kid, Dix." He glances over at me but his eyes are distant, as if seeing a different version of me than the one currently with him. "You barely spoke for an entire year after they died. Believe me, you missed them plenty. Thinking about what could have been different is a waste of time. Only thing we need to be thinking about right now is where Papa's brown suit is, the one he wore to weddings and funerals. Mr. Phillips needs one of us to bring it to the funeral home first thing tomorrow."

My brother's jaw flexes and I know he's uncomfortable. Dallas has always been able to focus on what needs to be done instead of his emotions. Somehow he's learned to keep them at arm's length. Shut them off and lock them away. Sometimes I wish I knew his secret.

"Okay. I'll handle it," I say quietly.

Dandelions can thrive almost anywhere, Dixie Leigh.

The funeral is held at Phillips Funeral Home on the edge of town and a surprising number of people show up to pay their respects. The men Papa used to sit with at the corner market café, eating breakfast and gossiping more than women, each give me a hug, holding their hats in their hands and telling Dallas and me how much they admired Papa for his service in the navy and how they enjoyed his stories. Papa never told us those stories, so I just nod and smile. After that, everyone becomes a blur. Faces in an endless stream flowing with tears and I'm so sorrys. The pastor of the Baptist church that Papa stopped attending after Nana died says a few words and invites everyone to the cemetery.

At his grave site, I play "Amazing Grace" on Oz and everyone ambles off to their cars with heads and hearts that seem significantly heavier. Mrs. Lawson and a few older ladies from the Junior League come by the house with casseroles, cakes, and more pies than I have room for in the fridge. I make coffee because a few of them linger, looking at old photo albums and discussing the way the world used to be. Glancing around I catch sight of Jaggerd sitting on the porch swing alone and Gavin making the rounds refilling coffee cups in the living room. I'm reeling a little from that odd sight when I hear my brother speaking harshly to someone in the backyard.

At first I think he's on the phone, but peering out the kitchen window I see the unmistakable red locks that belong to Robyn Breeland. She was at the funeral and hugged both mine and Dallas's necks, but he stepped away. Thanking her for coming without actually looking at her. Nana would've yanked his ear clean off for having such bad manners, but I know better. I don't know his exact reasoning because he's never told me. But I have a strong suspicion that Dallas keeps his distance from Robyn because he cares about her, not because he doesn't.

"If there's anything I can do—"

"There isn't," he tells her, cutting her off and causing a wounded look to cross her face. "We've got everything under control. Thank you, though."

At least he said thank you.

I sigh, knowing he doesn't understand how hurtful he's being. Or at least I hope he doesn't.

"Hey, stranger," Jaggerd says, surprising me in the kitchen.

"Hey, Jag." I turn and smile, offering him a piece of pie, but he shakes his head.

"Can we sit a minute? I have something I need to talk to you about."

"Sure." I sit gingerly on a kitchen chair and fold my hands on the table. I feel like I've hardly taken a breath since arriving at the hospital only to learn that Papa had passed away in his sleep. And that was three days ago.

"So it's not a big deal or anything you have to handle right away," Jaggerd begins, a messy lock of hair falling in his eyes. He needs a haircut, but he's the type that won't get one unless a girlfriend pushes the issue. "I just wanted to talk to you about the RV and let you know that I'm happy to keep it for as long as you need, but my dad will expect the space to be paid for and you know what a dick he can be about—"

"RV?" I wish I had a cup of coffee to sip or something; as it is, I just work my cuticles down absently with my fingernails.

Jaggerd looks at me like I'm trying to be funny and he doesn't get the joke. "Yeah, your grandparents' RV. The American Coach Heritage?"

I shake my head because I have absolutely no idea what he's talking about.

"They bought it right before you and Dallas moved here. They were going to travel the world but then . . ." He shrugs uncomfortably.

But then my parents died and they got stuck with two more kids after raising their own.

My chest compresses tightly with emotion and I try not to wince.

"You didn't know about this?"

"I didn't."

"Well it's a nice rig. Probably could get close to a hundred grand or so for it. It's been sitting in a spot your granddad rented out in the garage behind the shop for years. I take it out every now and then and flush the fluid lines and change the oil."

"Um, okay. Thanks . . . for that." I don't know what else to say. They were going to travel the world and Dallas and I kept them from being able to.

"Their map is still in it. They planned all these possible routes, circled the places they wanted to go. You can come see it anytime you like. Just let me know, okay?"

I nod, understanding for the first time what it means to be floored. I am floored.

"If you decide to sell it, I can probably find you a reliable buyer through the garage."

"Okay," I say for what feels like too many times. I force a smile and stand, ready for this conversation to be over so that I can be alone with this information about my grandparents.

Jag takes the hint and stands. "I'm sorry, Dixie. About your granddad and everything." The flecks of gold in his bourbon-colored eyes darken as he takes a step toward me. "And by everything, I mean acting like a jealous jackass when we were together. You didn't deserve that. You deserve a hell of a lot better than that."

I smooth the plain black dress I'm wearing and then finger the pearls that belonged to my grandmother. "Thanks . . . and it's really okay. The past is . . . the past."

"If you're going to be in town for a while, I'd love to take you to dinner. I know I missed your birthday."

Am I going to be in town for a while?

"Yeah, thanks. That sounds . . . nice."

Jag reaches an arm out and gives me a friendly hug. Someone clears his throat, and I straighten. Jaggerd tightens his grip for a brief instant before letting go.

Gavin stands in the doorway holding an empty coffeepot, his jaw feathering with tension. "You're out of coffee. Want me to make some more?"

"I can make it," I say, stepping away from Jaggerd and over to the coffeemaker.

"I'll call you," Jag says, his eyes darting to Gavin on his way out. My brother chooses that moment to enter the kitchen and I feel like I'm watching a very strange soap opera.

"Okay. Great." I toss Jag one last look of gratitude, hoping he won't mention the RV or my grandparents' plans in front of Dallas before I've had a chance to process it myself.

"Dallas," Jaggerd says, shaking my brother's hand and offering his condolences about Papa. "Hope to see you under better circumstances next time."

"Definitely." My brother walks him out and then returns to the kitchen just in time to see me spill coffee grounds all over the counter. Gavin tries to help clean it up and sets the coffeepot next to me, so of course I knock it off into the floor with my elbow and it shatters at my feet.

I didn't cry at the funeral. I even held it together through playing "Amazing Grace" at the grave site while everyone else fell apart. But now, with the knowledge that my very existence kept my grandparents from living their dream and that I might have been keeping Dallas from his all this time too, I begin to crumble amid shards of glass.

"I got it, Bluebird," Gavin says quietly just to me. "Don't move."

He grabs a nearby dish towel and uses it to pick up the larger pieces while my brother grabs a broom and dustpan for the smaller ones. Mrs. Lawson sticks her head in and asks if everything is okay.

I'm trembling, trying to keep myself in one piece—literally—with my arms around myself when Gavin whispers in my ear that I should go lie down.

"Here, dear," Mrs. Lawson says, reaching for me. "I'll clear these old biddies out of here so you can get some rest." She wraps a frail arm around my shoulders and escorts me out of the kitchen.

After thanking everyone for coming and for all of the food, I finally make it to the quiet safety of my room.

Except it isn't safe anymore. Because now when I lie in my bed, the sharp clean scent of Gavin wraps around me along with my quilt. And all I feel is loss.

I've barely started to slip into the murky place between awake and unconscious when my door opens slowly. Watching it angle open wider, my mind attempts to calculate the odds of it being Gavin. Before I have a concrete number, a redhead sporting a stylish side-sweep pops around the aged wood.

"Dix?" Robyn Breeland's emerald eyes are slightly pink around the rims but bright as always. "You in here?"

I sit up and shove my blankets into a heap at my feet. "Hey. Sorry for bailing on everyone out there. I wanted to see you. I just—"

"Do not apologize for not wanting to entertain guests after your grandfather's funeral."

I smile as she sits beside me on my bed, noticing how polished and sophisticated she looks. She's wearing more makeup than she used to and the light smattering of freckles across her nose is hidden beneath it. Her black dress and tweed jacket fit her petite figure perfectly.

"You look really great, Rob. I feel like I haven't seen you in forever."

She nods, slipping her high heels off and letting them fall to the floor. "It's been crazy with my new job and everything. But I saw the pictures from Austin online and I overheard someone saying y'all had a showcase in Nashville."

My chest aches at the memory of the showcase. "It wasn't just ours. It was kind of an audition type deal with several bands. We were just able to get a spot at the last minute."

Robyn's eyes scrutinize my face and I know she's looking for clues as to what I'm not saying. She's always been the kind of friend who just sort of *got* me without my having to explain much. "Gavin said it went well. He also said y'all signed with a manager. That sounds exciting."

I shrug because it was exciting, but not so much anymore. Not since the woman I thought would be my ticket to escaping music school basically benched me.

"I guess. It all seems kind of inconsequential right now, though."

"Well I think that's a sufficient amount of small talk." Robyn trains her concerned stare on me. "How are you doing? I mean, really doing."

This is where I'm supposed to smile and put on a brave face. I should tell her it's hard but I'm hanging in there. That he's with Nana and in a better place and that I've made my peace with that. But the thread I'm hanging by is in danger of snapping. And it's Robyn. So I pull my legs underneath me and wrap my arms around my pillow.

"I don't know, Rob. I'd just talked to him. I was going to make him meat loaf and he sounded fine. And then . . . and then . . . Mrs. Lawson called and the world stopped spinning."

The corners of Robyn's mouth turn down. "God, I'm so sorry, Dix. He was such an amazing man and I know how close the two of you were, how much he meant to you." She wraps an arm around me and leans over enough that we're shoulder to shoulder, holding each other up. "He was like a father to me after my dad passed away. I can remember walking in your house in sweats and with my hair in a sloppy bun on Saturday mornings and Papa always greeted me the same way."

The silence is broken by my sniffle.

"Hey, pretty girl," we say quietly together because that's how Papa greeted us no matter what. He was an old-school southern gentleman at heart. Always had been.

Robyn sits up a bit, allowing me to shift a little more of my weight onto her. "Remember that time he caught Dallas and Gavin trying to buy beer at the Stop-N-Shop?"

Half of a laugh escapes me. "Oh God. How could I forget? He made them sit at the kitchen table and drink that entire twelve-pack of that awful cheap junk they were trying to buy."

"Bet they wished they'd gone for a six-pack instead."

I nod against her shoulder. "Gavin held his own, even back then. But Dallas puked his guts up all night long."

"And then he had to escort me to my National Honor Society Luncheon at the Chamber of Commerce the next day. He had to wear a tie and everything. He was so hungover he tried to wear his sunglasses through the entire thing."

We both giggle a little. I'd forgotten that part. Robyn had won an award for planning a community service project that I think involved cleaning up litter or something and she'd given a speech in front of the mayor. Despite his condition, my brother had been there supporting her just as she sat through our band rehearsals and bowling alley and birthday party concerts. I remember envying the way they watched one another. It had looked like forever in their eyes to me back then. But maybe I was just young and naïve.

"I heard him," I say evenly. "Through the window earlier. I know he's being kind of an ass, but you know how he is about emotional situations."

Robyn waves her hand. "I know. And it's your grandfather's funeral. Like I said, y'all don't have to entertain folks and be friendly. You just lost a loved one. It's understandable."

Despite her words, I can hear the wounded undercurrent flowing beneath them. Whether she'll admit it or not, Dallas hurt her feelings. Nearly three years might have passed since they were technically a couple, but I could still hear the affection in her voice. Contemplating their issues is a welcome relief from my own.

"He never said why y'all broke up. I don't even think Gavin knows."

Robyn takes an audible breath that morphs into a sigh. "Some days, I don't even remember why. But mostly we were just young and heading in different directions. I was in college, and he wanted to focus more on the band. Dallas didn't want to leave Papa all alone so soon after your grandma died and he wanted to work until he had enough money to pay for a demo. I think he thought y'all would have some substantial plans lined up for the band before you left for Houston."

I frown even though she can't see my face directly. "But we didn't. We placed third in the State Fair Sound Off, which won us a thousand bucks but only really resulted in a few congratulatory handshakes since I'd already accepted my scholarship."

Mandy's words about me holding the band back steal into my mind.

"But now it sounds like things are looking up. For the band, at least." I stiffen and Robyn pulls back to look at me. "Aren't they?"

I try to force my shoulders to shrug nonchalantly. They're too heavy to cooperate. "Sort of. Actually our new manager is not really mine or Oz's biggest fan."

"Why? What do you mean, not your biggest fan?"

"She suggested I sit out the encore at the showcase."

Robyn's perfectly sculpted eyebrows rise almost to her hairline. "Did you suggest she go fuck herself?"

I can't help but smile at her outrage. I shake my head. "No." A heavy breath escapes, taking some of my shame at sitting out with it. Feels good to be able to tell someone. "I was nervous and kind of jittery so she said I should sit out and let Dallas have the spotlight. And she knew some stuff . . . about me and Gavin so . . ."

"So . . . there's *stuff* about you and Garrison now? Stuff she used to blackmail you into sitting out? What the hell, Dix? That's messed up."

I sit up straighter and watch my fingers twist into my comforter. "Yeah. I know. It's just, it was just one song and—"

"And nothing. Did you tell your brother?"

"Not exactly."

"Dixie Leigh Lark. You need to talk to Dallas. Like sooner rather than later."

I huff out my frustration and release the comforter. "And say what, Robyn? By the way, D, Gavin and I are sleeping together and our new manager threatened to tell you if I didn't sit my ass down and stop blowing your shot at making it big?"

I squeeze my eyes shut so I don't have to see the expression of shock on Robyn's face.

"I see," she says quietly. "So Garrison finally defied your brother and made a move. Can't say I didn't see it coming."

"No," I say softly while shaking my head. "*I* finally made a move."

"Nice," Robyn says grinning appreciatively at me. "Good for you, girl."

"It's complicated. With everything that's happened, I have no idea where we stand."

She smiles sympathetically at me. "I bet. But you'll figure it out. And you've loved each other forever, I can't imagine you won't have a happy ending."

"Enough about me," I say, eager to push away the messy confusion building inside of me. "Tell me what's been going on with you."

Robyn's eyes brighten several shades. "Um, I have the best job ever. And I just got a promotion. Midnight Bay is sponsoring Jason Wade's next tour, and they just put me in charge of the promotional campaign."

Midnight Bay Bourbon is a thriving liquor distributor out of Dallas that hired Robyn immediately after she interned there in college. I had no idea they were sponsoring Wade's next tour. I've seen him a few times in concert but don't know him personally.

"Robyn, that's awesome. Jason Wade is a huge freaking deal. What's he like?"

She shrugs and blushes. Robyn. Blushing. This is a new development.

"He's kind of a flirt. But you know, that country-boy macho-swag persona. Who knows if he means half of what he says?"

"Who knows if any of them mean half of what they say?"

We laugh and talk about her job for a few more minutes and I am grateful for the distraction. But soon she has to go, and I am alone again with memories and ghosts.

Chapter 31

"I DON'T KNOW, DAMN IT. I TOLD YOU I'M GOING TO TALK TO HER."

Raised voices nearby threaten to drag me from the safe womb of sleep and I try to burrow deeper into my covers.

"Because he was late and saw the encore where it was just the two of us. That's all she said."

Dallas. It's Dallas practically shouting at someone in the next room.

Groaning as I try to untangle myself from my quilt, I sit up and rub my eyes. The pearls I fell asleep in are cutting into the skin on my neck and my dress is twisted around my waist.

Glancing over at the alarm clock on my nightstand I see that it's a little past nine.

I expected to wake up in a hotel but it's my own bedroom that greets me. I can't believe I slept all night. The past twenty-four hours comes back all at once and my head throbs at the flood of memories of nodding and hugging and assuring everyone that I was okay.

Dallas is still arguing with the other voice that I've discerned as Gavin's while I strip off my pearls and my dress and find a pair of jeans and a clean shirt to put on. Once I'm dressed, I join them in the living room to see what all the fuss is about.

"I don't want us to miss out on this, either, but you can't afford to get—"

"Morning." Gavin cuts my brother off by greeting me with excess enthusiasm. It's an overly obvious attempt to ensure that my brother will pause his monologue long enough to turn around and see that I've entered the room.

"Morning, Dixie Leigh," my brother says gently. "Sleep okay?"

"I did until you woke me up hollering at each other. What's going on?"

They exchange wary glances and I get the distinct impression no one in this room plans to fill me in.

"Ugh. I'm going back to bed," I say, preparing to turn around and return to my quilt cocoon.

"Wait," Dallas begins in a resigned tone. "Dix, we need to talk."

Sighing, I perch on the edge of Papa's chair and nod at my brother. "Okay. Talk."

Gavin shoots me a concerned look, but I ignore it. I take in his jeans and human evolution shirt that shows man evolving from an ape to an upright and then sitting behind a drum kit. I wonder if he stayed here last night or went home and saw his mom. I don't get a chance to ask because Dallas rushes on.

"Barry Borscetti heard us at the showcase in Nashville. He was late but he caught the encore and he was really impressed. Mandy said he rarely reaches out to anyone and he wants to schedule a private audition with us to see if we'd be a good fit for an upcoming unsigned artists tour."

"Barry who?"

I look at Gavin to see if this is a new name to him as well but it looks as though he and my brother have already covered this part without me.

"He's a major label executive," Dallas informs me. "One of the founders of Clear the Air Records and now a higher-up for Universal."

Universal is a huge label—the largest in the business and it's a major deal that anyone there would be interested in us, but I nod for him to continue instead of fainting in surprise at the enormity of this. I can barely hear the rest of what he says, though, because one particular statement is playing on repeat and drowning him out.

He was late but he caught the encore and he was really impressed.

I struggle to hear much else. This guy liked the encore in Nashville, the one song that I wasn't a part of.

"Dixie? You still with me?" My brother is giving me the strangest look and I feel as if part of my mind might still be in bed asleep.

"Sorry, Dallas. Just tired. Go on. You were saying that Barry's a major player and was impressed."

My brother nods but his eyes are much less excited about continuing this conversation. "There's more. Mandy said if he gets us on this tour the next step is likely a major deal from Universal."

Rubbing my temples, I lean forward and prop my elbows on my knees. The thought of going back out on the road when there is so much to do here is unnerving to say the least.

"The thing is, we'd have to leave tonight. The audition is in Nashville . . . and it's tomorrow."

My head snaps up and Dallas nods like he was expecting my oncoming panic attack.

"Mandy couldn't buy us any more time than that? She couldn't explain that we just had a death in the family?"

"It's not like it's up to her, Dixie Leigh. This is just an opportunity. Gavin and I were discussing it and letting you rest. Now that we're all three here, we can decide whether we want to pursue it or not."

"There's just so much to do here, Dallas. There's so much . . ."

He nods his understanding. "I know there are a million things to deal with here—settling Papa's estate and handling the headstone order and all of that, but that will still be here when we get back."

"Which, if we get added to this tour, might be a while," Gavin points out.

I feel sick, dizzy, and overwhelmed. Like the train driving my life is barreling past me, driven by someone else, and I can either grab on or let go and watch it pass.

I just don't have the strength to chase after it right this second.

"Tell her all of it, D. She needs to know the truth."

Turning to Gavin for further explanation, and wondering if I'm finally going to hear what they've been behaving so strangely about, I'm annoyed when he puts his hands up and redirects the floor to my brother.

Dallas sighs and sinks onto the armchair Papa loved so much. "He doesn't . . . Barry didn't . . . Mandy wasn't able to convince Barry that he needed to see all three of us to make his decision about adding us to the tour."

I should feel something. Shocked maybe? Hurt? Anger? And yet, I feel slightly relieved. I don't want to run back out on the road and leave Papa's memory and his house in disarray. So if I can sit this audition out, I'm okay with that.

I give my brother the best reassuring smile that I can. "That's okay, Dallas. If this guy doesn't need me there to audition, then I don't need to be there. No big."

Both he and Gavin shift nervously as if they're attached at some location not visible to me.

"It's more complicated than that, Dix. But it doesn't matter." My brother's words come out in a jumbled mess resembling a multi-car pileup on the interstate. "Barry just wanted to put me and Gavin with another guitar player he's trying to get on the tour and then he'd probably just cut us loose. But like I told Mandy, and like I was just attempting to explain to Gavin, it doesn't matter. Great as it is that he's interested, we all go or none of us do."

"Dallas, I don't mind sitting out an audition, for goodness sakes. If this is a huge break then you should—"

"It's not a huge break *for the band*," my brother rushes out over the rest of my sentence. "It's not *the band* he wants added to the tour. The offer doesn't include plane tickets for all three of us, Dix. And it's not all three of us that would go on the tour if he likes the audition."

His shoulders slump as he watches me finally get it. Now I feel something. A lot of somethings that I can't accurately identify.

But mostly, I feel fear. Sheer terror, actually, at the idea of Dallas hanging around Amarillo forever waiting for the band to get discovered and passing up opportunities he should be grabbing on to with both hands.

"Dallas, maybe you should—"

"No," he says, reprimanding me with his tone and his glare simultaneously. "We all go or none of us go and that's that."

"But—"

My brother cuts me off sharply. "It's not up for discussion. I'm telling Mandy and Barry both thanks, but no thanks."

Gavin says something that I don't catch because there is another man's voice in my head.

"*Take care of each other*," the voice says. My breath hitches the moment I recognize it.

My dad's words. The command my brother has likely been trying to follow in honor of our parents' memory for the past ten years. He's done a good job taking care of me. But standing here watching him commit a completely selfless and completely foolish act of sacrifice, I know now that it's time I did the same for him.

Hours have passed and my brother paces across the living room floor, following the well-worn path in the hardwood. His suitcase is by the door. I know because I packed it.

"I told you, I'll handle this. We'll put you on keyboard or something until Barry warms up to the idea of a fiddle during live shows. You've got to be in the studio for recording sessions when it comes time to record the demo anyway, Dix. Please don't bail on me when I need you the most."

His eyes are dark with intensity while he pleads his case and as much as a part of me wants to do as I've always done and follow wherever he leads, I know it's time.

We've been having this same argument for the past two hours and we're out of time. Either they go now or they won't make their flight.

After an hour on the phone with Mandy, Dallas is still angry and nothing has really been resolved.

Barry has a daughter my age, Mandy told him, and he's an old-fashioned guy. Said the road was no place for a young lady. I checked online and sure enough, his label leaned much heavier on the male artist side. I suspected I would not like Barry very much.

"I'm not bailing on you, Dallas. I'm stepping aside so that I don't get in your way. I'm letting you go instead of holding you back."

"You're not in my way, Dix. You're part of this band. And once Barry sees what you can do and how talented you are—"

"I'm twenty years old, Dallas. I think it's time I stopped tagging along on your adventures. Don't you?" I don't believe the words coming out of my mouth, and they taste like I imagine poison might—bitter and acidic—but they have to be said. It's the only way. It's my turn to take care of him.

"We are the band. You, me, and Gavin. There is no band without you."

I wait quietly on the couch for him to accept that I'm not going. There is so much to handle here since Papa passed away and running back out on the road feels like abandoning his memory. As hard as it is to shove Dallas toward his dream, a part of me is thankful I can take care of all that Papa left behind.

Gavin taps his hands steadily on the couch across from me.

My brother shoots him a pleading look. "Gavin. Please tell her to get her ass in the truck and let's go."

I watch as Gavin stills and then shakes his head. "This is her decision. It's time you started letting her make her own."

I try to look at him with gratitude to let him know I appreciate his support, but I worry he'll see too much truth in my eyes when I'm busy trying to sell my brother a lie.

"He's right," I choke out. "And there are things you don't know about Nana and Papa. They had plans before us, Dallas. Plans we kept them from getting to live out. We held them back. I won't do that to you. Not anymore."

"What in the world are you even talking about? Nana and Papa chose to raise us. We could've went into foster care when Mom and Dad died or gone to live with Aunt Sheila in Oklahoma. They wanted us, Dix. So whatever parallel you're trying to draw here is moot."

"Moot?" I say, smirking at him and glad for the tension to be easing out of the room.

"Yes, moot," he confirms, folding his arms over his chest. "Now let's go."

I shake my head, then stand and open the front door for them. "I love you, big brother. I wish you the absolute best of luck—both of you. Really. But I have things I need to handle here. Go ahead and see this Barry guy and let me know how it goes. If he decides you desperately need a fiddle player in the band, I'll see what I can do. But right now I'd just be in your way."

The stare-down continues for several minutes until I flick my wrists toward the door in a shooing motion.

They both walk outside reluctantly, as if I've sentenced them to death. It's ridiculous since they've played without me several times and done just fine. After the showcase in Nashville, I'm grateful I never had to actually *see* any of those times for myself, but at least I know they can manage without me. And it feels good knowing that they care—that they want me even if record execs don't.

I sit on the porch swing and pull my legs to my chest, giving them both my biggest, bravest smile. "Call me and let me know how it goes, okay?"

My brother leans down to hug me goodbye and lingers before pulling away. "You don't have to do this, Dix. I really believe once he sees how great you are he'll be glad we have a fiddle in the band."

"You are going to blow him away, Dallas. You don't need me."

I start to ask what songs Dallas plans to play for the label executive when a startling and life-altering truth occurs to me. I'm having one of those moments—a glazed-over-eyes, out-of-body moment when the mysteries of the universe make complete sense and everything seems brilliantly connected by a grand design for one split second. It happens so quickly I almost miss it.

The lyrics I've been writing for Gavin came together the night Papa died. As much agony as I was in, something clicked for me when I realized that there is more to love than the fleeting instances of happiness—more than hugs, and violin lessons, and comfort. My parents, Nana, Papa, Dallas, and even Gavin—*especially* Gavin— have taught me a valuable lesson that it took losing them to realize.

Love isn't just about the good. It's fortified by the bad. I know how much I loved my parents and how much they must've loved me by the permanent stab I feel at having lost them, of living in a world without them. The same is true for my grandmother and granddad. And even though they aren't gone forever, when Dallas and Gavin walk out that door, it will be the biting teeth of loss that I feel. Because that's the other side of love. The pain and the loss and the missing. It's real and it's powerful—as undeniable and inevitable as a natural disaster that touches down leaving a path of permanent destruction in its wake.

It's dangerous to love, to allow yourself to be loved. But I dared to fly too close to the flames and I've decided it's better to burn—to have that all-consuming powerful kind of love that scars you for life even if it only lasts a little while, than to play it safe forever.

The last two lines I need to finish the song I've been working on are blazing to life behind my eyes when I grab my brother's arm.

"Wait," I say, squeezing him tightly. "Wait right there. Don't move."

Darting into the house, down the hallway, and into my room, I dig into my still half-packed bag until I find my notebook. Yanking a pen from my desk drawer where I used to do my homework, I pull the cap off with my teeth and write down the last two lines of the song I've been tinkering with, with a furious urgency before I lose them.

As soon as it's complete, I feel as if someone has lifted the weight of all the world's pain and suffering from my soul. Finishing a song always has a powerful effect on me, but this is different. This one I wrote for the people I love more than life itself. The people I would sacrifice my heart and soul for a thousand times over.

Tearing the paper carefully from the notebook, I fold it down once and carry it to where my brother is waiting on the porch.

"For you . . . For both of you," I say, handing it over to him. Dallas, being the King of Impatience that he is, opens it immediately and reads the lyrics my heart wrote while I stand there feeling exposed.

When he looks up from the page and back at me, the love and gratitude brimming over in his eyes touches me somewhere deep inside.

"I love you, Dixie Leigh. I should say it more." His voice hitches, and he stops, probably sensing that it's in danger of breaking as am I. "With everyone we've lost, I should tell you every day." He shakes his head as if disgusted with himself. "Christ. I should—"

"I know, Dallas. Me, too." I fling myself at him in one last good-bye hug, knowing he has to go now or I will cry and he will never leave. By the time our affectionate embrace ends, I'm not just letting him go. I'm practically pushing him off the porch.

Gavin stands awkwardly behind my brother and waits for him to head toward the truck before speaking to me.

"You really staying home to deal with your granddad's affairs? Or is it something else?"

I don't look him in the eyes. "Does it matter? I'm staying. The end."

He shakes his head. "No, not the fucking end. Tell me why."

"Tell me the truth about what happened while I was in Houston. Tell me and then I'll return the favor."

We stand there facing off until he mumbles. "I got into a minor accident. Now I'm on probation."

"What? What kind of accident? And probation for what?"

I try to recall everything I know about probation. It isn't much.

Tension tightens his jaw, and I can see the frustration building at my questions, but I don't care. "I made some poor decisions and I paid for them, okay? It doesn't matter."

It matters to me. I'm about to tell him this when a news report I saw about a man getting arrested for leaving the state while on probation comes to mind. "Wait a minute. If you're on probation, how come you're allowed to leave the state?"

Gavin's deafening silence is all the answer I need. It's so quiet I can hear my own heartbeat in my ears.

"Tell me you have not been risking jail time every time we leave the state. And that you're not about to risk it again." My voice is eerily calm considering the fact that my hands are shaking.

"I won't get caught. It's not like I'm hopping state lines to traffic heroin, Blue—"

"Don't fucking Bluebird me, Gavin. This is not a joke. We did that article for the *Indie Music Review*. They took our picture. We talked about playing gigs in Oklahoma, and Arkansas, and Tennessee. And now you're going to an airport full of cops when you're not supposed to leave the state. How do you not see what a bad idea this is?"

"I'll be fine."

"That's why you changed seats when you got pulled over." I feel so stupid for not realizing this sooner that I want to smack my palm to my forehead. "You'll be fine? Is that really what you believe? What if Dallas had been asleep? You would've been arrested on the spot."

"Possibly," is all he says.

"This have anything to do with your mom asking if you were holding? I'm assuming she meant drugs. Did she mean drugs?"

I can tell he thought I'd forgotten about this.

He runs a hand through his hair and looks over to where Dallas is loading his truck. "Sort of. It's complicated."

"Look at me." I wait until he does. "It's not really. It's actually quite simple. You're on probation and you shouldn't leave the state. Tell Mandy to work something out or contact the judge on your behalf. You need to talk to your probation officer first. See if you can work out a deal where you can leave the state due to your job."

Gavin shakes his head. "It doesn't work like that. It's not like I'm on some company payroll where I can prove it's necessary. I tried. Believe me."

"So you're just going to risk it? Jail time?"

"Some risks are worth it, Bluebird. But I think you already know that. Try and imagine how it will look from your brother's point of view. One day he'll find out about us—when that day comes, I'd like to at least be able to say that I risked my own ass to have his back when he needed me. Now tell me why you won't at least come with us."

"Don't you dare use what we did as an excuse to—"

Gavin's hands come up between us. "I'm not. I'm just saying that's a part of why I'm willing to do what I need to for my best friend. Now tell me why you won't come with us. I know you're hurting right now, I get that. But I don't think being alone is going to help."

My eyes meet his and I wonder if he knows that I don't have any other choice. When he looks at me the way he's looking at me now, all I can do is be honest. Even though I'm angry as hell at him.

"I'm afraid of holding Dallas back from his dream—of holding both of you back. No matter what he says, the fact is this guy liked what he saw when I wasn't performing with you." I shrug like I'm not being torn in two on the inside. Maybe this development that doesn't include me is Mandy's doing and maybe it isn't. But I'm not whole, not fully myself, and I need time to grieve my grandfather without the risk of letting my grief debilitate the band. "And I need more time to handle Papa's matters the way he would've wanted them handled. I'm not like Dallas. I can't channel my grief the way that he can."

The way he's staring makes me think he's about to make some grand profession about us or that he's going to take my advice and stay, but he only says, "Be careful in this house alone, okay? Lock up good. Windows and doors. And if you need anything, call me. No matter what time it is or what's going on."

"I will," I say, not knowing if that's the truth. "Gavin . . . I—"

His lips crash down onto mine and I lift onto the tips of my toes, savoring this one last taste. My small reason to hope. My hands hold tight to his hips, clutching his waistband. He drags out the end of our kiss, sucking my bottom lip gently before releasing it.

"I'm still pissed at you, Gavin Michael Garrison. This is a bad idea. It's not worth it. The right opportunity will come along when it's meant to. Dallas will understand."

He ignores every single one of my pleas and answers with one of his own. "Wait for me, Bluebird? Please?"

I glance over my shoulder, looking to see if my brother saw our kiss. Strangely Gavin doesn't seem as worried. Dallas's back is to us as he shoves something into the cab of his truck. Treacherous tears well in my throat on their promising journey toward the ducts in my eyes.

We're standing together, locked in one another's stares and breathing each other's air on the front porch, when my brother calls out to Gavin to get a move on. He gives me one more pleading look and then a soft kiss on the forehead when he realizes I'm really not going to go with them.

For the first time, I'm the one who pulls away. Frustration binds me and tugs at my nerves.

"You drive across the entire state to bail your mom out. You do everything and anything Dallas asks including breaking the law and risking jail time. You even gave me what I wanted, despite the many risks involved."

He gives me the what-are-you-getting-at look.

My voice is sharper than I intend for it to be when I ask him what I've been wondering for years.

"Who has your back, Gavin? Who's looking out for *you*? Tell me. Tell me who holds you up when you start to fall? Who is there for you when you need them? You're the man behind the beat, literally. You've always been the heart of this band, beating steadily behind us. Who's behind you?"

Me, I think to myself. *Let it be me.*

"I've got this, Bluebird. I don't need anyone. I never did."

The truth hurts. It punches me in the chest and bruises my heart. A solid lump of hurt forms instantly in my throat, blocking my attempts at swallowing my feelings. Inhaling his warmth one last time, I resist the urge to drag his face back to mine and kiss him until he agrees to stay and get legal permission to leave. An image of him being handcuffed and shoved into the back of a police car stifles my ability to breathe.

When he pulls away, I let him go.

Once Gavin climbs into the truck, I watch them drive off until they're out of sight. Feels like they pull a piece of my heart along with them and I can almost see it bouncing battered and bloody behind the truck.

It's then that I realize I didn't answer him, not with words. I didn't confirm whether or not I would wait. And he left anyway.

"I don't need anyone. I never did."

Breathing is suddenly harder, as if the air thickened once they were out of sight. My heart has to put forth a bit more effort to beat.

I can see it—how the audition will go. How excited they'll be when they find out they've been added to the tour. And where will I be? An image of myself appears unwelcome in my mind. I'm dressed in all black, my wild hair tamed and slicked back into a tight bun as I play the kind of music that the maestro demands instead of the kind I want—the kind that frees me.

No.

I shake my head to clear the stifling picture and start making a list of everything that needs to be done.

I'll have to call Jaggerd to take me to pick up Dallas's truck from the airport. The thought reminds me that I want to see my grandparents' RV. I'm grateful for Jag's friendship, for having someone here to help with the mountain of responsibilities I have to deal with now that Papa is gone. As much fun as turning into a younger version of Mrs. Lawson while Gavin and Dallas go on tour seems like it could be, or possibly to jail in Gavin's case, I'm going to do my best not to sit around and wallow.

I've never really thought much about what I'd do with myself without the band, other than my brief hiatus last year. And as much as my brother is going to fight me on it, and I know that he will, I'm not going back to Houston for fall semester. Life is short. My parents and grandparents are nonliving proof. Maybe my band doesn't need me anymore, maybe it never will again. But I will not move backward.

I meander slowly through the empty living room. Without Nana or Papa, I feel like the shadow of a ghost haunting their house.

Folding myself in a shawl-style chenille throw that we keep draped over the back of what was once Nana's favorite rocking chair, I peruse the pictures that have adorned these walls for as long as I can remember. When I come to one of me, Dallas, and Gavin at our first official band rehearsal in the shed out back when I was fifteen, I stop and run my fingers over us, passing my brother's dopey grin, my own worshipful expression turned toward the boy on my left, and linger on Gavin's smirking mouth below his soulful eyes. I move my fingers to my still-tingling lips.

Wait for me, Bluebird.

I don't know what's going to happen, with us, with the band, with my brother. But I have one memory, one solid piece of the past that I can hold on to and add to my internal memory box while I wait for the universe to help me figure it all out.

For one night, I held fire. And then a few nights ago, fire held me, too.

I thought it would destroy me, being that close to him. In some ways it did. But as I take a long, lonely walk down memory lane, I realize that the fire Gavin and I created has fueled me as well.

I will wait for him. Feels like I've been waiting on him for most of my life.

But I will not put off living for another second.

Chapter 32

"I'M GLAD THAT YOU CALLED," JAG TELLS ME AS I CLIMB INTO THE metallic blue classic Mustang he and his father rebuilt when we were dating.

"I'm glad you were in the neighborhood. And thanks again for having your guys get Dallas's truck. That was really sweet of you."

Her grins over at me as we back out of my driveway. "Anything for you, gorgeous."

"My hero," I say with an eye roll. "So tell me about this RV."

Jaggerd rakes his hair out of his eyes with one grease-stained hand. "Oh, you know. Standard American Coach. Kitchenette, bedroom, small bathroom. It was nice back when they first bought it, but it's aged a bit. I checked around online. Might be able to get more like seventy-five for it these days."

"I can't believe they never sold it."

Jaggerd gives me a strange look. I suspect he wants to ask what's going on with the band—the one that I so easily chose over him. But thankfully he doesn't.

"They put their life savings into that thing. Touring the world in it was their dream. Dreams aren't exactly easy to give up on or let go of. You of all people should know this."

The sentiment reminds me why I was so eager to see the RV. My dream no longer seems possible. Soon what once was my band will be touring without me and I'll be . . . on my own, I suppose.

I've submitted the life insurance policies and caught the house payment up to date. Papa had prepaid for everything from the funeral to his burial site beside Nana and his headstone. Soon after Gavin and my brother left I realized there wasn't as much to handle as I'd thought. But I still didn't know if I was ready to go back on the road, and I definitely couldn't go where the people making the decisions affecting the band's future didn't want me.

Dallas called to say the audition went well and that they should know something soon about whether or not they'd be joining the tour. I'm happy for them. I am. But a part of me is still that girl, still sitting on the side of the riverbank wishing she'd jumped. Still sitting in the audience wishing she hadn't sat out the encore. I can't change the past. But I don't have to put my future on hold.

After making meat loaf and eating leftovers for the third night in a row and crying all over Nana's piano, I decide it is time to get out of the house.

Out of town maybe.

"And tell me again why I can't tell anyone about this?" Jaggerd looks nervous when we pull behind his father's auto garage in the center of town.

"Because," I say climbing out of the car and grabbing my bag from the backseat, "Dallas has enough to worry about right now without adding me to it."

I follow Jag over to the oversized bay where the RV is parked. He unlocks the door and rolls it upward. The RV sits there in its massive glory. I don't know what I expected but I didn't think it would be in such pristine condition. I vaguely remember Jag saying he took it out and cleaned it up from time to time.

"Thank you. For taking such good care of it."

"Your granddad was a good guy. And I'd like to think that you and I are still friends."

"Of course we are," I say absently, running my hand along the side of the vehicle.

"Dixie, this isn't just something you can drive off in. You should really have a Class A or B for—"

"Relax. I just want to look at it, Jag." For now, that is. He opens the door and I follow him in. "Besides, I have my Class B. I got it when we were thinking about getting a larger van to tour in."

Jag steps aside and allows me to tour the home on wheels my grandparents considered the key to fulfilling their dreams.

When I move to the driver's seat, I see it. The map.

Unfolding it, a sense of holding something close to them clogs my throat with emotion. Various states and cities are circled across it with a few names of antique malls and monuments scrawled here and there.

When Dallas and Gavin left, I felt lost, with no direction and no idea what was next. I've felt that way ever since. Sitting in the leather captain's seat of the RV, the knowledge that I might never get to live my dream almost overwhelms me. But it doesn't.

Because even though I might not to get to live my dream, I can still fulfill theirs.

The lights of the nearly empty interstate guide me like a jet down the runway. As big as this RV is, I feel like a 747 about to take off. Turning down the radio, I glance at my map one more time.

Eleven states, almost two dozen cities, and several little-known landmarks, here I come. I grab the hand of the girl on the riverbank, pull the young woman from the audience, and bring them both along with me. We aren't sitting out anymore. We aren't standing still any longer.

As I approach the NOW LEAVING AMARILLO sign, my heart flutters in my chest and I begin to hum a song that used to signal the close of every show.

Nana used to say that every ending is really a new beginning—we just don't know it yet.

She was right.

Epilogue

Gavin

"WHO HAS YOUR BACK, GAVIN? WHO'S LOOKING OUT FOR YOU? Tell me. Tell me who holds you up when you start to fall? Who is there for you when you need them?"

You. I answer Dixie's questions in my mind for what feels like the thousandth time. They've played on repeat in my head since I walked away from her on that damned porch. The answer is the same. Every time.

But I didn't tell her. I should have. I wish to fuck I had.

"Garrison? Did you hear me?" Dallas sets his cell phone on the nightstand in our hotel room and lowers himself onto the bed across from mine. "Dude."

I heard him. He said, *"We're in."*

The audition went well. Dallas sang the song Dixie had handed him when we left, "Better to Burn" she'd titled it, and it fucked with me the entire time. And now we're going on tour. Without her.

I look up from the lyrics I've been reading. The ones that are breaking me apart and building me back up again.

"Yeah, man. I heard you. That's awesome." I offer him a half-hearted fist bump and he grins.

"There's more. Since Afton Tate's band joined up with the tour, more venues have signed on. Instead of three weeks it's going to be six. And instead of a dozen cities, it's going to be thirty-six. Thirty-six cities, man."

I glance at Dixie's lyrics again, then lift my eyes to Dallas. Dude is about to start jumping on the bed and squealing like a fucking five-year-old. Meanwhile I feel like the floor is being ripped out from underneath me. "Yeah. That's great."

"Stop bein' all broody. They loved us. Kind of a big deal here, brother. Thirty-six cities. Hear me? Three-six. You and me. On a sponsored tour."

His enthusiasm is contagious so I grin at him. But my Bluebird's words are burning a hole in my head and in my hands.

Even her handwriting is beautiful.

> *This one goes out to the one I love. These words I wrote while trying to rise above. You're the one I can't get past—the flame I knew would burn too fast. Deep down we both know I'm a dreamer, looking for the hope in world of doubt. But how will we know what we could be, if we're not willing to find out?*

Something fucked-up is happening to me. I don't know what it is, but it's akin to having my ass kicked while on a bad acid trip.

Dallas stands up and rattles off some shit about flights and times but I can't hear him over her lyrics coming to life in my mind. I can already feel the beat that belongs behind them. I rub one hand roughly across my denim-covered knee. It heats, but it would be better to set my leg on fire than hit something and alert Dallas to my five-alarm situation.

*I'd rather have one night of finally feeling alive than to
live forever holding everything inside. I finally get it, the
other half of love. It's pain and loss and all of the ugly
above. And when it ends, and you wish we'd stayed just
friends, I won't be able to deny the truth. There's no price
I wouldn't pay for you.*

A mirrored reflection of her gloriously naked body in front of
mine is permanently tattooed behind my eyes—imprinted as deep
as the ink on my skin. It's as if my blood has turned to kerosene and
Dixie Lark tossed a match at me.

Every line of her song is fuel to the flames in my chest.

*It's better to burn, better to risk it. 'Cause I'd rather have
scars than take a chance on missing this. I flew too close to
the flame. Just couldn't stay away. We ran out of time for
playin' it safe.*

"Dallas," I say on a wavering breath before clearing my throat.
"We gotta talk."

He stops his yammering about the tour and looks at me.
"What's up?"

My eyes fall to the paper in my hands. How it hasn't burnt to dust
is beyond me.

*You turned my night into bright blinding day. Let me be
the angel that chases the darkness away. We don't have
to live this life alone. You don't have to keep doin' this on
your own. If when it's all said and done, I turn to ashes,*

only ashes, scattered on the wind, it won't change a thing.
'Cause given the chance, baby, I'd do it all again.

The first verse repeats and I just stare.

"Did you tell her?" He nods to the paper in my hands. He means have I told Dixie about the shit that happened while she was in Houston. He has no idea what the words on this paper mean to me. Thank fuck. Except . . . I'm pretty sure I'm going to have to tell him.

"Some of it," I answer. "Not all."

He arches an eyebrow and folds his arm across his chest. I lay Dixie's lyrics beside Dallas's phone on the nightstand, feeling both relieved and bereft when I distance myself from them.

"Thirty-six cities, huh?" I rake my hand roughly over the top of my head. "That's a lot of state lines."

We both know I'm not supposed to cross a single one. Hell, even Dixie knows that now. She just doesn't know why.

Dallas's shoulders sag and his barely contained bravado vanishes as if he's been deflated. I glance up to see him giving me that same damn stare his sister pins on people. Somehow they both inherited the ability to see straight through my bullshit. I suspect they got it from their grandmother.

"It's just . . . I'm not sure, man. That's a fuck-ton of places where I could be—"

I lift a shoulder instead of finishing my sentence, leaving it there because he knows what could happen.

Dallas clears his throat and relaxes his stance. "I know." He looks away for a moment and then back at me again. "Maybe we should head back to Amarillo, help Dixie sort out Papa's stuff, and hold out for something else. There will be other tours, right?" His lips quirk up in a grin that I don't believe for a second because we both know this isn't necessarily true. The window of opportunity in our world is small. Like keyhole small.

"Dude. Stop. No." I shake my head because no fucking way am I going to let my mistakes hold him back. "Do your thing. Kick ass and take names. I have to take care of me, you take care of you."

Dallas nods. "You've always had my back. I appreciate that, but I understand. I don't know if I'd be willing to risk it if our roles were reversed, and I'm sure as hell not going to ask you to."

Dallas is a good friend. A great friend. A brother from another mother. I owe him the truth.

"Yeah. There's more. I would suggest sitting down or backing up because if you punch me, you might hurt your hand and playing guitar at your show in Omaha will be a bitch."

"Dude, you're on probation. I'm not going to punch you for—"

"It's about Dixie."

He sits.

All I can do is man up and tell him the truth. So I look him right in the eye and do that.

"I love her, Dallas. I fucking love her and I swear to God, I didn't mean for this to happen. I didn't even know it *could* happen. You were right, what you said last year, about my shit and her not needing that. You were right to tell me to keep my loser fucking hands off her when we were kids, too. But that was a promise I couldn't keep."

There is visible movement in his jaw. "I'm going to need a little more clarification than that," he says evenly.

I pull in a deep breath that has more to do with courage than oxygen. "I'm in love with your sister—maybe I always have been. I broke the promise I made you when we were kids *and* the one I made you last year in about a dozen different ways and as sorry as I am for that, I wouldn't take it back if my life depended on it."

I wait a beat for his reaction, wondering if my life *does* depend on it. A dozen emotions play across his expressive face. He's a lot like her, I realize. Neither of them has a poker face for shit.

Finally he seems to settle on a look of concern seasoned with determination. "I saw how you were at the funeral and after. Whatever you do, just be sure you mean it, Garrison. If this is just jealousy over McKinley, maybe shove that shit down deep and keep it to yourself."

"It's not," I answer abruptly, picturing McKinley with his arms around her in her kitchen. "But I'm not opposed to tearing his greasy fucking hands off if I ever see him touch her again, either."

Dallas gives me a half grin until he sees that I'm dead serious. Then his expression shifts to one of amused interest.

I shake my head and lift my hands in a gesture of helplessness. "She's my Bluebird, Dallas. I need to go home and get my shit straight so that I can be the kind of man she deserves."

"I can see that you care about her, and that's great. Really. I believe you'll protect her from your own bullshit like you promised—because otherwise I'd have to kill you here and now. But the nicknames or putting your hands all over her in front of me, that shit ain't gonna fly. Ever."

"I'll try my best. But I think we both need to go ahead and accept the fact that what Dixie wants, Dixie gets. From me at least. I can't put you first anymore."

"It's like you're breaking up with me, Garrison. Do I get break-up sex?"

"You wish," I tell him as I stand to pick up my bag.

"You leaving because you don't want to risk going to jail or for her?"

There's a good question. I give him the most honest answer that I can. "Both."

Sliding my phone into my pocket and lifting my bag onto my shoulder, I ask him to make sure someone gets my drum kit home. Most likely I'll have to hitchhike back to Amarillo.

Dallas promises that he will and leans on the wall by the door.

"You're not a bad guy, Gavin. And I trust you with my own life. But if you hurt my sister, you're fucking—"

"I know. I won't. Or I'll do everything in my power not to."

"You have to tell her," he says with a straight face. "All of it. Maybe not all at once, but eventually."

"I know. I will. I need to get my shit handled and then, I swear to God, I will tell her everything."

The lines etched into his face fade noticeably. "When I saw you with her in the alley at the showcase I thought it was like—"

"It wasn't," I say, cutting him off sharply. "And it never will be."

His mouth flattens into a straight line and he gives a quick nod. "Good. Better not be."

"After I tell her everything—once she knows everything that I did and what happened—she might tell me to stay the fuck away from her."

Dallas doesn't reassure me. Probably because he knows I'm right. "She might. But that's her decision to make."

"There are some sins even saints can't forgive," I mumble.

Dallas claps me on the shoulder and shakes my hand, pressing something into it. "Well let's just hope she loves your sorry ass back. Good luck, man."

Adjusting my bag on my shoulder, I nod to where Dallas's guitar is propped by the dresser. "Same to you, my friend."

S he answers on the second ring.

I'm sitting in the station where I used the money my best friend slipped me for bus fare to get a ticket home. I have about five minutes until my bus arrives so I decide to call the absolute last person I want to talk to. Well, one of the last people. Definitely not the first.

"Well, well. To what do I owe this honor?" She asks once I've told her it's me.

I stop tapping my drumstick on my knee. "We need to meet."

"Well that sounds promising. Dinner? Or just my place for dessert?"

My skin crawls at the sound of her voice. I shove a memory I wish I didn't have back into the deep, dark closet of my mind and ram the door shut. "Neither. This isn't about that."

"A girl can dream."

I don't have time for her bullshit. "Look, I'm not in the mood to play games with you."

"Too bad," she purrs through the phone. "We have so much fun when we play."

Jesus.

"Can you meet with me or not?"

"I have time tomorrow after lunch."

"Great. See you then." I disconnect the call without bothering with the formality of a goodbye. She doesn't need or deserve one.

My bus arrives and I lift my bag and climb on. Taking an empty seat, I glance out the gaping mouth that is the front windshield. There's a long road ahead of me, but for the first time in my life, I'm headed toward someone I love.

Someone I wish I didn't have to hurt.

Dixie, Gavin, and the band's story continues, but first . . . now that Dallas has his dreams within reach, does it mean anything if he's on his own? And what happens when a certain gorgeous redhead comes back into his life?

Loving Dallas

Coming Summer 2015

Dallas

THE AIRPORT IS ABOUT AS CROWDED AS I EXPECT HELL TO BE WHEN I get there. Everyone's either on their phone or eating or staring up at the electronic flight schedules. A few moms scream at their kids to stay the fuck where they are and not move. Even one who has hers on a leash attached to a teddy bear backpack. Christ. Why would anyone travel with these tiny gremlins?

My phone buzzes with a text from Mandy.

See you in Omaha! Safe travels, Superstar!

I stare at it for a full minute. This is it. I'm joining an actual tour paid for by someone other than myself. And if all goes well, a record deal will follow.

"We're now boarding passengers in group one. That includes all first-class passengers and those of you in our Elite and Platinum Traveler Rewards programs."

I take my place in line, and the attractive brunette with the microphone to her mouth makes eye contact as she rattles off more of the flight information. I tip my cowboy hat at her.

When I reach the entrance to the sky bridge connecting the building to the plane, I step out of line in a moment of panic. I watch as everyone else says their goodbyes and boards the plane.

"Sir? Will you be flying with us today?" The attractive brunette reaches for my boarding pass.

My mind and heart engage in an all-out war. Turn tail and head home to my sister and best friend—to my band—or get on this plane and leave them behind.

"Sir?" The flight attendant looks less interested and more irritated than before.

Handing over my boarding pass, I adjust the guitar on my back and take the first step toward a neon dream I've been chasing for as long as I can remember.

I knew I'd get here one day—I just didn't expect to be alone.

Leaving Amarillo Playlist

"The Devil Went Down to Georgia"—The Charlie Daniels Band
"If You're Gonna Play in Texas (You Gotta Have a Fiddle in the Band)"—Alabama
"Whataya Want from Me"—Adam Lambert
"Beneath Your Beautiful"—Labrinth feat. Emeli Sandé
"Ring of Fire"—Johnny Cash
"Set Fire to the Rain"—Adele
"Love Runs Out"—OneRepublic
"One Night"—Christina Perri
"All Your Life"—The Band Perry
"Metamorphosis"—Philip Glass
"Dust to Dust"—The Civil Wars
"Let the Drummer Kick"—Citizen Cope
"If I Lose Myself"—One Republic
"Somewhere in My Car"—Keith Urban
"Eavesdrop"—The Civil Wars
"Bluebird"—Christina Perri
"Lover Dearest"—Marianas Trench
"The End"—Kings of Leon
"Time to Go"—Sara Swenson
"Dream"—Priscilla Ahn
"Dust"—Eli Young Band

Acknowledgments

Writing the Neon Dreams series has been the most amazing experience for me. I've grown a great deal as a writer and as a human being. I've learned so much and been supported and challenged and I have so many people to thank for that.

I am so lucky to have the family that I have. Without them, I could never write the books that I do. I am so grateful for each and every one of you—there aren't even words to express how much you mean to me.

Without my rock star of an agent, this book would not be in your hands. Big hugs of love and gratitude to Kevan Lyon for taking a chance on some random lady from Alabama! I am so grateful to Kelly Simmon of InkSlinger PR for connecting us! Thanks, KP! Without Amanda Bergeron's tireless efforts and unfailing ability to see even more potential in my characters than I did, this book wouldn't be nearly as enjoyable as I hope you found it to be. Thank you, Amanda, for your patience and for your faith in me.

I have lots of teary hugs saved up for the ladies on the marketing team at HarperCollins as well! Thank you, ladies, for your enthusiasm and support. I can't even begin to describe how amazed I am by the art department and the perfection that they create. I am so excited to be a part of the Avon/William Morrow family. Speaking of which, I have to thank the sweet ladies who were so kind to me at RWA, many of whom made time in their own hectic writing schedules to read this novel. Thank you Jennifer Armentrout, Candis Terry, Jennifer Ryan, Cora Carmack, and Jay Crownover. I can't describe what it felt like to meet so many authors I admired, not to mention knowing that they were reading my words. (There was a lot of wine and anxiety medication involved.)

Thank you to the cover model, Louise, and photographer Mark Hare, for allowing us to use this image for the cover. I think I stared at it for a month straight.

I have a fabulous street team, the #BackwoodsBelles, made up of some of the most amazing ladies that I am beyond blessed to know. The same could be said for my beta reading group, CQ's Road Crew. I don't know what I did to deserve such a wonderful support system, but I'm glad I did it. Thank you, ladies, for always having my back!

Several of my critique partners were an essential part of making this novel the best that it could be. Elizabeth Lee and Emily Tippetts, thank you from the bottom of my heart for taking the time to read my hideous first drafts and for your honest feedback. Elizabeth, thank you for naming the band and for the hours on end you let me talk this series out over the phone.

I have a few other first-round readers that I have to send a tremendous thank you to. Amy, Erica, Chelcie, Jaclyn, Stephanie, Tricia, Marie, Kristy, Kelly, Mickey, Natalie, Jenna, Leah, and Rahab, y'all are precious to me and I love each of you! Just as I love and appreciate all of you who take the time to read and review books and blog and post about them. There aren't enough thank-yous in the world to say how much I appreciate y'all!

The dedicatee at the beginning is my brother and I have to thank him for driving me crazy all those years with constant guitar ballads coming from his bedroom and for explaining to me his many, *many* theories on the integrity and importance of music. Thanks for being you, little brother.

And here's where I get mushy. Music is such an integral part of who I am, it's almost impossible to articulate. When I was barely tall enough to sit in the front seat riding with my dad in an old pickup truck listening to what my mom referred to as "knee-slapping" music, I had no idea that one day he would be gone and those songs would forever be the music playing in my internal memory box. Just like I didn't know that one day anything and everything by Boyz II Men would remind me of that painful eighth-grade breakup, or that Aerosmith's "Crazy" would still conjure up the tingles of my very first kiss even fifteen years later. Shania Twain and Bryan White crooning "From This Moment" will always paint a clear portrait of my wedding day and there are so many songs on the soundtrack of my life that they'd be impossible to list here. I don't know how to go about thanking music, so I will thank the folks who support musicians. Thank you, music teachers. Whether you teach kindergarten kiddos to sing "The Wheels on the Bus" or you're the maestro of a world-renowned orchestra, what you do matters and I am grateful for it. Thank you to the many musicians who have struggled and overcome and made their music despite the odds. Every musician I've ever met has a story about "this one time" when someone gave them a chance or a shot that led to their lucky break. Thank y'all for giving me mine.

To those of you who sing in your car and don't get embarrassed when the guy next to you notices and to my family for letting me sing off key in the car at the top of my lungs—I love y'all.

And lastly and most important, if you read this book in its entirety and for some crazy reason you are still reading my overly emotional babbling nonsense, thank you. You are the ones I get emails and Facebook messages and tweets from and you make my world go 'round—literally. If I could see you in person I would hug you entirely too hard. If you come see me at a signing event, it's likely that I will!

This series is a lot of things. It's a glimpse at the backstory of a band. It's sexy, and gritty and romantic—sweet at times and ugly at others. But at its core, it's about dreams. Since I was a little girl writing silly stories and buying every single Babysitter's Club book I could get my hands on, I dreamt of being a writer. As I got older and the reality of how many writers actually got publishing deals and made a living with writing alone set in, my dream began to seem like just that—a pipe dream that was fun to imagine but not likely to happen in real life.

If you are reading this, my dream came true.

Never *ever* stop dreaming. And more important, never stop trying to achieve your dreams. While it might not be feasible to make it the central focus of your life (unfortunately, we can't pay bills with dreams or eat them), do something every day that keeps your dream alive. Your future self will thank you.

Y'all, I'm shutting up, I swear, but I know I forgot at least one person because I always do. To that person, or those several people I should have mentioned but forgot, please forgive me. You are likely the most important folks and I take you for granted! I am a flawed human being; thank you for loving me anyway.

Author bio

Author photograph by Lauren Perry, Perrywinkle Photography

Caisey Quinn lives in Birmingham, Alabama, with her husband, daughter, and other assorted animals. She is the bestselling author of the Kylie Ryans series as well as several new adult and contemporary romance novels featuring Southern girls finding love in unexpected places.

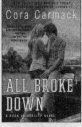

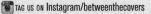

Available in eBook

Available in eBook

Available in eBook

Available in Paperback and eBook

Available in Paperback and eBook

Available in Paperback and eBook

Available in Paperback and eBook

Available in Paperback and eBook

Available in Paperback and eBook

Available in eBook

Available in eBook

Available in eBook

WAIT *for you*

Available in
eBook

TRUST *in me*

Available in
Paperback
and eBook

BE *with me*

Available in
Paperback
and eBook

STAY *with me*

Available in
Paperback
and eBook

Rule

Available in
Paperback
and eBook

Jet

Available in
Paperback
and eBook

Available in
Paperback
and eBook

Rowdy

Available in
Paperback
and eBook

Asa

Available in
Paperback
and eBook

Available in
Paperback
and eBook

Available in
Paperback
and eBook